NEVER
NEVER

NEVER NEVER

COLLEEN HOOVER

TARRYN FISHER

CANARY STREET PRESS

CANARY
STREET
PRESS™

Recycling programs
for this product may
not exist in your area.

ISBN-13: 978-1-335-01510-5

Never Never

First published in 2023. This edition published in 2025.

Copyright © 2023 by Tarryn Fisher

Canary Street Press
22 Adelaide St. West, 41st Floor
Toronto, Ontario M5H 4E3, Canada
CanaryStPress.com

Printed in U.S.A.

This book is dedicated to everyone
who isn't Sundae Colletti.

PART 1

1

Charlie

A crash. Books fall to the speckled linoleum floor. They skid a few feet, whirling in circles, and stop near feet. *My* feet. I don't recognize the black sandals, or the red toenails, but they move when I tell them to, so they must be mine. *Right?*

A bell rings. Shrill.

I jump, my heart racing. My eyes move left to right as I scope out my environment, trying not to give myself away.

What kind of bell was that? Where am I?

Kids with backpacks walk briskly into the room, talking and laughing. *A school bell.* They slide into desks, their voices competing in volume. I see movement at my feet and jerk in surprise. Someone is bent over, gathering up books on the floor; a red-faced girl with glasses. Before she stands up, she looks at me with something like fear and then scurries off. People are laughing. When I look around I think they're laughing at me, but it's the girl with glasses they're looking at.

"Charlie!" someone calls. "Didn't you see that?" And then, "Charlie…what's your problem…hello…?"

My heart is beating fast, so fast.

Where is this? Why can't I remember? "Charlie!" someone hisses. I look around. *Who is Charlie? Which one is Charlie?*

There are so many kids; blond hair, ratty hair, brown hair, glasses, no glasses…

A man walks in carrying a briefcase. He sets it on the desk.

The teacher. I am in a classroom, and that is the teacher. High school or college? I wonder.

I stand up suddenly. I'm in the wrong place. Everyone is sitting, but I'm standing…walking.

"Where are you going, Miss Wynwood?" The teacher is looking at me over the rim of his glasses as he riffles through a pile of papers. He slaps them down hard on the desk and I jump. I must be Miss Wynwood.

"She has cramps!" someone calls out. People snicker. I feel a chill creep up my back and crawl across the tops of my arms. They're laughing at me, except I don't know who these people are.

I hear a girl's voice say, "Shut up, Michael."

"I don't know," I say, hearing my voice for the first time. It's too high. I clear my throat and try again. "I don't know. I'm not supposed to be here."

There is more laughing. I glance around at the posters on the wall, the faces of presidents animated with dates beneath them. *History class? High school.*

The man—the teacher—tilts his head to the side like

I've said the dumbest thing. "And where else are you supposed to be on test day?"

"I… I don't know."

"Sit down," he says. I don't know where I'd go if I left. I turn around to go back. The girl with the glasses glances up at me as I pass her. She looks away almost as quickly.

As soon as I'm sitting, the teacher starts handing out papers. He walks between desks, his voice a flat drone as he tells us what percentage of our final grade the test will be. When he reaches my desk he pauses, a deep crease between his eyebrows. "I don't know what you're trying to pull." He presses the tip of a fat pointer finger on my desk.

"Whatever it is, I'm sick of it. One more stunt and I'm sending you to the principal's office." He slaps the test down in front of me and moves down the line.

I don't nod, I don't do anything. I'm trying to decide what to do. Announce to the whole room that I have no idea who and where I am—or pull him aside and tell him quietly. He said no more stunts. My eyes move to the paper in front of me. People are already bent over their tests, pencils scratching.

Fourth Period
History
Mr. Dulcott

There is a space for a name. I'm supposed to write my name, but I don't know what my name is. *Miss Wynwood*, he called me.

Why don't I recognize my own name? Or *where* I am? Or *what* I am?

Every head is bent over their papers except mine. So I sit and stare, straight ahead. Mr. Dulcott glares at me from his desk. The longer I sit, the redder his face becomes.

Time passes and yet my world has stopped. Eventually, Mr. Dulcott stands up, his mouth open to say something to me when the bell rings. "Put your papers on my desk on the way out," he says, his eyes still on my face. Everyone is filing out of the door. I stand up and follow them because I don't know what else to do. I keep my eyes on the floor, but I can feel his rage. I don't understand why he's so angry with me. I am in a hallway now, lined on either side by blue lockers.

"Charlie!" someone calls. "Charlie, wait up!" A second later, an arm loops through mine. I expect it to be the girl with the glasses; I don't know why. It's not. But, I know now that I am Charlie. *Charlie Wynwood.* "You forgot your bag," she says, handing over a white backpack. I take it from her, wondering if there's a wallet with a driver's license inside. She keeps her arm looped through mine as we walk. She's shorter than me, with long, dark hair and dewy brown eyes that take up half her face. She is startling and beautiful.

"Why were you acting so weird in there?" she asks. "You knocked the shrimp's books on the floor and then spaced out."

I can smell her perfume; it's familiar and too sweet, like a million flowers competing for attention. I think of the girl with the glasses, the look on her face as she bent to scoop up her books. If I did that, why don't I remember?

"I—"

"It's lunch, why are you walking that way?" She pulls

me down a different corridor, past more students. They all look at me…little glances. I wonder if they know me, and why *I* don't know me. I don't know why I don't tell her, tell Mr. Dulcott, grab someone random and tell them that I don't know who or where I am. By the time I'm seriously entertaining the idea, we're through a set of double doors in the cafeteria. Noise and color; bodies that all have a unique smell, bright fluorescent lights that make everything look ugly. *Oh, God.* I clutch at my shirt.

The girl on my arm is babbling. Andrew this, Marcy that. She likes Andrew and hates Marcy. I don't know who either of them is. She corrals me to the food line. We get salad and Diet Cokes. Then we are sliding our trays on a table. There are already people sitting there: four boys, two girls. I realize we are completing a group with even numbers. All the girls are matched with a guy. Everyone looks up at me expectantly, like I'm supposed to say something, do something. The only place left to sit is next to a guy with dark hair. I sit slowly, both hands flat on the table. His eyes dart toward me and then he bends over his tray of food. I can see the finest beads of sweat on his forehead, just below his hairline.

"You two are so awkward sometimes," says a new girl, blonde, across from me. She's looking from me to the guy I'm sitting next to. He looks up from his macaroni and I realize he's just moving things around on his plate. He hasn't taken a bite, despite how busy he looks. He looks at me and I look at him, then we both look back at the blonde girl.

"Did something happen that we should know about?" she asks. "No," we say in unison.

He's my boyfriend. I know by the way they're treating

us. He suddenly smiles at me with his brilliantly white teeth and reaches to put an arm around my shoulders.

"We're all good," he says, squeezing my arm. I automatically stiffen, but when I see the six sets of eyes on my face, I lean in and play along. It's frightening not knowing who you are—even more frightening thinking you'll get it wrong. I'm scared now, really scared. It's gone too far. If I say something now I'll look...*crazy*. His affection seems to make everyone relax. Everyone except...him. They go back to talking, but all the words blend together: football, a party, more football. The guy sitting next to me laughs and joins in with their conversation, his arm never straying from my shoulders. They call him Silas. They call me Charlie. The dark-haired girl with the big eyes is Annika. I forget everyone else's names in the noise.

Lunch is finally over and we all get up. I walk next to Silas, or rather he walks next to me. I have no idea where I'm going. Annika flanks my free side, winding her arms through mine and chatting about cheerleading practice. She's making me feel claustrophobic. When we reach an annex in the hallway, I lean over and speak to her so only she can hear. "Can you walk me to my next class?" Her face becomes serious. She breaks away to say something to her boyfriend, and then our arms are looped again.

I turn to Silas. "Annika is going to walk me to my next class."

"Okay," he says. He looks relieved. "I'll see you... later." He heads off in the opposite direction.

Annika turns to me as soon as he's out of sight. "Where's he going?"

I shrug. "To class."

She shakes her head like she's confused. "I don't get you guys. One day you're all over each other, the next you're acting like you can't stand to be in the same room. You really need to make a decision about him, Charlie."

She stops outside a doorway.

"This is me…" I say, to see if she'll protest. She doesn't. "Call me later," she says. "I want to know about last night."

I nod. When she disappears into the sea of faces, I step into the classroom. I don't know where to sit, so I wander to the back row and slide into a seat by the window. I'm early, so I open my backpack. There's a wallet wedged between a couple of notebooks and a makeup bag. I pull it out and flip it open to reveal a driver's license with a picture of a beaming, dark-haired girl. *Me.*

Charlize Margaret Wynwood
2417 Holcourt Way
New Orleans, LA

I'm seventeen. My birthday is March twenty-first. I live in Louisiana. I study the picture in the top left corner and I don't recognize the face. It's my face, but I've never seen it. I'm…*pretty.* I only have twenty-eight dollars.

The seats are filling up. The one beside me stays empty, almost like everyone is too afraid to sit there. I'm in Spanish class. The teacher is pretty and young; her name is Mrs. Cardona. She doesn't look at me like she hates me, like so many other people are looking at me. We start with tenses.

I have no past. I have no past.

Five minutes into class the door opens. Silas walks in, his eyes downcast. I think he's here to tell me something, or to bring me something. I brace myself, ready to pretend, but Mrs. Cardona comments jokingly about his lateness. He takes the only available seat next to me and stares straight ahead. I stare at him. I don't stop staring at him until finally, he turns his head to look at me. A line of sweat rolls down the side of his face.

His eyes are wide. Wide...*just like mine.*

2

Silas

Three hours.

It's been almost three hours, and my mind is still in a haze.

No, not a haze. Not even a dense fog. It feels as if I'm wandering around in a pitch-black room, searching for the light switch.

"You okay?" Charlie asks. I've been staring at her for several seconds, attempting to regain some semblance of familiarity from a face that should apparently be the *most* familiar to me.

Nothing.

She looks down at her desk and her thick black hair falls between us like blinders. I want a better look at her. I need something to grab me, something familiar. I want to predict a birthmark or a freckle on her before I see it, because I need *something* recognizable. I'll grasp at any piece of her that might convince me I'm not losing my mind.

She reaches her hand up, finally, and tucks her hair behind her ear. She looks up at me through two wide and completely unfamiliar eyes. The crease between her brows deepens and she begins biting at the pad of her thumb.

She's worried about me. About us, maybe.

Us.

I want to ask her if she knows what might have happened to me, but I don't want to scare her. How do I explain that I don't know her? How do I explain this to *anyone*? I've spent the last three hours trying to act natural. At first I was convinced I must have used some kind of illegal substance that caused me to black out, but this is different from blacking out. This is different from being high or drunk, and I have no idea how I even know that. I don't remember anything beyond three hours ago.

"Hey." Charlie reaches out like she's going to touch me, then draws back. "Are you okay?"

I grip the sleeve of my shirt and wipe the sheen of moisture off my forehead. When she glances back up at me, I see the concern still filling her eyes. I force my lips to form a smile.

"I'm fine," I mutter. "Long night."

As soon as I say it, I cringe. I have no idea what kind of night I had, and if this girl sitting across from me really is my girlfriend, then a sentence like that probably isn't very reassuring.

I see a small twitch in her eye and she tilts her head. "Why was it a long night?"

Shit.

"Silas." The voice comes from the front of the room. I look up. "No talking," the teacher says. She returns to her instruction, not too concerned with my reaction to being singled out. I glance back at Charlie, briefly, and then immediately stare down at my desk. My fingers trace over names carved into the wood. Charlie is still staring at me, but I don't look at her. I flip my hand over, and I run two fingers over the callouses across the inside of my palm.

Do I work? Mow lawns for a living?

Maybe it's from football. During lunch I decided to use my time to observe everyone around me, and I learned I have football practice this afternoon. I have no idea what time or where, but I've somehow made it through the last few hours without knowing when or where I'm supposed to be. I may not have any sort of recollection right now, but I'm learning that I'm very good at faking it. *Too* good, maybe.

I flip my other hand over and find the same rough callouses on that palm.

Maybe I live on a farm.

No. I don't.

I don't know how I know, but even without being able to recall anything, I seem to have an immediate sense of what assumptions of mine are accurate and which are not. It could just be process of elimination, rather than intuition or memory. For example, I don't feel like someone who lives on a farm would be wearing the clothes I have on. Nice clothes. *Trendy?* Looking down at my shoes, if someone asked me if I have rich parents, I'd tell them, "Yes, I do." And I don't know how, because I don't remember my parents.

I don't know where I live, who I live with, or if I look more like my mother or my father.

I don't even know what I look like.

I stand abruptly, shoving the desk a few loud inches

forward in the process. Everyone in the class turns to face me other than Charlie, because she hasn't stopped staring at me since I sat down. Her eyes aren't inquisitive or kind.

Her eyes are accusing.

The teacher glares at me, but doesn't seem at all surprised by the loss of everyone's attention to me. She just stands, complacent, waiting for me to announce my reason for the sudden disruption.

I swallow. "Bathroom." My lips are sticky. My mouth is dry. My mind is wrecked. I don't wait for permission before I begin to head in that direction. I can feel everyone's stares as I push through the door.

I go right and make it to the end of the hall without finding a restroom. I backtrack and pass by my classroom door, continuing until I round the corner and find the restroom. I push open the door, hoping for solitude, but someone is standing at the urinal with his back to me. I turn to the sink, but don't look into the mirror. I stare down at the sink, placing my hands on either side of it, gripping tightly. I inhale.

If I would just look at myself, my reflection could trigger a memory, or maybe just give me a small sense of recognition. Something. *Anything.*

The guy who was standing at the urinal seconds before is now standing next to me, leaning against a sink with his arms folded. When I glance over at him, he's glaring at me. His hair is so blond, it's almost white. His skin is so pale, it reminds me of a jellyfish. Translucent, almost.

I can remember what jellyfish look like, but I have no idea what I'll find when I look at myself in the mirror?

"You look like shit, Nash," he says with a smirk.

Nash?

Everyone else has been calling me Silas. Nash must be my last name. I would check my wallet, but there isn't one in my pocket. Just a wad of cash. A wallet is one of the first things I looked for after…well, after it happened.

"Not feeling too hot," I grumble in response.

For a few seconds, the guy doesn't respond. He just continues to stare at me the same way Charlie was staring at me in class, but with less concern and way more contentment. The guy smirks and pushes off the sink. He stands up straight, but is still about an inch shy of reaching my height. He takes a step forward, and I gather by the look in his eye that he isn't closing in on me out of concern for my health.

"We still haven't settled Friday night," the guy says to me. "Is that why you're here now?" His nostrils flare when he speaks and his hands drop to his sides, clenching and unclenching twice.

I have a two-second silent debate with myself, aware that if I step away from him, it'll make me look like a coward. However, I'm also aware that if I step forward, I'll be challenging him to something I don't want to deal with right now. He obviously has issues with me and whatever it was that I chose to do Friday night that pissed him off.

I compromise by giving him no reaction whatsoever. *Look unaffected.*

I lazily move my attention to the sink and turn one of the knobs until a stream of water begins to pour from the faucet. "Save it for the field," I say. I immediately want to take back those words. I hadn't considered he might not even play football. I assumed he did based on his size, but if he doesn't, my comment will have not made a damn bit of sense. I hold my breath and wait for him to correct me, or call me out.

Neither of those things happens.

He stares for a few more seconds, and then he shoulders past me, purposefully bumping me on his way out the door. I cup my hands under the stream of water and take a sip. I wipe my mouth with the back of my hand and glance up. At *myself*.

At Silas Nash.

What the hell kind of name is that, anyway?

I'm staring, emotionless, into a pair of unfamiliar, dark eyes. I feel as though I'm staring at two eyes I've never seen before, despite the fact that I've more than likely looked at these eyes on a daily basis since I was old enough to reach a mirror.

I'm as familiar with this person in the reflection as I am with the girl who is—*according to some guy named Andrew*—the girl I've been "banging" for two years now.

I'm as familiar with this person in the reflection as I am with every single aspect of my life right now.

Which is not familiar at all. "Who *are* you?" I whisper to him.

The bathroom door begins to open slowly, and my eyes move from my reflection to the reflection of the door. A hand appears, gripping the door. I recognize the sleek, red polish on the tips of her fingers. *The girl I've been "banging" for more than two years.*

"Silas?"

I stand up straight and turn to face the door full-on as she peeks around it. When her eyes meet mine, it's only for two seconds. She glances away, scanning the rest of the bathroom.

"It's just me," I say. She nods and makes it the rest of the way through the door, albeit extremely hesitantly. I wish I knew how to reassure her that everything is okay so she won't grow suspicious. I also wish I remembered her, or anything about our relationship, because I want to tell her. I *need* to tell her. I need for someone else to know, so that I can ask questions.

But how does a guy tell his girlfriend he has no idea who she is? Who he himself is?

He doesn't tell her. He pretends, just like he's been pretending with everyone else.

One hundred silent questions fill her eyes at once, and I immediately want to dodge them all. "I'm fine, Charlie." I smile at her, because it feels like something I should do. "Just not feeling so hot. Go back to class."

She doesn't move. She doesn't smile.

She stays where she is, unaffected by my instruction. She reminds me of one of those animals on springs you'd ride on a playground. The kind you push, but they just bounce right back up. I feel like if someone were to shove her shoulders, she'd lean straight back, feet in place, and then bounce right back up again.

I don't remember what those things are called, but I do make a mental note that I somehow remember them. I've made a lot of mental notes in the last three hours.

I'm a senior.

My name is Silas.

Nash might be my last name. My girlfriend's name is Charlie. I play football.

I know what jellyfish look like.

Charlie tilts her head and the corner of her mouth twitches slightly. Her lips part, and for a moment, all I hear are nervous breaths. When she finally forms words,

I want to hide from them. I want to tell her to close her eyes and count to twenty until I'm too far away to hear her question.

"What's my last name, Silas?"

Her voice is like smoke. Soft and wispy and then gone.

I can't tell if she's extremely intuitive or if I'm doing a horrible job of covering up the fact that I know nothing. For a moment, I debate whether or not I should tell her. If I tell her and she believes me, she might be able to answer a lot of questions I have. But if I tell her and she *doesn't* believe me…

"Babe," I say with a dismissive laugh. *Do I call her babe?* "What kind of question is that?"

She lifts the foot I was positive was stuck to the floor, and she takes a step forward. She takes another. She continues toward me until she's about a foot away; close enough that I can smell her.

Lilies.

She smells like lilies, and I don't know how I can possibly remember what lilies smell like, but somehow not remember the actual person standing in front of me who smells like them.

Her eyes haven't left mine, not even once. "Silas," she says. "What's my last name?"

I work my jaw back and forth, and then turn around to face the sink again. I lean forward and grip it tightly with both hands. I slowly lift my eyes until they meet hers in the reflection.

"Your last name?" My mouth is dry again and my words come out scratchy.

She waits.

I look away from her and back at the eyes of the unfamiliar guy in the mirror. "I… I can't remember."

She disappears from the reflection, followed immediately by a loud smack. It reminds me of the sound the fish make at Pike Place Market, when they toss and catch them in the wax paper.

Smack!

I spin around and she's lying on the tile floor, eyes closed, arms splayed out. I immediately kneel down and lift her head, but as soon as I have her elevated several inches off the floor, her eyelids begin to flutter open.

"Charlie?"

She sucks in a rush of air and sits up. She pulls herself out of my arms and shoves me away, almost as if she's afraid of me. I keep my hands positioned near her in case she attempts to stand, but she doesn't. She remains seated on the floor with her palms pressed into the tile.

"You passed out," I tell her.

She frowns at me. "I'm aware of that."

I don't speak again. I should probably know what all her expressions mean, but I don't. I don't know if she's scared or angry or…

"I'm confused," she says, shaking her head. "I… Can you…" She pauses, and then makes an attempt to stand. I stand with her, but I can tell she doesn't like this by the way she glares at my hands that are slightly lifted, waiting to catch her should she start to fall again.

She takes two steps away from me and crosses an arm over her chest. She brings her opposite hand up and begins chewing on the pad of her thumb again. She studies me quietly for a moment and then pulls her thumb from her mouth, making a fist. "You didn't know we had class together after lunch." Her words are spoken with a layer of accusation. "You don't know my last name."

I shake my head, admitting to the two things I can't deny. "What can you remember?" she asks.

She's scared. Nervous. Suspicious. Our emotions are reflections of one another, and that's when the clarity hits.

She may not feel familiar. *I* may not feel familiar. But our actions—our demeanor—they're exactly the same.

"What do I remember?" I repeat her question in an attempt to buy myself a few more seconds to allow my suspicions to gain footing.

She waits for my answer.

"History," I say, attempting to remember as far back as I can. "Books. I saw a girl drop her books." I grab my neck again and squeeze.

"Oh, God." She takes a quick step toward me. "That's...that's the first thing *I* remember."

My heart jumps to my throat.

She begins to shake her head. "I don't like this. It doesn't make sense." She appears calm—calmer than I feel. Her voice is steady. The only fear I see is in the stretched whites of her eyes. I pull her to me without thinking, but I think it's more for my own relief rather than to put her at ease. She doesn't pull away, and for a second, I wonder if this is normal for us. I wonder if we're in love.

I tighten my hold until I feel her stiffen against me. "We need to figure this out," she says, separating herself from me.

My first instinct is to tell her it'll be okay, that I'll figure it out. I'm flooded with an overwhelming need to protect her—only I have no idea how to do that when we're both experiencing the same reality.

The bell rings, signaling the end of Spanish. Within seconds, the bathroom door will probably open. Lockers will be slamming shut. We'll have to figure out what classes we're supposed to be in next. I take her hand and pull her behind me as I push open the bathroom door.

"Where are we going?" she asks.

I look at her over my shoulder and shrug. "I have no idea. I just know I want to leave."

3

Charlie

This dude—this guy, Silas—he grabs my hand like he knows me and drags me behind him like I'm a little kid. And that's what I feel like—a little kid in a big, big world. I don't understand anything, and I most certainly don't recognize anything. All I can think, as he pulls me through the understated halls of some anonymous high school, is that I fainted; keeled over like some damsel in distress. And on the boys' bathroom floor. *Filthy.* I'm evaluating my priorities, wondering how my brain can fit germs into the equation when I clearly have a much larger problem, when we burst into the sunlight. I shield my eyes with my free hand as the Silas dude pulls keys from his backpack. He holds them above his head and makes a circle, clicking the alarm button on his key fob. From some far corner of the parking lot we hear the shriek of an alarm.

We run for it, our shoes slapping the concrete with urgency, as if someone is chasing us. And they might be. The car turns out to be an SUV. I know it's impressive because it sits above the other cars, making them look small and insignificant. A Land Rover. Silas is either driving his dad's car, or floating in his dad's money. Maybe he doesn't have a dad. He wouldn't be able to tell me anyway. And how do I even know how much a car like this costs? I have memories of how things work: a car, the rules of the road, the presidents, but not of who I am.

He opens the door for me while looking over his shoulder toward the school, and I get the feeling I'm being pranked. He could be responsible for this. He could have given me something to cause me to lose my memory temporarily, and now he's only pretending.

"Is this for real?" I ask, suspended above the front seat. "You don't know who you are?"

"No," he says. "I don't."

I believe him. Kind of. I sink into my seat.

He searches my eyes for a moment longer before slamming my door and running around to the driver's side. I feel rough. Like after a night of drinking. Do I drink? My license said I was only seventeen. I chew on my thumb as he climbs in and starts the engine by pressing a button.

"How'd you know how to do that?" I ask.

"Do what?"

"Start the car without a key."

"I… I don't know."

I watch his face as we pull out of the spot. He blinks a lot, glances at me more, runs a tongue over his bottom lip. When we're at a stoplight, he finds the home button on the GPS and hits it. I'm impressed that he thought to do that.

"Redirecting," a woman's voice says. I want to lose it, jump out of the moving car and run like a frightened deer. I am so afraid.

His home is large. There are no cars in the driveway as we linger on the curb, the engine purring quietly.

"Are you sure this is you?" I ask. He shrugs.

"Doesn't look like anyone is home," he says. "Should we?"

I nod. I shouldn't be hungry, but I am. I want to go inside and have something to eat, maybe research our symptoms and see if we've come in contact with some brain-eating bacteria that's stolen our memories. A house like this should have a couple of laptops lying around. Silas turns into the driveway and parks. We climb out timidly, looking around at the shrubs and trees like they're going to come alive. He finds a key on his key ring that opens the front door. As I stand behind him and wait, I study him. In his clothes and hair, he wears the cool look of a guy who doesn't care, but he carries his shoulders like he cares too much. He also smells like the outside: grass, and pine, and rich black dirt. He's about to turn the knob.

"Wait!"

He turns around slowly, despite the urgency in my voice. "What if there's someone in there?"

He grins, or maybe it's a grimace. "Maybe they can tell us what the hell is happening…"

Then we are inside. We stand immobile for a minute, looking around. I cower behind Silas like a wimp. It's not cold but I'm shivering. Everything is heavy and impressive—the furniture, the air, my book bag, which hangs off my shoulder like dead weight. Silas moves forward.

I grab onto the back of his shirt as we skirt through the foyer and into the family room. We move from room to room, stopping to examine the photos on the walls. Two smiling, sun-kissed parents with their arms around two smiling, dark-haired boys, the ocean in the background.

"You have a little brother," I say. "Did you know you have a little brother?"

He shakes his head no. The smiling in the photos becomes more scarce as Silas and his mini-me brother get older. There is plenty of acne and braces, photos of parents who are trying too hard to be cheerful as they pull stiff-shouldered boys toward them. We move to the bedrooms…the bathrooms. We pick up books, read the labels on brown prescription bottles we find in medicine cabinets. His mother keeps dried flowers all over the house; pressed into the books on her nightstand, in her makeup drawer, and lined up on the shelves in their bedroom. I touch each one, whispering their names under my breath. I remember all the names of the flowers. For some reason, this makes me giggle. Silas stops short when he walks into his parents' bathroom and finds me bent over laughing.

"I'm sorry," I say. "I had a moment."

"What kind of moment?"

"A moment where I realized that I've forgotten everything in the world about myself, but I know what a hyacinth is."

He nods. "Yeah." He looks down at his hands, creases forming on his forehead.

"Do you think we should tell someone? Go to a hospital, maybe?"

"Do you think they'd believe us?" I ask. We stare at

each other then. And I hold back the urge once again to ask if I'm being pranked. This isn't a prank. It's too real.

We move to his father's study next, scouring over papers and looking in drawers. There is nothing to tell us why we are like this, nothing out of the ordinary. I keep a close watch on him from the corner of my eye. If this is a prank, he's a very good actor. *Maybe this is an experiment*, I think. I'm part of some psychological, government experiment and I'm going to wake up in a lab. Silas watches me too. I see his eyes darting over me, wondering…assessing. We don't speak much. Just, *Look at this*. Or, *Do you think this is something?*

We are strangers and there are few words between us.

Silas's room is last. He clutches my hand as we enter and I let him because I'm starting to feel light-headed again. The first thing I see is a photo of us on his desk. I am wearing a costume—a too-short leopard print tutu and black angel wings that spread elegantly behind me. My eyes are lined with thick, glittery lashes. Silas is dressed in all white, with white angel wings. He looks handsome. *Good vs. evil*, I think. Is that the sort of life game we played? He glances at me and raises his eyebrows.

"Poor costume choice," I shrug. He cracks a smile and then we move to opposite sides of the room.

I lift my eyes to walls where there are framed photos of people: a homeless man slouched against a wall, holding a blanket around himself; a woman sitting on a bench, crying into her hands. A fortune teller, her hand clamped around her own neck as she looks into the camera lens with empty eyes. The photos are morbid. They make me want to turn away, feel ashamed. I don't understand why anyone would *want* to take a photo of such morbidly sad things, never mind hang them on their walls to look at every day.

And then I turn and see the expensive camera perched on the desk. It's in a place of honor, sitting atop a pile of glossy photography books. I look over to where Silas is also studying the photos. An artist. Is this his work? Is he trying to recognize it? No point in asking. I move on, look at his clothes, look in the drawers in the rich mahogany desk.

I'm so tired. I make to sit down in the desk chair, but he's suddenly animated, beckoning me over.

"Look at this," he says. I get up slowly and walk to his side. He's staring down at his unmade bed. His eyes are bright and should I say…shocked? I follow them to his sheets. And then my blood runs cold.

"Oh, my God."

4

Silas

I toss the comforter out of the way to get a better look at the mess at the foot of the bed. Smears of mud caked into the sheet. Dried. Pieces of it crack and roll away when I pull the sheet taut.

"Is that…" Charlie stops speaking and pulls the corner of the top sheet from my hand, tossing it away to get a better look at the fitted sheet beneath it. "Is that *blood*?"

I follow her eyes up the sheet, toward the head of the bed. Next to the pillow is a smeared ghost of a handprint. I immediately look down at my hands.

Nothing. No traces of blood or mud whatsoever.

I kneel down beside the bed and place my right hand over the handprint left on the mattress. It's a perfect match. Or *imperfect*, depending on how you look at it. I glance at Charlie and her eyes drift away, almost as if she doesn't want to know whether or not the handprint belongs to me. The fact that it's mine only adds to the questions. We have so many questions piled up at this point, it feels as though the pile is about to collapse and bury us in everything but answers.

"It's probably my own blood," I say to her. Or maybe I say it to myself. I try to dismiss whatever thoughts I know are developing in her head. "I could have fallen outside last night."

I feel like I'm making excuses for someone who isn't me. I feel like I'm making excuses for a friend of mine. This *Silas* guy. Someone who definitely isn't me.

"Where were you last night?"

It's not a real question, just something we're both thinking. I pull at the top sheet and comforter and spread them out over the bed to hide the mess. The evidence. The clues. Whatever it is, I just want to cover it up.

"What does this mean?" she asks, turning to face me. She's holding a sheet of paper. I walk to her and take it out of her hands. It looks like it's been folded and unfolded so many times, there's a small, worn hole forming in the very center of it. The sentence across the page reads, *Never stop. Never forget.*

I drop the sheet of paper on the desk, wanting it out of my hands. The paper feels like evidence, too. I don't want to touch it. "I don't know what it means."

I need water. It's the only thing I remember the taste of. Maybe because water has no taste.

"Did you write it?" she demands.

"How would I know?" I don't like the tone in my voice. I sound aggravated. I don't want her to think I'm aggravated with her.

She turns and walks swiftly to her backpack. She digs around inside and pulls out a pen, then walks back to me, shoving it into my hand. "Copy it."

She's bossy. I look down at the pen, rolling it between my fingers. I run my thumb across the embossed words printed down the side of it.

WYNWOOD-NASH FINANCIAL GROUP

"See if your handwriting matches," she says. She flips the page over to the blank side and pushes it toward me. I catch her eyes, fall into them a little. But then I'm angry.

I hate that she thinks of this stuff first. I hold the pen in my right hand. It doesn't feel comfortable. I switch the pen to my left hand and it fits better. *I'm a leftie.*

I write the words from memory, and after she gets a good look at my handwriting, I flip the page back over.

The handwriting is different. Mine is sharp, concise. The other is loose and uncaring. She takes the pen and rewrites the words.

It's a perfect match. We both stare quietly at the paper, unsure if it even means anything. It could mean nothing. It could mean *everything.* The dirt on my sheets could mean everything. The blood-smeared handprint could mean everything. The fact that we can remember basic things but not people could mean everything. The clothes I'm wearing, the color of her nail polish, the camera on my desk, the photos on the wall, the clock above the door, the half-empty glass of water on the desk. I'm turning, taking it all in. It could *all* mean everything.

Or it could all mean absolutely nothing.

I don't know what to catalog in my mind and what to ignore. Maybe if I just fall asleep, I'll wake up tomorrow and be completely normal again.

"I'm hungry," she says.

She's watching me; strands of hair stand between

me and a full view of her face. She's beautiful, but in a shameful way. One I'm not sure I'm supposed to appreciate. Everything about her is captivating, like the aftermath of a storm. People aren't supposed to get pleasure out of the destruction Mother Nature is capable of, but we want to stare anyway. Charlie is the devastation left in the wake of a tornado.

How do I know that?

Right now she looks calculating, staring at me like this. I want to grab my camera and take a picture of her. Something twirls in my stomach like ribbons, and I'm not sure if it's nerves or hunger or my reaction to the girl standing next to me.

"Let's go downstairs," I tell her. I reach for her backpack and hand it to her. I grab the camera from the dresser. "We'll eat while we search our things."

She walks in front of me, pausing at every picture between my room and the bottom of the stairwell. With each picture we pass, she trails her finger over my face, and my face alone. I watch as she quietly tries to figure me out through the series of photographs. I want to tell her she's wasting her time. Whoever is in those pictures, it isn't me.

As soon as we reach the bottom of the stairs, our ears are assaulted by a short burst of a scream. Charlie comes to a sudden halt and I bump into the back of her. The scream belongs to a woman standing in the doorway of the kitchen.

Her eyes are wide, darting from me to Charlie, back and forth. She's clutching her heart, exhaling with relief.

She's not from any of the photographs. She's plump and older, maybe in her sixties. She's wearing an apron that reads *I put the "hor" in hors d'oeuvres.*

Her hair is pulled back, but she brushes away loose gray strands as she blows out a calming breath. "Jesus, Silas! You scared me half to death!" She spins and heads into the kitchen. "You two better get back to school before your father finds out. I'm not lying for you."

Charlie is still frozen in front of me, so I place a hand against her lower back and nudge her forward. She glances at me over her shoulder. "Do you know…"

I shake my head, cutting off her question. She's about to ask me if I know the woman in the kitchen. The answer is no. I don't know *her*, I don't know *Charlie*, I don't know the family in the photos.

What I *do* know is the camera in my hands. I look down at it, wondering how I can remember everything there is to know about operating this camera, but I can't remember how I learned any of those things. I know how to adjust the ISO. I know how to adjust shutter speed to give a waterfall the appearance of a soft stream, or make each individual drop of water stand on its own. This camera has the ability to put the smallest detail in focus, like the curve of Charlie's hand, or the eyelashes lining her eyes, while everything else about her becomes a blur. I know that I somehow know the ins and outs of this camera better than I know what my own little brother's voice should sound like.

I wrap the strap around my neck and allow the camera to dangle against my chest as I follow Charlie toward the kitchen. She's walking with purpose. So far, I've concluded that everything she does has a purpose. She wastes nothing. Every step she takes appears to be planned out before she takes it. Every word she says is necessary. Whenever her eyes land on something, she focuses on it with all of her senses, as though her eyes alone could determine how something tastes, smells, sounds, and feels. And she only looks at things when there's a reason for it. Forget the floors, the curtains, the photographs in the hall that don't have my face in them. She doesn't waste time on things that aren't of use to her.

Which is why I follow her when she walks into the kitchen. I'm not sure what her purpose is right now. It's either to find out more information from the housekeeper or she's on the hunt for food.

Charlie claims a seat at the massive bar and pulls out the chair next to her and pats it without looking up at me. I take the seat and set my camera down in front of me. She drops her backpack onto the counter and begins to unzip it. "Ezra, I'm starving. Is there anything to eat?"

My entire body swivels toward Charlie's on the stool, but it feels like my stomach is somewhere on the floor beneath me. *How does she know her name?*

Charlie glances at me with a quick shake of her head. "Calm down," she hisses. "It's written right there." She points at a note—a shopping list lying in front of us. It's a pink stationery pad, personalized, with kittens lining the bottom of the page. At the top of the personalized stationery, it reads *Things Ezra needs right meow.*

The woman closes a cabinet and faces Charlie. "Did you work up an appetite while you were upstairs? Because in case you weren't aware, they serve lunch at the school you should both be attending right now."

"You mean right *meow*," I say without thinking. Charlie spatters laughter, and then I'm laughing too. And it feels like someone finally let air into the room. Ezra, less amused, rolls her eyes. It makes me wonder if I used to be funny. I also smile, because the fact that she didn't appear confused by Charlie referring to her as Ezra means Charlie was right.

I reach over and run my hand along the back of Charlie's neck. She flinches when I touch her, but relaxes almost immediately when she realizes it's part of our act. *We're in love, Charlie. Remember?*

"Charlie hasn't been feeling well. I brought her here so she could nap, but she hasn't eaten today." I return my attention to Ezra and smile. "Do you have anything to make my girl feel better? Some soup or crackers, maybe?"

Ezra's expression softens when she sees the affection I'm showing Charlie. She grabs a hand towel and tosses it over her shoulder. "I'll tell you what, Char. How about I make you my grilled cheese specialty? It was your favorite back when you used to visit."

My hand stiffens against Charlie's neck. *Back when you used to visit?* We both look at each other, more questions clouding our eyes. Charlie nods. "Thank you, Ezra," she says.

Ezra shuts the refrigerator door with her hip and begins dropping items onto the counter. Butter. Mayonnaise. Bread. Cheese. *More* cheese. *Parmesan* cheese. She lays a pan on the stove and ignites the flame. "I'll make you one, too, Silas," Ezra says. "You must have caught whatever bug Charlie has, because you haven't spoken to me this much since you hit puberty." She chuckles after her comment.

"Why don't I speak to you?"

Charlie nudges my leg and narrows her eyes. I shouldn't have asked that.

Ezra slides the knife into the butter and retrieves a slab of it. She smears it across the bread. "Oh, you know," she says, shrugging her shoulders. "Little boys grow up. They become men. Housekeepers stop being *Aunt Ezra* and return to just being housekeepers." Her voice is sad now.

I grimace, because I don't like learning about this side of myself. I don't want *Charlie* learning about this side of me.

My eyes fall to the camera in front of me. I power it on. Charlie begins rifling through her backpack, inspecting item after item.

"Uh oh," she says.

She's holding a phone. I lean over her shoulder and look at the screen with her, just as she switches the ringer to the on position. There are seven missed calls and even more texts, all from "Mom."

She opens the latest text message, sent just three minutes ago.

You have three minutes to call me back.

I guess I didn't think about the ramifications of us ditching school. The ramifications of parents we don't even remember. "We should go," I say to her.

We both stand at the same time. She throws her backpack over her shoulder and I grab my camera.

"Wait," Ezra says. "The first sandwich is almost done." She walks to the refrigerator and grabs two cans of Sprite. "This will help with her stomach." She hands me both sodas and then wraps the grilled cheese in a paper towel. Charlie is already waiting at the front door. Just as I'm about to walk away from Ezra, she squeezes my wrist. I face her again, and her eyes move from Charlie to me. "It's good to see her back here," Ezra says softly. "I've been worried how everything between both your fathers might have affected the two of you. You've loved that girl since before you could walk."

I stare at her, not sure how to process all the information I just received. "Before I could walk, huh?"

She smiles like she has one of my secrets. I want it back. "Silas," Charlie says.

I shoot a quick smile at Ezra and head for Charlie. As soon as I reach the front door, the shrill ring on her phone startles her and it falls from her hands, straight to the floor. She kneels to pick it up. "It's her," she says, standing. "What should I do?"

I open the door and urge her outside by her elbow. Once the door is shut, I face her again. The phone is on its third ring. "You should answer it."

She stares at the phone, her fingers gripping tightly around it. She doesn't answer it, so I reach down and swipe right to answer. She crinkles up her nose and glares at me as she brings it to her ear. "Hello?"

We begin walking to the car, but I listen quietly at the broken phrases coming through her phone: "ou know better," and "Skip school," and "How could you?" The words continue to come out of her phone, until we're both seated in my car with the doors shut. I start the car and the woman's voice grows quiet for several seconds. Suddenly, the voice is blaring through the speakers of my car. *Bluetooth. I remember what Bluetooth is.*

I place the drinks and sandwich on the center console and begin to back out of the driveway. Charlie still hasn't had a chance to respond to her mother, but she rolls her eyes when I look at her.

"Mom," Charlie says flatly, attempting to interrupt

her. "Mom, I'm on my way home. Silas is taking me to my car."

There's a long silence that follows Charlie's words, and somehow her mother is much more intimidating when words *aren't* being yelled through the phone. When she does begin speaking again, her words come out slow and overenunciated. "Please tell me you did not allow *that* family to buy you a *car*."

Our eyes meet and Charlie mouths the word *shit*. "I… No. No, I meant Silas is bringing me home. Be there in a few minutes." Charlie fumbles with the phone in her hands, attempting to return to a screen that will allow her to end the call. I press the disconnect button on the steering wheel and end it for her.

She inhales slowly, turning to face her window. When she exhales, a small circle of fog appears against the window near her mouth. "Silas?" She faces me and arches a brow. "I think my mother may be a bitch."

I laugh, but offer no reassurance. I agree with her.

We're both quiet for several miles. I repeat my brief conversation with Ezra over and over in my head. I'm unable to push the scene out of my head, and she's not even my parent. I can't imagine what Charlie must be feeling right now after speaking to her actual mother. I think both of us have had the reassurance in the backs of our minds that once we came in contact with someone as close to us as our own parents, it would trigger our memory. I can tell by Charlie's reaction that she didn't recognize a single thing about the woman she spoke to on the phone.

"I don't have a car," she says quietly. I look over at her and she's drawing a cross with her fingertip on the fogged-up window. "I'm seventeen. I wonder why I don't have a car."

As soon as she mentions the car, I remember that I'm still driving in the direction of the school, rather than wherever I need to be taking her. "Do you happen to know where you live, Charlie?"

Her eyes swing to mine, and in a split second the confusion on her face is overcome by clarity. It's fascinating how easily I can read her expressions now in comparison to earlier this morning. Her eyes are like two open books and I suddenly want to devour every page.

She pulls her wallet from her backpack and reads the address from her driver's license. "If you pull over we can put it in the GPS," she says.

I push the navigation button. "These cars are made in London. You don't have to idle to program an address into the GPS." I begin to enter her street number and I feel her watching me. I don't even have to see her eyes to know they're overflowing with suspicion.

I shake my head before she even asks the question. "No, I don't know how I knew that."

Once the address is entered, I turn the car around and begin to head in the direction of her house. We're seven miles away. She opens both sodas and tears the sandwich in half, handing me part of it. We drive six miles without speaking. I want to reach over and grab her hand to comfort her. I want to say something reassuring to her. If this were yesterday, I'm sure I would have done that without a second thought. But it's not yesterday. It's today, and Charlie and I are complete strangers today.

On the seventh and final mile, she speaks, but all she says is, "That was a really good grilled cheese. Make sure you tell Ezra I said so."

I slow down. I drive well below the speed limit until we reach her street, and then I stop as soon as I turn onto the road. She's staring out her window, taking in each and every house. They're small. One-story houses, each with a one-car garage. Any one of these houses could fit inside my kitchen and we'd still have room to cook a meal.

"Do you want me to go inside with you?"

She shakes her head. "You probably shouldn't. It doesn't sound like my mother likes you very much."

She's right. I wish I knew what her mother was referring to when she said *that* family. I wish I knew what Ezra was referring to when she mentioned our fathers.

"I think it's that one," she says, pointing to one a few houses down. I let off the gas and roll toward it. It's by far the nicest one on the street, but only because the yard was recently mowed and the paint on the window frames isn't peeling off in chunks.

My car slows and eventually comes to a stop in front of the house. We both stare at it, quietly taking in the vast separation between the lives we live. However, it's nothing like the separation I feel knowing we're about to have to split up for the rest of the night. She's been a good buffer between me and reality.

"Do me a favor," I tell her as I put the car in park. "Look for my name in your caller ID. I want to see if I have a phone in here."

She nods and begins scrolling through her contacts. She swipes her finger across the screen and brings her phone to her ear, pulling her bottom lip in with her teeth to hide what looks like a smile.

Right when I open my mouth to ask her what just made her smile, a muffled ring comes from the console.

I flip it open and reach in until I find the phone. When I look at the screen, I read the contact.

Charlie baby

I guess that answers my question. She must also have a nickname for me. I swipe answer and bring the phone to my ear. "Hey, *Charlie baby*."

She laughs, and it comes at me twice. Once through my phone and again from the seat next to me.

"I'm afraid we might have been a pretty cheesy couple, *Silas baby*," she says.

"Seems like it." I run the pad of my thumb around the steering wheel, waiting for her to speak again. She doesn't. She's still staring at the unfamiliar house.

"Call me as soon as you get a chance, okay?"

"I will," she says.

"You might have kept a journal. Look for anything that could help us."

"I will," she says again.

We're both still holding our phones to our ears. I'm not sure if she's hesitating to get out because she's scared of what she'll find inside or because she doesn't want to leave the only other person who understands her situation.

"Do you think you'll tell anyone?" I ask.

She pulls the phone from her ear, swiping the end button. "I don't want anyone to think I'm going crazy."

"You're not going crazy," I say. "Not if it's happening to both of us." Her lips press into a tight, thin line. She gives her head the softest nod, as if it's made from glass. "Exactly. If I were going through this alone, it would be easy to just say I'm going crazy. But I'm *not* alone. We're both experiencing this, which means it's something else entirely. And that scares me, Silas."

She opens the door and steps out. I roll the window down as she closes the door behind her. She folds her arms over the windowsill and forces a smile as she gestures over her shoulder toward the house behind her. "I guess it's safe to say I won't have a housekeeper to cook me grilled cheese."

I force a smile in return. "You know my number. Just call if you need me to come rescue you."

Her fake smile is swallowed up by a genuine frown. "Like a damsel in distress." She rolls her eyes. She reaches through the window and grabs her backpack. "Wish me luck, *Silas baby.*" Her endearment is full of sarcasm, and I kind of hate it.

5

Charlie

"Mom?" My voice is weak, a squeak. I clear my throat. "Mom?" I call again.

She comes careening around the corner and I immediately think of a car without brakes. I retreat two steps until my back is flush against the front door.

"What were you doing with that boy?" she hisses. I can smell the liquor on her breath.

"I… He brought me home from school." I wrinkle my nose and breathe through my mouth. She's all up in my personal space. I reach behind me and grab the doorknob in case I need to make a quick exit. I was hoping to feel something when I saw her. She was my incubating uterus and birthday party thrower for the last seventeen years. I half expected a rush of warmth or memories, some familiarity. I flinch away from the stranger in front of me.

"You skipped school. You were with *that* boy! Care to explain?" She smells like a bar just vomited on her.

"I don't feel like…myself. I asked him to bring me

home." I back up a step. "Why are you drunk in the middle of the day?"

Her eyes splay wide and for a minute I think it's a real possibility that she might hit me. At the last moment she stumbles back and slides down the wall until she's sitting on the floor. Tears invade her eyes and I have to look away.

Okay, I wasn't expecting that.

Yelling I can deal with. Crying makes me nervous. Especially when it's a complete stranger and I don't know what to say. I creep past her just as she buries her face in her hands and begins to sob hard. I'm not sure if this is normal for her. I hesitate, hovering right where the foyer ends and the living room starts. In the end, I leave her to her tears and decide to find my bedroom. I can't help her. I don't even know her.

I want to hide until I figure something out. Like who the hell I am. The house is smaller than I thought. Just past where my mother is crying on the floor, there is a kitchen and a small living room. They sit squat and orderly, filled to the max with furniture that doesn't look like it belongs. Expensive things in an inexpensive house. There are three doors. The first is open. I peer in and see a plaid bedspread. My parents' bedroom? I know from the plaid bedspread that it isn't mine. I like flowers. I open the second of the doors: a bathroom. The third is another bedroom on the left side of the hallway. I step inside. Two beds. I groan. I have a sibling.

I lock the door behind me, and my eyes dart around the shared space. I have a sister. By the looks of her things she is younger than me by at least a few years. I stare at the band posters that adorn her side of the room with distaste. My side is simpler: a twin bed with a dark

purple comforter and a framed black and white print
that hangs on the wall over the bed. I immediately know
it's something Silas photographed. A broken gate that
hangs on its hinges; vines choking their way through
the rusted metal prongs—not as dark as the prints in his
bedroom, perhaps more suited to me. There is a stack
of books on my nightstand. I reach for one to read the
title when my phone pings.

Silas: You okay?

Me: I think my mom is an alcoholic and I have a sister.

His response comes a few seconds later.

Silas: I don't know what to say. This is so awkward.

I laugh and set my phone down. I want to dig around,
see if I can find anything suspicious. My drawers are
neat. I must have OCD. I toss around the socks and underwear to see if I can piss myself off.

There is nothing in my drawers, nothing in my nightstand. I find a box of condoms stuffed in a purse under
my bed. I look for a journal, notes written by friends—
there is nothing. I am a sterile human, boring if not for
that print above my bed. A print which Silas gave to me,
not one I picked out myself.

My mother is in the kitchen. I can hear her sniffling
and making herself something to eat. *She's drunk*, I
think. Maybe I should ask her some questions and she
won't remember I asked them.

"Hey, er... Mom," I say, coming to stand near her. She
pauses in her toast-making to look at me with bleary eyes.

"So, was I being weird last night?"

"Last night?" she repeats.

"Yeah," I say. "You know…when I came home."

She scrapes the knife over the bread until it is smeared with butter.

"You were dirty," she slurs. "I told you to take a shower."

I think of the dirt and leaves in Silas's bed. That means we were probably together.

"What time did I get home? My phone was dead," I lie.

She narrows her eyes. "Around ten o'clock."

"Did I say anything…unusual?"

She turns away and wanders over to the sink, where she bites into her toast and stares down the drain.

"Mom! Pay attention. I need you to answer me." Why does this feel familiar? Me begging, her ignoring.

"No," she says simply. Then I have a thought: my clothes from last night. Off the kitchen there is a small closet with a stacked washer and dryer inside of it. I open the lid to the washing machine and see a small mound of wet clothes clumped at the bottom. I pull them out. They are definitely my size. I must have thrown them in here last night, tried to wash away the evidence. *Evidence of what?* I pry the pockets of the jeans open with my fingers and reach inside. There is a wad of paper, clumped in a thick, damp mess. I drop the jeans and carry the wad back to my room. If I try to unfold it, it might fall apart. I decide to set it on the windowsill and wait for it to dry.

I text Silas.

Me: Where are you?

I wait a few minutes and when he doesn't text back, I try again.

Me: Silas!

I wonder if I always do this; harass him until he answers.

I send five more and then I toss my phone across the room, burying my face in Charlie Wynwood's pillow to cry. Charlie Wynwood probably never cried. She has no personality from the looks of her bedroom. Her mother is an alcoholic and her sister listens to crappy music. And how do I know that the poster above my sister's bed compares love to a *boom* and a *clap*, but I don't remember said sister's name? I wander over to her side of the small bedroom and rummage around in her things.

"Ding, ding, ding!" I say, pulling a pink polka dot journal out from under her pillow.

I settle down on her bed and flip open the cover.

Property of Janette Elise Wynwood.
DO NOT READ!

I ignore the warning and page to her first entry, titled:

Charlie sucks.
My sister is the worst person on the planet. I hope she dies.

I close the book and put it back underneath the pillow. "That went well."

My family hates me. What type of human are you when your own family hates you? From across the room my phone tells me that I have a text. I jump up, thinking it's Silas, suddenly feeling relieved. There are two texts. One is from Amy.

Where r u?!!

And the other is from a guy named Brian.

Hey, missed u today. Did you tell him?

Him who? And tell him what?

I set my phone down without answering either of them. I decide to give the journal another try, skipping all the way to Janette's last entry, which was last night.

Title: I might need braces but we're too broke. Charlie had braces.

I run my tongue over my teeth. Yup, they feel pretty straight.

Her teeth are all straight and perfect and I'm going to have a snaggle tooth forever. Mom said she'd see about financing but ever since that thing happened with dad's company we don't have money for normal things. I hate taking packed lunch to school. I feel like a kindergartener!

I skip a paragraph in which she details her friend Payton's last period.

She's ranting about her lack of menstruation when her journaling is disturbed by yours truly.

I have to go. Charlie just got home and she's cry-ing. She hardly ever cries. I hope Silas broke up with her—would serve her right.

So I was crying when I came home last night? I walk over to the windowsill where the paper from my pocket has somewhat dried. Carefully smoothing it out, I lay it on the desk my sister and I seem to share. Part of the ink has washed away, but it looks like a receipt. I text Silas.

Me: Silas, I need a ride.

I wait again, growing irritated with his delay in re-sponse. *I am impatient*, I think.

Me: There's a guy named Brian who's texting me. He's really flirty. I can ask him for a ride if you're busy...

My phone pings a second later.

Silas: Hell no. OMW!

I smile.

It shouldn't be a problem slipping out of the house since my mother has passed out on the sofa. I watch her for a moment, studying her sleeping face, trying des-perately to remember it. She looks like Charlie, only older. Before I head outside to wait for Silas, I cover her with a blanket and grab a couple of sodas from the barren fridge.

"See ya, Mom," I say quietly.

6

Silas

I can't tell if I'm going back to her because I feel protective over her or possessive of her. Either way, I don't like the idea of her reaching out to someone else. It makes me wonder who this Brian guy is, and why he thinks it's okay to send her flirty texts when Charlie and I are obviously together.

My left hand is still clutching my phone when it rings again. There's no number on the screen. Just the word "Bro." I slide my finger across it and answer the phone.

"Hello?"

"Where the hell are you?"

It's a guy's voice. A voice that sounds a lot like mine. I look left and right, but nothing is familiar about the intersection I'm passing through. "I'm in my car."

He groans. "No shit. You keep missing practice, you'll be benched." Yesterday's Silas probably would have been pissed off about this.

Today's Silas is relieved. "What day is today?"

"Wednesday. Day before tomorrow, day after yesterday. Come get me, practice is over."

Why does he not have his own car? I don't even know this kid and he already feels like an inconvenience. He's definitely my brother.

"I have to pick up Charlie first," I tell him.

There's a pause. "At her house?"

"Yeah."

Another pause. "Do you have a death wish?"

I really hate not knowing what everyone else seems to know. Why would I not be allowed at Charlie's house?

"Whatever, just hurry up," he says, right before hanging up.

She's standing in the street when I turn the corner. She's staring at her house. Her hands are resting gently at her sides, and she's holding two sodas. One in each hand. She's holding them like weapons, like she wants to throw them at the house in front of her in hopes that they're actually grenades. I slow the car down and stop several feet from her.

She's not wearing the same clothes she had on earlier. She's wearing a long, black skirt that covers her feet. A black scarf is wrapped around her neck, falling over her shoulder. Her shirt is tan and long-sleeved, but she still looks cold. A gust of wind blows and the skirt and scarf move with it, but she remains unaffected. She doesn't even blink. She's lost in thought.

I'm lost in her.

When I put the car in park, she turns her head, looks at me and then immediately casts her eyes at the ground. She walks toward the passenger door and climbs inside. Her silence seems to be begging for my silence, so I don't say anything as we head toward the school. After a couple of miles, she relaxes against the seat and props one of her booted feet against the dash. "Where are we going?"

"My brother called. He needs a ride." She nods.

"Apparently I'm in trouble for not showing up to football practice today." I'm sure she can tell by the lackadaisical tone of my voice that I'm not too concerned about missing practice. Football isn't really on my list of priorities right now, so being benched is probably the best outcome for everyone.

"You play football," she says, matter of fact. "I don't do anything. I'm boring, Silas. My room is boring. I don't keep a journal. I don't collect anything. The only thing I have is a picture of a gate, and I didn't even take the picture. *You* did. All I have with any personality in my whole room is something you gave me."

"How do you know the picture is from me?"

She shrugs and tugs her skirt taut across her knees. "You have a unique style. Kind of like a thumbprint. I could tell it was yours because you only take pictures of things that people are too scared to stare at in real life."

She doesn't like my photographs, I guess.

"So…" I ask, staring straight ahead. "Who's this Brian guy?"

She picks up her phone and opens her texts. I'm trying to look over at them, knowing I'm too far away to read them, but I make the effort, anyway. I notice she tilts her phone slightly to the right, shielding it from my view. "I'm not sure," she says. "I tried to scroll back and see if I could figure out anything from texts, but our messages are confusing. I can't tell if I was dating him or you."

My mouth is dry again. I take one of the drinks she

brought with her and pop the top of it. I take a long sip and set it back in the cup holder.

"Maybe you were messing around with both of us." There's an edge to my voice. I try to soften it. "What do his texts from today say?"

She locks the phone and turns it face down in her lap, almost as if she's ashamed to look at it. She doesn't answer me. I can feel my neck flush, and I recognize the warmth of the jealousy creeping through me like a virus. I don't like it.

"Text him back," I say to her. "Tell him you don't want him to text you anymore and that you want to work it out with me."

She cuts her eyes in my direction. "We don't know our situation," she says. "What if I didn't like you? What if we were both ready to break up?"

I look back at the road and grind my teeth together. "I just think it's better if we stick together until we figure out what happened. You don't even know who this Brian guy is."

"I don't know you, either," she bites back.

I pull into the parking lot of the school. She's watching me closely, waiting on my response. I feel like I'm being baited.

I park the car and turn it off. I grip the steering wheel with my right hand and my jaw with my left hand. I squeeze both. "How do we do this?"

"Can you be a little more specific?" she says.

I give my head the slightest shake. I don't know if she's even looking at me to notice. "I can't be specific, because I'm referring to everything. To us, our families, our lives. How do we figure this out, Charlie? And how do we do it without finding things out about each other that are going to piss us off?"

Before she can answer me, someone exits a gate and begins walking toward us. He looks like me, but younger. Maybe a sophomore. He's not as big as me yet, but from the looks of him, he's probably going to surpass me in size.

"This should be fun," she says, watching my little brother approach the car. He walks straight to the back passenger side and swings open the door. He tosses in a backpack, an extra pair of shoes, a gym bag, and finally, himself.

The door slams.

He pulls out his phone and begins scrolling through his texts. He's breathing heavily. His hair is sweaty and matted to his forehead. We have the same hair. When he looks up at me, I see that we also have the same eyes.

"What's your problem?" he asks.

I don't respond to him. I turn back around in my seat and glance at Charlie. She has a smirk on her face and she's texting someone. I almost want to grab her phone and see if she's texting Brian, but my phone vibrates from her text as soon as she hits send.

Charlie: Do you even know your little brother's name?

I have absolutely no idea what my own little brother's name is. "Shit," I say.

She laughs, but her laugh is cut short when she spots something in the parking lot. My gaze follows hers and lands on a guy. He's stalking toward the car, glaring hard at Charlie.

I recognize him. He's the guy from the bathroom this morning. The one who tried to provoke me.

"Let me guess," I say. "Brian?"

He walks straight to the passenger door and opens it. He steps back and crooks his finger at Charlie. He ignores me completely, but he's about to get to know me really well if he thinks he can summon Charlie this way.

"We need to talk," he says, his words clipped.

Charlie puts her hand on the door to pull it shut. "Sorry," she says. "We were just about to leave. I'll talk to you tomorrow."

Disbelief registers on his face, but so does a hefty dose of anger. As soon as I see him grab her by the arm and yank her toward him, I'm out of the vehicle and rounding the front of my car. I'm moving so fast, I slip on the gravel and have to grab the hood of the car to prevent myself from falling. *Smooth.* I rush around the passenger door, prepared to grab the bastard by his throat, but he's bent over, groaning. His hand is covering his eye. He straightens up and glares at Charlie through his good eye.

"I told you not to touch me," Charlie says through clenched teeth.

She's standing next to her door, her hand still clenched in a fist.

"You don't want me to touch you?" he says with a smirk. "That's a first."

Just as I begin to lunge toward him, Charlie shoves a hand against my chest. She shoots me a warning look, giving her head the slightest shake. I force a deep, calming breath and step back.

Charlie focuses her attention back on Brian. "That was yesterday, Brian. Today's a brand-new day and I'm leaving with Silas. Got it?" She turns around and climbs back into the passenger seat. I wait until her door is shut and locked before I begin to walk back to the driver's side.

"She's cheating on you," Brian yells after me. I stop in my tracks.

I slowly turn and face him. He's standing upright now, and from the looks of his posture, he's expecting me to hit him. When I don't, he continues to provoke me.

"With me," he adds. "More than once. It's been going on for over two months now."

I stare at him, trying to remain calm on the outside, but internally, my hands are wrapped around his throat, squeezing the last drop of oxygen from his lungs.

I glance at Charlie. She's begging me with her eyes not to do anything stupid. I turn back to face him and somehow, I smile. "That's nice, Brian. You want a trophy?"

I wish I could bottle up the expression on his face and release it any time I need a good laugh.

Once I'm back inside the car, I pull out of the parking lot more dramatically than I probably should. When we're back on the road, heading toward my house, I finally find it in me to look at Charlie. She's staring right back at me. We keep our eyes locked for a few seconds, gauging one another's reaction. Right before I'm forced to look back at the road in front of me, I see her smile.

We both start laughing. She relaxes against her seat and says, "I can't believe I was cheating on you with that guy. You must have done something that really pissed me off."

I smile at her. "Nothing short of murder should have made you cheat on me with that guy."

A throat clears in the backseat, and I immediately glance in the rearview mirror. I forgot all about my brother. He leans forward until he's positioned between the front and middle seats. He looks at Charlie, and then at me.

"Let me get this straight," he says. "You two are *laughing* about this?"

Charlie glances at me out of the corner of her eye. We both stop laughing and Charlie clears her throat. "How long have we been together now, Silas?" she asks.

I pretend to count on my fingers when my brother speaks up. "Four years," he interjects. "Jesus, what's gotten into the two of you?"

Charlie leans forward and locks eyes with me. I know exactly what she's thinking.

"Four years?" I mutter.

"Wow," Charlie says. "Long time."

My brother shakes his head and falls back against his seat. "The two of you are worse than an episode of *Jerry Springer.*"

Jerry Springer is a talk show host. How do I know this? I wonder if Charlie remembers this.

"You remember Jerry Springer?" I ask her.

Her lips are tight, pressed together in contemplation. She nods and turns toward the passenger window.

None of this makes sense. How can we remember celebrities? People we've never met? How do I know that Kanye West married a Kardashian? How do I know that Robin Williams died?

I can remember everyone I've never met, but I can't remember the girl I've been in love with for over four years? Uneasiness takes over inside of me, pumping through my veins until it settles in my heart. I spend the next few miles silently naming off all the names and faces of people I remember. Presidents. Actors. Politicians. Musicians. Reality TV stars.

But I can't for the life of me remember the name of my little brother, who is climbing out of the backseat right now. I watch him as he makes his way inside our house. I continue to watch the door, long after it closes behind him. I'm staring at my house just like Charlie was staring at hers.

"Are you okay?" Charlie asks.

It's as if the sound of her voice is suction, pulling me out of my head at breakneck speed and shoving me back into the moment. The moment where I picture Charlie and Brian and the words he said that I had to pretend didn't affect me at all. *"She's cheating on you."*

I close my eyes and lean my head against the headrest. "Why do you think it happened?"

"You really do need to learn how to be more specific, Silas."

"Okay," I reply, lifting my head and looking directly at her. "Brian. Why do you think you slept with him?"

She sighs. "You can't be mad at me for that."

I tilt my head and look at her in disbelief. "We were together for *four* years, Charlie. You can't blame me for being a little upset."

She shakes her head. "*They* were together for four years. Charlie and Silas. Not the two of us," she says. "Besides, who's to say you were an angel? Have you even looked through all your own texts?"

I shake my head. "I'm afraid to now. And don't do that."

"Don't do what?"

"Don't refer to us in the third person. You *are* her. And I'm him. Whether we like who we were or not."

As soon as I begin to pull out of the driveway, Charlie's phone rings. "My sister," she says right before she answers it with a hello. She listens quietly for several seconds, eyeing me the entire time. "She was drunk when I got home. I'll be there in a few minutes." She ends the call. "Back to the school," she says. "My alcoholic mother was supposed to pick my sister up after her swim practice. Looks like we're about to meet another sibling."

I laugh. "I feel like I was a chauffeur in my past life."

Charlie's expression tightens. "I'll stop referring to us in the third person if you stop referring to it as a past life. We didn't *die*, Silas. We just can't remember anything."

"We can remember *some* things," I clarify.

I begin to head back in the direction of the school. At least I'll know my way around with all of this back and forth.

"There was this family in Texas," she says. "They had a parrot, but he went missing. Four years later, he showed up out of the blue—speaking Spanish." She laughs. "Why do I remember that pointless story but I can't remember what I did twelve hours ago?"

I don't respond, because her question is rhetorical, unlike all the questions in my head.

When we pull up to the school again, a spitting image of Charlie is standing by the entrance with her hands crossed tightly over her chest. She climbs into the backseat and sits in the same spot where my brother was just sitting.

"How was your day?" Charlie asks her.

"Shut up," her sister says.

"Bad, I take it?"

"Shut up," she says again.

Charlie looks at me wide-eyed, but with a mischievous grin on her face. "Were you waiting long?"

"Shut *up*," her sister says again.

I realize now that Charlie is just instigating her. I smile when she keeps at it.

"Mom was pretty wasted when I got home today."

"What's new?" her sister says.

At least she didn't say shut up *this time.*

Charlie fires a couple more questions, but her sister ignores her completely, giving her full attention to the phone in her hands. When we pull into Charlie's driveway, her sister begins to open her door before the car even comes to a stop.

"Tell Mom I'll be late," Charlie says as her sister climbs out of the car. "And when do you think Dad will be home?"

Her sister pauses. She stares at Charlie with contempt. "Ten to fifteen, according to the judge." She slams the door.

I wasn't expecting that, and apparently neither was Charlie. She slowly turns around in her seat until she's facing forward again. She inhales a slow breath and carefully releases it. "My sister hates me. I live in a dump. My mom's an alcoholic. My father is in prison. I cheat on you." She looks at me. "Why the hell are you even dating me?"

If I knew her better, I'd hug her. Hold her hand. *Something.* I don't know what to do. There's no protocol on how to console your girlfriend of four years who you just met this morning.

"Well, according to Ezra, I've loved you since before I could walk. I guess that's hard to let go of."

She laughs under her breath. "You must have some fierce loyalty, because *I'm* even beginning to hate me."

I want to reach over and touch her cheek. Make her look at me. I don't, though. I put the car in reverse and keep my hands to myself. "Maybe there's a lot more to you than just your financial status and who your family is."

"Yeah," she says. She glances at me and the disappointment is momentarily replaced by a brief smile. "Maybe."

I smile with her, but we both glance out our respective windows to hide them. Once we're on the road again, Charlie reaches for the radio. She scrolls through several stations, settling on one song that we both immediately begin singing. As soon as the first line of lyrics comes out of our mouths, we both immediately turn and face one another.

"Lyrics," she says softly. "We remember song lyrics."

Nothing is adding up. At this point, my mind is so exhausted I don't even feel like attempting to figure it out at the moment. I just want the respite the music provides. Apparently so does she, because she sits quietly beside me for most of the drive. After several minutes pass, I can feel her look at me.

"I hate that I cheated on you." She immediately turns up the volume on the radio and settles against her seat. She doesn't want a response from me, but if she did I would tell her it was okay. That I forgive her. Because the girl sitting next to me right now doesn't seem like she could be the girl who previously betrayed me.

She never asks where we're going. I don't even know

where we're going. I just drive, because driving seems to be the only time my mind settles down. I have no idea how long we drive, but the sun is finally setting when I decide to turn around and head back. We're both lost in our heads the entire time, which is ironic for two people who have no memories.

"We need to go through our phones," I say to her. It's the first thing spoken between us in over an hour. "Check old text messages, emails, voicemail. We might find something that could explain this."

She pulls her phone out. "I tried that earlier, but I don't have a fancy phone like yours. I only get text messages, but I barely have any."

I pull the car over at a gas station and park off to the side where it's darker. I don't know why I feel like we need privacy to do this. I just don't want anyone approaching if they recognize us, because chances are, we won't know them in return.

I turn off the car and we both begin scrolling through our phones. I start with text messages between the two of us first. I scroll through several, but they're all short and to the point. Schedules, times to meet up. *I love you*'s and *miss you*'s. Nothing revealing anything at all about our relationship.

Based on my call log, we talk for at least an hour almost every night. I go through all the calls stored in my phone, which is well over two weeks' worth.

"We talked on the phone for at least an hour every night," I tell her.

"Really?" she says, genuinely shocked. "What in the world could we have talked about for an hour every night?"

I grin. "Maybe we don't actually do a whole lot of *talking*."

She shakes her head with a quiet laugh. "Why do your sex jokes not surprise me, even though I remember absolutely nothing about you?"

Her half laugh turns into a groan. "Oh, God," she says, tilting her phone toward me. "Look at this." She scrolls through her phone's camera roll with her finger. "Selfies. Nothing but selfies, Silas. I even took *bathroom* selfies." She exits out of her camera app. "Kill me now."

I laugh and open the camera on my own phone. The first picture is of the two of us. We're standing in front of a lake, taking a selfie, naturally. I show her and she groans even louder, dropping her head dramatically against the headrest. "I'm starting to not like who we are, Silas. You're a rich kid who's a dick to your house-keeper. I'm a mean teenager with absolutely no person-ality who takes selfies to make herself feel important."

"I'm sure we aren't as bad as we seem. At least we appear to like each *other*."

She laughs under her breath. "I was cheating on you. Apparently we weren't that happy."

I open the email on my phone and find a video file labeled "Do not delete." I click on it.

"Check this out." I lift the armrest and scoot closer to her so she can see the video. I turn the car stereo up so the sound can be heard through Bluetooth. She lifts her armrest and scoots closer to get a better look.

I hit play. My voice comes through the speakers of my car, making it apparent that I'm the one holding the cam-era in the video. It's dark, and it looks like I'm outside.

"It's officially our two year anniversary." My voice is hushed, like I don't want to be caught doing whatever

it is I'm doing. I turn the camera on myself and the light from the recorder is on, illuminating my face. I look younger, maybe by a year or two. I'm guessing I was sixteen based on the fact that I just said it was our two-year anniversary. I look like I'm sneaking up to a window.

"I'm about to wake you up to tell you happy anniversary, but it's almost one o'clock in the morning on a school night, so I'm filming this in case your father murders me."

I turn the camera back around and face it toward a window. The camera goes dark, but we can hear the window being raised and the sound of me struggling to climb inside. Once I'm inside the room, I shine the camera toward Charlie's bed. There's a lump under the covers, but she doesn't move. I move the camera around the rest of the room. The first thing I notice is that the room on the camera doesn't look like it would be a room in the house Charlie lives in now.

"That's not my bedroom," Charlie says, looking closer at the video playing on my phone. "My room now isn't even half that size. And I share with my little sister."

The room on the video definitely doesn't look like a shared room, but we don't get a good enough look because the camera points back at the bed. The lump under the covers moves and from the angle of the camera, it looks as though I'm crawling onto the bed.

"Charlie baby," I whisper to her. She pulls the covers over her head but shields her eyes from the light of the camera.

"Silas?" she whispers. The camera is still pointed at her from an awkward angle, as if I forgot I was even holding it. There are kissing sounds. I must be kissing up her arm or neck.

Just the sound alone of my lips touching her skin is enough reason to turn off the video. I don't want to make this awkward for Charlie, but she's focused on my phone with as much intensity as I am. And not because of what's happening between us on the video, but because we don't *remember* it. It's me…it's her…it's us together. But I don't remember a single thing about this encounter, so it feels like we're watching two complete strangers share an intimate moment.

I feel like a voyeur.

"Happy anniversary," I whisper to her. The camera pulls away and it looks like I move it to the pillow beside her head. The only view we have now is the profile of Charlie's face as her head rests against her pillow.

It's not the best view, but it's enough to see that she looks exactly the same. Her dark hair is splayed out across the pillow. She's looking up and I assume I'm hovering over her, but I can't see myself in the video. I just see her mouth as it curls up into a smile.

"You're such a rebel," she whispers. *"I can't believe you snuck in to tell me that."*

"I didn't sneak in to tell you that," I whisper quietly. *"I snuck in to do this."* My face finally appears in the video, and my lips rest softly against hers.

Charlie shifts in her seat next to me. I swallow the lump in my throat. I suddenly wish I were alone right now, watching this. I'd be replaying this kiss over and over and over.

My nerves are tight, and I realize it's because I'm jealous of the guy in the video, which makes absolutely no sense. It feels like I'm watching a complete stranger make out with her, even though it's me. Those are my lips against hers, but it's pissing me off because I don't remember what that feels like.

I debate whether or not to stop the video, especially because the kiss that's happening right now looks like it's turning into more than just a simple kiss. My hand, which was resting against her cheek, is now out of view. From the sounds coming out of Charlie's mouth in the video, it seems like she knows exactly where my hand is.

She pulls her mouth from mine and glances into the camera, just as her hand appears in front of the lens, knocking the camera face down onto the bed. The screen goes black, but the sound is still recording.

"The light was blinding me," she murmurs.

My finger is right next to the pause button on my phone. I should press pause, but I can feel the warmth of her breath escaping her mouth, flirting with the skin on my neck. Between that and the sounds coming from my speakers, I never want the video to end.

"Silas," she whispers.

We're both still staring at the screen, even though it's been pitch black since she knocked the camera over. There's nothing to see, but we can't look away. The sounds of our voices are playing all around us, filling the car, filling us.

"Never never, Charlie," I whisper. A moan.

"Never never," she whispers in response. A gasp.

Another moan.

Rustling.

The sound of a zipper.

"I love you so much, Charlie."

Sounds of bodies shifting on the bed.

Heavy breaths. Lots of them. They're coming from

the speakers surrounding us and also from our mouths as we sit here and listen to this.

"Oh, God... Silas."

Two sharp intakes of breath. Desperate kissing.

A horn blaring, swallowing up the sounds coming from my speakers.

I fumble with the phone and it falls to the floorboard. Headlights are shining into my car. Fists are suddenly beating on Charlie's window and before I can retrieve the phone from the floorboard, her door is being jerked open.

"You feel incredible, Charlie." My voice barrels through the speakers.

Loud bursts of laughter escape the mouth of the girl who is now holding open Charlie's door. She sat with us at lunch today, but I can't remember her name.

"Oh, my God!" she says, shoving Charlie in the shoulder. "Are you guys watching a sex tape?" She turns around and yells at the car whose headlights are still shining through the windows. "Char and Si are watching a sex tape!" She's still laughing when I finally have the phone back in my hands and press pause. I turn the volume down on the car radio. Charlie looks from the girl to me, wide-eyed.

"We were just leaving," I say to the girl. "Charlie has to get home."

The girl laughs with a shake of her head. "Oh, please," she says, looking at Charlie. "Your mom is probably so drunk she thinks you're in bed right now. Follow us, we're headed out to Andrew's."

Charlie smiles with a shake of her head. "I can't, Annika. I'll see you at school tomorrow, okay?" Annika looks overly offended. She scoffs when Charlie continues to pull the door shut, despite her being in the way. The girl steps aside and Charlie slams her door and locks it.

"Drive," she says. I do. Gladly.

We're about a mile away from the gas station when Charlie clears her throat. It doesn't help her voice because it still comes out in a raspy whisper. "You should probably delete that video."

I don't like her suggestion. I was already planning on replaying it tonight when I get home. "There could be a clue in it," I say to her. "I think I should watch it again. Listen to how it ends."

She smiles, just as my phone indicates an incoming text. I flip it over and see a notification at the top of the screen from "Father." I open my text messages.

Father: Come home. Alone, please.

I show the text to Charlie and she just nods. "You can drop me off at home."

The rest of the ride is slightly uncomfortable. I feel like the video we just watched together has somehow made us see one another in a different light. Not necessarily a bad one, just a different one. Before, when I looked at her, she was just the girl who was experiencing this weird phenomenon with me. Now when I look at her, she's the girl I supposedly make love to. The girl I've apparently made love to for a while. The girl I apparently *still* love. I just wish I could remember what it's supposed to feel like.

After seeing the obvious connection we once had, it only further confuses me that she was involved with that Brian guy. Thinking about him now fills me with a whole lot more anger and jealousy than it did before seeing us together in that video.

When we pull into her driveway and stop, she doesn't immediately get out. She stares up at the dark house in front of us. There's a faint light on in a front window, but no sign of movement anywhere inside the house.

"I'll try to talk to my sister tonight. Maybe get more of an idea about what happened last night when I came home."

"That's probably a good idea," I tell her. "I'll do the same with my brother. Maybe figure out what his name is while I'm at it."

She laughs.

"Want me to pick you up for school tomorrow?"

She nods. "If you don't mind."

"I don't."

It's quiet again. The silence reminds me of the soft sounds that were escaping her in the video that's still on my phone, thank God. I'll be hearing her voice in my head all night. I'm kind of looking forward to it, actually.

"You know," she says, tapping the door with her fingers. "We could wake up tomorrow and be perfectly fine. We might even forget today happened and everything will be back to normal."

We can hope for it, but my instincts lead me to believe that won't happen. We're going to wake up tomorrow just as confused as we are right now.

"I'd bet against it," I say. "I'll go through the rest of my emails and messages tonight. You should do the same."

She nods again, finally turning her head to make direct eye contact with me. "Goodnight, Silas."

"Goodnight, Charlie. Call me if you…"

"I'll be fine," she says quickly, cutting me off. "See you in the morning." She exits the car and begins walking toward her house. I want to yell after her, tell her to wait. I want to know if she's wondering the same thing I'm wondering: *What does "never never" mean?*

7

Charlie

I think if you cheat, it should be with someone worthy of your sin. I'm not sure if this is old Charlie's thoughts or new Charlie's thoughts. Or maybe, because I'm observing Charlie Wynwood's life as an outsider, I'm able to think of her cheating with detachment rather than judgment. All I know is if you're going to cheat on Silas Nash it had better be with Ryan Gosling.

I turn back to look at him before he drives away and catch a glimpse of his profile, the dim streetlamp behind the car illuminating his face. The bridge of his nose isn't smooth. At school, the other boys had pretty noses, or noses that were still too big for their faces. Or worse, noses pocked with acne. Silas has a grown-up nose. It makes you take him more seriously.

I turn back to the house. My stomach feels oily. No one is around when I open the door and peer inside. I feel like I'm an intruder breaking into somebody's house.

"Hello?" I say. "Anyone here?" I close the door quietly behind me and tiptoe into the living room.

I jump.

Charlie's mother is on the couch watching *Seinfeld* on mute, and eating pinto beans straight from the can. I'm suddenly reminded that all I've eaten today is the grilled cheese I split with Silas.

"Are you hungry?" I ask her tentatively. I don't know if she's still mad at me or if she's going to cry again. "Do you want me to make us something to eat?"

She leans forward without looking at me and slides her beans onto the coffee table. I take a step toward her and force out the word, "Mom?"

"She's not going to answer you."

I spin around to see Janette stroll into the kitchen, a bag of Doritos in her hand.

"Is that what you ate for dinner?"

She shrugs.

"What are you, like fourteen?"

"What are you, like brain-dead?" she shoots back. And then, "Yes, I'm fourteen."

I grab the Doritos from her hand and carry them over to where drunken mommy is staring at the TV screen. "Fourteen-year-old girls can't eat chips for dinner," I say, dropping the bag on her lap. "Sober up and be a mom."

No response.

I stalk over to the fridge, but all that's inside it is a dozen cans of Diet Coke and a jar of pickles. "Get your jacket, Janette," I say, glaring at the mother. "Let's get you some dinner."

Janette looks at me like I'm speaking Mandarin. I figure I need to throw something mean in there just to keep up appearances. "Hurry up, you little turd!"

She scampers back to our room while I search the house for car keys. What type of life was I living? And who was that creature on the couch? Surely she hadn't always been that way. I glance at the back of her head and feel a spurt of sympathy. Her husband—*my father*—is in prison. *Prison!* That's a big deal. Where are we even getting money to live?

Speaking of money, I check my wallet. The twenty-eight dollars is still there. That should be enough to buy us something other than Doritos.

Janette comes out of the bedroom wearing a green jacket just as I find the keys. Green is a good color on her—makes her look less angsty teen.

"Ready?" I ask.

She rolls her eyes.

"Okay then, Mommy Dearest. Going to get some grub!" I call out before I close the door—mostly to see if she'll try to stop me. I let Janette lead the way into the garage, anticipating what kind of car we drive. It isn't going to be a Land Rover, that's for sure.

"Oh, boy," I say. "Does this thing work?" She ignores me, popping her earbuds in as I eye the car. It's a really old Oldsmobile. Older than me. It smells of cigarette smoke and old people. Janette climbs into the passenger side wordlessly and stares out the window. "Okay then, Chatty Cathy," I say. "Let's see how many blocks we can go before this thing breaks down."

I have a plan. The receipt I found is dated last Friday and is from The Electric Crush Diner in the French Quarter. Except this piece of crap car doesn't have GPS. I'll have to find it on my own.

Janette is quiet as we pull out of the driveway. She traces patterns on the window with her fingertip, fog-

ging and re-fogging the glass with her breath. I watch
her out of the corner of my eye; poor kid. Her mom's
an alcoholic and her dad is in prison—kind of sad. She
also hates me. That pretty much leaves her alone in the
world. I realize with surprise that Charlie is in the same
situation. Except maybe she has Silas—or *did* have Silas
before she cheated on him with Brian. *Ugh.* I shake my
shoulders to get rid of all my feels. I hate these people.
They're so annoying. Except I kind of like Silas.

Kind of.

The Electric Crush Diner is on North Rampart Street.
I find a parking spot on a crowded corner and have to
parallel park between a truck and a Mini Cooper. *Charlie is an excellent parallel parker*, I think proudly. Janette climbs out after me and stands on the sidewalk,
looking lost. The diner is across the street. I try to peer
in through the windows, but they're mostly blacked out.
The Electric Crush flashes in pink neon over the front
door.

"Come on," I say. I hold out my hand to her and she
draws back. "Janette! Let's go!" I march up to her in
what can only be an aggressive Charlie move, and grab
her hand. She tries to pull away from me, but I hold on
tight, dragging her across the street.

"Let. Me. Go!"

As soon as we reach the other side, I spin around to
face her. "What's your problem? Stop acting like a...,"
fourteen-year-old, I finish in my head.

"What?" she says. "And why do you even care what I
act like?" Her bottom lip is puffing out like she's about
to cry. I suddenly feel very sorry for being so rough

with her. She's just a little kid with tiny boobs and a hormone-addled brain.

"You're my sister," I say gently. "It's time we stick together, don't you think?" For a minute, I think she's going to say something—maybe something soft and nice and sisterly—but then she stomps toward the diner ahead of me and flings open the door. *Damn.* She's a tough cookie. I follow her in—a little sheepishly—and stop dead in my tracks.

It's not what I thought it was going to be. It's not really a diner—more like a club with booths lining the walls. In the middle of the room is what looks like a dance floor. Janette is standing near the bar, looking around in bewilderment. "You come here often?" she asks me.

I look from the black leather booths to the black marble floors. Everything is black aside from the bright pink signs on the walls. It's morbid and bubblegum.

"Help you?" A man steps out from a door at the far end of the bar, carrying an armful of boxes. He's young—maybe early twenties. I like him on sight because he's wearing a black vest over a pink t-shirt. *Charlie must like pink.*

"We're hungry," I blurt.

He half smiles and nods over to a booth. "Kitchen doesn't usually open for another hour, but I'll see what he can whip up for you if you'd like to sit."

I nod and beeline over to the booth, pulling Janette along with me. "I was here," I tell her. "Last weekend."

"Oh" is all she says before studying her fingernails.

A few minutes later, the pink t-shirt guy comes out of the back, whistling. He walks over and places two hands on the table.

"Charlie, right?" he asks. I nod dumbly. *How does he...? How many times have I...?*

"The kitchen was making me a roast chicken. What do you say I share it with you guys? We won't get busy for a couple more hours, anyway."

I nod again.

"Good." He hits the table with his palm and Janette jumps. He points to her. "Coke? Sprite? Shirley Temple?"

She rolls her eyes. "Diet Coke," she says.

"And you, Charlie?"

I don't like the way he says my name. It's too...familiar. "Coke," I say quickly.

When he leaves, Janette leans forward, her eyebrows drawn together. "You always get diet," she says accusatorily.

"Yeah? Well, I'm not quite feeling like myself."

She makes a little noise in the back of her throat. "No kidding," she says. I ignore her and try to get a good look around. What were Silas and I doing here? Is it a place we came often? I lick my lips.

"Janette," I say. "Have I ever told you about this place?"

She looks surprised. "You mean all the times we have heart-to-hearts when we put the lights out at night?"

"Okay, okay, I get it. I'm a really crappy sister. Geez. Get over it already. I'm extending the olive branch here."

Janette scrunches up her nose. "What's that mean?"

I sigh. "I'm trying to make it up to you. Start fresh."

Just then the pink t-shirt dude brings us our drinks. He brought Janette a Shirley Temple even though she asked for a Diet Coke. Her face registers disappointment.

"She wanted a Diet Coke," I say.

"She'll like that," he says. "When I was a kid..."

"Just get her a Diet Coke."

He holds up his hands in surrender. "Sure thing, princess."

Janette glances at me from under her eyelashes. "Thanks," she says.

"No problem," I say. "You can't trust a guy who wears a pink shirt."

She sort of smirks and I feel triumphant. I can't believe I thought I liked that guy. I can't believe I liked Brian. What the hell was wrong with me?

I pick up my phone and see that Silas has texted me multiple times. *Silas.* I like Silas. Something about his soothing voice and good-boy manners. And his nose— he has a wicked cool nose.

Silas: My dad...

Silas: Where are you?

Silas: Hello?

The guy comes back with the chicken and a plate of mashed potatoes.

It's a lot of food.

"What's your name again?" I ask.

"You're such a bitch, Charlie," he says, laying a plate down in front of me. He glances at Janette. "Sorry," he says.

She shrugs. "What *is* your name?" she asks through a mouthful of food.

"Dover. That's what my friends call me."

I nod. *Dover.*

"So last weekend...," I say.

Dover bites. "Yeah, that was crazy. I didn't expect to see you back here this soon."

"Why not?" I ask. I'm trying to be casual, but my insides are jumping around like they're being shocked.

"Well, your man was pretty pissed. I thought he was going to blow his shit before he got kicked out."

"Blow his shit…?" I change my tone so it's not so much a question. "Blow his shit. Yeah. That was…"

"You looked pretty pissed," Dover says. "I can't blame you. You might have liked it here if Silas hadn't ruined it for you."

I sit back, the chicken suddenly unappealing. "Yeah," I say, glancing at Janette, who is watching us both curiously.

"You finished, brat?" I ask her. She nods, wiping her greasy fingers on a napkin. I pull a twenty out of my purse and drop it on the table.

"No need," Dover says, waving it away.

I lean down till we are eye to eye. "Only my boyfriend gets to buy me dinner," I say, leaving the money on the table. I walk to the door, Janette trailing behind me.

"Yeah, well," Dover calls, "you live by that rule, you can eat for free seven days a week!"

I don't stop until I reach the car. Something happened in there. Something that made Silas almost lose his shit. I start the car and Janette lets out a loud burp. We both start laughing at the same time.

"No more Doritos for dinner," I tell her. "We can learn to cook."

"Sure," she shrugs.

Everyone breaks their promises to Janette. She's got that bitter air about her. We don't speak for the rest of the ride home, and when I pull into the garage, she jumps out before I've turned off the engine.

"Nice spending time with you, too," I call after her. I imagine that when I walk in, Charlie's mother will be waiting for her—perhaps to chew her out for taking the car—but when I step into the house, everything is dark except for the light underneath the door to Janette's and my bedroom. Mother has gone to sleep. Mother doesn't care. It's perfect for the situation I'm in. I get to snoop around and try to figure out what happened to me without the questions and rules, but I can't help thinking about Janette, about how she's just a little kid who needs her parents. Everything is so screwed up.

Janette is listening to music when I open the door.

"Hey," I say. I suddenly have an idea. "Have you seen my iPod?" Music tells a lot about a person. I don't have to have a memory to know that.

"I don't know." She shrugs. "Maybe it's with all your other crap in the attic."

My other crap? The attic?

I suddenly feel excited.

Maybe there's more to me than a bland bedspread and a stack of bad novels. I want to ask her what kind of crap, and why my crap is in the attic instead of in our shared bedroom, but Janette has stuck the buds back in her ears and is working hard to ignore me.

I decide the best route would be to go up to the attic to check things out for myself. *Now, where is the attic?*

8

Silas

The front door to my house opens as I'm putting my car in park, and Ezra walks outside, wringing her hands together nervously. I get out of the car and walk to where she's standing, wide-eyed.

"Silas," she says, her voice quivering. "I thought he knew. I wouldn't have mentioned Charlie was here, but you didn't seem to be hiding it, so I thought things had changed and she was allowed over here…"

I hold up my hand to stop her from more unnecessary apologies. "It's fine, Ezra. Really."

She sighs and runs her hand across the apron she's still wearing. I don't understand her nervousness, or why she anticipated I would be angry with her. I shove more reassurance into my smile than is probably necessary, but she looks as if she needs it.

She nods and follows me inside the house. I pause in the foyer, not quite familiar enough with the house to know where my father would be at the moment. Ezra passes me, muttering a "goodnight," and heads up the stairs. She must live here.

"Silas."

It sounds like my voice, but more worn. I turn and am suddenly face to face with the man in all the family photos lining the walls. He's missing the brilliantly fake smile, though.

He eyes me up and down, as if the mere sight of his son disappoints him.

He turns and walks through a door leading out of the foyer. His silence and the assurance in his steps demand I follow him, so I do. We walk into his study, and he slowly edges around his desk and takes a seat. He leans forward and folds his arms over the mahogany wood. "Care to explain?"

I'm tempted to explain. I really am. I want to tell him that I have no idea who he is, no idea why he's angry, no idea who *I* am.

I should probably be nervous or intimidated by him. I'm sure yesterday's Silas would have been, but it's hard to feel intimidated by someone I don't know at all. As far as I'm concerned, he has no power over me, and power is the primary ingredient of intimidation.

"Care to explain what?" I ask.

My eyes move to a shelf of books on the wall behind him. They look like classics. Collectibles. I wonder if he's read any of the books or if they're just more ingredients for his intimidation.

"Silas!" His voice is so deep and sharp; it feels like the tip of a knife piercing my ears. I press my hand against the side of my neck and squeeze before looking at him again. He eyes the chair across from him, silently commanding me to sit down.

I get the feeling yesterday's Silas would be saying *Yes, sir* right about now.

Today's Silas smiles and walks slowly to his seat.

"Why was she inside this house today?"

He's referring to Charlie like she's poison. He's referring to her the same way her mother referred to me. I look down at the arm of the chair and pick at a piece of worn leather. "She wasn't feeling well at school. She needed a ride home, and we took a quick detour."

This man…*my father*…leans back in his chair. He brings a hand up to his jaw and rubs it.

Five seconds pass. Ten seconds pass. *Fifteen.*

He finally leans forward again. "You seeing her again?"

Is this a trick question? Because it feels like one.

If I say yes, it'll obviously piss him off. If I say no, it feels like I'll be letting him win. I don't know why, but I really don't want this man to win. He seems like he's accustomed to winning.

"What if I am?"

His hand is no longer rubbing his jaw because it's now moving across the desk, fisting into the collar of my shirt. He yanks me toward him just as my hands grip the edges of the desk for resistance. We're eye to eye now, and I expect he's about to hit me. I wonder if this type of interaction with him is common.

Instead of hitting me like I know he wants to, he pushes his fist against my chest and releases me. I fall back into my seat, but only for a second. I push out of my chair and take a few steps back.

I probably should have hit the asshole, but I don't hate him enough to do that yet. I also don't like him enough to be affected by his reaction. It does confuse me, though.

He picks up a paperweight and hurls it across the room, luckily not in my direction. It smashes against a wooden shelf and knocks the contents to the floor. A few books. A picture frame. A rock.

I stand still and watch him pace back and forth, beads of sweat dripping from his forehead. I don't understand why he could possibly be this upset over the fact that Charlie was here today. Especially since Ezra said we grew up together.

His palms are now flat against the desk. He's breathing heavily, nostrils flaring like a raging bull. I expect him to start kicking up dust with his foot any second now. "We had an understanding, Silas. Me and you. I wasn't going to push you to testify if you swore to me you wouldn't see that man's daughter again." One of his hands flails toward a locked cabinet while his other hand runs through what's left of his thinning hair. "I know you don't think she took those files from this office, but I know she did! And the only reason I haven't pursued it further is because you *swore* to me we wouldn't have to deal with that family again. And here you are…" He shudders. *Literally* shudders. "Here you are bringing her to this house like the last twelve months never even happened!" More frustrated hand flailing, twisted facial expressions. "That girl's father almost *ruined* this family, Silas! Does that not mean a damn thing to you?"

Not really, I want to say.

I make a mental note to never get this angry. It's not an attractive look on a Nash.

I search for some sort of emotion that conveys remorse, so that he can see it on my face. It's hard, though, when the only thing I'm experiencing is curiosity.

The door to the office opens and we both move our attention to whomever is entering.

"Landon, this doesn't concern you," my father says, his voice soft. I briefly face my father again, just to make sure the words actually fell from his mouth and not someone else's. It almost sounds like the voice of a caring father, rather than the monster I just witnessed.

Landon—*nice to finally know my little brother's name*—looks at me. "Coach is on the phone for you, Silas."

I glance back at my father, who now has his back turned to me. I assume that means our conversation is over. I walk toward the door and gladly exit the room, followed closely by Landon.

"Where's the phone?" I ask him when I reach the stairs. Valid question, though. How am I supposed to know if he called on a cell phone or a landline?

Landon laughs and moves past me. "There's no phone call. I was just getting you out of there."

He continues up the stairs and I watch as he reaches the top and then turns left, disappearing down the hall. *He's a good brother*, I think. I make my way to what I assume is his room, and I knock lightly on the door. It's slightly ajar, so I push it open. "Landon?" I open the door all the way and he's seated at a desk. He looks over his shoulder briefly and then returns his attention to his computer. "Thanks," I say, stepping into the room. *Do brothers thank each other?* Probably not. I should have said something along the lines of *Took you long enough, asshole*.

Landon turns in his chair and tilts his head. A combination of confusion and admiration plays out in his smile. "I'm not sure what your deal is. You aren't showing up for practice, and that's never happened. You act like you don't give a shit that Charlie has been screwing Brian Finley. And then you have the balls to bring her *here*? After all the shit Dad and Brett went through?" He shakes his head. "I'm surprised you escaped his office without a bloodbath."

He spins back around and leaves me to process everything. I turn and rush toward my bedroom.

Brett Wynwood, Brett Wynwood, Brett Wynwood.

I repeat his name in my head so I'll know exactly what to search when I get to my computer. *Surely I have a computer.*

When I reach my room, the first thing I do is walk to my dresser. I pick up the pen Charlie handed me earlier today and read the imprint again.

WYNWOOD-NASH FINANCIAL GROUP

I search the room until I finally find a laptop stuffed in the drawer of my bedside table. I power it on and enter the password.

I remember the password? Add that to the list of *shit that makes no sense.*

I type *Wynwood-Nash Financial Group* into the search engine. I click on the first result and am taken to a page that reads *Nash Finance*, with the *Wynwood* noticeably absent. I scroll quickly through the page and discover nothing that helps. Just a bunch of useless company contact information.

I back out of the page and scroll through the rest of the results, reading each of the leading headlines and the articles that follow:

*Finance gurus Clark Nash and Brett Wynwood,
co-founders of Wynwood-Nash Financial Group,
have been charged with four counts of conspiracy,
fraud, and illegal trading.*

*Partners for over twenty years, the two business
moguls are now placing the blame on each other,
both claiming to have no knowledge of the illegal
practices uncovered during a recent investigation.*

I read another.

*Clark Nash cleared of charges. Company co-
chair, Brett Wynwood, sentenced to fifteen years
for fraud and embezzlement.*

I make it to the second page of search results when
the battery light begins to flash on the laptop. I open the
drawer, but there's no charger. I look everywhere. Under
the bed, in the closet, in my dresser drawers.

The laptop dies during my search. I begin to use my
phone to research, but it's about to die, too, and the only
phone charger I can find plugs into a laptop. I keep looking because I need to know exactly what happened to
make these two families hate each other so much.

I lift the mattress, thinking maybe the charger could
be stuck behind the bed somehow. I don't find the charger, but I do find what looks like a notebook. I slide it
out from under the mattress and then take a seat on top
of the bed. Right when I open it up to the first page, my
phone vibrates with an incoming text.

Charlie: How are things with your father?

I want to learn more before deciding what I want to share with her. I ignore the text and open the notebook to find stacks of papers stuffed into a folder. Across the top, the papers all read *Wynwood-Nash Financial Group*, but I don't understand any of them. I also don't understand why these were hidden beneath my mattress.

Clark Nash's words from downstairs repeat in my head—*I know you don't think she took those files from this office, Silas, but I know she did.*

Looks like he was wrong, but why would *I* have taken them? What would I have needed with them?

Who was I trying to protect?

My phone buzzes again with another text.

Charlie: There's this really neat feature on your phone called "read receipts." If you're going to ignore texts, you should probably turn that off. ☺

At least she put a winky face.

Me: Not ignoring you. Just tired. We have a lot to figure out tomorrow.

Charlie: Yeah

That's all she says. I'm not sure if I should respond to her effortless reply, but I don't want her to be irritated if I *don't* respond.

Me: Goodnight, Charlie baby. ☺

As soon as I hit send, I want to retract it. I don't know what I was going for with that reply. Not sarcasm, but definitely not flirtation, either.

I decide to regret it tomorrow. Right now I just need sleep so I can make sure I'm awake enough in the morning to deal with all of this.

I shove the notebook back under the mattress and see a wall charger, so I plug it into my phone. I'm too exhausted to keep searching tonight, so I kick off my shoes. It isn't until I lie down that I notice Ezra changed my sheets.

As soon as I turn the lamp off and close my eyes, my phone vibrates.

Charlie: Goodnight, Silas.

Her lack of endearment doesn't go unnoticed, but for some inexplicable reason, the text still makes me smile. Typical Charlie.

I think.

9

Charlie

It is not a good night.

The trapdoor to the attic is in the closet I share with my sister. After I text Silas goodnight, I climb the three shelves—which are bursting with fabric—and push upward with my fingertips until it shifts left. I glance back over my shoulder and see that Janette hasn't looked up from her phone. This must be normal—me climbing into the attic, leaving her behind. I want to ask if she'll come with me, but it was exhausting just to get her to come to dinner. *Another time*, I think. I'll figure out how to fix things between us.

I don't know why, but as I hoist myself through the hole and into an even smaller space, I picture Silas's face; the tan, smooth skin. His full lips. How many times had I tasted his mouth and yet I can't remember a single kiss.

The air is warm and stuffy. I crawl on my knees to a pile of pillows and press my back to them, straightening my legs out in front of me. There's a flashlight standing atop a pile of books. I click it on, examining their spines; stories I know, but don't remember reading. How odd to be made of flesh, balanced on bone, and filled with a soul you've never met.

I pick up her books one by one and read the first page of each. I want to know who she is—who *I* am. When I've exhausted the pile, I find a larger book at the bottom, bound in creased red leather. My immediate thought is that I've found a journal. My hands shake as I fold open the pages.

Not a journal. A scrapbook. Letters from Silas.

I know this because he signs each one with a sharp *S* that almost looks like a lightning bolt. And I know I like his handwriting, direct and distinct. Paper-clipped to the top of each note is a photo—presumably one that Silas has taken. I read one note after another, pouring over words. Love letters. Silas is in love.

It's beautiful.

He likes to imagine a life with me. In one letter, written on the back of a brown paper sack, he details the way we will spend Christmas when we have our own place: spiked apple cider by the Christmas tree, raw cookie dough that we eat before we get the chance to bake it. He tells me he wants to make love to me with only candles lighting the room so that he can see my body glow in the candle light. The photo paper clipped to the note is of a tiny Christmas tree that looks like it's in his bedroom. We must have set it up together.

I find another written on the back of a receipt in which he details what it feels like to be inside of me. My face grows warm as I read the note over and over, reveling in his lust. The photo paper clipped to this one is of my bare shoulder. His photos pack a punch—just like his words. They take my breath, and I'm not sure if the part of me I can't remember is in love with him. I feel only curiosity toward the dark-haired boy who looks at me so earnestly.

I set the note aside, feeling like I'm snooping on someone else's life, and close the book. This belonged to Charlie. I'm not her. I fall asleep surrounded by Silas's words, the sprinkling of letters and sentences swirling around in my head until…

A girl drops to her knees in front of me. "Listen to me," she whispers. "We don't have much time…"

But I don't listen to her. I push her away and then she's gone. I am standing outside. There is a fire burning from an old metal trash can. I rub my hands together to get warm. From somewhere behind me I can hear a saxophone playing, but the sound morphs into a scream. That's when I run. I run through the fire that was in the trash can, but now it is everywhere, licking the buildings along the street. I run, choking on smoke until I see one pink-faced storefront that is free of flame and smoke, though everything around it burns. It is a shop of curiosities. I open the door without thought because it is the only place safe from the flames. Silas is there waiting for me. He leads me past bones and books and bottles and takes me to a back room. A woman sits on a throne made of broken mirrors, staring down at me with a thin smile on her lips. The pieces of mirror reflect slices of light across the walls where they jiggle and dance. I turn to look at Silas, to ask him where we are, but he's gone. "Hurry!"

I wake with a start.

Janette is leaning through the slat of space in the closet roof, shaking my foot. "You have to get up," she says. "You don't have any more skip days left."

I am still in the dank attic space. I wipe the sleep from my eyes and follow her down the three shelves to our room. I'm touched she knows I'm out of skip days, and that she cared enough to wake me up. I'm shaking when I reach the bathroom and turn on the shower. I haven't shaken the dream. I can still see my reflection in the broken shards of her throne.

The fire swims in and out of my vision, waiting behind my eyelids every time I blink. If I concentrate, I can smell the ash above the body wash I'm using, above the sickeningly sweet shampoo I pour into my hand. I close my eyes and try to remember Silas's words… *You are warm and wet, and your body grips me like it doesn't want me to leave.*

Janette pounds on the door. "Late!" she yells.

I hurry to dress and we're tumbling out the front door before I realize I don't even know how Janette expects we're getting to school today. I told Silas to pick me up yesterday.

"Amy should be here already," Janette says. She folds her arms across her chest and peers down the street. It's like she can't even stand to look at me. I pull out my phone and text Silas to let him know not to pick me up. I also check to see if this Amy has texted me, right as a little silver Mercedes whips around the corner.

"Amy," I say. I wonder if she's one of the girls I sat with at lunch yesterday. I hardly noticed names and faces. The car pulls to the curb and we walk forward. Janette climbs into the backseat without a word, and after a few seconds of deliberation I open the front door. I stare at her in surprise for a minute before I climb into the car.

"Hey," she says, without looking over. I'm grateful for her distraction because I have a moment to study her.

"Hi."

She's pretty; her hair, which is lighter than her skin, is braided to her waist. She seems at ease with me—not to mention she's giving my sour sister and me a ride to school. We must be good friends, I decide.

"Glad to see you're feeling better. Did you figure out what you're going to do about Silas?" she asks me.

"I… I…er… Silas?"

"Uh huh," she says. "That's what I thought. You still don't know. It's a shame, too, because you guys can be really good together when you try."

I sit in silence until we've almost reached the school, wondering what she means. "Amy," I say. "How would you describe my relationship with Silas to someone who has never met us?"

"See, this is your problem," she says. "You always want to play games." She pulls up to the front of the school and Janette climbs out. It's all like clockwork.

"Bye," I call as the door closes. "She's so mean," I say, facing forward again.

Amy pulls a face. "And you're queen of nice? Seriously, I don't know what's come over you. You're even more out of it than normal."

I chew on my lips as we pull into the high school parking lot. I open the door before the car has even stopped.

"What the hell, Charlie?"

I don't wait to hear what else she has to say. I run for the school, my arms wrapped tightly around my torso.

Did *everyone* hate me? I duck my head as I push through the doors. I need to find Silas. People are looking at me as I walk the hallway. I don't look left or right, but I can feel their eyes. When I reach for my phone to text Silas, it's gone. I ball up my fists. I had my phone when I texted and told him I didn't need a ride. I must have left it in Amy's car.

I'm on my way back toward the parking lot when someone calls my name.

Brian.

I glance around to see who's watching us as he jogs toward me. His eye still looks a little bruised from where I punched him. I like that.

"What?" I say.

"You hit me." He stops a few feet away like he's afraid I'm going to do it again. I suddenly feel guilty. I shouldn't have done that. Whatever game I'd been playing with him before all of this happened wasn't his fault.

"I'm sorry," I say. "I haven't been myself lately. I shouldn't have done that."

It looks like I've told him exactly what he wants to hear. His face relaxes and he runs a hand along the back of his neck as he looks at me.

"Can we go somewhere more private to talk?"

I look around at the crowded hallway and shake my head. "No."

"All right," he says. "Then we can do this here." I shift from one foot to another and look over my shoulder. Depending on how long he takes, I can still catch Amy and get the keys to her car and…

"It's Silas or me."

My head jerks back to look at him. "What?"

"I love you, Charlie."

Oh, God. I feel itchy all over. I take a step back, looking around for someone to help me get out of this. "Now is a really bad time for me, Brian. I need to find Amy and—"

"I know you guys have history, but you've been unhappy for a long time. That guy's a dick, Charlie. You saw what happened with the shrimp. I'm surprised—"

"What are you talking about?"

He looks put out that I've interrupted his speech. "I'm talking about Silas and—"

"No, the shrimp thing." People are stopping to watch us now. Clusters of nosiness form at lockers; eyes, eyes, eyes on my face. I'm so uncomfortable with this. I hate it.

"Her." Brian jerks his head left just as a girl pushes through the doors and makes her way past us. When she sees me looking, her face turns a bright pink color, like a shrimp. I recognize her from my class yesterday. She was the one on the floor, picking up the books. She's tiny. Her hair is an ugly shade of greenish brown, like she tried to dye it herself and it went terribly wrong. But even if she hadn't dyed it, it looks…sad. Jagged, uneven bangs, oily and lank. She has a smattering of pimples across her forehead and a nose that's pugged. My first thought is *Ugly*. But it's more of a fact than a judgment. She skitters away before I can blink, disappearing into a crowd of onlookers. I have a feeling she hasn't left. She's waiting right behind their backs—she wants to hear. I felt something…when I saw her face I felt something.

My head is swimming when Brian reaches for me. I let him grab me by the elbow and pull me toward his chest.

"It's me or Silas," he says again. He's being bold since I already punched him for touching me. But I'm not thinking about him. I'm thinking about the girl, the shrimp, wondering if she's back there, hiding behind everyone else. "I need an answer, Charlie." He has me so close that when I look into his face I can see the freckles in his eyes.

"Then my answer is Silas," I say softly.

He freezes. I can feel the stiffening of his body.

10

"You gonna show up for practice today?" Landon asks. He's already standing outside my door and I don't even remember pulling into the parking lot of the school, much less turning off the car. I nod, but fail to make eye contact with him. I'd been so lost inside my own thoughts during the drive over, I didn't even think to prod him for information.

I've been hung up on the fact that I didn't wake up with memories. I was hoping Charlie was right—that we would wake up and everything would be back to normal. But we didn't and it's not.

Or at least *I* didn't wake up with memories. I haven't spoken to Charlie since last night, and her text this morning revealed nothing.

I didn't even open the text. It flashed on my lock screen and I read enough of the first sentence to know I didn't like how it made me feel. My thoughts immediately wandered to who might be picking her up and if she was okay with it.

My protective instincts kick in whenever it comes to her, and I don't know if it's always been that way or if it's because she's the only one I can relate to right now.

I get out of the car, determined to find her. Make sure she's okay, even though I know she more than likely is. I don't have to know any more about her to know that she doesn't really need me to take care of her. She's fiercely independent.

That doesn't mean I won't still try.

When I enter the school, it occurs to me that I don't know where to begin searching for her. Neither of us can remember which lockers are ours, and considering this happened to us both during fourth period yesterday, we have no idea where our first, second, or third period classes are.

I decide to walk to the administration office and see about getting a new copy of my schedule. Hopefully Charlie thought to do the same, because I doubt they'll give me hers.

The secretary is unfamiliar, but she smiles knowingly at me. "Here to see Ms. Ashley, Silas?"

Ms. Ashley.

I start to shake my head no, but she's already pointing me in the direction of an open office door. Whoever Ms. Ashley is, I must visit her enough that my presence in the office isn't unusual.

Before I make it to the open office door, a woman steps out. She's tall, attractive and appears extremely young to be an employee. Whatever she does here, she hasn't been doing it long. She barely looks old enough to be out of college.

"Mr. Nash," she says with a vague smile, flicking her blonde hair back over her shoulder. "Do you have an appointment?"

I pause and stop my advancement toward her. I glance back at the secretary right when Ms. Ashley waves it off. "It's fine, I have a few minutes. Come inside."

I move gingerly past her, taking in the nameplate on the door as I enter her office.

AVRIL ASHLEY, GUIDANCE COUNSELOR

She closes the door behind me and I look around the office, which is decorated in motivational quotes and typical posters portraying positive messages. I suddenly feel uncomfortable. Trapped. I should have said I didn't need to see her, but I'm hoping this counselor—*one I apparently visited regularly*—will know a few things about my past that may be of help to Charlie and me.

I turn, just as Ms. Ashley's hand slides down the door and reaches the lock. She turns it and then begins to saunter toward me. Her hands meet my chest and right before her mouth connects with mine, I stumble backward and catch myself on a filing cabinet.

Whoa.

What the hell?

She looks offended that I just shook off her advance. This must not be unusual behavior with us.

I'm sleeping with the guidance counselor?

I immediately think of Charlie and, based on our obvious noncommitment to one another, I question what kind of relationship we had. *Why were we even together?*

"Is something wrong?" Ms. Ashley says.

I turn slightly and take a few steps away from her,

toward the window. "Not feeling very well today." I look her in the eyes and force a smile. "Don't want to get you sick."

My words put her at ease and she closes the space between us again, this time leaning in and pressing her lips against my neck. "Poor thing," she purrs. "Want me to make you feel better?"

My eyes are wide, darting around the room, mapping out my escape route. My attention falls to the computer on her desk, and then a printer behind her chair. "Ms. Ashley," I say, gently pushing her away from my neck.

This is wrong on so many levels.

She laughs. "You never call me that when we're alone. It's weird." She's too comfortable with me. I need to get out of here.

"Avril," I say, smiling at her again. "I need a favor. Can you print a copy of mine and Charlie's schedules?"

She immediately straightens up, her smile whisked away at the mention of Charlie's name. *Point of contention, apparently.*

"I'm thinking about switching a couple of my classes so I won't have to be around her as much." *Couldn't be further from the truth.*

Ms. Ashley—*Avril*—slides her fingers down my chest, the smile reappearing on her face. "Well, it's about time. Finally decided to take the counselor's advice, I see."

Her voice drips with sex. I can see how things must have started up with her, but it makes me feel shallow. It makes me hate who I was.

I shift on my feet as she works her way to her seat and begins clicking at her keyboard.

She pulls freshly printed pages from the printer and

walks them over to me. I attempt to take the schedules from her hand, but she pulls them away with a grin. "Uh-uh," she says, shaking her head slowly. "These are gonna cost you." She leans against her desk and lays the sheets of paper beside her, face down. She brings her eyes back to mine and I can see I'm not leaving without appeasing her, which is the last thing I want to do right now.

I take two slow steps toward her and rest my hands on either side of her. I lean in to her neck and can hear her gasp when I begin to speak. "Avril, I only have five minutes left before I have to be in class. There's no way I can do all the things I want to do to you in just five minutes."

I slip my hand to the schedules lying on her desk and I back away with them. She's tugging on her bottom lip, staring up at me with heated eyes. "Come back during lunch," she whispers. "Will an hour be sufficient, Mr. Nash?"

I wink at her. "I guess it'll have to do," I say as I head out the door. I don't pause until I'm down the hallway and around the corner, out of her line of sight.

The eighteen-year-old irresponsible side of me wants to high five myself for having apparently snagged the school counselor, but the reasonable side of me wants to punch myself for doing something like that to Charlie.

Charlie is obviously the better choice, and I hate knowing that I was putting that relationship at risk.

But then again, so was Charlie.

Luckily, the schedules list our locker numbers and combinations. Hers is 543 and mine is 544. I'm guessing that was intentional.

I open my locker first, and find three textbooks

stacked inside. There's a half-empty coffee in front of the books and an empty Cinnamon Roll wrapper. There are two pictures taped to the inside of the locker: one of Charlie and me, the other just of Charlie.

I pull the picture of her down and stare at it. Why, if we weren't happy together, do I have pictures of her in my locker? Especially this one. I obviously took it, as it's similar in style to the pictures hanging around my room.

She's sitting cross-legged on a couch. Her head is tilted slightly and she's staring directly at the camera.

Her eyes are intense—looking into the camera as if she's looking into me. She's both confident and comfortable, and although she isn't smiling or laughing in the photo, I can tell she's happy. Whenever this was taken, it was a good day for her. For us. Her eyes are screaming a thousand things in this photo, but the loudest is *I love you, Silas!*

I stare at it a while longer and then place the photo back inside the locker. I check my phone to see if she's texted. She hasn't. I look around, just as Landon approaches from down the hall. He tosses words over his shoulder as he passes me. "Looks like Brian isn't quite out of the picture yet, brother."

The bell rings.

I look in the direction Landon came from and see a heavier crowd of students at that end of the hallway. People seem to be stalling, glancing over their shoulders. Some are looking at me, some are fixated on whatever is at the end of the hallway. I begin to walk in that direction and everyone's attention falls on me as I pass.

A break in the crowd begins to shape and that's when I see her. She's standing against a row of lockers, hugging herself with her arms. Brian is leaning against one of the lockers, looking at her intently. He looks deep in conversation, whereas she just appears guarded. He spots me almost immediately and his posture stiffens along with his expression. Charlie follows his gaze until her eyes land on mine.

As much as I can assume she doesn't need rescuing, relief falls over her as soon as we lock eyes. A smile tugs at her lips, and I want nothing more than to get him away from her. I spend two seconds deliberating. Should I threaten him? Should I hit him like I wanted so badly to hit him yesterday in the parking lot? Neither of these actions feels as though they'll make the point I want to make.

"You should get to class," I hear her say to him. Her words are quick, a warning, as if she's afraid I've decided to punch him. She doesn't have to worry. What I'm about to do will hurt Brian Finley a hell of a lot more than if I were to just hit him.

The second bell rings. No one moves. There are no students rushing to class to avoid being late. No one around me shuffles down the hall at the sound of the bell.

They're all waiting. Watching. Expecting me to start a fight. I wonder if that's what the old Silas would do. I wonder if that's what the new Silas should do.

I ignore everyone but Charlie and walk confidently toward her, keeping my eyes trained on her the entire time. As soon as Brian sees me approaching, he takes two steps away from her. I look directly at him while I stretch out my hand toward her, giving her the choice to take it and go with me or remain where she is.

I feel her fingers slide between mine and she grips my hand tightly. I pull her away from the lockers, away from

Brian, away from the crowd of students. As soon as we round the corner, she drops my hand and stops walking.

"That was a little dramatic, don't you think?" she says.

I turn to face her. Her eyes are narrowed, but her mouth could pass for smiling. I can't tell if she's amused or angry.

"They expected a certain reaction from me. What'd you want me to do, tap him on the shoulder and ask politely if I could cut in?"

She folds her arms over her chest. "What makes you think I needed you to do anything?"

I don't understand her hostility. It seemed like we left on good terms last night, so I'm confused as to why she seems so angry with me.

She rubs her hands up and down her arms and then her eyes fall to the floor. "Sorry," she mutters. "I just…" She looks up at the ceiling and groans. "I was just prodding him for information. That's the only reason I was with him in the hallway just now. I wasn't flirting."

Her response catches me off guard. I don't like the look of guilt in her expression. That's not why I pulled her away from him, but I realize now that she thinks I really am upset with her for being with him. I could tell she didn't want to be there, but maybe she doesn't realize how well I've learned to read her.

I take a step toward her. When she lifts her eyes to meet mine, I smile. "Would it make you feel better to know I was cheating on you with the guidance counselor?"

She sucks in a quick rush of air and shock registers on her face.

"You weren't the only one who wasn't committed to

us, Charlie. Apparently we both had issues we needed to work out, so don't be so hard on yourself."

Relief probably isn't the reaction a girl should have to finding out her boyfriend has been cheating on her, but it's definitely what Charlie feels right now. I can see it in her eyes and I can hear it in the pent-up breath she releases.

"Wow…," she says, her hands falling to her hips. "So technically, we're tied?"

Tied? I shake my head. "This isn't a game I want to win, Charlie. If anything, I'd say we both lost."

Her lips spread into a ghostly grin, and then she looks over her shoulder. "We should figure out where our classes are."

I remember the schedules and pull hers out of my back pocket. "We're not together until fourth period History. You have English first. It's back in the other hallway," I say, motioning toward her first period classroom.

She nods appreciatively and unfolds the schedule. "Smart thinking," she says, glancing it over. She looks back up at me with a wicked smile. "I guess you got these from your guidance counselor mistress?"

Her words make me wince, even though I shouldn't really feel remorse for whatever happened before yesterday.

"*Ex* guidance counselor mistress," I clarify with a grin. She laughs, and it's a laugh of solidarity. As screwed up as our situation is, and as confusing as the new information about our relationship is, the fact that we can laugh about it proves that we at least share in the absurdity of it all. And the only thought I have as I walk away from her is how much I wish Brian Finley could choke on her laugh.

* * *

The first three classes of the day felt foreign. No one in them and nothing discussed seemed familiar to me. I felt like an imposter, out of place.

But the instant I walked into fourth period and took a seat next to Charlie, my mood changed. She's familiar. My only familiar thing in a world of inconsistency and confusion.

We stole a few glances at each other, but we never spoke during class. We aren't even speaking now as we enter the cafeteria together. I glance at our table and everyone from yesterday is already seated, save our two empty seats.

I nudge my head toward the lunch line. "Let's get our food first."

She glances up at me, briefly, before looking back at the table. "I'm not really hungry," she says. "I'll just wait for you at the table." She heads in the direction of our group and I head toward the cafeteria line.

After grabbing my tray and a Pepsi, I walk over to the table and take a seat. Charlie is looking down at her phone, excluding herself from the surrounding conversation.

The guy to my right—*Andrew, I think*—elbows me. "Silas," he says, jabbing me repeatedly. "Tell him how much I benched Monday."

I look up at the guy sitting across from us. He rolls his eyes and downs the rest of his soda before slamming it on the table. "Come on, Andrew. You think I'm stupid enough to believe your best friend wouldn't lie for you?"

Best friend.

Andrew is my best friend, yet I wasn't even sure of his name thirty seconds ago.

My attention moves from the two of them to the food in front of me. I open my soda and take a sip, just as Charlie clenches her waist. It's loud in the cafeteria, but I still hear the rumble of her stomach. She's hungry.

If she's hungry, why isn't she eating?

"Charlie?" I lean in close to her. "Why aren't you eating?" She dismisses my question with a shrug. I lower my voice even more. "Do you have money?"

Her eyes dart up to mine as if I just revealed a huge secret to the entire room. She swallows and then looks away, embarrassed. "No," she says quietly. "I gave my last few dollars to Janette this morning. I'll be fine until I get home."

I set my drink down on the table and push my tray in front of her. "Here. I'll go get another one."

I stand and go back to the line and get another tray. When I return to the table, she's taken a few bites of the food. She doesn't tell me thank you, and I feel relieved. Making sure she has food to eat isn't a favor I want to be thanked for. It's something I hope she would expect from me.

"Do you want a ride home today?" I ask her, just as we're finishing up our meal.

"Dude, you can't miss practice again," Andrew shoots in my direction. "Coach won't let you play tomorrow night if you do."

I rub a palm down my face, and then I reach in my pocket and retrieve my keys. "Here," I tell her, placing them in her hand. "Drive your sister home after school. Pick me up when practice is over."

She tries to hand the keys back to me, but I won't take them. "Keep them," I tell her. "You might need a car today and I won't be using it."

Andrew interrupts. "You're letting her drive your car? Are you kidding me? You've never even let me sit behind the damn wheel!"

I look over at Andrew and shrug. "You aren't the one I'm in love with."

Charlie spits out her drink with a burst of laughter. I glance over at her, and her smile is huge. It lights up her entire face, somehow even making the brown of her eyes seem less dark. I may not remember anything about her, but I would bet her smile was my favorite part of her.

This day has been exhausting. It feels like I've been on a stage for hours, acting out scenes I have no script for. The only thing that appeals to me right now is either being in my bed or being with Charlie. Or maybe a combination of both.

However, Charlie and I both still have a goal, and that's to figure out what the hell happened to us yesterday. Despite the fact that neither of us really wanted to bother with school today, we knew school could lead to an answer. After all, this did happen in the middle of the school day yesterday, so the answer could be related somehow.

Football practice may be of some help. I'll be around people I haven't spent much time with in the last twenty-four hours. I might learn something about myself or about Charlie that I didn't know before. Something that could shed some light on our situation.

I'm relieved to find all the lockers have names on them, so it isn't hard to locate my gear. What is hard is trying to figure out how to put it on. I struggle with the pants, all the while trying to look like I know what I'm doing. The locker room slowly empties out as all the guys make their way to the field until I'm the only one left.

When I think I've got everything situated, I grab my jersey off the top shelf of the locker to pull it on over my head. A box catches my eye, located in the back of the top shelf of my locker. I pull it toward me and take a seat on the bench. It's a red box, much larger than a box that would just contain a piece of jewelry. I pull the lid off and find a few pictures at the very top.

There aren't any people in the pictures. They seem to be of places. I flip through them and come to a picture of a swing set. It's raining, and the ground beneath the swing is covered in water. I flip it over, and written on the back, it says, *Our first kiss.*

The next picture is of a backseat, but the view is from the floorboard, looking up. I flip it over. *Our first fight.*

Third is a picture of what looks like a church, but it's only the picture of the doors. *Where we met.*

I flip through all the pictures until finally I get to a letter, folded at the bottom of the box. I pick it up and unfold it. It's a short letter in my handwriting, addressed to Charlie. I begin to read it, but my phone buzzes, so I reach over and unlock it.

Charlie: What time is your practice over?

Me: Not sure. I found a box of stuff in the locker room. Don't know if it'll help, but there's a letter in it.

Charlie: What does it say?

"Silas!" someone yells from behind me. I spin around and drop two of the pictures in my hands. There's a man standing at the door with an angry look on his face. "Get on the field!"

I nod and he continues on down the hall. I put the pictures back in the box and set it back inside my locker. I take a deep, calming breath and make my way out to the practice field.

Two lines are formed on the field, both rows of guys hunched forward and staring at the guy in front of them. There's an obvious opening, so I jog toward the empty spot and copy what the other players are doing.

"For shit's sake, Nash! Why are you not wearing your shoulder pads?" someone yells.

Shoulder pads. Crap.

I skip out of line and run back to the locker room. This is going to be the longest hour of my life. It's odd I can't remember the rules of football. Can't be that hard, though. Just run back and forth a few times and practice will be over.

I locate pads behind the row of lockers. Luckily, they're easy to put on. I rush back out onto the field and everyone is scattering, running around like ants. I hesitate before walking onto the field. When a whistle blows, someone shoves me from behind. "Go!" he yells, frustrated.

The lines, the numbers, the goal posts. They mean nothing to me as I stand on the field amongst the other guys. One of the coaches shouts an order and before I know it, the ball is being thrown in my direction. I catch it.

What now?

Run. I should probably run.

I make it three feet before my face meets the Astro-turf. A whistle blows.

A man yells.

I stand up, just as one of the coaches stalks in my direction. "What the hell was that? Get your damn head in the play!"

I look around me, the sweat beginning to trickle down my forehead. Landon's voice rings out behind me. "Dude. What the hell is wrong with you?"

I turn and look at him, just as everyone huddles around me. I follow their motions and lay my arms over the backs of the guys to my left and right. No one speaks for several seconds, and then I realize they're all looking at me. Waiting. I think they want me to say something? I get the feeling it's not a prayer circle.

"You gonna call a play or what?" the guy to my left says.

"Uh...," I stutter. "You...," I point to Landon. "Do that...thing." Before they can question me, I pull apart and the huddle breaks.

"Coach is gonna bench him," I hear someone mumble behind me. A whistle blows and before the sound even leaves my ears, a freight train crashes into my chest.

Or at least it feels that way.

The sky is above me, my ears are ringing, I can't pull in a breath.

Landon is hovering over me. He grabs my helmet and shakes it. "What the hell is *wrong* with you?" He looks around and then back down at me. His eyes narrow. "Stay on the ground. Act sick."

I do what he says and he jumps up to a stand. "I told him not to come to practice, Coach," Landon says. "He's had strep all week. I think he's dehydrated."

I close my eyes, relieved for my brother. I kind of like this kid.

"What the hell are you even doing here, Nash?" The coach is kneeling now. "Go to the locker room and get hydrated. We've got a game tomorrow night." He stands and motions for one of the assistant coaches. "Get him a Z-Pak and make sure he's ready for the field tomorrow."

Landon pulls me up. My ears are still ringing, but I'm able to breathe now. I make my way toward the locker rooms, relieved to be off the field. I should have never walked on in the first place. *Not smart, Silas.*

I make it back to the locker room and change out of my gear. As soon as I get my shoes on, I hear footsteps nearing the locker room from down the hall. I glance around and spot an exit on the far wall, so I rush to it and push it open. Luckily, it leads right out to the parking lot.

I'm immediately relieved to see my car. I rush over to it just as Charlie climbs out of the driver side, hopping onto her feet as I approach. I'm so relieved to see her—to just have someone to relate to—that I don't even think about what I do next.

I grab her wrist and pull her to me, wrapping my arms around her in a tight hug. My face is buried in her hair and I let out a sigh. She feels familiar. Safe. Makes me forget that I can't even remember…

"What are you doing?"

She's stiff against me. Her cold reaction reminds me that we don't do things like this. Silas and Charlie did things like this.

Shit.

I clear my throat and release her, taking a quick step back. "Sorry," I mutter. "Force of habit."

"We *have* no habits." She pushes past me and walks around my car.

"Do you think you've always been this mean to me?" I ask her.

She looks at me from over the hood and nods. "My money's on yes. You're probably a glutton for punishment."

"More like a masochist," I mutter.

We both climb into my car, and I have two places I plan on going tonight. The first being my house to shower, but I'm sure if I asked her if she wanted to come along, she'd say no just to spite me. Instead, I head in the direction of my house and don't give her a choice.

"Why are you smiling?" she asks, three miles into our drive. I didn't realize I was. I shrug. "Just thinking."

"About what?"

I glance at her and she's waiting for my answer with an impatient frown.

"I was wondering how the old Silas ever broke through your hard exterior."

She laughs. "What makes you think he did?"

I would smile again, but I don't think I've stopped. "You saw the video, Charlie. You loved him." I pause for a second, then rephrase. "*Me.* You loved *me.*"

"*She* loved you," Charlie says, and then smiles. "I'm not even sure if I *like* you yet."

I shake my head with a soft laugh. "I don't know myself very well, but I must have been extremely competitive. Because I just took that as a challenge."

"Took *what* as a challenge? You think you can make me like you again?"

I look over at her and give my head the slightest shake. "No. I'm gonna make you fall in love with me again."

I can see the gentle roll of her throat as she swallows,

but just as fast as she let her guard down, it flies back up. "Good luck with that," she says, facing forward again. "I'm pretty sure you'll be the first guy to ever compete with himself over the affection of a girl."

"Maybe so," I say as we pull into my driveway. "But my money's on me."

I turn the car off and get out. She doesn't unbuckle. "You coming? I need to take a quick shower."

She doesn't even look at me. "I'll wait in the car."

I don't argue. I close the door and head inside to shower, thinking about the small smile I could swear was playing in the corner of her mouth.

And while winning her over again isn't my main priority, it's definitely the new back-up plan in case neither of us can figure out how to revert back to who we were before yesterday. Because even through all the bullshit— her cheating on me with Brian, me cheating on her with the counselor, our families in turmoil—we still obviously tried to make it work. There had to be something there, something deeper than attraction or a simple childhood bond, that made me fight to keep her.

I want to feel that again. I want to remember what it feels like to love someone like that. And not just anyone. I want to know what it feels like to love *Charlie*.

11

Charlie

I'm standing on the edge of the lawn, looking down his street when he walks up behind me. I don't hear him approach, but I smell him. I don't know how, since he smells just like the outdoors.

"What are you looking at?" he asks.

I stare at the houses, each of them immaculate and manicured to the point of irritation. It makes me want to shoot a gun into the air, just to see all the quiet people inside scramble out. This neighborhood needs a little life breathed into it. "It's strange how money seems to silence a neighborhood," I say quietly. "On my street, where no one has money, it's so loud. Sirens blaring, people shouting, car doors slamming, stereos thumping. There's always someone, somewhere, making noise." I turn and look up at him, not expecting the reaction I have to seeing his damp hair and smooth jaw. I focus on his eyes, but that isn't much better. I clear my throat and look away. "I think I prefer the noise."

He takes a step until we're shoulder to shoulder, both staring at the taciturn street. "No, you don't. You don't prefer either." He says this like he knows me, and I want to remind him he doesn't know me at all, but he puts his hand on my elbow. "Let's get out of here," he says. "Go do something that doesn't belong to Charlie and Silas. Something that's ours."

"You're talking about us like we're body invaders."

Silas closes his eyes and tilts his head back. "You have no idea how many times a day I think about invading your body."

I don't intend to laugh as hard as I do, but I trip over my own feet and Silas reaches down to catch me. We're both laughing as he rights me on my feet and rubs his hands up and down my arms.

I look away. I'm tired of liking him. I only have a day and a half worth of memories, but they're all filled with me not hating Silas. And now he's made it his personal mission to make me love him again. It's annoying that I like it.

"Go away," I say.

He raises his hands in surrender and takes a step back. "This far?"

"Farther."

Another step. "Better?"

"Yes," I smart.

Silas grins. "I don't know myself well, but I can tell I have a lot of game."

"Oh, please," I say. "If you were a game, Silas, you'd be Monopoly. You just go on and on and everyone ends up cheating just to be over with it."

He's quiet for a minute. I feel bad for saying something so awkward even if it was a joke.

"You're probably right," he laughs. "That's why you cheated on me with that asshat, Brian. Lucky for you, I'm not Monopoly Silas anymore. I'm Tetris Silas. All my pieces and parts are going to fit into all of your pieces and parts."

I snort. "And the guidance counselor's, apparently."

"Low blow, Charlie," he says, shaking his head.

I wait a few seconds, chewing on my lip. Then I say, "I don't think I want you to call me that."

Silas turns to look at me. "Charlie?"

"Yeah." I look over at him. "Is that weird? I don't feel like I'm her. I don't even know her. It just doesn't feel like my name."

He nods as we walk toward his car. "So, I get to re-name you?"

"Until we figure all this out…yeah."

"Poppy," he says.

"No."

"Lucy."

"Hell no, what's wrong with you?"

He opens the passenger side door to his Rover and I climb in. "Okay…okay. I can see you don't like tradition-ally cute names. We can try for something tougher." He walks around to the driver side and climbs in. "Xena…"

"No."

"Rogue."

"Ugh. No."

We go back and forth like this until Silas's GPS tells us that we've arrived. I look around, surprised that I was too engaged with him to notice the drive here. When I look down at my phone I see that Brian has texted me six times. I don't want to deal with him right now. I shove my phone and wallet under the seat, out of view.

"Where are we?"

"Bourbon Street," he says. "Most happening place in New Orleans."

"How do you know that?" I ask suspiciously.

"I Googled it." We stare at each other over the hood, and then both shut our doors at the same time.

"How did you know what Google was?"

"I thought that's what we're supposed to be figuring out together." We meet at the front of the car.

"I think we're aliens," I say. "That's why we don't have any of Charlie's and Silas's memories. But we remember things like Google and Tetris because of the computer chips in our brains."

"So, can I rename you Alien?"

Before I can think about what I'm doing, I send the back of my hand into his chest. "Focus, Silas!"

He *uumphs*, and then I'm pointing straight ahead. "What's that?" I walk ahead of him.

It's a building, castle-like in structure, and white. There are three spires jutting up toward the sky.

"Looks like a church," he says, taking out his phone.

"What are you doing?"

"Taking a picture…in case we forget again. I figure we should document what's happening and where we go."

I'm quiet as I think about what he said. It's a really good idea. "That's where we should go, right? Churches help people…" My voice trails off.

"Yes," says Silas. "They help *people*, not aliens. And since we're—"

I hit him again. I wish he would take this seriously. "What if we're angels and we're supposed to help someone, and we were given these bodies to fulfill our mission?"

He sighs. "Are you listening to yourself?"

We've reached the doors to the church, which are ironically locked. "Okay," I say, spinning around. "What's *your* suggestion for what's happened to us? Did we boink our heads together and lose our memories? Or maybe we ate something that really messed us up!" I storm down the stairs.

"Hey! Hey!" he calls. "You're not allowed to get mad at me. This is not my fault." He runs down the stairs after me.

"How do we know that? We don't know *anything*, Silas! This could be all your fault!"

We're standing at the bottom of the stairs now, staring at each other. "Maybe it is," he says. "But whatever I did, you did it too. Because in case you haven't noticed, we're in the same boat."

I clench and unclench my fists, take deep breaths, concentrate on staring at the church until my eyes water.

"Look," Silas says, stepping closer. "I'm sorry for turning this into a joke. I want to figure it out as much as you do. What are some of your other ideas?"

I close my eyes. "Fairy tales," I say, looking back up at him. "Someone is always cursed. To break the spell they have to figure something out about themselves... then..."

"Then what?"

I can tell he's trying to take me seriously, but this somehow makes me angrier. "There's a kiss..."

He grins. "A kiss, huh? I've never kissed anyone before."

"Silas!"

"*What?* If I can't remember, it doesn't count!"

I fold my arms across my chest and watch a street musician pick up his violin. He remembers the first time he picked up a violin, the first notes he played, who gave it to him. I envy his memories.

"I'll be serious, Charlie. I'm sorry."

I look at Silas out of the corner of my eye. He looks genuinely sorry, hands shoved into his pockets, neck dropping like it's suddenly too heavy.

"So, what do you think we need to do? Kiss?"

I shrug. "It's worth a try, right?"

"You said in fairy tales they have to figure something out first…"

"Yeah. Like, Sleeping Beauty needed someone brave to kiss her and wake her from the sleeping curse. Snow White needed true love's kiss to bring her back to life. Ariel needed to get Eric to kiss her to break the spell the sea witch put on her."

He perks up. "Those are movies," he says. "Do you remember watching them?"

"I don't remember watching them, I just know I've seen them. Mr. Deetson spoke about fairy tales in English today. That's where I got the idea."

We start walking toward the street musician, who is playing something slow and mournful.

"Sounds like the breaking of the curse is mostly up to the guy," Silas says. "He needs to mean something to her."

"Yeah…" My voice drops off as we stop to listen. I wish I knew the song he was playing. It sounds like something I've heard, but I have no name for it.

"There's a girl," I say softly. "I want to talk to her…

I think maybe she knows something. A few people have referred to her as The Shrimp."

Silas's eyebrows draw together. "What do you mean? Who is she?"

"I don't know. She's in a couple of my classes. It's just a feeling."

We stand among a group of onlookers, and Silas reaches for my hand. For the first time, I don't pull away from him. I let his warm fingers intertwine with mine. With his free hand, he takes a picture of the violinist, then he looks down at me. "So I can remember the first time I held your hand."

12

Silas

We've walked two blocks and she hasn't let go of my hand yet. I don't know if it's because she likes holding it, or if it's because Bourbon Street is...*well*...

"Oh, God," she says, turning toward me. She fists my shirt in her hand and presses her forehead against my arm. "That guy just flashed me," she says, laughing into the sleeve of my shirt. "Silas, I just saw my first penis!"

I laugh as I continue steering her through the inebriated crowd of Bourbon Street. After walking a ways, she peeks up again. We're now approaching an even larger group of belligerent men, all without shirts. In the place of shirts are mounds of beads draped around their necks. They're all laughing and screaming at the people perched on the balconies above us. She squeezes my hand tighter until we've successfully navigated through them. She relaxes and puts more space between us.

"What's with the beads?" she asks. "Why would anyone spend money on such tacky jewelry?"

"It's part of the Mardi Gras tradition," I tell her. "I read about it when I was researching Bourbon Street. It started as a celebration for the last Tuesday before Lent, but I guess it's turned into a year-round thing." I pull her against my side and point down to the sidewalk in front of her. She sidesteps around what looks like puke.

"I'm hungry," she says.

I laugh. "Stepping over vomit made you hungry?"

"No, vomit made me think of food, and food made my stomach growl. Feed me." She points to a restaurant up the street. The sign is flashing in red neon. "Let's go there."

She steps ahead of me, still gripping my hand. I glance down at my phone and follow her lead. I have three missed calls. One from "Coach," one from my brother, and one from "Mom."

It's the first time I've thought about my mother. I wonder what she's like. I wonder why I haven't met her yet.

My whole body crashes into the back of Charlie's after she stops short to let a vehicle pass. Her hand flies up to the back of her head, where my chin smashed against it. "Ouch," she says, rubbing her head.

I rub my chin and watch from behind her as she pushes her hair forward, over her shoulder. My eyes fall to the tip of what appears to be a tattoo peeking out from the back of her shirt.

She begins walking again, but I grab her shoulder. "Wait," I tell her. My fingers trail to the collar of her shirt and I pull it down a couple of inches. Right below the nape of her neck is a small silhouette of trees in black ink. I run my fingers over their outline. "You have a tattoo."

Her hand flies to the spot I'm touching. "What?!" she shrieks. She spins around and looks up at me. "I do not."

"You do." I turn her back around and pull the shirt down again. "Here," I say as I trace the trees again. This time I notice as chills break out on her neck. I follow the line of tiny bumps with my eyes, running over her shoulder and hiding beneath her shirt. I look back at the tattoo again, because her fingers are now attempting to feel what I'm feeling. I take two of them and press them against her skin. "A silhouette of trees," I tell her. "Right here."

"Trees?" she says, cocking her head to the side. "Why would I have trees?" She turns around. "I want to see it. Take a picture with your phone."

I pull her shirt down enough so that she can see the entire tattoo, even though it's no more than three inches wide. I brush her hair over her shoulder again, not for the sake of the picture, but because I've really been wanting to do that. I also reposition her hand so that it's coming across the front of her body, draping over her shoulder.

"Silas," she grumbles. "Just take the damn picture. This isn't art class."

I grin and wonder if I'm always like this—if I refuse to take a simple picture, knowing it only takes a little bit more effort to make it exceptional. I bring the phone up and snap the picture, then look at the screen, admiring how good the tattoo looks on her. She spins around and takes the phone from my hands.

She looks down at the picture and gasps. "Oh, my God."

"It's a very nice tattoo," I tell her. She hands me back my phone and rolls her eyes, walking again in the direction of the restaurant.

She can roll her eyes all she wants. It doesn't change how she reacted to my fingers trailing across the back of her neck.

I watch her walk toward the restaurant, and realize that I have her figured out already. The more she likes me, the more closed off she becomes. The more sarcasm she inflicts on me. Vulnerability makes her feel weak, so she's pretending to be tougher than she really is. I think the old Silas knew this about her, too. Which is why he loved her, because apparently he liked the game they played.

Apparently I do too, because once again, I'm following her.

We walk through the door of the restaurant and Charlie says, "Two people, booth please," before the hostess even has a chance to ask. *At least she said please.*

"Right this way," the woman says.

The restaurant is quiet and dark, a stark contrast to the noise and neon lights of Bourbon Street. We both breathe a collective sigh of relief once we're seated. The waitress hands us our menus and takes our drink order. Every now and then, Charlie lifts a hand to the back of her neck as if she can feel the outline of the tattoo.

"What do you think it means?" she says, still staring at the menu in front of her.

I shrug. "I don't know. Maybe you liked forests?" I glance up at her. "These fairy tales you talked about. Did they all take place in forests? Maybe the man who needs to break your spell with a kiss is a strapping lumberjack, living in the woods."

Her eyes meet mine and I can tell my jokes are aggravating her. Or maybe she's aggravated because she thinks I'm funny. "Stop making fun of me," she says.

"We woke up without our memories at the exact same time, Silas. Nothing is more absurd than that. Even fairy tales with lumberjacks."

I smile innocently and look down at my hand. "I have callouses," I tell her, lifting my hand and pointing at the rough skin of my palm. "*I* could be your lumberjack."

She rolls her eyes again, but laughs this time. "You probably have callouses from jerking off too much."

I hold up my right hand. "But they're on both hands, not just my left."

"Ambidextrous," she deadpans.

We both grin as our drinks are placed in front of us. "Ready to order?" the waitress asks.

Charlie quickly scans the menu and says, "I hate that we can't remember what we like." She looks up at the waitress. "I'll take a grilled cheese," she says. "It's safe."

"Burger and fries, no mayo," I tell her. We hand her back our menus and I refocus on Charlie. "You aren't eighteen yet. How could you get a tattoo?"

"Bourbon Street doesn't seem to be a stickler for the rules," she says. "I probably have a fake ID hidden somewhere."

I open the search engine on my phone. "I'll try to figure out what it means. I've gotten pretty good at this Google thing." I spend the next few minutes searching every possible meaning of trees and forests and clusters of trees. Just when I think I'm onto something, she pulls my phone away and sets it on the table.

"Get up," she says as she stands. "We're going to the bathroom." She grabs my hand and pulls me out of the booth.

"Together?"

She nods. "Yep."

I look at the back of her head as she walks away from me, then back at the empty booth. *What the...*

"Come *on*," she says over her shoulder.

I follow her to the hallway that leads to the restrooms. She pushes open the women's and peeks inside, then pulls her head out. "It's a single stall. It's empty," she says, holding the door open for me.

I pause and look at the men's restroom, which looks perfectly fine, so I don't know why she's— "Silas!" She grabs my arm and pulls me inside the restroom. Once we're inside, I half expect her to wrap her arms around my neck and kiss me because...*why else would we be in here together?*

"Take off your shirt."

I look down at my shirt.

I look back up at her. "Are we...are we about to make out? Because I didn't picture it going down like this."

She groans and reaches forward, pulling at the hem of my shirt. I help her pull it over my head when she says, "I want to see if you have any tattoos, dumbass."

I deflate.

I feel like an eighteen-year-old who's just been blue-balled. I guess I kind of am...

She turns me around and, when I face the mirror, she gasps. Her eyes are fixated on my back. My muscles tense beneath her touch as her fingertips meet my right shoulder blade. She traces a circle, spanning a radius of several inches. I squeeze my eyes shut and try to control my pulse. I suddenly feel drunker than everyone on Bourbon Street combined. I'm gripping the counter in front of me because her fingers...my skin.

"Jesus," I groan, dropping my head between my shoulders. *Focus, Silas.*

"What's wrong?" she asks, pausing her inspection of my tattoo. "It doesn't hurt does it?"

I release a laugh, because her hands on me are the opposite of pain. "No, Charlie. It doesn't hurt."

My eyes meet hers in the mirror and she stares at me for several seconds. When what she's doing to me finally registers, she glances away and pulls her hand from my back. Her cheeks flush.

"Put your shirt on and go wait for our food," she demands. "I have to pee."

I release my grip on the counter and inhale deeply as I pull my shirt back over my head. On my walk back to our table, I realize I never even asked her what the tattoo was.

"A strand of pearls," she says as she slides into the booth. "Black pearls. It's about six inches in diameter."

"Pearls?"

She nods.

"Like a...*necklace*?"

She nods again and takes a sip of her drink. "You have a tattoo of a woman's necklace on your back, Silas." She's smiling now. "Very lumberjack-esque."

She's enjoying this. "Yeah, well. You have trees on your back. Not much to brag about. You'll probably get termites."

She laughs out loud and it makes me laugh, too. She moves the straw around in her drink and looks down at her glass. "Knowing me..." She pauses. "Knowing *Charlie*, she wouldn't have gotten a tattoo unless it really meant something to her. It had to be something she knew she would *never* grow tired of. *Never* stop loving."

Two familiar words stick out in her sentence. "Never never," I whisper.

She looks up at me, recognizing the phrase we repeated to each other in the video. She tilts her head to the side. "You think it had something to do with you? With Silas?" She shakes her head, silently disagreeing with my suggestion, but I begin scrolling through my phone. "Charlie wouldn't be that stupid," she adds. "She wouldn't ink something into her skin that was related to a guy. Besides, what would trees have to do with you?"

I find exactly what I'm looking for and, as much as I'm trying to keep a straight face, I can't stop the smile. I know it's a smug smile and I probably should not be looking at her like this, but I can't help it. I hand her the phone and she looks down at the screen and reads out loud.

"'From a Greek name meaning *forests* or *woods.*'" She looks up at me. "So it's the meaning of a name?"

I nod. *Still smug.* "Scroll up."

She scrolls up the screen with a swipe of her finger and her lips part with a gasp. "'Derived from the Greek term—Silas.'" Her mouth clamps shut and her jaw hardens. She hands me back the phone and closes her eyes. Her head moves slowly back and forth. "She got a tattoo of the meaning of your *name*?"

As expected, she's pretending to be disappointed in herself. As expected, I feel triumphant.

"*You* got a tattoo," I tell her, pointing my finger in her direction. "It's on *you. Your* skin. *My* name." I can't stop with the stupid smile plastered across my face. She rolls her eyes again, just as our food is laid in front of us.

I push mine aside and search the meaning for the name Charlie. I don't pull anything up that could mean pearls. After a few minutes, she finally sighs and says, "Try Margaret. My middle name."

I search the name Margaret and read the results out loud. "'Margaret, from the Greek term meaning *pearl*.'"

I set my phone down. I don't know why it seems like I've just won a bet, but I feel victorious.

"It's a good thing you're giving me a new name," she says, matter of fact.

A new name my ass.

I pull my plate in front of me and pick up a french fry. I point it at her and wink. "We're branded. You and me. We are so in *love*, Charlie. You feeling it yet? Do I make your heart go pitter patter?"

"These aren't *our* tattoos," she says.

I shake my head. "Branded," I repeat. I raise my index finger as if I'm gesturing over her shoulder. "Right there. Permanently. Forever."

"God," she groans. "Shut up and eat your damn burger." I eat it. I eat the entire thing with a shit-eating grin.

"What now?" I ask, leaning back in my seat. She's barely touched her food and I'm pretty sure I just broke a record with how fast I ate mine.

She looks up at me and I can see by the trepidation in her expression that she already knows what she wants to do next, she just doesn't want to bring it up.

"What is it?"

Her eyes narrow. "I don't want you to make a smart-ass comment in response to what I'm about to suggest."

"No, Charlie," I say immediately. "We aren't eloping tonight. The tattoos are enough commitment for now."

She doesn't roll her eyes at my joke this time. She sighs, defeated, and leans back in her seat.

I hate her reaction. I like it a whole lot more when she rolls her eyes at me.

I reach across the table and cover her hand with mine, rubbing my thumb over hers. "I'm sorry," I say. "Sarcasm just makes this whole thing feel a little less frightening." I remove my hand from hers. "What did you want to say? I'm listening. Promise. Lumberjack's honor."

She laughs with a small roll of her eyes and I'm relieved. She glances up at me and shifts in her seat, then begins playing with her straw again. "We passed a few... *tarot* shops. I think maybe we should get a reading."

I don't even start at her comment. I just nod and pull my wallet out of my pocket. I lay enough money on the table to cover our bill and then I stand up. "I agree," I tell her, reaching out for her hand.

I actually *don't* agree, but I feel bad. These last two days have been exhausting and I know she's tired. The least I can do is make this easier for her, despite knowing this hocus pocus bullshit isn't going to enlighten us in any way.

We pass a few tarot shops during our search, but Charlie shakes her head each time I point one out. I'm not sure what she's looking for, but I actually like walking the streets with her, so I'm not complaining. She's holding my hand, and sometimes I put my arm around her and pull her against me when the paths become too narrow. I don't know if she's noticed, but I've been leading us through a lot of these narrow paths unnecessarily.

Any time I see a big crowd, I aim for it. After all, she's still my back-up plan.

After about half an hour longer of walking, it looks like we're reaching the end of the French Quarter. The crowds are dwindling, giving me fewer excuses to pull her to me. Some of the shops we're passing have already closed. We make it to St. Philip Street when she pauses in front of an art gallery window.

I stand next to her and stare at the displays illuminated inside the building. There are plastic body parts suspended from the ceiling, and giant, metal sea life clinging to the walls. The main display, which is directly in front of us, just happens to be a small corpse—wearing a strand of pearls.

She taps her finger against the glass, pointing at the corpse. "Look," she says. "It's me." She laughs and moves her attention to somewhere else inside the store.

I'm not looking at the corpse anymore. I'm not looking inside the store anymore.

I'm looking at her.

The lights from inside the gallery are illuminating her skin, giving her a glow that really does make her look like an angel. I want to run my hand across her back and feel for actual wings.

Her eyes move from one object to another as she studies everything beyond the window. She's looking at each piece with bewilderment. I make a mental note to bring her back here when they're actually open. I can't imagine what she'd look like actually being able to touch one of the pieces.

She stares into the window a few minutes longer and I continue to stare at her, only now I've taken two steps and I'm standing directly behind her. I want to see her tattoo again, now that I know what it means. I wrap my hand around her hair and brush it forward, over her shoulder. I half expect her to reach behind her and slap my hand away, but instead, she sucks in a quick rush of air and looks down at her feet.

I smile, remembering what it felt like when she ran her fingers over my tattoo. I don't know if I make her feel the same, but she's standing still, allowing my fingers to slip inside the collar of her shirt again.

I swallow what feels like three entire heartbeats. I wonder if she's always had this effect on me.

I pull her shirt down, revealing her tattoo. A pang shoots through my stomach, because I hate that we don't have this memory. I want to remember the discussion we had when we decided to make such a permanent decision. I want to remember who brought the idea up first. I want to remember what she looked like as the needle pierced her skin for the first time. I want to remember how we felt when it was over.

I run my thumb over the silhouette of trees while curving the rest of my hand over her shoulder—over skin covered in chills again. She tilts her head to the side and the tiniest of whimpers escapes her throat.

I squeeze my eyes shut. "Charlie?" My voice is like sandpaper. I clear my throat to smooth it out. "I changed my mind," I say quietly. "I don't want to give you a new name. I kind of love your old one now."

I wait.

I wait for her snarky response. For her laughter.

I wait for her to push my hand away from the nape of her neck. I get no reaction from her. Nothing. *Which means I get everything.*

I keep my hand on her back as I slowly step around her. I'm standing between her and the window now, but she keeps her eyes focused on the ground. She doesn't look up at me, because I know she doesn't like to feel weak. And right now, I'm making her weak. I bring my free hand to her chin and graze my fingers up her jaw, tilting her face to mine.

When we lock eyes, I feel like I'm meeting a brand-new side of her. A side of her without resolve. A vulnerable side. A side that's allowing herself to feel something. I want to grin and ask her how it feels to be in love, but I know teasing her in this moment would piss her off and she'd walk away and I can't let that happen. Not right now. Not when I finally get to catalog an actual memory with all the numerous fantasies I've had about her mouth.

Her tongue slides across her bottom lip, causing jealousy to flutter through me, because I really wanted to be the one to do that to her lip.

In fact… I think I will.

I begin to dip my head, just as she presses her hands against my forearms. "Look," she says, pointing at the building next door. The flickering light has stolen her attention and I want to curse the universe for the simple fact that a *light bulb* just interfered with what was about to become my absolute favorite of very few memories.

I follow her gaze to a sign that doesn't look any different from all of the other tarot signs we've passed. The only thing different about this one is it just completely ruined my moment. And *dammit*, it was a good moment. A *great* one. One I know Charlie was also feeling, and I don't know how long it'll take me to get back to that.

She's walking in the direction of the shop now. I follow behind her like a lovesick puppy.

The building is unmarked and it makes me wonder what it was about the unreliable, asshole lighting that drew her away from my mouth. The only words indicating this is even a store are the "No Cameras" signs plastered on every blackened window.

Charlie puts her hands on the door and pushes it open. I follow her inside and we're soon standing in what looks like the center of a touristy voodoo gift shop. There's a man standing behind a register and a few people browsing the aisles.

I try to take everything in as I follow Charlie through the store. She fingers everything, touching the stones, the bones, the jars of miniature voodoo dolls. We silently make our way down each aisle until we reach the back wall. Charlie stops short, grabs my hand and points at a picture on the wall. "That gate," she says. "You took a picture of that gate. It's the one hanging on my wall."

"Can I help you?"

We both spin around and a large—*really large*—man with gauged ears and a lip ring is staring down at us.

I kind of want to apologize to him and leave as fast as we can, but Charlie has other plans. "Do you know what this gate is guarding? The one in the picture?" Charlie asks him, pointing over her shoulder. The man's eyes lift to the picture frame. He shrugs.

"Must be new," he says. "I've never noticed it before." He looks at me, arching an eyebrow adorned with multiple piercings. One being a small…*bone*? *Is that a bone sticking through his eyebrow*? "You two looking for anything in particular?"

I shake my head and begin to respond, but my words are cut off by someone else's.

"They're here to see me." A hand reaches through a beaded curtain to our right. A woman steps out, and Charlie immediately sidles against me. I wrap my arm around her. I don't know why she's allowing this place to freak her out. She doesn't seem like the type to believe in this sort of thing, but I'm not complaining. A frightened Charlie means a very lucky Silas.

"This way," the woman says, motioning for us to follow her. I start to object, but then remind myself that places like this…they're all about theatrics. It's Halloween 365 days a year. She's just playing a part. She's no different than Charlie and me, pretending to be two people we aren't.

Charlie glances up at me, silently asking for permission to follow her. I nod and we follow the woman through the curtain of—*I touch one of the beads and take a closer look*—plastic skulls. *Nice touch.*

The room is small and every wall is covered with thick, velvet black curtains. There are candles lit around the room, flickers of light licking the walls, the floor, us. The woman takes a seat at a small table in the center of the room and gestures for us to sit in the two chairs across from her. I keep Charlie's hand wrapped tightly in mine as we both sit.

The woman begins to slowly shuffle a deck of tarot cards. "A joint reading, I assume?" she asks.

We both nod. She hands Charlie the deck and asks her to hold them. Charlie takes them from her and clasps her hands around them. The woman nudges her head toward me. "Both of you. Hold them."

I want to roll my eyes, but instead I reach my hand across Charlie and place it on the deck with her.

"You need to want the same thing out of this reading. Multiple readings can sometimes overlap when there isn't cohesiveness. It's important your goal is the same."

Charlie nods. "They are. It is."

I hate the desperation in her voice, like we're actually going to get an answer. *Surely she doesn't believe this.*

The woman reaches across to take the cards from our hands. Her fingers brush mine and they're ice cold. I pull my hand back and grab Charlie's, moving it onto my lap.

She begins laying cards out on the table, one by one. They're all face down. When she's finished, she asks me to pull a card from the deck. When I hand her the card, she sets it apart from the others. She points at it. "This card will give you your answer, but the other cards explain the path to your question."

She puts her fingers on the card in the middle. "This position represents your current situation." She flips it over.

"Death?" Charlie whispers. Her hand tightens around mine.

The woman looks at Charlie and tilts her head. "It isn't necessarily a bad thing," she says. "The Death card represents a major change. A reformation. The two of you have experienced a loss of sorts."

She touches another card. "This position represents the immediate past." She flips it over and before I look down at the card, I can see the woman's eyes narrow. My eyes fall to the card. *The Devil.*

"This indicates something or someone was enslaving you in the past. It could represent a number of things close to you. Parental influence. An unhealthy relationship." Her eyes meet mine. "Inverted cards reflect a negative influence, and although it represents the past, it can also signify something you're currently transitioning through."

Her fingers fall to another card. "This card represents your immediate future." She slides the card toward her and flips it over. A quiet gasp falls from her mouth and I feel Charlie flinch. I glance down at her and she's staring intently at the woman, waiting for an explanation. She looks terrified.

I don't know what kind of game this woman is playing, but it's beginning to piss me off...

"The Tower card?" Charlie says. "What does it mean?"

The woman flips the card back over as if it's the worst card in the deck. She closes her eyes and blows out a long breath. Her eyes pop open again and she's staring right at Charlie. "It means...destruction."

I roll my eyes and push back from the table. "Charlie, let's get out of here."

Charlie looks at me pleadingly. "We're almost finished," she says. I relent and scoot back toward the table.

The woman flips over two more cards, explaining them to Charlie, but I don't hear a single word she says. My eyes wander around the room as I try to remain patient and let her finish, but I feel like we're wasting time.

Charlie's hand begins squeezing the life out of mine, so I return my attention to the reading. The woman's eyes are closed tight and her lips are moving. She's mumbling words I can't decipher.

Charlie scoots closer to me, and I instinctively wrap my arm around her. "Charlie," I whisper, making her look up at me. "It's theatrics. She gets paid to do this. Don't be scared."

My voice must have broken the woman out of her conveniently timed trance. She's tapping the table, trying to get our attention as if she wasn't off in la-la land for the last minute and a half.

Her fingers fall to the card I pulled out of the deck. Her eyes meet mine, and then they move to Charlie's. "This card," she says slowly. "Is your outcome card. Combined with the other cards in the reading, this gives you the answer to why you are here." She flips the card over.

The woman doesn't move. Her eyes are locked on the card beneath her fingertips. The rooms grows eerily quiet, and as if on cue, one of the candles loses its flame. *Another nice touch*, I think.

I look down at the outcome card. There aren't any words on it. No title. No picture.

The card is blank.

I can feel Charlie stiffen in my arms as she stares at the blank card on the table. I shove back from the table and pull Charlie up. "This is ridiculous," I say loudly, accidentally knocking my chair over.

I'm not pissed that the woman is trying to scare us. It's her job. I'm pissed because she's *actually* scaring Charlie, yet she's keeping up this ridiculous façade.

I take Charlie's face in my hands and look her in the eyes. "She planted that card to scare you, Charlie. This is all bullshit." I take both her hands and begin to turn her toward the exit.

"There *are* no blank cards in my tarot deck," the woman says.

I pause in my tracks and turn around to face her. Not because of what she said, but because of the *way* she said it. She sounded scared.

Scared for us?

I close my eyes and exhale. *She's an actress, Silas. Calm your shit.*

I push open the door and pull Charlie outside. I don't stop walking until we're around the building and on another street. When we're away from the store and away from the damn flickering of the sign, I stop walking and pull her against me. She wraps her arms around my waist and buries her head against my chest.

"Forget all of that," I say, rubbing my hand in reassuring circles over her back. "Fortune-telling, tarot readings…it's ridiculous, Charlie."

She pulls her face from my shirt and looks up at me. "Yeah. Ridiculous like the both of us waking up at school with no memory of who we are?"

I close my eyes and pull away from her. I run my hands through my hair, the frustration from the day catching up to me. I can make light of it all with my jokes. I can dismiss her theories—from tarot readings to fairy tales—simply because it doesn't make sense to me. But she's right. None of this makes sense. And the more we try to uncover the mystery, the more I feel like we're wasting our damn time.

13

Charlie

His lips fold in and he shakes his head. He wants out of here. I can feel his edginess.

"Maybe we should go back and ask her more detailed questions," I suggest.

"No way," he says. "I'm not entertaining that again." He starts to walk away, and I consider going back in there myself. I'm just about to take my first step toward the shop when the "Open" sign in the window turns off. The shop is in sudden darkness. I chew on the inside of my cheek. I could come back when Silas isn't around. Maybe she'd talk to me more.

"Charlie!" he calls.

I run after him until we're walking side by side again. We can see our breath as we walk. When did it get this cold? I rub my hands together.

"I'm hungry," I say.

"You're always hungry. I've never seen someone so

small eat so much." He doesn't offer to feed me this time, so I continue to walk beside him.

"What just happened back there?" I ask. I'm trying to make a joke of it, but my stomach feels funny.

"Someone tried to scare us. That's it."

I look up at Silas. Mostly everything together except those shoulders, which are tense. "But what if she's right? What if there weren't any blank cards in her tarot deck?"

"No," he says. "Just no."

I bite my lip and sidestep a man dancing backward down the sidewalk. "I don't understand how you can dismiss something so easily, considering our circumstances," I say from between my teeth. "Don't you think—"

"Why don't we talk about something else," Silas says.

"Right, like what we're going to do next weekend? Or how about we talk about what we did *last* weekend? Or maybe we talk about…" I smack my hand against my forehead. "The Electric Crush Diner." *How could I forget about that?*

"What?" Silas asks. "What's that?"

"We were there. You and me, last weekend. I found a receipt in my jeans pocket." Silas is watching me recount all of this with a look of mild annoyance on his face. "I took Janette there for dinner last night. A server recognized me."

"Hey!" he yells over my shoulder. "If you touch her with that I'll break you in half!"

I glance behind me and see a man pointing a foam finger at my butt.

He backs off when he sees the look on Silas's face.

"Why didn't you tell me that?" Silas says under his breath, directing his attention back to me. "That's not like tarot readers, that's something important."

"I really don't know. I meant to..."

He grabs my hand, but this time it's not for the pleasure of our palms pressing together. He drags me down the street with one hand while typing something into his phone with the other. I'm both impressed and mildly annoyed at being spoken to like that. We may have been something in our other life, but in this life I don't even know his middle name.

"It's on North Rampart Street," I say helpfully.

"Yeah."

He's pissed. I kind of like the emo-ness of it. We pass through a park with a fountain. Street vendors have set up their artwork along the fence; they stare at us as we pass by. Silas is taking one step to my three. I trot to keep up. We walk so far until my feet hurt and finally I yank my hand free of his.

He stops and turns around.

I don't know what to say, or what I'm mad at, so I place my hands on my hips and glare at him.

"What's wrong with you?" he says.

"I don't know!" I shout. "But you can't just drag me around the city! I can't walk as fast as you and my feet hurt."

This feels familiar. Why does this feel familiar?

He looks away and I can see the muscles working in his jaw. He turns back to me and everything happens quickly. He takes two steps and scoops me off my feet. Then he resumes his pace with me bouncing ever so slightly in his arms. After my initial squeal, I settle down and clasp my arms around his neck. I like it up here where I can smell his cologne and touch his skin. I don't recall seeing perfume among Charlie's things, and I doubt I would have thought to put any on. *What does that say about Silas?* That in the midst of all of this, he thought to pick up a bottle and spray cologne on his neck before he left the house this morning. Was he always the type of person who cared about the little things—like smelling good?

As I think these thoughts, Silas stops to ask a woman who has fallen in the street if she's all right. She's drunk and sloppy. When she tries to stand up, she steps on the hem of her dress and falls back down. Silas sets me down on the sidewalk and goes to help her.

"Are you bleeding? Did you hurt yourself?" he asks. He helps her stand, leads her back to where I'm waiting. She slurs her words and pats him on the cheek, and I wonder if he knew when he went to help her that she was homeless. I wouldn't touch her. She smells. I step away from both of them, and watch him watch her. He's concerned. He keeps his eyes on her until she's stumbled off down the next street, and then he swings his head around to find me.

In this moment—right now—it's so clear to me who Charlie is. She's not as good as Silas. She loves him because he's so different from her. Maybe that's why she went to Brian, because she couldn't live up to Silas.

Like I can't.

He half smiles at me, and I think he's embarrassed to be caught caring. "Ready?"

I want to tell him that what he did was nice, but *nice* is such a silly word for kindness. Anyone could pretend to be nice. What Silas did was innate. Boldfaced kindness. I haven't had any thoughts like that. I think about the girl in class the first morning who dropped her books at my feet. She'd looked at me with fear. She expected me not to help. And more. What else?

Silas and I walk in silence. He checks his phone every few minutes to make sure we're headed in the right direction and I check his face. I wonder if this is what a crush feels like. If watching a man help a woman is supposed to elicit these types of feelings. And then we're here. He points across the street and I nod.

"Yeah, that's it."

But it's almost not. The diner has transformed since I was here with Janette. It's loud and pumping. There are men lined up on the sidewalk smoking; they part for us as we walk by. I can feel the bass in my ankles as we stand outside the doors. They open for us as a group leaves. A girl walks past me laughing, her pink fur jacket brushing against my face. Inside, people are defending their space with widened elbows and jutted hips. People glare at us as we walk by. *This is my space, back off. I'm waiting for the rest of my group—keep moving.* We bypass the few empty seats in favor of walking deeper into the building. We press through the crowd, walking sideways, and flinching when raucous laughter erupts next to us. A drink spills on my shoes, someone says sorry. I don't even know who, because it's so dark. And then someone calls our names.

"Silas! Charlie! Over here!"

A boy and…who was that girl who picked me up this morning?

Annie… Amy?

"Hey," she says, as we draw close. "I can't believe you actually came back here after last weekend."

"Why wouldn't we?" Silas asks.

I take the seat I am offered and stare up at the three of them.

"You punch a guy, throw over a couple of tables and wonder why you shouldn't come back?" the boy says, along with a laugh. I think he's Annie/Amy's boyfriend by the way he looks at her—like they're in on something together. Life, maybe.

It's how Silas and I look at each other. Except we really are in on something together.

"You acted like an ass," she says.

"Amy," the spare boy says. "Don't."

Amy!

I want to know more about this person Silas punched.

"He deserved it," I say. Amy raises her eyebrows and shakes her head. Whatever she's thinking, she's too afraid to say it, because she turns away. I try her boyfriend next. "Don't you think so?" I ask innocent-like. He shrugs. Goes to sit next to Amy. *They're all scared of me*, I think, *but why?*

I order a Coke. Amy's head snaps around to look at me when she hears.

"Regular Coke? Not diet?"

"Do I look like I need to drink diet?" I snap. She shrinks back. I don't know where that came from—honest to God. I don't even know how much I weigh. I decide to shut up and let Silas do the detective work before I offend someone again. He drops down next to Amy's boyfriend and they begin to talk. The music makes it impossible to eavesdrop, and Amy is doing her best not to look at me, so I people-watch. People…they all have memories…know who they are. I'm jealous.

"Let's go, Charlie." Silas is standing above me, waiting. Amy and her boyfriend are watching us from across the table. It's a big table, I wonder who else is coming to join them and how many of those people hate me.

Out of the restaurant and back onto the street. Silas clears his throat. "I got into a fight."

"I heard," I say. "Did they tell you who it was?"

"Yeah."

I wait and, when he doesn't offer the information, I say, "Well…?"

"I punched the owner in the face. Brian's father."

My head snaps around. "What the hell?"

"Yeah," he says. He rubs the scruff on his chin thoughtfully. "Because he said something about you…"

"Me?" I get a sick feeling in my stomach. I know what's coming, but I don't know what's coming.

"He told me he was giving you a job as a waitress…"

Okay, that's not so bad. We need the money.

"Because you were Brian's girl. So I punched him, I guess."

"Damn."

"Yeah. That kid—Eller—told me we needed to leave before Brian's dad called the cops."

"The cops?" I echo.

"I guess Brian's dad and my dad have worked together on some stuff. He agreed not to press charges last week because of it, but I'm not supposed to go back there. Also, Landon has been calling around, looking for me. Apparently my dad is wondering why I left practice. Everyone's pretty pissed about that."

"Oops," I say.

"Yeah, oops." He says it like he doesn't care.

We go back the way we came, both of us quiet. We pass a few street artists I didn't notice before. Two of them look like a couple. The man is playing the bagpipes while the woman draws pictures in colored chalk on the sidewalk. We step over the drawings, both of our heads down, examining. Silas takes out his camera and snaps a few pictures while I watch her turn a few lines into a couple kissing.

A couple kissing. That reminds me. "We need to kiss," I say to him.

He almost drops his phone. His eyes are big when he looks at me.

"To see if something happens…like in the fairy tales we talked about."

"Oh," he says. "Yeah, sure. Okay. Where? Now?"

I roll my eyes and walk away from him, toward a fountain near a church. Silas follows behind. I want to see his face, but I don't look. This is all business. I can't make it into something else. It's an experiment. That's it.

When we reach the fountain, we both sit down on the rim of it. I don't want to do it this way, so I stand up and face him.

"Okay," I say, coming to stand in front of him. "Close your eyes." He does, but there's a grin on his face.

"Keep them closed," I instruct. I don't want him to see me. I barely know what I look like; I don't know if my face contorts under pressure.

His head is tilted up, and mine is tilted down. I put my hands on his shoulders and feel his hands lift to my waist as he pulls me closer, between his knees. His hands slide up without warning, his thumbs grazing my stomach and then making a quick swipe along the underside of my bra. My stomach clenches.

"Sorry," he says. "I can't see what I'm doing."

I smirk this time and I'm glad he can't see my reaction right now. "Put your hands back on my waist," I command.

He puts them too low and now his palms are on my ass. He squeezes a little, and I smack his arm.

"What?" He laughs. "I can't see!"

"Up," I say. He slides them a little higher, but slowly. I tingle down to my toes. "Higher," I say, again.

He takes them up a quarter of an inch. "Is this—"

Before he can finish his sentence, I lean my face down and kiss him. He's smiling at first, still in the middle of his little game, but when he feels my lips, his smile dissolves.

His mouth is soft. I lift my hands to his face and cup it as he pulls me tighter, wrapping his arms around my backside. I'm kissing down and he's kissing up. At first, I expect to just give him a peck. That's all they ever show in the fairy tales—a quick peck and the curse is broken. We'd have gotten our memories back by now if this were going to work. The experiment should be over, but neither of us stops.

He kisses with soft lips and a firm tongue. It's not sloppy or wet, it moves in and out of my mouth sensually as his lips suck softly on mine. I run my fingers up the back of his neck and into his hair, and that's when he stands, forcing me to take a step back and change position. I do a good job of hiding my gasp.

Now I'm kissing up and he's kissing down. Except he's holding me to him, his arm wrapped around my waist, his free hand curled around the back of my neck. I cling to his shirt, dizzy. Soft lips, dragging…tongue between my lips…pressure on my back…something pressing between us that makes me feel a riot of heat. I push away, gasping.

I stand there looking at him, he looking at me.

Something has happened. It's not our memories that have awoken, but something else that makes us feel drunk.

And it occurs to me as I stand here, wanting him to kiss me again, that this is exactly what doesn't need to happen. We're going to want more of the new us and we'll lose focus.

He slides a hand down his face as if to sober himself up. He smiles. "I don't care what our real first kiss was," he says. "That's the one I want to remember."

I stare at his smile long enough to remember it, and then I turn and walk away.

"Charlie!" he yells.

I ignore him and keep walking. That was stupid. What was I thinking?

A kiss isn't going to bring our memories back. This isn't a fairy tale.

He grabs my arm. "Hey. Slow down." And then, "What are you thinking?"

I keep walking in the direction I'm certain we came from. "I'm thinking I need to get home. I have to make sure Janette has eaten dinner...and..."

"About *us*, Charlie."

I can feel him staring at me. "There *is* no us," I say. I bring my eyes back to his. "Haven't you heard? We were obviously broken up and I was dating Brian. His dad was giving me a job. I..."

"We were an us, Charlie. And holy shit, I can see why."

I shake my head. *We can't lose focus.* "That was your first kiss," I say. "It could feel like that with anyone."

"So it felt that way for you too?" he asks, running around to stand in front of me.

I consider telling him the truth. That if I were dead like Snow White and he kissed me like that, surely my heart would kick back to life. That I'd be the one to slay dragons for that kiss.

But we don't have time to kiss like that. We need to find out what's happened and how to reverse it.

"I didn't feel anything," I say. "It was just a kiss and it didn't work." *A lie that burns my insides it's so foul.* "I have to go."

"Charlie…"

"I'll see you tomorrow." I lift a hand over my head and wave because I don't want to turn around and look at him. I'm afraid. I want to be with him, but it's not a good idea. Not until we figure more of this out. I think he's going to follow me, so I wave over a cab. I open the door and look back at Silas to show him that I'm fine. He nods, and then lifts his phone to snap a picture of me. *The first time she left me*, he's probably thinking. He then buries his hands in his pockets and turns in the direction of his car.

I wait until he's past the fountain before I lean down to speak to the driver. "Sorry, I changed my mind." I slam the door and step back to the curb. I don't have money for a cab anyway. I'll go back to the diner and ask Amy for a ride.

The cabbie peels off and I duck down a different street so Silas won't see me. I need to be alone. I need to think.

14

Silas

Another night of shitty sleep. Only this time, my lack of sleep wasn't because I was worried about myself, or even worried about what made Charlie and me lose our memories. My lack of sleep was strictly because I had two things on my mind: our kiss, and Charlie's reaction to our kiss.

I don't know why she walked away, or why she preferred to take a cab over riding with me. I could tell by the way she responded during the kiss that she felt what I was feeling. Of course it wasn't like the kisses in fairy tales that could end a curse, but I don't think either of us really expected it to. I'm not sure we really had any expectations for the kiss at all—just a little bit of hope.

What I certainly didn't expect was for everything else to take a backseat once her lips pressed against mine, but that's exactly what happened. I stopped thinking about the reason we were kissing and everything we had been through all day. All I could think about was how she was clenching my shirt in her fists, pulling me closer, wanting more. I could hear the small gasps of air she was sucking in between kisses, because as soon as our mouths met, we were both breathless. And even though she stopped the kiss and stepped away, I could still see the dazed look on her face and the way her eyes lingered on my mouth.

Despite all of it, though, she still turned and walked away. But if I've learned anything about Charlie in these last two days, it's that there's a reason for every move she makes. And it's usually a good reason, which is why I didn't try to stop her.

My phone receives a text, and I almost fall as I scramble out of the shower to get to it. I haven't heard from her since we parted ways last night, and I'd be lying if I said I wasn't beginning to worry.

My hope bleeds out of me when I see the text isn't from Charlie. It's from the kid I talked to at the diner last night, Eller.

Eller: Amy wants to know if Charlie rode with you to school. She's not at home.

I turn off the water, despite not even having rinsed off yet. I grab a towel with one hand and respond to his text with the other.

Me: No, I haven't even left my house yet. Has she tried her cell?

As soon as I send the text, I dial Charlie's number and hit speaker, then set the phone down on the counter. I'm dressed by the time her voicemail picks up.

"Shit," I mutter as I end the call. I open the door and stop by my bedroom long enough to get into my shoes and grab my keys. I make it downstairs, but freeze before I reach the front door.

There's a woman in the kitchen, and she isn't Ezra. "Mom?"

The word comes out of my mouth before I realize I'm even speaking. She spins around, and even though I only recognize her from the pictures on the wall, I think I might feel something. I don't know what it is. It's not love or recognition. I'm just overcome with a sense of calmness.

No…it's *comfort*. That's what I feel.

"Hey, sweetie," she says with a bright smile that reaches the corners of her eyes. She's preparing breakfast—or maybe she's cleaning after just finishing up breakfast. "Did you see the mail I put on your dresser yesterday? And how are you feeling?"

Landon looks more like her than I do. His jaw is soft, like hers. Mine is harsh, like my father's. Landon carries himself like she does, too. Like life has been good to them.

She tilts her head and then closes the distance between us. "Silas, are you okay?"

I take a step back when she tries to touch her hand to my forehead. "I'm fine."

She tucks her hand to her chest like it offends her that I backed away. "Oh," she says. "Okay. Well, good. You already missed school this week and you have a game tonight." She walks back into the kitchen. "You shouldn't stay out so late when you're sick."

I stare at the back of her head, wondering why she would say that. This is the first time I've even seen her since all of this started. Ezra or my father must have told her about Charlie being here.

I wonder if Charlie being here upset her. I wonder if she and my father share the same opinion of Charlie.

"I feel fine now," I reply. "I was with Charlie last night, that's why I was home late."

She doesn't react to my baited comment. She doesn't even look at me. I wait a few more seconds to see if she's going to respond. When she doesn't, I turn and head for the front door.

Landon is in the front seat already when I reach the car. I open the back door and throw my backpack inside. When I open the front, he reaches his hand out to me. "This was ringing. Found it under your seat."

I take the phone from him. It's Charlie's. "She left her phone in my car?"

Landon shrugs. I stare at the screen and there are several missed calls and texts. I see Brian's name, along with Amy's. I try to open them, but I'm prompted for a password.

"Get in the damn car, we're already late!"

I climb inside and set Charlie's phone on the console while I back out. When I pick it back up again to try and figure out the password, Landon snatches it out of my hands.

"Did you not learn anything from your fender bender last year?" He slaps the phone back down on the console.

I'm uneasy. I don't like that Charlie doesn't have her phone with her. I don't like that she didn't ride to school with Amy. If she already left her house before Amy got there, who did she ride to school with? I'm not sure how I'll react if I find out she caught a ride with Brian.

"I mean this in the nicest way possible," Landon says.

I glance over at him—at the cautious look on his face. "But…is Charlie pregnant?"

I slam on my breaks. Luckily there's a light in front of us that turns red, so my reaction appears intentional.

"Pregnant? Why? Why would you ask that? Did you hear that from someone?"

Landon shakes his head. "No, it's just… I don't know. I'm trying to figure out what the hell is going on with you and that seemed like the only justifiable answer."

"I miss practice yesterday, so you assume it's because Charlie is pregnant?"

Landon laughs under his breath. "It's more than just that, Silas. It's everything. You fighting with Brian, the practices you've missed all week, you ditching school half a day Monday, all day Tuesday, half a day Wednesday. It's not like you."

I ditched school this week?

"Also, you and Charlie have been acting strange when you're together. Not like your usual selves. You forgot to pick me up after school, you stayed out past curfew on a school night. You've been really off this week, and I don't know if you want to tell me what the hell is going on, but it's really starting to worry me."

I watch as the disappointment fills his eyes.

We were close. He's definitely a good brother, I can tell. He's used to knowing all my secrets—all my thoughts. I wonder if these rides to and from school are when we normally share them. I wonder if I were to tell him what I'm really thinking—if he would even believe me.

"The light's green," he says, facing forward.

I begin driving again, but I don't share any secrets with him. I don't know what to say or how to even begin telling him the truth. I just know I don't want to lie to him because that doesn't seem like something the old Silas would do.

When I pull into a parking spot, he opens his door and gets out. "Landon," I say before he shuts the door. He leans down and looks at me. "I'm sorry. I'm just having an off week."

He nods thoughtfully and turns his attention toward the school. He works his jaw back and forth and then locks eyes with me again. "Hopefully your week is back on before the game tonight," he says. "You have a lot of pissed-off teammates right now."

He slams the door and begins walking in the direction of the school. I grab Charlie's phone and head inside.

I couldn't find her in the halls, so I went to my first two classes. I'm headed to my third now, still with no word from her. I'm sure she just slept late and I'll see her when we have class together fourth period. But still something doesn't feel right. Everything feels off.

She could just be avoiding me, but that doesn't seem like something she would do. She would go out of her way to let me know she doesn't want to speak to me. She'd throw it in my face.

I go to my locker to find my third period math book. I would check her locker to see if any of her textbooks are missing, but I don't know the combination to her lock. It was written on her schedule, but I gave that to her yesterday.

"Silas!"

I turn around to see Andrew fighting his way through the crowded hallway like a fish swimming upstream.

He finally gives up and yells, "Janette wants you to call her!" He turns and heads in the opposite direction again.

Janette… Janette… Janette…

Charlie's sister!

I find her name in the contacts in my phone. She answers on the first ring.

"Silas?" she says.

"Yeah, it's me."

"Is Charlie with you?"

I close my eyes, feeling the panic begin to settle in the pit of my stomach. "No," I reply. "She didn't come home last night?"

"No," Janette says. "I normally wouldn't be worried, but she usually tells me if she's not coming home. She never called and now she's not responding to my texts."

"I have her phone."

"Why do you have her phone?"

"She left it in my car," I say. I close my locker and begin to head toward the exit. "We got into an argument last night and she got in a cab. I thought she was going straight home."

I stop walking when it hits me. She didn't have lunch money yesterday—which means she wouldn't have had cab fare last night.

"I'm leaving school," I tell Janette. "I'll find her."

I hang up before I even give her a chance to respond. I sprint down the hallway toward the door that leads to the parking lot, but as soon as I round the corner, I stop short.

Avril.

Shit. Now is not the time for this. I try to duck my head and walk past her, but she grabs the sleeve of my shirt. I stop walking and face her.

"Avril, I can't right now." I point to the exit. "I need to leave. Kind of an emergency."

She releases my shirt and folds her arms over her chest. "You never showed up during lunch yesterday. I thought maybe you were running late, but when I checked the cafeteria, you were there. With *her*."

Christ, I don't have time for this. In fact, I think I'll save myself any future trouble and just end it now.

I sigh and run a hand through my hair. "Yeah," I say. "Charlie and I...we decided to work things out."

Avril tilts her head and shoots me an incredulous look. "*No*, Silas. That isn't what you want, and it's definitely not going to work for me."

I look left, down the hall, and then right. When I see no one's around, I take a step toward her. "Listen, Ms. Ashley," I say, taking care to address her professionally. I look her directly in the eyes. "I don't think you're in any position to tell me how things are going to be between the two of us."

Her eyes immediately narrow. She stands silently for several seconds as though she's waiting for me to laugh and tell her I'm only kidding. When I don't falter, she huffs and shoves her hands against my chest, pushing me out of the way. The click of her heels begins to fade the farther I sprint away from her—toward the exit.

I'm knocking for a third time on Charlie's front door when it finally flies open. Her mother is standing in front of me. Wild hair, wilder eyes. It's as if hatred spews from her soul the moment she realizes I'm standing here.

"What do you want?" she spits.

I try to glance past her to get a look inside the house.

She moves to block my view, so I point over her shoulder. "I need to talk to Charlie. Is she here?"

Her mother takes a step outside and pulls the door shut behind her so that I can't see inside at all. "That's none of your business," she hisses. "Get the hell off my property!"

"Is she here or not?"

She folds her arms over her chest. "If you aren't out of my driveway in five seconds, I'm calling the police."

I throw my hands up in defeat and groan. "I'm worried about your daughter, so can you please put your anger aside for one minute and tell me if she's inside?"

She takes two quick steps toward me and pokes a finger into my chest. "Don't you dare raise your voice at me!"

Jesus Christ.

I push past her and kick open the door. The first thing I'm hit with is the smell. The air is stale. A fog of thick cigarette smoke fills the air and assaults my lungs. I hold my breath as I make my way through the living room. There's a bottle of whiskey open on the bar, sitting next to an empty glass. Mail is scattered across the table—what looks like several days' worth. It's like this woman doesn't even care enough to open any of it. The envelope on the top of the stack is addressed to Charlie.

I move to pick it up, but hear the woman stalking into the house behind me. I make my way down the hall and see two doors to my right and one on the left. I push open the door to my left, just as Charlie's mother begins screaming from behind me. I ignore her and make my way into the bedroom.

"Charlie!" I yell. I glance around the room, knowing she isn't here, but still hoping I'm wrong. If she isn't here, I don't know where else to look. I don't remember any of the places we used to hang out.

But neither would Charlie, I guess.

"Silas!" her mother yells from the doorway to the bedroom. "Get out! I'm calling the police!" She disappears from the doorway, probably to retrieve a phone. I continue my search for... I don't even know. Charlie obviously isn't here, but I keep looking around anyway, hoping to find something that could help.

I know which side of the room is Charlie's because of the picture of the gate above her bed. The one she said I took.

I look around for clues, but find nothing. I remember her mentioning something about an attic in her closet, so I check the closet. There's a small hole at the top of it. It looks like she uses her shelves as steps. "Charlie!" I call out.

Nothing.

"Charlie, are you up there?"

Just as I check the sturdiness of the bottom shelf with my foot, something slams against the side of my head. I turn, but immediately duck again when I see a plate fly out of the woman's hand. It crashes against the wall next to my head. "Get out!" she screams. She's looking for more things to throw, so I put my hands up in surrender.

"I'm leaving," I tell her. "I'll leave!"

She moves out of the doorway to let me pass. She's still yelling as I make my way down the hall. As I walk toward the front door, I swipe the letter off the bar that was addressed to Charlie. I don't even bother telling Charlie's mother to have her call me if she makes it home.

I get in my car and pull back onto the street.

PART 2

Where the hell is she?

I wait until I'm a few miles away and then I pull over to check her phone again. Landon mentioned he heard it ringing under the seat, so I lean over and reach my hand beneath the seat. I pull out an empty soda can, a shoe and then finally—her wallet. I open it and sift through it, but find nothing I don't already know.

She's somewhere out there, without her phone or her wallet. She doesn't have anyone's numbers memorized. If she didn't come home, where would she have gone?

I punch the steering wheel. "Dammit, Silas!" I should have never let her leave by herself. This is all my fault.

My phone receives an incoming text. The text is from Landon, wondering why I left school.

I drop the phone back onto the seat and notice the letter I stole from Charlie's house. There's no return address. The date stamp in the top corner is from Tuesday—the day before all of this happened.

I open the envelope and find several pages inside, folded together.

Across the front, it reads *Open immediately.*

I unfold the pages and my eyes instantly fall to the two names written at the top of the page.

Charlie and Silas. It's addressed to both of us? I keep reading.

If you don't know why you're reading this, then you've forgotten everything. You recognize no one, not even yourselves.

Please don't panic, and read this letter in its entirety. We will share everything we know, which right now isn't much.

What the hell? My hands begin to shake as I continue reading.

> *We aren't sure what happened, but we're afraid if we don't write it down, it might happen again. At least with everything written down and left in more than one place, we'll be more prepared if it does happen again.*
>
> *On the following pages, you'll find all the information we know. Maybe it will help in some way.*

Charlie and Silas

I stare at the names at the bottom of the page until my vision is blurry. I look at the names at the top of the page again. *Charlie and Silas*.

I look at the names at the bottom. *Charlie and Silas*. We wrote ourselves a letter?

It makes no sense. If we wrote ourselves a letter…

I immediately flip to the pages that follow. The first two pages are things I already know. Our addresses, our phone numbers. Where we go to school, what our classes are, our siblings' names, our parents' names. I read through it all as fast as I possibly can.

My hands are shaking so badly by the third page, I can hardly read the handwriting. I set the page in my lap to finish. It's more personal information—a list of things we've figured out about one another already, our relationship, how long we've been together. The letter mentions Brian's name as someone who keeps texting Charlie. I skip over all the familiar information until I get close to the end of the third page.

*The first memories either of us can recall are from
Saturday, October 4th, around 11am. Today is
Sunday, October 5th. We're going to make a copy
of this letter for ourselves, but will also mail copies in the morning, just to be safe.*

I flip to the fourth page and it's dated Tuesday, October 7th.

*It happened again. This time, it happened dur-
ing history class on Monday, October 6th. It appears to have happened at the same time of day, 48
hours later. We don't have anything new to add to
the letter. We both did our best to stay away from
friends and family the past day, faking illnesses.
We've been calling one another with any information we know, but so far it seems this has happened
twice. The first time being Saturday, the second
being Monday. Wish we had more information, but
we're still kind of freaked out that this is happening and aren't sure what to do about it. We'll do
what we did last time and mail copies of this letter to ourselves. Also, there will be a copy in the
glove box of Silas's car. That's the first place we
looked this time, so there's a good chance you'll
look there again.*

I never checked the glove box.

*We'll keep the original letters somewhere safe so
no one will find them. We're afraid if anyone sees
the letters, or if anyone suspects anything, they'll
think we're going crazy. Everything will be in a box*

*on the back of the third shelf of Silas's bedroom
closet. If this pattern continues, there's a chance
it could happen again on Wednesday at the same
time. In case it does, this letter should arrive to
both of you that day.*

I look at the time stamp on the envelope again. It was
mailed first thing Tuesday morning. And Wednesday at
11am is exactly when this happened to us.

*If you find anything out that will help, add it to the
next page and keep this going until we figure out
what started it. And how to stop it.*

I flip to the last page, but it's blank.
I look at the clock. It's 10:57am. It's Friday. This happened to us almost forty-eight hours ago.
My chest is heaving. This can't be happening.
Forty-eight hours will be up in less than three minutes.
I flip open my console and search for a pen. I don't
find one, so I yank open the glove box. Right on top is
a copy of the same letter with Charlie's and my names
on it. I lift it up and there are several pens, so I grab
one and flatten the paper out against the steering wheel.
It happened again, I write. My hands are shaking so
bad, I drop the pen. I pick it up again and keep writing.

*At 11am, Wednesday, October 8th, Charlie and
I both lost our memories for what appears to be
the third time in a row. Things we've learned in
the last 48 hours:*

-Our fathers used to work together.

-Charlie's father is in prison.

I'm writing as fast as I can, trying to figure out which points I need to write down first—which are the most important, because I'm almost out of time.

-We visited a tarot reader on St. Philip Street. That might be worth checking out again.

-Charlie mentioned a girl at school—called her The Shrimp. Said she wanted to talk to her.

-Charlie has an attic in her bedroom closet. She spends a lot of time in there.

I feel like I'm wasting time. I feel like I'm not adding anything of importance to this damn list. If this is true and it's about to happen again, I won't have time to mail a letter, much less make copies. Hopefully if I have it in my hands, I'll be smart enough to read it and not just toss it aside.

I bite the tip of the pen, attempting to focus on what to write next.

-We grew up together, but now our families hate each other. They don't want us together.

-Silas was sleeping with the guidance counselor, Charlie with Brian Finley. We broke it off with both of them.

-*Landon is a good brother, you can probably trust
  him if you have to.*

I continue to write. I write about our tattoos, The
Electric Crush Diner, Ezra, and anything and everything
I can recall from the last forty-eight hours.

I look at the clock. 10:59.

Charlie doesn't know about this letter. If everything
in this letter so far is accurate and this really has been
happening to us since last Saturday, that means she's
about to forget everything she's learned in the past forty-
eight hours. And I have no idea how to find her. How
to warn her.

I press the pen to the paper again and write one last
thing.

-*Charlie got into a cab on Bourbon Street last
  night and no one has seen her since. She doesn't
  know about this letter. Find her. The first thing
  you need to do is find her. Please.*

15

Silas

It starts slowly. The rain.

A splatter here, a splash there. First on the windshield in front of me and then against the windows surrounding me. The drops begin to sound like thousands of fingertips tapping the top of my car out of unison. *Tap-tatap-tap-ta-ta-tap-tap-tap.* The sound is all around me now. It feels like it's coming from inside me, trying to get out. The rain begins to trickle down the windshield, thick enough to mix together in long lines that resemble tears. They slide to the bottom and disappear beyond the glass. I attempt to turn my wipers on, but my car is off.

Why isn't my car on?

I wipe the fog off my window with the palm of my hand to see outside, but the rain is falling so hard now I can't see anything.

Where am I?

I turn around and look in the backseat, but there's no one there.

Nothing there. I face forward again.

Think, think, think.

Where was I headed? I must have fallen asleep.

I don't know where I am.

I don't know where "I" am. I... I... I...

Who am I?

It seems so natural to think thoughts that contain the word *I*. But each of my thoughts are hollow and weightless, because the word *I* is attached to no one. No name, no face. I am...*nothing*.

The hum of an engine steals my attention as a car slows next to mine on the road. Water splashes across the windshield as it passes. I make out taillights as the car slows and then pulls over in front of me.

Reverse lights.

My heart begins to beat in my throat, my fingertips, my temples. The lights atop the car breathe to life. *Red, blue, red, blue.* I watch as someone exits the vehicle. All I can make out is their silhouette as they begin to approach my car. I barely move my neck as they walk toward my passenger door, keeping my eyes trained on them as they reach the window.

A tap.

Tap, tap, tap.

I press the ignition button to give power to the windows—*how did I know how to do that?* I roll the window down.

A cop.

Help, I want to say.

I forgot where I was going, I want to say.

"Silas?"

His voice startles me. It's loud. He's trying to compete with the sound of the rain by yelling the word *Silas.*

What does that word mean? *Silas*. Maybe he's French. Maybe I'm in France and *Silas* is a greeting. Maybe I should say *Silas* in return.

The man clears his throat and then says, "Your car broke down?"

Not French.

I look at the controls on my dash. I force my lips apart so that I can form a word. Instead, I gasp for air, unaware I've been holding my breath. When I release the air in my lungs, it comes out shaky…embarrassing. I look back at the officer standing at the window. "No," I say. My voice scares me. I don't recognize it.

The officer leans down and motions to my lap. "What you got there?" he asks. "Directions somewhere? You lost?"

I look down at an unfamiliar stack of papers resting on my lap. I push them to the passenger seat, wanting them off me, and I shake my head again. "I, um. I was just…"

My words are interrupted by a ring. A loud ring, coming from inside the car. I follow the sound, moving the papers from the seat to find a cell phone beneath them. I look at the caller ID. "Janette."

I don't know a Janette.

"You need to get off the side of the road, son," the officer says, taking a step back. I push a button on the side of the phone to get it to silence. "Go on ahead and get back to the school. Big game tonight."

Big game. School.

Why does neither seem familiar?

I nod.

"Rain should let up soon," he adds. He taps the roof of my car as if he's sending me off. I nod again and put my finger on the button that controls the windows. "Tell your father to save me a seat tonight."

I nod again. *My father.*

The officer stares at me for a few seconds longer, a quizzical look on his face. He finally shakes his head and then begins to retreat back to his car.

I look down at the phone. Just as I'm about to hit a button, it begins ringing again.

Janette.

Whoever Janette is, she really wants someone to answer this phone. I swipe the screen and bring it to my ear.

"Hello?"

"Did you find her?" I don't recognize the voice on the phone. I wait a few seconds before responding, hoping it clicks. "Silas? Hello?"

She just said the same word the officer said. *Silas.* Except she said it like a name.

My name?

"What?" I say into the phone, confused by everything.

"Did you find her?" There's panic in her voice.

Did I find her? Who am I supposed to be looking for? I turn around and check the backseat once more, even though I know there isn't anyone in the car with me. I face forward again, not sure how to respond to the question just posed to me. "Did I find her?" I ask, repeating the question. "I... Did *you* find her?"

A groan comes from Janette. "Why would I be calling you if I found her?"

I pull the phone away from my ear and look at it. I'm so confused. I press it against my ear again.

"No," I say. "I didn't find her."

Maybe this girl is my little sister. She sounds young.

Younger than me. Maybe she lost her dog and I was out looking for her? Maybe I hydroplaned in the rain and hit my head.

"Silas, this isn't like her," Janette says. "She would tell me if she wasn't going to come home or show up for school today."

Okay, I guess we're not talking about a dog here. And the fact that I'm pretty sure we're discussing a person who is apparently missing makes me really uncomfortable, considering I'm not even sure who I am right now. I need to hang up before I say something wrong. Something incriminating.

"Janette, I have to go. I'll keep looking." I press end and set the phone down on the seat next to me. The papers that were sitting on my lap catch my eye. I reach over and grab for them. The pages are stapled together, so I flip to the front page. It's a letter, addressed to me and some other guy named Charlie.

Charlie and Silas, If you don't know why you're reading this, then you've forgotten everything.

What the hell? The first sentence isn't what I was expecting to read. I don't know what I was expecting to read.

You recognize no one, not even yourselves. Please don't panic, and read this letter in its entirety.

It's a little late for the *don't panic* part.

We aren't sure what happened, but we're afraid if we don't write it down, it might happen again.

At least with everything written down and left in more than one place, we'll be more prepared if it does happen again.

On the following pages, you'll find all the information we know. Maybe it will help in some way.

Charlie and Silas

I don't immediately flip to the next page. I drop the pages into my lap and bring my hands to my face. I rub them up and down, up and down. I glance in the rearview mirror and then immediately look away when I don't recognize the eyes staring back at me.

This can't be happening.

I squeeze my eyes shut and bring my fingers to the bridge of my nose. I wait for myself to wake up. This is a dream, and I need to wake up.

A car passes, and more water is tossed across the windshield. I watch as it trickles down again and disappears beneath the hood.

I can't be dreaming. Everything is too vivid, too detailed to be a dream. Dreams are splotchy, and they don't flow from one moment to the next like everything is doing right now.

I pick the pages up again, and with each sentence it becomes harder to read. My hands become increasingly unsteady. My mind is all over the place as I scan over the next page. I find out Silas is definitely my name and that Charlie is actually the name of a girl. I wonder if she's the girl who is missing. I continue to read, even though I can't suspend disbelief long enough to accept the words I'm reading. And I don't know why I won't

allow myself to believe it, because everything I'm reading certainly coincides with the fact that I have no recollection of any of it. It's just that if I were to suspend
my disbelief, I would be admitting that this is possible.
That according to what I'm reading, I've just lost my
memory for the fourth time in a row.

My breathing is almost as erratic as the rain falling
against the roof of my car. I bring my left hand up to the
back of my neck and squeeze as I read the last paragraph.
One I apparently just wrote a matter of ten minutes ago.

*-Charlie got into a cab on Bourbon Street last
night and no one has seen her since. She doesn't
know about this letter. Find her. The first thing
you need to do is find her. Please.*

The last few words of the letter are scrawled, barely
legible, like I was running out of time when I wrote it. I
set the letter down on the seat, contemplating everything
I've just learned. The information is racing in my mind
faster than my heart is beating in my chest. I can feel the
onset of a panic attack coming, or maybe a breakdown.
I grip the steering wheel with both hands and breathe
in and out through my nose. I don't know how I know
that's supposed to produce a calming effect. At first, it
doesn't seem to be working, but I sit like this for several minutes, thinking about everything I just learned.
*Bourbon Street, Charlie, my brother, The Shrimp, the
tarot reading, the tattoos, my penchant for photography.* Why does none of it seem familiar? This has to be
a joke. This has to be referring to someone else. I can't
be Silas. If I were Silas, I would *feel* like I'm him. I

wouldn't feel this complete separation from the person I'm supposed to be.

I grab my phone again and open up the camera app. I lean forward and reach behind me, pulling my shirt forward and over my head. I hold the camera behind me and snap a picture of my back, then pull my shirt back into place and look at the phone.

Pearls.

A strand of black pearls is tattooed on my back, just like the letter said. "Shit," I whisper, staring down at the picture.

My stomach. I think I'm about to be…

I open up the car door just in time. The contents of whatever I had for breakfast are now on the ground at my feet. My clothes are being soaked as I stand here, waiting to get sick again. When I think the worst is over, I climb back into the car.

I look at the clock, and it reads 11:11am.

I'm still not sure what to believe, but the more time that passes without recollection, the more I begin to entertain the idea that I may have just a little over forty-seven hours before this happens again.

I reach across the seat and open my glove box. I don't know what I'm looking for, but sitting here doing nothing seems like a waste of time. I pull out the contents, tossing aside vehicle and insurance information. I find an envelope with our names written across it. *A duplicate of everything I just read.* I continue to flip through the papers until a folded piece of paper tucked at the very bottom of the glove box steals my attention. It has my name written across the top of it. I open it, first reading the signature at the bottom. It's a letter from Charlie. I start back at the top of the page and begin reading.

Dear Silas, This is not a love note. Okay? No matter how much you try to convince yourself that it is—it's not. Because I'm not that type of girl. I hate those girls, always so lovesick and disgusting. Ew.

Anyway, this is the anti-love note. For instance, I do not love the way you brought me orange juice and medicine last week when I was sick. And what was with that card? You hope I feel better and you love me? Pfft.

And I definitely do not love the way you pretend that you can dance when you really look like a malfunctioning robot. It's not adorable and it doesn't make me laugh at all.

Oh, and when you kiss me and pull away to tell me I'm pretty? Don't like that one damn bit. Why can't you just be like other guys who ignore their girlfriends? It's so unfair that I have to deal with this.

And speaking of how you do everything wrong, remember when I hurt my back during cheerleading practice? And you skipped David's party to rub Biofreeze on my back and watched Pretty Woman *with me? It was a clear sign of how needy and selfish you can really be.*

How dare you, Silas!

I will also no longer tolerate the things you say about me around our friends. When Abby made fun of my outfit that day and you told her that I could wear a plastic bag and make it look couture, it was way out of line. And it was even more out of line when you drove Janette to the eye doctor when she kept getting headaches. You need to

*get a grip. All of this caring and consideration is
so unattractive.*

*So I am here to tell you that I absolutely do not
love you more than any human on this planet. And
that it's not butterflies I feel every time you walk
into a room, but sick, one-winged, drunken moths.
Also, you're very, very unattractive. I flinch every
time I see your unblemished skin and think—Oh
my god, that kid would be so much more attractive with some pimples and crooked teeth. Yeah,
you're gross, Silas.*

Not in love.

Not at all.

Never Never.

Charlie

I stare at the way she signed off and read those words
through a few more times.

Not in love.

Not at all.

Never Never.

Charlie

I flip the note over, hoping to see a date. There's nothing to indicate when it was written. If this girl wrote me

letters like this, then how could everything I just read in my notes about the current state of our relationship even be true? I'm obviously in love with her. Or at least I *was* in love with her.

What happened to us? What happened to *her*?

I fold the letter up and put it back where I found it. The first place I go is to the address listed on the paper for Charlie's house. If I don't find her there, maybe I can get more information from her mother, or from anything I can find that we might have overlooked before.

The garage door is shut when I pull into her driveway. I can't tell if anyone is home. The place is grungy. Someone's trash can sits sideways next to the curb, trash spilling out onto the street. A cat is pawing at the bag. When I step out of the car, the cat dashes down the street. I look around as I make my way to the front door. No one is around, the neighbor's windows and doors are all shut tight. I knock several times, but no one answers.

I look around one last time before I turn the knob. *Unlocked.* I quietly push the door open.

In the letters we wrote to ourselves, we mention Charlie's attic a few times, so that's the first place I search for. *Charlie's attic.* I'm meeting the attic before I meet the girl. One of the doors is open in the hallway. I walk in and find the bedroom empty. Two beds—this must be where Charlie and her sister sleep.

I walk to the closet and look up at the ceiling, finding the entrance to the attic. I push clothes aside, and a smell fills my nose. Her smell? Floral. It smells familiar, but that's crazy, right? If I can't remember her, I can't possibly remember her smell. I use the closet shelves as stairs and make my way up.

The only light inside the attic comes from the window on the other side of the room. It's enough to illuminate where I'm going, but not by much, so I pull out my phone and open the flashlight app.

I pause and stare down at the open app on my phone. *How did I know that was there?* I wish there were rhyme or reason to why I remember some things and not others. I try to find a common link in the memories but come up completely empty.

I have to hunch over because the ceiling is too low for me to stand upright. I continue across the attic, toward a makeshift sitting area on the far side of the room. There's a pile of blankets lined with pillows.

She actually sleeps up here?

I shudder trying to imagine anyone willingly spending time in a place this isolated. She must be a loner.

I have to bend over more to avoid hitting my head on the rafters. When I reach the area she's made up for herself, I look around. There are stacks of books beside the pillows. Some of the books she uses as tables, topped with picture frames.

Dozens of books. I wonder if she's read them all, or if she just needs them for comfort. Maybe she uses them as an escape from her real life. From the looks of this place, I don't blame her.

I bend down and pick one up. The cover is dark, of a house and a girl, merging together as one. It's creepy. I can't imagine sitting up here alone, reading books like this in the dark.

I set the book down where I found it, and my attention falls on a cedar chest pushed up against the wall. It looks heavy and old, like maybe it's something that's been passed down in her family. I walk over to it and open the lid. Inside, there are several books, all with blank covers. I pick up the top one and open it.

January 7th–July 15th, 2011

I flip through the pages and see that it's a journal. In the box beneath this one, there are at least five more.

She must love to write.

I look around, lifting pillows and blankets, searching for something to put the journals in. If I want to find this girl, I need to know where she frequents. Places she might be, people she might know. Journals are the perfect way to find out that information.

I find an empty, worn backpack on the floor a few feet away, so I grab it and stuff all the journals inside. I begin pushing things aside, shaking out books, looking around for anything and everything that might help me. I find several letters in various places, a few stacks of pictures, random sticky notes. I take everything I can fit into the backpack and make my way back to the attic opening. I know there are also a few things in the bedroom at my own house, so I'll go there next and sort through it all as fast as I can.

When I reach the opening, I drop the backpack through the attic hole first. It hits the ground with a loud thud and I flinch, knowing I should be quieter. I begin to descend the shelves one by one, trying to imagine Charlie making the journey up and down these makeshift stairs every night. Her life must be pretty bad if she escapes to the attic by choice. When I make it to the bottom, I grab the backpack and stand up straight. I pull it over my shoulder and start toward the door.

I freeze.

I'm not sure what to do, because the officer who tapped on my window earlier is now staring straight at me.

Is being inside my girlfriend's house illegal?

A woman appears in the doorway behind the officer. Her eyes are frantic and they're lined with mascara—like she just woke up. Her hair is wild, and even from several feet away, the scent of alcohol finds its way across the room.

"I told you he was up there!" she yells, pointing at me. "I warned him just this morning to stay off my property, and he's back again!"

This morning?

Great. Wish I had informed myself of that fact in the letter. "Silas," the officer says. "You mind coming outside with me?"

I nod and proceed cautiously toward them. It doesn't seem like I've done anything wrong, since he's only asking me to speak with him. If I did anything wrong, he would have immediately read me my rights.

"He knows he's not supposed to be here, Grant!" the woman yells, walking backward down the hall, toward the living room. "He knows this, but he keeps coming back! He's just trying to get a rise out of me!"

This woman hates me. A lot. And not knowing why makes it hard not to just apologize for whatever the hell I did to her.

"Laura," he says. "I'll have a talk with Silas outside, but you need to calm down and move aside so that I can do that."

She steps to the side and glares at me as we pass her. "You get away with everything, just like your daddy," she says. I look away from her so she won't see the confusion on my face, and I follow Officer Grant outside, clutching the backpack over my shoulder.

Luckily the rain has let up. We keep walking until we're standing next to my car. He turns to face me, and I have no idea if I'll be able to answer the questions he's about to throw at me, but hopefully they aren't too specific.

"Why are you not at school, Silas?"

I purse my lips together and think about the answer to that. "I, um…" I look over his shoulder at a passing car. "I'm looking for Charlie."

I don't know if I should have said that. Surely if the cops weren't supposed to know she was missing, I would have clarified that in the letter. But the letter only stated that I needed to do whatever I could to find her, and reporting her missing seems like it would be the first step.

"What do you mean you're looking for her? Why isn't she at school?"

I shrug. "I don't know. She hasn't called, her sister hasn't heard from her, she didn't show up for school today." I throw a hand behind me in the direction of the house. "Her own mother is obviously too drunk to notice she's missing, so I thought I'd try to find her myself."

He tilts his head, more out of curiosity than concern. "Who was the last person to see her? And when?"

I swallow as I shift uncomfortably on my feet, trying to recall what was written about last night in the letter. "Me. Last night. We got into an argument and she refused to ride home with me."

Officer Grant motions for someone behind me to come toward us. I turn around, and Charlie's mother is standing in the open doorway. She crosses the threshold and makes her way out to the yard.

"Laura, do you know where your daughter is?"

She rolls her eyes. "She's at school where she's supposed to be."

"She is not," I interject.

Officer Grant keeps his eyes trained on Laura. "Did Charlie come home last night?"

Laura glances at me and then looks back at the officer. "Of course she did," she says. Her voice tapers off at the end like she's not sure.

"She's lying," I blurt out.

Officer Grant holds up a hand to hush me, still directing his questions at Laura. "What time did she come home?"

I can see the confusion wash over Laura's face. She shrugs. "I grounded her for skipping school this week. So she was up in her attic, I guess."

I roll my eyes. "She wasn't even home!" I say, raising my voice. "This woman was obviously too drunk to know if her own daughter was even inside the house!"

She closes the distance between us and begins pounding her fists against my arms and chest. "Get off my property, you son of a bitch!" she screams.

The officer grabs her by the arms and motions his eyes to my truck. "For the last time, Nash. Go back to school."

Laura is thrashing in his arms, trying to break free. She's not even fazing him as he keeps her in a tight grip. This seems so normal to him; it makes me wonder if she's called the cops on me before.

"But…what about Charlie?" I'm confused as to why no one else seems to be concerned about her. Especially her own mother.

"Like her mother said, she's probably at school," he

says. "At any rate, she'll show up to the game tonight. We'll talk there."

I nod, but I know good and well I'm not going back to the school. I'm taking my bag of Charlie's secrets and I'm going straight to my house to find more.

16

Silas

The first thing I do when I walk through the door to my home is pause. None of it looks familiar, not even the pictures on the walls. I wait for a few seconds, letting everything sink in. I could search the house or browse the pictures, but I've probably already done that. I'm on a time crunch, and if I want to figure out what happened to Charlie—what happened to *us*—I need to keep focused on the things we haven't wasted time doing before.

I find my bedroom and walk straight to the closet—to the shelf that contains all the other stuff we've collected. I dump everything out onto my bed, including the contents of the duffel bag. Sifting through it all, I try to figure out where to begin. There's so much stuff. I grab a pen so I can make notes of anything I find that might be of use if I end up forgetting this all over again.

I know a lot of things about my relationship with Charlie as of late, but that seems to be it. I know almost nothing about how we got together or how our families were torn apart. I don't know if any of that is even a factor in what's happened to us, but I feel like the best place to start is from the beginning.

I grab one of the older-looking notes addressed to Charlie—something I wrote myself. It's dated over four years ago and is just one of the many letters I grabbed from her attic. Maybe reading something from my point of view will help me figure out what type of person I am, even if this letter is over four years old.

I sit down on the bed and lean against my headboard, and I begin to read.

Charlie, Can you recall a single time we went on vacation without each other? I've been thinking about that today. About how it's never just my immediate family and me. It's always both sets of our parents, Landon, Janette, you and me.

One big happy family.

I'm not sure we've ever spent a holiday apart, either. Christmas, Easter, Thanksgiving. We've always shared them together, either at our house or yours. Maybe that's why I've never felt like it's just been my little brother and me. I've always felt like I had a brother and two sisters. And I can't imagine not feeling that way—like you're part of my family.

But I'm scared that I've ruined that. And I don't even know what to say to you, because I don't want to apologize for kissing you last night. I know I should regret it, and I know I should be doing whatever I can to make up for the fact that I might have officially ruined our friendship, but I don't regret it. I've wanted to make that mistake for a long time now.

I've been trying to figure out when my feelings for you changed, but I realized tonight that they haven't changed. My feelings for you as my best friend haven't changed at all—they've just evolved.

Yes, I love you, but now I'm in love with you. And instead of looking at you like you're just my best friend, now you're my best friend who I want to kiss.

And yes, I've loved you like a brother loves his sister. But now I love you like a guy loves a girl.

So despite that kiss, I promise nothing has changed between us. It's just become something more. Something so much better.

Last night, when you were lying next to me on this bed, looking up at me in breathless laughter, I couldn't help myself. So many times you've taken my breath away or made it feel like my heart was trapped inside my stomach. But last night was more than any fourteen-year-old boy could handle. So I took your face in my hands and I kissed you, just like I've been dreaming of doing for over a year now.

Lately, when I'm around you, I feel too drunk to speak to you. And I've never even tasted alcohol before, but I'm sure kissing you is what being drunk feels like. If that's the case, I'm already worried for my sobriety because I can see myself becoming addicted to kissing you.

I haven't heard from you since the moment you pulled yourself out from under me and walked straight out of my bedroom last night, so I'm beginning to worry that you don't remember that kiss like I do. You haven't answered your phone.

You haven't responded to my texts. So I'm writing you this letter in case you need to be reminded of how you really feel about me. Because it seems like you're trying to forget.

Please don't forget, Charlie.

Never allow your stubbornness to talk you into believing that our kiss was wrong.

Never forget how right it felt when my lips finally touched yours. Never stop needing me to kiss you like that again.

Never forget the way you pulled closer—wanting it to feel like my heart was beating inside your chest.

Never stop me from kissing you in the future when one of your laughs makes me wish I could be a part of you again.

Never stop wanting me to hold you like I finally got to hold you last night.

Never forget that I was your first real kiss. Never forget that you'll be my last.

And never stop loving me between all of them.

Never stop, Charlie.

Never forget.

Silas

I don't know how long I stare at the letter. Long enough to grow confused as to how it makes me feel. How even though I don't know this girl at all, I somehow believe every word of this letter. And maybe even feel it a little. My pulse begins to quicken, because I've done all I know how to do in the past hour to find her, and the need to know she's okay is imminent.

I'm worried about her.

I need to find her.

I grab another letter for more clues when my phone rings. I pick it up and answer it without looking at the caller ID. There's no point in screening the calls, since I don't know any of the people who would even be calling me.

"Hello?"

"You do realize tonight is one of the most important games of your football career, right? Why in the hell are you not at school?"

The voice is heavy and angry.

Must be my father.

I pull the phone away from my ear and look down at it. I have no idea what to say. I need to read more of these letters before I would know how Silas would normally respond to his father. I need to find out more about these people who seem to know everything about me.

"Hello?" I repeat.

"Silas, I don't know what's gotten—"

"I can't hear you," I say louder. "Hello?"

Before he can speak again, I end the call and drop the phone onto the bed. I grab all of the letters and journals that will fit into the backpack. I rush to leave because I shouldn't be here. Someone might show up who I'm not prepared to interact with yet.

Someone like my father.

17

Charlie

Where am I?

That's the first question. Then, *Who am I?*

I shake my head from side to side, like this simple act could jar my brain back into working order. People normally wake up and know who they are...*right*? My heart aches, it's pounding so fast. I'm scared to sit up, afraid of what I'll see when I do.

I'm confused...overwhelmed, so I start to cry. Is it weird to not know who you are, but to understand that you're not a crier? I am so mad at myself for crying that I swipe hard at my tears and sit up, banging my head pretty hard on the metal bars of a bed in the process. I flinch, rubbing my head.

I'm alone. That's good.

I don't know how I'd explain to someone that I have no clue who or where I am. I'm on a bed. In a room. It's hard to tell what kind of room, because it's so dark. No windows. A bulb flickers on the ceiling in a struggling

Morse code. It's not strong enough to really illuminate the small room, but I can tell that the floor is made of shiny white tile, and the walls are painted white, bare except for a small television bolted to the wall.

There is a door. I stand up to go to it, but there is a heavy feeling in my stomach as I place my feet one in front of the other. *It's going to be locked, it's going to be locked...*

It's locked.

I feel panic, but I calm myself, tell myself to breathe. I'm shaking as I press my back against the door and look down at my body. I'm wearing a hospital gown, socks. I run my hands over my legs to check how hairy they are—not very. Which means I shaved recently? I have black hair. I pull a piece of it in front of my face to examine it. I don't even know my name. This is crazy. Or maybe I'm crazy. *Yes. Oh, my God.* I'm in a mental hospital. That's the only thing that makes sense. I turn around and pound on the door.

"Hello?"

I press my ear against the door and listen for a noise. I can hear the soft humming of something. A generator? An air conditioner? It's some kind of machinery. I get chills.

I run for the bed and fold myself into the corner so I can see the door. I pull my knees up to my chest, breathing hard. I'm scared, but there's nothing I can do but wait.

18

Silas

The strap of my backpack digs into my shoulder as I push myself through the swarm of students in the hallway. I pretend I know what I'm doing—where I'm going—but I know nothing. As far as I'm concerned, this is the first time I've ever stepped foot in this school. The first time I'm seeing these people's faces. They smile at me, bob their heads in greeting. I reciprocate the best I can.

I glance up at the numbers on the lockers, navigating my way through the halls until I find mine. According to everything I wrote, I was here just this morning, searching through this locker, hours ago. I obviously didn't find anything then, so I'm sure I won't find anything now.

When I'm finally facing my locker, I feel the hope that I didn't even know I had evaporate. I guess a part of me was hoping I would find Charlie standing there, laughing at this genius prank she pulled off. I was hopeful that this mess would be over with.

I'm not that lucky, obviously.

I enter the combination on Charlie's locker first and open it in an attempt to find something we missed earlier. As I'm digging through her locker, I can feel someone approach me from behind. I don't want to turn around and have to interact with an unfamiliar face, so I pretend I don't notice they're standing here in hopes that they'll walk away.

"What are you looking for?"

It's a girl's voice. Since I have no idea what Charlie sounds like, I turn around, hoping it's her. Instead, I find someone who isn't Charlie staring back at me. Based on her looks, I assume this is Annika. She fits the description Charlie wrote of our friends in the notes.

Big eyes, dark curly hair, looks at you like she's bored.

"I'm just looking for something," I mutter, turning back to face Charlie's locker. I find no clues whatsoever, so I close the locker and begin to enter the combination on my own lock.

"Amy said Charlie wasn't home this morning when she went to pick her up. Janette didn't even know where she was," Annika says. "Where is she?"

I shrug and pull open my locker, trying to make it inconspicuous that I'm reading the combination from a sheet of paper in my hand. "I don't know. Still haven't heard from her."

Annika stands silently behind me until I'm finished searching my own locker. My phone begins to ring in my pocket. My father is calling again.

"Silas!" someone yells as he passes by. I look up to see a reflection of myself, only younger and not as... *intense. Landon.* "Dad wants you to call him!" he yells, walking backward in the opposite direction.

I hold up my phone, screen facing him, so he knows I'm already aware. He shakes his head with a laugh and disappears down the hall. I want to tell him to come back. I have so many questions I want to ask him, but I know how crazy all of it would sound.

I press a button to ignore the call and I slide it back into my pocket. Annika is still standing here, and I have no idea how to shake her. The old Silas seemed to have an issue with commitment, so I'm hoping Annika wasn't one of his conquests.

The old me is sure making things difficult for the current me.

Right when I begin to tell her I need to get to my last period class, I catch sight of a girl over Annika's shoulder. My eyes lock with hers, and she quickly looks in the other direction. I can tell by the way she slinks away that she must be the girl Charlie referred to as The Shrimp in our notes. Because she really does kind of resemble a shrimp: pinkish skin, light hair, and dark, beady eyes.

"Hey!" I yell.

She keeps moving in the other direction.

I push past Annika and rush after the girl. I yell, "Hey," again, but she just picks up her pace and tucks into herself even more, never turning around. I should know her name. She'd probably stop if I just called out her name. I'm sure if I yelled *Hey, Shrimp!* that wouldn't win me any favors.

What a nickname. Teenagers can be so cruel. I'm embarrassed to be one of them.

Right before her hand reaches the doorknob of a classroom, I slide in front of her, my back against the door. She takes a quick step back, surprised to see me directing my attention at her. She hugs her books to her chest and glances around, but we've reached the end of the hallway and there aren't any students around us.

"What…what do you want?" she asks, her voice a scattered whisper.

"Have you seen Charlie?" The question seems to surprise her more than the fact that I'm talking to her. She immediately distances herself from me with another step.

"What do you mean?" she asks again. "She's not looking for me, is she?"

Her voice sounds fearful. *Why would she be afraid of Charlie?*

"Listen," I say, glancing down the hallway to ensure our privacy. I look back at her and can tell she's holding her breath. "I need a favor, but I don't want to talk about it here. Can you meet me after school?"

Again with the surprised expression. She immediately shakes her head no. Her hesitance to want to have anything to do with Charlie or me piques my interest. She either knows something and she's hiding it, or she knows something that she has no idea could help me.

"Just for a few minutes?" I ask. She shakes her head again when someone begins walking in our direction. I cut the conversation short and don't give her a chance to say no again. "Meet me at my locker after class. I have a couple of questions," I say before walking away.

I don't look back at her. I head down the hallway but have no idea where I'm actually going. I should probably go to the athletic department and find my locker there. According to what I read in our notes, there's a letter I haven't read yet in the locker room, along with some pictures.

I round the corner in a hurry and bump into a girl,

causing her to drop her purse. I mutter an apology and step around her, continuing down the hallway.

"Silas!" she yells. I pause.

Crap. I have no idea who she is.

I slowly turn on my heels and she's standing upright, pulling her purse strap higher up on her shoulder. I wait for her to say something else, but she just stares at me. After a few seconds, she throws her palms up in the air. "Well?" she says, frustrated.

I tilt my head in confusion. Is she expecting an apology? "Well...*what*?"

She huffs and folds her arms over her chest. "Did you find my sister?" *Janette. This is Charlie's sister, Janette. Crap.*

I can imagine it's hard enough searching for a missing person, but trying to search for them when you have no idea who you are, who they are, or who anyone else is kind of feels like shooting for the impossible.

"Not yet," I tell her. "Still looking. You?"

She takes a step toward me and tucks her chin in. "Don't you think if I found her I wouldn't have asked you if *you* found her?"

I take a step back, putting a safe distance between that glare and me.

Okay. So Janette is not a very pleasant person. I should write that in the notes for future reference.

She pulls a phone from her purse. "I'm calling the police," she says. "I'm really worried about her."

"I already spoke to the police."

She darts her eyes up to mine. "When? What did they say?"

"I was at your house. Your mother called the police when she found me in the attic looking for Charlie. I told the officer she's been missing since last night, but your mother made it sound like I was overreacting, so they didn't take it seriously."

Janette groans. "Figures," she says. "Well, I'm calling them again. I need to go outside to get a better signal. I'll let you know what they say." She steps around me to head outside.

Once she's gone, I head in the direction of where I think the athletic building might be.

"Silas," someone says from behind me.

Are you kidding me? Can I not make it five feet in this hallway without having to answer to someone?

I turn to face whoever is wasting my time, only to find a girl—or woman, rather—who perfectly matches the description of Avril Ashley.

This is exactly what I *don't* need right now. "Can I see you in my office, please?"

I squeeze the back of my neck and shake my head. "I can't, Avril."

She reveals nothing of what is going through her head. She stares at me with a stoic expression and then says, "My office. Now." She turns on her heel and heads down the hall.

I contemplate running in the other direction, but drawing attention to myself won't do me any favors. I reluctantly follow her until she reaches the door to administration. I follow her past the secretary and into an office. I step aside as she closes the door, but I don't sit. I'm watching her carefully, and she still hasn't looked back at me.

She makes her way to the window and stares outside, wrapping her arms around herself. The silence is awkward at best.

"Do you want to explain what happened Friday night?" she asks.

I immediately begin searching my infant memory for what she could be talking about.

Friday, Friday, Friday.

Without my notes in front of me, I come up empty. There's no way I can remember every detail of what I've read in the past two hours.

When I fail to respond, she lets out a soft laugh. "You are unreal," she says, turning to face me now. Her eyes are red, but so far they're dry. "What in the world possessed you to punch my father?"

Oh. The diner. The fight with the owner, Brian's father.

Wait.

I stand up straighter, the hairs prickling up across the skin of my neck. Avril Ashley is Brian Finley's *sister*? How is that even possible? And why would Charlie and I be involved with them?

"Did it have to do with her?" she asks.

She's throwing too much at me at once. I grip the back of my neck with my hands again and squeeze away some of the nerves. She doesn't seem to care that I'm not in the mood to discuss this right now. She takes several quick steps toward me until her finger is poking me in the chest.

"My father was offering her a job, you know. I don't know what you're up to, Silas." She spins and walks back to the window but then throws her hands up in frustration and faces me. "First, you waltz in here three weeks ago and act like Charlie is destroying your life because of her involvement with Brian. You make me feel sorry for you. You even make me feel guilty just for being his sister. And then you use that to manipulate me into kissing you, and once I finally cave, you show up every single day for more. Then you go to my father's restaurant and attack him, then follow that up by breaking things off with me." She takes a step back and puts her hand against her forehead. "Do you realize how much trouble I could be in, Silas?" She begins pacing back and forth. "I liked you. I risked my *job* for you. Hell, I risked my relationship with my own *brother* for you." She stares up at the ceiling, placing her hands on her hips. "I'm an idiot," she says. "I'm married. I'm a married woman with a degree, and here I am messing around with a student simply because he's attractive and I'm too damn foolish to know when someone is using me."

Information overload. I can't even respond as everything she just said sinks in.

"If you tell anyone about this, I'll make sure my father presses charges against you," she says with a threatening glare.

I find my tongue with that comment. "I'll never tell anyone, Avril. You know that."

Does she know that? The old me didn't seem to be very trustworthy.

She keeps her eyes locked with mine for several moments until she seems satisfied with my response. "Leave. And if you need a counselor for the rest of the school year, do us both a favor and transfer schools."

I put my hand on the doorknob and wait for her to say something else. When she doesn't, I try and make up for the old Silas. "For what it's worth… I'm sorry."

Her lips press into a tight line. She spins and walks angrily to her desk. "Get the hell out of my office, Silas."

Gladly.

19

Charlie

I must have drifted off. I hear a soft beep and then the sound of metal sliding against metal. My eyes snap open and instinctually I press myself harder against the wall. I can't believe I fell asleep. They had to have drugged me.

They. I'm about to find out who *they* are.

The door opens and my breathing gets faster as I squirm against the wall. A foot, plain white tennis shoes, and then…the smiling face of a woman. She comes in humming, kicking the door closed behind her. I relax a little. She looks like a nurse, dressed in pale yellow scrubs. Her hair is dark and pulled back in a low pony-tail. She's older, maybe in her forties. For a brief second I wonder how old I am. My hand travels up to my face, as if I could feel my age on my skin.

"Hello," she says cheerfully. She hasn't looked at me yet. She's busying herself with the tray of food.

I wrap my arms tighter around my knees. She sets a

tray down on a little table next to the bed and glances up for the first time.

"I brought your lunch. Are you hungry?"

Lunch? I wonder what happened to breakfast.

When I still don't answer, she smiles and lifts the lid off one of the plates as if to tempt me.

"It's spaghetti today," she says. "You like spaghetti."

Today? Like, how many days have I been here? I want to ask her, but my tongue is frozen in fear.

"You're confused. That's okay. You're safe here," she says. Funny, I don't *feel* safe.

She offers me a paper cup. I stare at it.

"You have to take your meds," she says, shaking the cup. I can hear the rattling of more than one pill inside. *I am being drugged.*

"What's it for?" I startle at the sound of my voice. Raspy. I haven't used it in a while, or I've been screaming a lot.

She smiles again. "The usual, silly." She frowns down at me, suddenly serious. "We know what happens when you don't take your medication, Sammy. You don't want to go down that path again."

Sammy!

I want to cry because I have a name! I reach for the cup. I don't know what she means, but I don't want to go down *that* path again. That path is probably why I'm here.

"Where am I?" I ask. There are three pills: one white, one blue, one brown.

She cocks her head to the side as she hands me a plastic cup of water. "You're in the Saint Bartholomew hospital. Don't you remember?"

I stare at her. Am I supposed to? If I ask her questions,

she may think I'm crazy, and by the looks of things, I may already be crazy. I don't want to make things worse, but— She sighs. "Look, I'm trying really hard with you, kid. But you have to do better this time. We can't have any more incidents."

I'm a kid. I cause incidents. That must be why I'm locked up here.

I tilt the cup 'til I feel the pills on my tongue. She hands me the water and I drink it. I'm thirsty.

"Eat up," she says, clapping her hands together. I pull the tray toward me. I am very hungry.

"Would you like to watch some television?"

I nod. She's really nice. And I *would* like to watch television. She pulls a remote control out of her pocket and switches it on. The show is about a family. They are all sitting around a table having dinner. *Where is my family?*

I'm starting to feel sleepy again.

20

Silas

It's amazing how much I can learn just by keeping my mouth shut. Avril and Brian are brother and sister.

Avril is married, yet I somehow still talked her into some sort of jacked-up relationship. And it's fairly new, which I didn't expect. It also seems odd that I would have gone to her for comfort, knowing Charlie and Brian were together.

Based on what I've learned of Silas—or myself—I don't see me wanting to be with anyone but Charlie.

Revenge? Maybe I was just using Avril to get information on Charlie and Brian.

I spend the next ten minutes contemplating what I've learned as I make my way around the campus in search of the athletic department. Everything looks the same: faces, buildings, stupid motivational posters. I finally give up and duck into an empty classroom. I take a seat at a table along the back wall and unzip the backpack filled with my past. I pull out the journals and a few letters, organizing them by date. The majority of the letters are between Charlie and myself, but some of them are from her father, written to her from prison. This makes me sad. There are a few from random people—friends of hers, I'm assuming. Their notes to her annoy me, filled with shallow teenage angst and bad spelling. I toss them aside, frustrated. I have a feeling whatever is going on with us has little to do with anyone else.

I grab one of the letters Charlie's father wrote to her and read it first.

Dear Peanut, You remember why I call you that, right? You were so small when you were born. I'd never held a baby before you, and I remember saying to Mom, "She's tiny, just like a little human peanut!"

I miss you, baby girl. I know this must be hard for you. Be strong for your sister and your mom. They're not like us, and they'll need you to figure things out for them for a while. Until I come home. Trust me, I'm working hard to get home to you guys. In the meantime, I've been doing a lot of reading. I even read that book you liked so much. The one with the apple on the cover. Wow! That Edward is...how did you put it...dreamy?

Anyway, I wanted to talk to you about something important. So please listen to me. I know you've known Silas for a very long time. He's a good boy. I don't blame him for what his father did. But you have to stay away from that family, Charlize. I don't trust them. I wish I could explain everything, and I will one day. But please, stay away from the Nashes. Silas is just a pawn in his father's game. I'm afraid they'll use you to get to me. Promise me, Charlize, that you'll stay away from them. I told Mom to use the money in the other account to get by for a while. If you have to, sell her rings. She won't want to, but do it anyway.

I love you,

Dad

I read the letter twice to make sure I don't miss anything. Whatever happened between my father and her father was serious. The man is in prison, and from reading the letter, he doesn't think his sentence is justified. It makes me wonder if my father is really to blame.

I place the letter in a new pile to keep it separate. If I keep all the letters that could mean something in their own pile, then if we lose our memories again, we won't have to waste time reading letters that serve no purpose.

I open up another letter that looks like it's been read a hundred times.

Dear Charlie baby, You get really angry when you're hungry. You get hangry. It's like you're not even the same person. Can we keep granola bars in your purse or something? It's just that I worry about my balls. The guys are starting to say I'm whipped. And I know what it looks like. I ran like a young buck to get you a bucket of chicken yesterday and missed the best part of the game. I missed seeing the greatest comeback in the history of football. All because I'm ~~scared~~—so in love with you. Maybe I am whipped. You looked really sexy with

*all that chicken grease on your face. Ripping the
meat away with your teeth like a savage. God. I
just want to marry you.*

Never Never,

Silas

I can feel a smile begin to form on my face, and I immediately shake it away. The fact that this girl is somewhere out there and has no idea who or where she is
leaves no room for smiles. I grab another letter, this time
wanting to read something from her to me.

*Dear Silas baby, Best. Concert. Ever. You may
be cuter than Harry Styles, especially when you
do that shoulder move and pretend you're smoking a cigar. Thank you for locking us in a broom
closet and then keeping your promise. I REALLY
liked the broom closet. I hope we can replicate it
in our house one day. Just go in there and make
out while the kids nap. Except with snacks, because...hangry. Speaking of food, I have to go because the kids I'm babysitting are dumping a jar
of pickles down the toilet. Oops! Maybe we should
just have a dog.*

Never Never,

Charlie

I like her. I even kind of like myself with her.

A dull ache begins to make its way across my chest.
I rub it while staring at her handwriting. It's familiar.

It's sadness. *I remember what it feels like to be sad.*

I read another letter from me to her, hoping to gain more insight into my personality.

Charlie baby, I missed you today more than I've ever missed you. It was a hard day. It's been a hard summer, actually. The upcoming trial coupled with not being allowed to see you has officially made this the worst year of my life.

And to think it started out so good.

Remember that night I snuck in your window? I remember it vividly, but that might be because I still have it on video and I watch it every single night. But I know that whether or not I had it on video at all, I'd still remember every detail of it. It was the first time we ever spent the night together as a couple, even though I wasn't actually supposed to be spending the night.

But waking up and seeing the sun shining through the window and across your face made it feel like a dream. Like this girl I had been holding in my arms for the past six hours wasn't real. Because life couldn't possibly feel as perfect and as carefree as it did in that moment.

I know you sometimes give me a hard time about how much I loved that night, but I think it's because I never really told you why.

After you fell asleep, I moved the video camera closer to us. I wrapped my arms around you and listened to you breathe until I fell asleep.

Sometimes when I have trouble sleeping, I'll play that video.

I know that's weird, but that's what you love about me. You love how much I love you. Because yes. I love you way too much. More than anyone deserves to be loved. But I can't help it. You make normal love hard. You make me psycho-love you.

One of these days all of this mess will pass. Our families will forget how much they've hurt each other. They'll see the bond we continue to have and they'll be forced to accept it.

Until then, never lose hope. Never stop loving me. Never forget.

Never Never,

Silas

I squeeze my eyes shut and release a slow breath. How is it possible to miss someone you can't remember?

I set the letters aside and begin to sift through Charlie's journals. I need to find the ones surrounding the events with our fathers. It seems to have been the catalyst in our relationship. I grab one and open it up to a random page.

I hate Annika. Oh my god, she's so stupid.

I flip to a different page. I kind of hate Annika too, but that's not important right now.

Silas baked me a cake for my birthday. It was awful. I think he forgot the eggs. But it was the most beautiful chocolate failure I've ever seen. I was so happy that I didn't even make a gag face while I ate a slice. But, oh god, it was so bad. Best boyfriend ever.

I want to keep reading that one, but I don't. What type of idiot forgets the eggs? I flip a few pages forward. *They took my dad today.* I sit up straighter.

They took my dad today. I don't feel anything. Will the feelings come? Or maybe I feel everything. All I can do is sit here and stare at the wall. I feel so helpless, like I should be doing something. Everything has changed, and my chest hurts. Silas keeps coming to the house, but I don't want to see him. I don't want to see anyone. It's not fair. Why have kids if you're just going to do stupid shit and leave them? Dad says it's all a misunderstanding and that the truth will come out, but Mom hasn't stopped crying. And we can't use any of our credit cards, because everything has been frozen. The phone won't stop ringing, and Janette is sitting on her bed, sucking her thumb like when she was little. I just want to die. I hate whoever did this to my family. I can't even—

I flip a few pages forward.

We have to move out of our house. Dad's lawyer told us today. The court is seizing it to pay off his debt. I only know this because I was listening outside of the office door when he told Mom. As soon as he left, she locked herself in her bedroom and hasn't come out in two days. We have to be

out of our house in five. I started packing some
of our stuff, but I'm not even sure what we're al-
lowed to keep. Or where we are supposed to go.
My hair started falling out about a week ago. In
big chunks when I brush it and when I'm in the
shower. And yesterday, Janette got in trouble at
school for scratching a girl on the face when she
made fun of the fact our dad is in prison.

I have a couple thousand dollars in my savings
account, but seriously, who is going to rent me an
apartment? I don't know what to do. I still haven't
seen Silas, but he comes every day. I make Janette
tell him to go away. I'm so embarrassed. Everyone
is talking about us, even my friends. Annika ac-
cidentally included me in a group text where they
were sending each other prison memes. Come to
think of it, I don't think it was an accident. She'd
love to get her claws into Silas. Now's her chance.
As soon as he realizes what an embarrassment
my family has become, he won't want anything to
do with me.

Ugh. Was that the type of person I was? Why did she
think that? I would never... I don't think I would ever...
Would I...? I close the journal and rub my forehead.
I'm getting a headache, and I don't feel any closer to figuring this out. I decide to read one more page.

I miss my house. It's not my house anymore,
so can I still say that? I miss what used to be my
house. Sometimes I go there, just stand across
the street, and remember. I don't even know if life
was so great pre Dad in prison, or if I was just

living in a luxurious bubble. At least I didn't feel like this. Like some loser. All Mom does is drink. She doesn't even care about us anymore. And you have to wonder if she ever did, or if we were just fixtures in her glamorous life, Janette and me. Because she only cares about the way she feels now.

I feel bad for Janette. I at least had a real life, with real parents. She's still little. It's going to mess her up because she's not even going to know what it's like to have a whole family. She's so mad all the time. I am too. Yesterday I made fun of this kid until he cried. It felt good. It felt bad too. But like Daddy said, as long as I'm meaner than they are, they can't touch me. I'll just beat them down until they leave me alone.

I saw Silas for a little bit after school. He took me for a burger and then drove me home. It was the first time he'd seen the shit pit we're living in now. I could see the shock on his face. He dropped me off, and then an hour later I heard a mower outside. He went home and picked up a mower and some tools to fix the place up. I wanted to love him for it, but it just embarrassed me.

He pretends he doesn't care about how much my life has changed, but I know he does. He has to. I'm not what I used to be.

My dad has been writing to me. He's said some things, but I don't know what to believe anymore. If he's right... I don't even want to think about it.

I look through the letters from her father. Which one is she talking about? Then I see it. My stomach churns.

Dear Charlize, I spoke to your mother yesterday. She said you were still seeing Silas. I'm disappointed. I warned you about his family. His father is the reason I'm in prison, yet you continue to love him. Do you realize how much that hurts me?

I know you think you know him, but he's no different from his father. They're a family of snakes. Charlize, please understand that I'm not trying to hurt you. I want to keep you safe from those people, and here I am, locked up behind these bars, unable to take care of my own family. A warning is really all I can give you, and I hope that you heed my words.

We lost everything—our house, our reputation, our family. And they still have everything that was theirs as well as everything that was ours. It's not right. Please, stay away from them. Look what they did to me. To all of us.

Please tell your sister that I love her.

Dad

I feel sympathy for Charlie after reading the letter. A girl torn between a boy who obviously loved her and a father who manipulated her.

I need to visit her father. I find a pen and write down the return address from the letters he's sent to her. I pull out my phone and Google it. The prison is a good two-and-a-half-hour drive from New Orleans.

Two and a half hours one way is a lot of wasted time when I only have forty-eight hours total. And it feels like I've already wasted a lot of that. I make a note of visiting hours and decide if I haven't found Charlie by to-morrow morning, I'll be paying her father a visit. Based on the letters I just read, Charlie is closer to her father than anyone. Well, besides the old Silas. And if *I* don't have a clue where she is, her father is probably one of the few who might. I wonder if he would even agree to meet with me.

I flinch in my seat when the final bell rings, sig-naling the end of school. I keep the letters separated and put them all neatly inside the backpack. It's the last class period, and I'm hoping The Shrimp will be where I asked her to be.

21

Charlie

I'm locked in a room with a boy. The room is tiny and it smells like bleach. Tinier even than the room I was in before I fell asleep. I don't remember waking up and being moved, but here I am, and let's be honest—I don't remember a whole lot lately. He's sitting on the floor with his back against the wall, and his knees spread apart. I watch as he tilts his head back and belts out the chorus to "Oh Cecelia."

He's pretty hot.

"Oh, my God," I say. "If we're going to be locked in here, can you at least sing something good?"

I don't know where that came from. I don't even know this boy. He finishes, punctuating the last word with a really off-key *eh-eh-eh-eh*. It's then that I realize that I not only recognize the song he's singing but also know the lyrics. Things change, and suddenly I'm not the girl anymore. I'm watching the girl watch the boy.

I'm dreaming.

"I'm hungry," she says.

He lifts his hips off the ground and digs around in his pocket. When he pulls out his hand, he's holding a Life Saver.

"You're such a lifesaver," she says, taking it from him. She kicks his foot, and he grins at her.

"How come you're not mad at me?" he asks.

"For what? Ruining our night by making us miss the concert so you could make out with me in a broom closet? Why the hell would I be mad?" She makes a show of slipping the mint between her lips. "Do you think they'll hear us in here when the concert's over?"

"I hope so. Or you'll get really hangry and be mean to me all night."

She laughs, and then they're both smiling at each other like idiots. I can hear the music playing. It's something slower this time. They got locked in here making out. Very cute. I feel envious.

She crawls over to him, and he lowers his legs to accommodate her. When she's straddling him, he runs his hands up and down her back. She's wearing a purple dress and black boots. A couple of grimy mops and a giant yellow bucket are propped next to them.

"I promise this won't happen when we see One Direction," he says seriously.

"You hate One Direction."

"Yeah, but I guess I have to make this up to you. Be a good boyfriend and such." His hands tease the exposed skin on her legs. He makes a walking motion up her thigh with his fingers. I can almost feel the goose bumps for her.

She throws back her head this time and starts to sing

a One Direction song. It clashes with the music playing behind them, and she's a worse singer than he is.

"Oh, God," he says, covering her mouth. "I love you, but no." He pulls his hand away, and she grabs it back to kiss his palm.

"Yeah you do. I love you back."

It's when they kiss that I wake up. I feel intense disappointment. I lie very still, hoping to fall asleep again so I can see what happens to them. I need to know if they got out in time to see The Vamps play at least one song. Or if he kept his word and took her to One Direction. Their togetherness has made me feel so incredibly lonely that I bury my face in the pillow and cry. I liked their stuffy little room better than mine. I begin to hum out the tune of the song that was playing, and then I suddenly bolt upright in bed.

They *did* get out. During intermission. I can hear his laughter and see the confusion on the face of the janitor who opened the door for them. How do I know that? How can I see something that never happened? Unless…

That wasn't a dream. It happened. To me.

Oh, my God. That girl was *me*.

I reach up to touch my face, smiling a little. He loved me. He was so…full of life. I lie back down, wondering what happened to him and if he's the reason I'm here. Why hasn't he come to find me? Can a person forget that kind of love?

And how exactly did my life go from that…to this nightmare?

22

Silas

School has been out for over fifteen minutes. The hall-way is empty, yet here I stand, still waiting for The Shrimp to show up. I'm not sure what I would even ask her if she did show up. I just got a feeling when I saw her, a feeling that she was hiding something. Maybe it's something she doesn't even realize she's hiding, but I want to find out what she knows. Why she hates Charlie so much. Why she hates *me* so much.

My phone rings. My father again. I press ignore, but then see that I've somehow missed a few texts. I open them, but none are from Charlie. Not that they could be, since I have her phone. I've simply accepted the fact that I still have a little bit of hope that this is all a joke. That she'll either call or text or show up to laugh about it.

The most recent text is from Landon.

Get your ass to practice. I'm not covering for you again, and we have a game in three hours.

I have no idea what move will be the most efficient use of my time. Surely practice won't be, considering I couldn't care less about football right now. But if practice is where I normally am at this hour, I should probably be there in case Charlie shows up. After all, everyone seems to think she'll be at the game tonight. And since I don't know where else to look or what else to do, I guess I'll look for her there. Doesn't look like The Shrimp agreed to my request, anyway.

I finally locate the locker rooms, and I'm relieved to find them empty. Everyone else is out on the field, so I use the privacy to search for the box I wrote about in the letters to myself. When I locate it at the top of the locker, I pull it down and take a seat on the bench, lifting the lid.

I flip quickly through the pictures. *Our first kiss. Our first fight. Where we met.* I finally get to a letter at the bottom of the box. Across the top is Charlie's name, written in the handwriting I've come to recognize as my own.

I look around to ensure I still have complete privacy, and then I unfold the letter.

It's dated last week. Just one day before we lost our memories for the first time.

Charlie, Well, I guess this is it. The end of us. The end of Charlie and Silas.

At least it didn't come as a surprise. We've both known, since the day your father was sentenced, that we wouldn't be able to move past that. You blame my father, I blame yours. They blame each other. Our mothers, who used to be best friends, won't even speak each other's names out loud.

But hey, at least we tried, right? We tried hard, but when two families are torn apart like ours were, it's a little difficult to look ahead at the future we could possibly have and actually be excited about it.

Yesterday, when you approached me about Avril, I denied it. You accepted my denial, because you know I never lie to you. Somehow, you've always seemed to know what's going on in my head before I even do, so you never question whether or not I'm telling the truth, because you already know.

And that's what bothers me, because you so easily accepted my lie, when I know you know it's true. And that leads me to believe that I was right. You aren't seeing Brian because you like him. You aren't seeing him behind my back to get revenge on me. The only reason you're with him is because you're trying to punish yourself. And you accepted my lie, because if you broke up with me, it would relieve you of your guilt.

You don't want to be relieved of your guilt. Your guilt is your way of punishing yourself for your recent behavior, and without it, you won't be able to treat people the way you've been treating them.

I know this about you, because me and you, Charlie? We're the same. No matter how tough you've been trying to act lately, I know that deep down you have a heart that bleeds in the presence of injustice. I know that every time you lash out at someone, it makes you cringe inside. But you do it because you think you have to.

Because your father is manipulating you into

believing that if you're vindictive enough, people won't touch you.

You told me once that too much good in a person's life will stunt their growth. You said pain is necessary, because in order for a person to succeed, they must first learn to conquer adversity. And that's what you do...you deliver adversity where you see fit. Maybe you do it to gain respect. To intimidate. Whatever your reasons, I can't do this anymore. I can't watch you tear people down in order to build yourself up.

I'd rather love you at the bottom than despise you at the top.

It doesn't have to be this way, Charlie. You're allowed to love me, despite what your father says. You're allowed to be happy. What you can't allow is for negativity to choke you until we no longer breathe the same air.

I want you to stop seeing Brian. But I also want you to stop seeing me. I want you to stop trying to find a way to free your father. I want you to stop allowing him to mislead you. I want you to stop resenting me every time I defend my own father.

You act one way in front of everyone else, but at night when I'm on the phone with you, I get the real Charlie. It's going to be absolute torture not dialing your number and hearing your voice before I go to sleep each night, but I can't do this anymore. I can't only love that part of you—the real part of you. I want to love you when I talk to you at night and I also want to love you when I see you during the day, but you're beginning to show two different sides of yourself.

And I only like one of those sides.

As much as I try, I can't possibly imagine how hurt you must be since your father went away. But you can't let that change who you are. Please stop caring about what other people think. Stop allowing your father's actions to define you. Figure out what you did with the Charlie I fell in love with. And when you find her, I'll be here. I told you before I'll never stop loving you. I'll never forget what we have.

But lately, it seems that you've forgotten.

I've enclosed some pictures I want you to go through. Hopefully they'll help remind you of what we could have again someday. A love that wasn't dictated by our parents or defined by our family status. A love we couldn't stop if we tried. A love that got us through some of the hardest moments of our lives.

Never forget, Charlie.

Never stop.

Silas

23

Silas

"Silas, Coach wants you suited up and on the field in five."

I sit up straight at the sound of the voice. I'm not at all surprised that I don't recognize the guy standing in the doorway to the locker room, but I nod as if I do. I begin shoving all the pictures and the letter from the box into the backpack, stowing it away in my locker.

I was going to break up with her.

I wonder if I did break up with her. I still have the letter, though. It was written the day before we lost our memories. Our relationship was obviously on a rapid decline. Maybe I gave her the box and she read the letter and then gave it back to me?

Endless possibilities and theories plague my mind as I attempt to put on the football gear. I end up having to Google how to do it on my phone. Ten minutes have easily passed by the time I'm dressed and walking onto the field. Landon is the first to notice me. He breaks formation and jogs in my direction. He puts his hands on my shoulders and leans in.

"I'm tired of covering for you. Get whatever shit is screwing up your head out of there. You need to focus, Silas. This game is important, and Dad will be pissed if you blow it."

He releases my shoulders and jogs back onto the field. The guys are all lined up, doing what looks like a whole lot of nothing. Some of them are passing footballs back and forth. Others are sitting in the grass, stretching. I take a seat in the grass next to where Landon has just plopped down, and I begin to mock his movements.

I like him. I can only recall two conversations we've had in our life, and they've both consisted of Landon spitting some sort of direction at me. I know I'm the older brother, but he seems to act like I treat him with respect. We had to have been close. I can tell by the way he's looking at me that he's suspicious of my behavior. He knows me well enough to know something is up.

I try to use this to my advantage. I stretch my leg out in front of me and lean forward. "I can't find Charlie," I say to him. "I'm worried about her."

Landon laughs under his breath. "I should have known this had to do with her." He switches legs and faces me. "And what do you mean you can't find her? Her phone was in your car this morning. She can't very well call you from it. She's probably at home."

I shake my head. "No one has heard from her since last night. She never made it home. Janette reported her missing an hour ago."

His eyes are locked with mine, and I see them shift to concern. "What about her mom?"

I shake my head. "You know how she is. She's no help."

Landon nods. "True," he says. "Damn shame what this has turned her into."

His words make me contemplate. If she hasn't always been this way, what made her change? Maybe the sentencing destroyed her. I feel a small shred of sympathy for the woman. More than I did this morning.

"What did the police say? I doubt they'll consider her a missing person if all she's done is skip school today. They have to have more evidence than that."

The word *evidence* sticks with me as it falls from his mouth.

I haven't wanted to admit this to myself, because I want to focus on finding her, but deep down I've been a little concerned how this looks for me. If she really is missing and she doesn't show up soon, I have a feeling the only person the police will be interested in questioning is the last person to see her. And considering I have her wallet, her phone, and every letter and journal entry she's ever written—that doesn't bode well for Silas Nash.

If they question me—how will I know what to tell them? I don't remember our last words. I don't remember what she was wearing. I don't even have a valid excuse as to why I have all of her belongings. Any answer I give them would be a lie on a polygraph because I don't remember any of it.

What if something happened to her and I really am responsible? What if I've suffered some kind of shock, and that's why I can't remember anything? What if I hurt her and this is my mind's way of convincing me I didn't?

"Silas? Are you okay?"

My eyes flick up to Landon's. *I have to hide the evidence.*

I push my palms into the ground and immediately stand. I turn and run in the direction of the locker rooms.

"Silas!" he yells after me. I keep running. I run until I reach the building, and I push open the door so hard it slaps the wall behind it. I run straight to my locker and swing it open.

I reach inside but feel nothing.

No.

I touch the walls, the floor of the locker; I swipe my hands around every empty inch of it.

It's gone.

I run my hands through my hair and spin around, looking all around the locker room, hoping maybe I left the backpack on the floor. I swing open Landon's locker and pull everything out of it. It's not in there, either. I open the next locker and do the same. I open the next. Nothing.

The backpack is nowhere.

I'm either going crazy or someone was just in here. "Shit. Shit, shit, shit."

When all of the contents from the entire row of lockers are on the floor, I move to the other wall of lockers and begin doing the same to them. I look inside other people's backpacks. I empty gym bags, watching as gym clothes tumble to the floor. I find anything and everything, from cell phones to cash to condoms.

But no letters. No journals. No photographs.

"Nash!"

I spin around to see a man filling the doorway, looking at me like he has no idea who I am or what's gotten into me. *That makes two of us.*

"What in the hell are you doing?"

I look around at the mess I've made. It looks like a tornado just ripped through the locker room.

How am I going to get out of this?

I've just destroyed every single locker in here. And what explanation would I give them? *I'm looking for stolen evidence so the police won't arrest me for my girlfriend's disappearance?*

"Someone…" I squeeze the back of my neck again. This must be one of my old ticks—squeezing the stress out of my neck. "Someone stole my wallet," I mutter.

The coach looks around the locker room, the anger never once leaving his face. He points at me. "Clean this up, Nash! Now! And then get your ass to my office!" He walks away, leaving me alone.

I waste no time. I'm relieved I left all my clothes on the bench and not in my locker with the stuff that was stolen. My keys are still in my pants pocket. As soon as I'm out of my football gear and back into my clothes, I walk out the door, but I don't go in the direction of the offices. I head straight for the parking lot.

Straight for my car.

I have to find Charlie. Tonight.

Otherwise, I could be sitting completely helpless in a jail cell.

24

Charlie

I hear the lock open again, and I sit up. The pills the nurse gave me make me feel drowsy. I don't know how long I was asleep, but it couldn't have been long enough to already be time for another meal. However, she comes in carrying another tray. I'm not even hungry. I wonder if I finished my spaghetti earlier. I can't even remember eating it. I must be a lot crazier than I thought. But I did have a memory. I debate telling her, but it feels private. Something I want to keep for myself.

"Dinner time!" she says, setting it down. She lifts the lid to reveal a plate of rice and sausage. I eye it warily, wondering if I'm going to have to take more pills. As if reading my mind, she hands me the teeny paper cup.

"You're still here," I say, trying to stall. These pills make me feel like crap.

She smiles. "Yes. Take your pills so that you can eat before it gets cold." I pour them into my mouth while she watches, and I take a sip of water.

"If you behave today, you may be able to go to the rec room for a while tomorrow. I know you must be itching to get out of this room."

What constitutes behaving? So far there hasn't been much mischief to get up to.

I eat my dinner with a plastic fork while she watches me. I must be a real delinquent if I have to be supervised during dinner.

"I'd rather use the restroom than the rec room," I tell her.

"Eat first. I'll be back to take you to the restroom and to have a shower."

I feel like a prisoner rather than a patient. "Why am I here?" I ask.

"You don't remember?"

"Would I be asking if I remembered?" I snap. I wipe my mouth as her eyes narrow.

"Finish your food," she says coldly.

I grow immediately angry at my situation—at the way she's dictating every second of my life as if it's hers to live.

I fling the plate across the room. It smashes against the wall by the television. Rice and sausage fly everywhere.

That felt good. That felt *more* than good. That felt like *me*.

I laugh then. Throw my head back and laugh. It's a deep laugh, wicked.

Oh, my God! This is why I'm here. *Craaaaazy.*

I can see the muscles in her jaw clench. I've made her mad. *Good.* I stand up and run for a broken shard of plate. I don't know what's come over me, but this feels right. Defending myself feels right.

She tries to grab me, but I slip out of her grasp. I pick up a sharp piece of porcelain. What type of mental hospital gives you porcelain plates? It's a disaster waiting to happen. I hold the shard toward her and take a step forward. "Tell me what's going on."

She doesn't move. Looks quite calm, actually.

That's when the door behind me must open, because the next thing I know there's a sharp sting in my neck and I'm falling to the ground.

25

Silas

I pull over on the side of the road. I grip the steering wheel, trying to calm myself down.

Everything is gone. I have no idea who took it. Someone is probably reading our letters right now. They'll read everything we wrote to ourselves, and depending on who took it, I probably look certifiably insane.

I grab a sheet of blank paper I find in the backseat, and I begin to write things down. Anything I can remember. I'm pissed, because I can't remember even a fraction of what was in the notes inside the backpack. Our addresses, our locker codes, our birthdays, all the names of our friends and family—I can't remember any of it. What little I can recall, I write down. I can't let this stop me from finding her.

I have no idea where to go next. I could visit the tarot shop again; see if she returned there. I could try and find the address to whatever property has the gate that's in the picture in her bedroom. There has to be a connection with the tarot shop displaying that same picture.

I could drive to the prison and visit Charlie's father, see what he knows.

Prison is probably the last place I should go right now, though.

I grab my phone and begin scrolling through it. I pass the pictures from just last night. A night I don't recall a single second of. There are pictures of me and Charlie, pictures of our tattoos, pictures of a church, pictures of a street musician.

The last picture is of Charlie, standing next to a cab. It appears that I'm on the other side of the street, snapping a picture of her as she prepares to climb inside it.

This had to be the last time I saw her. In the letter it said she got into a cab on Bourbon Street.

I zoom in on the picture, my excitement getting caught in my throat. There's a license plate on the front of the cab and a phone number on the side of the cab.

Why didn't I think of this already?

I jot down the phone number and license plate, and dial the number. I feel like I'm finally making progress.

The cab company almost refused to give me information. I finally convinced the operator that I was a detective and needed to question the driver regarding a missing person. That's only half of a lie. The guy on the phone said he had to ask around and call me back. It took about thirty minutes before my phone rang again.

It was the actual driver of the cab I spoke to this time. He said a girl matching the description of Charlie hailed his cab last night, but before he could take her anywhere, she told him never mind and she shut the door and walked away.

She just...walked away?

Why would she do that? Why would she not catch up to me? She had to know I was probably just around the next corner if that's where we parted ways.

She had to have an agenda. I don't remember a thing about her, but based on what I've read, everything she does seems to have a purpose. But what could her purpose have been on Bourbon Street at that time of night?

The only things that come to mind are the tarot shop and the diner. But in the notes, it states that Charlie never showed back up to the diner, based on information from someone named Amy. Was she going to find Brian? I feel a prickle of jealousy at the thought, but I'm almost confident she wouldn't have done that.

It has to be the tarot shop.

I search Google on my phone, unable to remember the exact name of the place written in our notes. I mark two of them in the French Quarter and set my GPS to take me there.

I can tell almost immediately upon entering that this is the shop we described in the notes. The one we visited just last night.

Last night. *God.* Why can't I remember something that just happened one day ago?

I make my way up and down each aisle, taking in everything around me, not even sure what I'm in search of. When I reach the last aisle, I recognize the photo hanging on the wall. The picture of the gate.

It's here for decoration. Not something for sale. I lift up on my toes until my fingers grab at the frame, and I pull it down to inspect it closer. The gate is tall, guarding a house in the background that I can barely make out in the picture. In the corner of one of the massive columns attached to the gate is the name of the house. *Jamais Jamais.*

"Can I help you?"

I look up to see a man towering over me, which is impressive. I'm six foot one, according to my driver's license. He has to be six foot five.

I point down to the photograph in my hands. "Do you know what this picture is of?"

The man snatches the frame out of my hands. "Seriously?" He seems agitated. "I didn't know what it was when your girlfriend asked me last night, and I still don't know what it is tonight. It's a damn picture." He hangs it back on the wall.

"Don't touch anything unless it's for sale and you plan to purchase it." He begins to walk away, so I follow him.

"Wait," I say, taking two steps to his long, single strides. "My girlfriend?"

He doesn't stop walking toward the register. "Girlfriend. Sister. Cousin. Whatever."

"Girlfriend," I clarify, even though I don't know why I'm clarifying. He obviously doesn't care. "Did she come back in here last night? After we left?"

He makes his way behind the register. "We closed right after the two of you left." He plants his gaze on mine and arches an eyebrow. "You gonna buy anything, or are you just gonna follow me around with stupid questions the rest of the night?"

I swallow. He makes me feel younger. Immature. He's the epitome of man, and the bone in his eyebrow makes me feel like a frightened child.

Suck it up, Silas. You're not a pussy.

"I just have one more stupid question."

He begins ringing up a customer. He doesn't respond, so I continue. "What does *Jamais Jamais* mean?"

He doesn't even look at me.

"It means *Never Never*," someone says from behind me.

I immediately turn, but my feet feel heavy, like I've sunken into my shoes. *Never Never?*

This can't be a coincidence. Charlie and I repeat this phrase over and over in our letters.

I look at the woman the voice belongs to, and she's staring at me, chin lifted, face straight. Her hair is pulled back. It's dark, sporadically streaked with gray strands. She's wearing a long, flowing piece of material that pools around her feet at the floor. I'm not even sure it's a dress. It looks as if she just fashioned something out of a sheet and a sewing machine.

She has to be the tarot reader. She's playing the part well.

"Where is that house located? The one in the photo on the wall?" I point to the photograph. She turns and stares at it for several long seconds. Without facing me again, she crooks her finger for me to follow her, and she begins to head toward the back of the store.

I reluctantly follow her. Before we pass through a doorway of beaded curtains, my phone begins to vibrate in my pants pocket. It rattles against my keys, and the woman turns and looks at me over my shoulder. "Turn it off."

I look down at the screen and see that it's my father again. I silence the phone. "I'm not here for a reading," I clarify. "I'm just looking for someone."

"The girl?" she says, taking a seat on the other side of a small table in the center of the room. She motions for me to sit, but I refuse the offer.

"Yes. We were here last night."

She nods and begins to shuffle a deck of cards. "I remember," she says. A small smirk plays at the corner of her mouth. I watch as she separates the cards into stacks. She lifts her head and her face is expressionless. "But that only makes one of us, doesn't it."

The statement sends chills over my arms. I take two quick steps forward and grab the back of the empty chair. "How do you know that?" I blurt out.

She motions to the chair again. This time I sit. I wait for her to speak again, to tell me what she knows. She's the first one to be clued in to what's happening to me.

My hands begin to shake. My pulse is throbbing behind my eyes. I squeeze them shut and pull my hands through my hair to hide my nerves. "Please," I tell her. "If you know something, please tell me."

She begins to shake her head slowly. Back and forth, back and forth. "It's not that easy, Silas," she says.

She knows my name. I want to scream *Victory*, but I still don't have any answers.

"Last night, your card was blank. I've never seen that before." She runs her hand across a stack of cards, smoothing them out in a line. "I've heard of it. We've *all* heard of it happening. But I don't know anyone who has actually *seen* it."

Blank card? I feel like I remember reading that in our notes, but it doesn't help when I no longer have the notes in my possession. And who is she referring to when she says *we've* all heard of it.

"What does it mean? What can you tell me? How do

I find Charlie?" My questions tumble out of my mouth and trip over each other.

"That picture," she says. "Why are you so curious about that house?"

I open my mouth to tell her about the picture in Charlie's room, but I clamp it shut. I don't know if I can trust her. I don't know her. She's the first one to know what's going on with me. That could be an answer, or it could be an indication of guilt. If Charlie and I are under some sort of spell, she's probably one of the few who would know how to do something of that magnitude.

God, this is ridiculous. A spell? Why am I even allowing myself these thoughts?

"I was just curious about the name," I say, lying to her about my inquiry of the house in the picture. "What else can you tell me?"

She continues realigning stacks of cards, never flipping them over. "What I can tell you…the *only* thing I will tell you…is that you need to remember what it is that someone so desperately wanted you to forget." Her eyes meet mine, and she lifts her chin again. "You may go now. I am of no further help to you."

She scoots away from the table and stands. Her frock billows out with the swift movement, and the shoes she has on underneath make me question her authenticity. I would assume a fortune teller would be barefoot. Or is she a witch? A wizard? Whatever she is, I want desperately to believe that she can help me more than she has. I can tell based on my hesitation that I'm not the type of person to buy into this shit. But my desperation is heavier than my skepticism. If it takes believing in dragons to find Charlie, then I'll be the first to wield a sword in the face of its fire.

"There has to be *something*," I tell her. "I can't find Charlie. I can't remember anything. I don't even know where to start looking. You have to give me more information than this." I stand, my voice desperate and my eyes even more so.

She simply tilts her head and smiles.

"Silas, the answers to your questions lie with someone who is very close to you." She points to the doorway. "You may go now. You have a lot of searching to do."

Very close to me?

My father? Landon? Who else am I close with besides Charlie? I glance at the beaded curtains and then back at her. She's already walking away, toward a door in the back of the building. I watch her as she leaves.

I run my hands up my face. I want to scream.

26

Charlie

When I wake up, everything is clean. No rice, no sausage, no shards of porcelain to cut a bitch.

Whoa! Where did that come from? I feel loopy. She's got this timed down to a T.

Knock Sammy out, bring her crappy food, knock Sammy out, bring her crappy food.

But this time when she returns, she doesn't have crappy food. She's carrying a towel and a small bar of soap.

Finally! A restroom.

"Shower time," she says. She's not as friendly this time. Her mouth is a tight line across her face. I stand up, expecting to sway a little. The needle to the neck was stronger than the other stuff they've been giving me, but I don't feel as foggy. My mind is sharp; my body is ready to react.

"Why are you the only one who comes?" I say. "If you're a nurse, you must work in shifts."

She turns away, walks to the door.

"Hello…?"

"Behave," she says. "Next time things won't go as well for you."

I shut my mouth because she's taking me out of this box, and I really, really want to see what's behind that door.

She opens the door and lets me walk out first. There's another door in front of me. I'm confused. She turns right and I see there's a hallway. Just to my right is a bathroom. I haven't used the toilet in hours, and the minute I see it my bladder starts to ache. She hands me the towel. "Shower only has cold water. Don't take long."

I close the door. It's like a bunker. No windows, raw concrete. The toilet doesn't have a lid or a seat, just a rimless hole with a sink next to it. I use it anyway.

On top of the sink is a new hospital gown and underwear. I study everything as I pee, looking for something. Anything. There's a rusted pipe near the floor, jutting out of the wall. I flush the toilet and move toward it. Sticking my hand inside, I feel around. *Gross.* A piece of the pipe has corroded away.

I go to turn the water on in the shower in case she's listening. It's a tiny little bit of metal, but with some effort I'm able to detach it from the wall. It's something, at least.

I carry it into the shower with me, holding it in one hand while I wash. The water is so cold; I can't stop my teeth from chattering. I try to clench my jaw tighter, but my teeth still rattle inside my head despite how much I try to still them.

How pathetic am I? I have no control over my own

teeth. No control over my own memories. No control over when I eat, sleep, shower or pee.

The only thing I feel I can control is my eventual escape from wherever it is that I am. I clutch the pipe in my hands with all my strength, knowing it could be the only thing that gets me back some form of control.

When I walk out of the bathroom, it's wrapped in toilet paper and stuffed in my underwear, a simple pair of white panties she left for me. I don't have a plan yet; I'll just wait for the right moment.

27

Silas

It's dark now. I've been driving for over two hours without a clue as to where to go next. I can't go back home. I can't go to Charlie's house. I don't know anyone else, so the only thing I can do is drive.

I have eight missed calls. Two are from Landon. One from Janette. The rest are from my father.

I also have eight voicemails, none of which I've listened to yet. I don't want to worry about any of them right now. None of them has any clue what's really going on, and no one would believe me if I told them. I don't blame them. I keep repeating the entire day in my head, and it seems too ridiculous for me to even believe—and I'm the one *living* it.

It's all too ridiculous, but way too real.

I pull over at a gas station to fill up my car. I'm not even sure if I've eaten anything today, but I feel lightheaded, so I grab a bag of chips and a bottle of water while inside the store.

The entire time I fill my tank with gas, I wonder about Charlie. When I'm back on the road, I'm still wondering about Charlie. I wonder if Charlie's eaten anything.

I wonder if she's alone.

I wonder if she's being taken care of.

I wonder how I'm possibly supposed to find her when she could be anywhere in the entire world right now. All I'm doing is driving in circles, slowing every time I pass a girl walking on a sidewalk. I don't know where to look. I don't know where to go. I don't know how to be the guy who saves her.

I wonder what people do when they have no place to go and no place to be.

I wonder if this is what it's like to be crazy. Certifiably insane. I feel as though I have absolutely zero control over my own mind.

And if I'm not the one in control…who is?

My phone rings again. I look at the caller ID and see that it's Landon. I don't know why I pick it up to answer it. Maybe I'm just tired of being inside my own head and not getting any answers. I pull over to the side of the road to talk to him.

"Hello?"

"Please tell me what the hell is going on."

"Can anyone hear you?"

"No," he says. "The game just ended. Dad is talking to the police. Everyone's worried about you, Silas."

I don't respond. I feel bad that they're worried, but even worse that no one seems to be worried about Charlie.

"Have they found Charlie yet?"

I can hear people shouting in the background. It

sounds like he called me the second the game ended. "They're looking," he says.

But there's something else in his voice. Something unspoken. "What is it, Landon?"

He sighs again. "Silas…they're looking for you too. They think…" His voice is heavy with worry. "They think you know where she is."

I close my eyes. I knew this would happen. I wipe my palms down my jeans. "I don't know where she is."

Several seconds pass before Landon speaks again. "Janette went to the police. She said she thought you were acting strange, so when she found Charlie's things in a backpack inside your gym locker, she turned them in to the police. You had her wallet, Silas. And her phone."

"Finding Charlie's things in my possession is hardly proof that I'm responsible for her disappearance. It's proof that I'm her boyfriend."

"Come home," he says. "Tell them you have nothing to hide. Answer their questions. If you cooperate, they'll have no reason to accuse you."

Ha. If only answering their questions was that easy.

"Do you think I have something to do with her disappearance?"

"*Do* you?" he asks immediately.

"No."

"Then no," he says. "I don't think you have anything to do with it. Where are you?"

"I don't know."

I hear a muffled noise, like he's covering the phone with his hand. I can hear voices in the background.

"Did you get hold of him?" a man asks.

"Still trying, Dad," Landon says.

More muttering.

"You there, Silas?" he asks.

"Yeah. I have a question," I say. "Have you ever heard of a place called *Jamais Jamais*?"

Silence. I wait for him to respond, but he doesn't. "Landon? Have you heard of it?"

Another heavy sigh. "It's Charlie's old house, Silas. What the hell is wrong with you? You're on drugs, aren't you? Jesus Christ, Silas. What the hell did you take? Is that what happened to Charlie? Is that why…"

I hang up the phone while he's still in the middle of spouting off questions. I search Brett Wynwood's home address on the Internet. It takes me a while, but two addresses pop up in the results. One I remember, because I was just there earlier today. It's where Charlie lives now.

The other is one I don't recognize. It's the address to *Jamais Jamais.*

THE HOUSE SITS ON SIX ACRES, OVERLOOKING LAKE BORGNE. IT WAS BUILT IN 1860, EXACTLY ONE YEAR BEFORE THE CIVIL WAR BEGAN. THE HOUSE WAS ORIGINALLY NAMED "LA TERRE RENCONTRE L'EAU," WHICH MEANS "LAND MEETS WATER."

IT WAS USED AS A HOSPITAL DURING THE WAR, HOUSING WOUNDED CONFEDERATE SOLDIERS. YEARS AFTER THE WAR, THE HOUSE WAS PURCHASED BY A BANKER, FRANK WYNWOOD, IN 1880. THE HOME REMAINED IN THE FAMILY, PASSED DOWN THREE GENERATIONS, ULTIMATELY LANDING IN THE HANDS OF THEN THIRTY-YEAR-OLD BRETT WYNWOOD IN 1998.

BRETT WYNWOOD AND HIS FAMILY OCCUPIED THE HOME UNTIL 2005, WHEN HURRICANE KATRINA CAUSED EXTENSIVE DAMAGE TO THE PROPERTY. THE FAMILY WAS FORCED TO ABANDON THE HOME, AND IT SAT UN-

TOUCHED FOR SEVERAL YEARS BEFORE RENOVATIONS BEGAN. THE ENTIRE HOUSE WAS GUTTED AND REBUILT, WITH ONLY PORTIONS OF THE ORIGINAL OUTER WALLS AND ROOF SALVAGED.

IN 2011, THE WYNWOOD FAMILY MOVED BACK INTO THEIR HOME. DURING THE UNVEILING, BRETT WYNWOOD ANNOUNCED THE HOME HAD BEEN GIVEN A NEW NAME: "JAMAIS JAMAIS."

WHEN ASKED WHY HE CHOSE THE FRENCH TRANSLATION OF "NEVER NEVER," HE SAID HIS DAUGHTER, FOURTEEN-YEAR-OLD CHARLIZE WYNWOOD, ACTUALLY DECIDED ON THE NAME. "SHE SAYS IT'S AN HOMAGE TO FAMILY HISTORY. NEVER FORGET THOSE WHO PAVED THE WAY BEFORE YOU. NEVER STOP TRYING TO BETTER THE WORLD FOR THOSE WHO WILL INHABIT IT AFTER YOU."

THE WYNWOOD FAMILY OCCUPIED THE HOME UNTIL 2013, WHEN IT WENT INTO FORECLOSURE FOLLOWING AN INVESTIGATION INTO WYNWOOD-NASH FINANCIAL GROUP. THE HOME WAS SOLD IN AUCTION IN LATE 2013 TO AN ANONYMOUS BIDDER.

I add the page to my favorites in my phone and make a note of the article. I found it after I pulled up to the property—right up to the locked gate.

The height of the gate is impressive, as if it's letting visitors know that the people beyond this gate are mightier than the people who are not.

I wonder if that's how Charlie's father felt living here. I wonder how mighty he felt when someone else took ownership of the property that's been in his family for generations.

The property is located at the end of an isolated road, as if the road belongs to the gate, too. After attempting to find a way around or through the gate, I conclude that there isn't one. It's dark now, so I could be missing a path or an alternate entrance. I'm not even sure why I want past the gate, but I can't help but feel like the pictures of this property are clues.

Considering I'm wanted for questioning, it's probably best if I don't drive around any more than I have to tonight, so I decide to stay here until morning. I turn off my car. If I'm going to be worth anything tomorrow, I need to try and get at least a few hours of sleep.

I lean my seat back, close my eyes and wonder if I'm going to dream tonight. I don't even know what I would dream about. I can't dream if I don't sleep, and I have a feeling falling asleep tonight is going to be impossible.

My eyes flick back open with that thought.

The video.

In one of my letters, I mentioned falling asleep to a video of Charlie sleeping. I search my phone until I find it. I press play and wait to hear Charlie's voice for the first time.

28

Charlie

More sleeping.

Not because of pills this time. I pretended to swallow them and kept them in my cheek. She stayed so long they were starting to dissolve. As soon as the door closed behind her, I spit them into my hand.

No more drowsiness. I need to be clear of mind.

I slept of my own accord and had more dreams earlier. Dreams of the same guy as in the first dream. Or should I say the first memory? In my dream, the guy was leading me through a dirty street. He wasn't looking at me, he was looking ahead, his whole body pulling forward like some invisible force had hold of him. In his left hand was a camera. He stopped suddenly and looked across the street. I followed his gaze.

"There," he said. "Look."

But I didn't want to look. I turned my back on what he was seeing, looked at a wall instead. Then all of a sudden, his hand was no longer in mine. I turned and watched him cross the street and approach a woman sitting cross-legged against a wall. In her arms she cradled a tiny baby wrapped in a woolen blanket. The guy crouched down in front of her. They spoke for a long time. He handed her something and she smiled. When he stood up, the baby started to cry. That's when he snapped the picture.

I could still see her face when I woke up, but it wasn't a real-life image, it was a photo. The one he took. A ragged mother with knotted hair, staring down at her infant, his tiny mouth open in a scream, their backdrop the chipped paint of a bright blue door.

When the dream was over, I wasn't sad like last time. I wanted to meet the boy who documented suffering in such vivid color.

I lie awake most of what I assume is the night. She returns with breakfast.

"You again," I say. "Never a day off…or an hour."

"Yup," she says. "We're understaffed, so I'm working doubles. Eat."

"Not hungry."

She offers me the cup of pills. I don't take them. "I want to see a doctor," I say.

"The doctor is very busy today. I can make an appointment for you. He can probably see you sometime next week."

"No. I want to see a doctor today. I want to know what medication you're giving me and I want to know why I'm here."

It's the first time I've seen anything but bored friendliness on her face. She leans forward, and I can smell the coffee on her breath. "Don't be a brat," she hisses.

"You don't get to make demands here, do you understand me?" She shoves the pills at me.

"I'm not taking those until a doctor tells me why I am," I say, nodding toward the cup. "Do *you* understand *me*?"

I think she's going to hit me. My hand feels for the piece of pipe under my pillow. The muscles in my shoulders and back tense, the balls of my feet press down on the tile. I am ready to spring if I need to. But the nurse turns, inserts her key into the door, and is gone. I hear the click of the lock, and then I'm alone again.

29

"I can't believe you got away with that," I say to her. I drop my hands to her waist, pushing her until her back is against her bedroom door. She places her palms against my chest and looks up at me with an innocent grin.

"Got away with what?"

I laugh and press my lips against her neck. "It's an *homage* to family *history*?" I laugh, moving my lips up her neck, drawing closer to her mouth. "What are you going to do if you ever want to break up with me? You'll be stuck living in a house that was named after the phrase you use with your ex-boyfriend."

She shakes her head and pushes against me so she can walk past me. "If I ever want to break up with you, I'll just have Daddy change the name of our house."

"He would never do that, Char. He thought the b.s. meaning you gave him was genius."

She shrugs. "Then I'll burn it to the ground." She sits on the edge of her mattress, and I take a seat next to her, pushing her onto her back. She giggles as I lean over her and cage her in with my hands. She's so beautiful.

I've always known she was beautiful, but this year has been really good to her. *Really* good. I look down at her chest. I can't help it. They've just gotten so...*perfect* this year.

"Do you think your boobs are finished growing?" I ask her. She laughs and slaps me on the shoulder. "You're disgusting."

I bring my fingers up to where her t-shirt scoops down at her neck. I trail my fingers across her chest until I meet the dip in her shirt. "When do you think you'll let me see them?"

"Jamais, jamais," she says with a laugh.

I groan. "Come on, Charlie baby. I've loved you for fourteen years now. That should earn me something— a quick peek, a hand up the shirt."

"We're fourteen, Silas. Ask me again when we're fifteen."

I smile. "That's only two months away for me." I press my lips to hers and can feel her chest rise against mine with her quick intake of breath. *God, the torture.*

Her tongue slips inside my mouth as her hand cradles the back of my head, pulling me closer. *The sweet, sweet torture.*

I lower my hand to her waist, inching her shirt up little by little until my fingers have access to her skin. I splay my hand out across her waist, feeling the heat from her body against my palm.

I continue to kiss her as my hand explores more of her, inch by inch, until one of my fingertips meets the fabric of her bra.

I want to keep going—to feel the softness beneath my fingertips. I want to— "Silas!"

Charlie sinks into the mattress. Her entire body is absorbed by the sheets, and I'm left palming her empty pillow.

What the hell? Where did she go? People don't just disappear into thin air.

"Silas, open the door!"

I squeeze my eyes shut. "Charlie? Where are you?"

"Wake up!"

I open my eyes and I'm no longer in Charlie's bed.

I'm no longer a fourteen-year-old boy about to touch a boob for the first time.

I'm… Silas. Lost and confused and sleeping in a damn car.

A fist pounds against my driver-side window. I allow my eyes a few more seconds to adjust to the sunlight pouring into my car before I look up.

Landon is standing at my door. I immediately sit up and turn around, looking behind me, to the sides of me.

It's only Landon. No one else is with him.

I reach for the handle on the door and wait for him to step aside before I swing it open. "Did you find her?" I ask, stepping out of my car.

He shakes his head. "No, they're still looking." He squeezes the back of his neck, just like I do when I'm nervous or stressed.

I open my mouth to ask him how he knew where to find me. But then I close my mouth after remembering I asked him about this house right before I hung up on him. Of course he would look here.

"You need to help them find her, Silas. You have to tell them everything you know."

I laugh. *Everything I know.* I lean against my car and fold my arms across my chest. I stop smiling at the ridiculousness of the situation, and I lock eyes with my little brother. "I don't know anything, Landon. I don't even know *you*. And as far as my memory is concerned, I've never even *met* Charlize Wynwood. How am I supposed to tell the police that?"

Landon's head is tilted. He's staring at me…silent and curious. He thinks I've gone crazy; I can see it in his eyes.

He might be right.

"Get in the car," I tell him. "I have a lot to tell you. Let's go for a drive."

I open my door and climb back inside. He waits several seconds, but then he walks to the car parked in the ditch. He locks it and then makes his way to my passenger door.

"Let me get this straight," he says, leaning forward in the booth. "You and Charlie have both been losing your memories for over a week now. You've both been writing yourselves letters. Those letters were in the backpack Janette found and turned in to the police. The only person who knows about this is some random tarot reader. It happens at the same time of day, every forty-eight hours, and you claim to have no recollection of what happened the day before she went missing?"

I nod.

Landon laughs and falls back against his seat. He shakes his head and picks up his drink, sticking the straw into his mouth. He takes a long sip and then sighs heavily as he returns his glass to the table.

"If this is your way of trying to get away with her

murder, you're going to need a much stronger alibi than a damn voodoo curse."

"She's not dead."

He raises a questioning eyebrow. I can't blame him. If the tables were turned, there's no way in hell I would believe everything that just came out of my mouth.

"Landon, I don't expect you to believe me. I really don't. It's ridiculous. But for the sake of shits and giggles, will you just humor me for a few hours? Just pretend you believe me and answer questions for me, even if you think I already know the answers. Then tomorrow you can turn me in to the police if you still think I'm crazy."

He shakes his head and looks disappointed. "Even if I thought you were crazy, I would never turn you in to the police, Silas. You're my brother." He motions for the waiter to come over and refill his drink. He takes a sip and then gets comfortable. "Okay. Fire away."

I smile. I knew I liked him for a reason.

"What happened between Brett and our father?"

Landon laughs under his breath. "This is ridiculous," he mutters. "You know more about that than I do." But then he leans forward and begins to answer my question. "An investigation was launched a couple of years ago due to an external audit. A lot of people lost a lot of money. Dad was cleared and Brett was charged with fraud."

"Is Dad really innocent?"

Landon shrugs. "I'd like to think he is. His name was dragged through the mud and he lost the majority of his business after what happened. He's been trying to rebuild it, but no one trusts him with their money now. But I guess we can't complain. We still fared better than Charlie's family did."

"Dad accused Charlie of taking some files from his office. What was he talking about?"

"They couldn't figure out where the money went, so they assumed Brett or Dad was hiding it in offshore accounts. There was a stretch before the trial where Dad didn't sleep for three days. He went through every detail of every transaction and every receipt recorded for the past ten years. One night he came out of his office holding a file. He said he found it, found where Brett was keeping the money. He finally had the information he needed to hold Brett responsible for the entire thing. He called his lawyer and told him he would deliver the evidence as soon as he got a couple hours of sleep. The next day…he couldn't find the files. He blew up on you, assuming you had warned Charlie about it. He believes to this day that Charlie took those files. She denied it. You denied it. And without the evidence he claimed to have, they could never charge Brett on all counts. He'll probably be out of jail in five years with good behavior, but from what Dad says, those files would have put him away for life."

Jesus. This is a lot to remember.

I hold up a finger. "I'll be right back." I slip out of the booth and run out of the restaurant, straight to my car. I search for more paper to take notes on. Landon is still at the booth when I return. I don't ask another question until I write everything down he just told me. And then I feed him a tidbit of information just to see how he responds.

"I'm the one who took those files," I say to Landon. I look up at him and his eyes are narrowed.

"I thought you said you can't remember anything."

I shake my head. "I can't. But I made a note about

some files I found that I was hiding. Why do you think I would take them if they would have proved Dad's innocence?"

Landon ponders my question for a moment then shakes his head. "I don't know. Whoever took them never did anything with them. So the only reason you would have hid them is to protect Charlie's father."

"Why would I want to protect Brett Wynwood?"

"Maybe you weren't protecting him for his own sake. Maybe you were doing it for Charlie."

I drop the pen. *That's it.* The only reason I would have taken those files is if I were doing it to protect Charlie.

"Was she close to her father?"

Landon laughs. "Very. She was a daddy's girl through and through. In all honesty, I think the only person she loved more than you was her father."

This feels like I'm unraveling a piece of a puzzle, even if it's not the puzzle I should be unraveling. Knowing the old Silas, he would have done anything to make Charlie happy. Which includes protecting her from knowing the truth about her father.

"What happened with me and Charlie after that? I mean…if she loved her father that much, you would think my father putting him behind bars would have made her never want to speak to me again."

Landon shakes his head. "You were all she had," he says. "You stuck by her side through it all, and nothing pissed Dad off more than knowing you didn't stand by his side a hundred percent."

"Did I think Dad was innocent?"

"Yeah," Landon says. "You just made it a point not to take sides when it came to him and Charlie. Unfortunately, to Dad that meant you were taking *their* side. The two of you haven't been on the best terms for the past year or two. The only time he speaks to you is when he's yelling at you from the stands at Friday night games."

"Why is he so obsessed with me playing football?"

Landon laughs again. "He's been obsessed with his sons attending his alma matter since before he knew he was having sons. He's shoved football down our throats since we could walk. I don't mind it, but you always hated it. And that makes him resent you even more, because you have a talent for it. It's in your blood. But you've never wanted anything more than to just be able to walk away from it." He smiles. "God, you should have seen him when he showed up last night and you weren't out on that field. He actually tried to have the game stopped until we could find you, but the officials wouldn't allow it."

I make a note of this. "You know... I can't remember how to play football."

A smirk plays on Landon's lips. "Now, that's the first thing you've said today that I actually believe. The other day when we were in a huddle, you seemed lost. *You. Do that thing.*" He laughs out loud. "So add that to your list. You forgot how to play football. How convenient."

I add it to the list.

Remember song lyrics.
Forgot people we know.
Remember people we don't know.
Remember how to use a camera.
Hate football, but I'm forced to play.
Forgot how to play football.

I stare at the list. I'm sure I had a lot more stuff written down on my old list, but I can hardly remember any of it.

"Let me see that," Landon says. He scrolls over the notes I've already taken. "Shit. You're really taking this seriously." He stares at it for a few seconds and then hands it back to me. "It seems like you can remember things you wanted to learn yourself, like song lyrics and your camera. But anything else you were taught, you forgot."

I pull the list in front of me and look at it. He might have a point, other than the fact that I can't remember people. I make a note of that and then continue with my questions.

"How long has Charlie been seeing Brian? Were we broken up?"

He runs his hand through his hair and takes a sip of his soda. He pulls his feet up and leans against the wall, stretching his legs out on the seat. "We're gonna be here all day, aren't we."

"If that's what it takes."

"Brian's always had a thing for Charlie and everyone knows it. You and Brian have never gotten along because of it, but you make it work for the sake of the football team. Charlie started to change after her father went to prison. She wasn't as nice...not that she's ever been the nicest. But lately, she's actually turned into somewhat of a bully. The two of you do nothing but fight now. I honestly think she hasn't been seeing him for that long. It started with her just giving him attention when you were around, so she could piss you off. I guess for her to continue that, she had to keep up appearances with him when they were alone. I don't buy it that she likes him, though. She's a hell of a lot smarter than he is, and if anyone was being used, it was Brian."

I'm writing everything down, but I'm also nodding

my head. I had a feeling she wasn't really into the guy. It seems like my relationship with Charlie was stretched as thin as air, and she was just doing what she could to test our strength.

"What are Charlie's religious beliefs? Was she known to be into voodoo or spells or anything like that?"

"Not that I know of," he says. "We were all raised Catholic. We don't really practice unless it's a significant holiday."

I make note of that and try to think of another question. I still have so many, and I don't know what to go with next. "Is there anything else? Anything out of the ordinary that happened last week?"

I can immediately tell he's hiding something by the change in his facial expression and the way he shifts in his seat.

"What is it?"

He pulls his feet off the seat and leans forward, lowering his voice. "The police...they were at the house today. I heard them questioning Ezra about finding anything unusual. At first she denied it, but I think her guilt got the best of her. She mentioned finding sheets in your room. She said there was blood on them."

I lean back against my booth and stare up at the ceiling. This isn't good. "Wait," I say, leaning forward again. "That was last week. Before Charlie went missing. It can't be tied to her if that's what they're thinking."

"No, I know that. Ezra told them that too. That it was last week and she saw Charlie that day. But still, Silas. What the hell were you doing? Why was there blood on your sheets? The way police think, they're probably assuming you beat Charlie or something, and that it finally went too far."

"I'd never hurt her," I say defensively. "I love that girl."

As soon as the words leave my mouth, I shake my head, not understanding why I even said them. I've never even met her. I've never even spoken to her.

But I'll be damned. I just said I love her, and I meant it straight to my core.

"How can you love her? You claim you can't remember her."

"I may not remember her, but I sure as hell still feel her." I stand up. "And that's why we need to find her. Starting with her father."

Landon tries to calm me down, but he has no idea how frustrating it is to lose eight entire hours when you only have forty-eight hours total.

It's after eight o'clock at night already, and we've officially wasted the entire day. As soon as we left the restaurant, we headed toward the prison to pay Brett Wynwood a visit. A prison that's almost three hours away. Couple that with a two-hour wait, only to be told we aren't on the visitor list and there's nothing we can do today to change it… I'm more than pissed.

I can't afford to make mistakes when I have just hours left to figure out where she is before I lose everything I've learned since yesterday.

We pull up next to Landon's car. I kill my ignition, step out of the car, and walk to the gate. There are two padlocks on it, and it looks like they're never used.

"Who bought this house?" I ask Landon.

I hear him laugh behind me, so I turn around. He sees that I lack humor in this situation, so he rolls his head.

"Come on, Silas. Drop the act, already. You know who bought the house."

I breathe steadily in through my nose and out my mouth, reminding myself that I can't blame him for thinking I'm making all of this up. I nod and then turn to face the gate again. "Humor me, Landon."

I can hear him kick at the gravel and groan. And then he says, "Janice Delacroix."

The name means nothing to me, but I walk back to my truck and open the door to make a note of the name. "Delacroix. Is that a French name?"

"Yeah," he says. "She owns one of those tourist shops downtown. Reads tarots or some shit like that. No one knows how she was able to afford the place. Her daughter goes to our school."

I stop writing. *The tarot reader.* That explains the picture, and also why she wouldn't give me more information on the house—because it seemed weird to her that I was asking about her home.

"So people actually *live* here?" I say, turning around to face him.

He shrugs. "Yeah. It's just the two of them, though—her and her daughter. They probably use a different entrance. Doesn't look like this gate gets opened much."

I stare past the gate…at the house. "What's her daughter's name?"

"Cora," he says. "Cora Delacroix. But everyone calls her The Shrimp."

30

Charlie

No one comes for a long time. I think I'm being punished. I'm thirsty and I need to go to the bathroom. After holding it as long as I can, I finally pee in the plastic cup on my breakfast tray and set the full cup in the corner of the room. I pace back and forth, pulling at my hair until I think I'm going to go crazy.

What if no one comes back? What if they've left me here to die?

The door won't budge; I bruise my fists pounding on it. I scream for someone to help me until my voice grows hoarse.

I'm sitting on the floor with my head in my hands when the door finally opens. I jump up. It's not the nurse—it's someone else this time, younger. Her scrubs hang off her small body. She looks like a little kid playing dressup. I eye her warily as she moves across my small room. She notices the cup in the corner and raises her eyebrows.

"Do you need to use the facilities?" she asks.

"Yes."

She sets the tray down and my stomach grumbles. "I asked to see the doctor," I say.

Her eyes dart left to right. *She's nervous. Why?*

"The doctor is busy today," she says, not looking at me.

"Where is the other nurse?"

"It's her day off," she says.

I can smell the food. I am so hungry. "I need to use the bathroom," I say. "Can you take me?"

She nods her head, but she looks afraid of me. I follow her out of the little room and into the small hallway. What kind of hospital has the toilets in a separate area from their patients' rooms? She stands off to the side while I use the restroom, wringing her hands and turning an awful shade of pink.

When I'm finished, she makes the mistake of turning toward the door. When she opens it, I pull the piece of pipe from my hospital gown and hold it toward her neck.

She faces me again and her beady eyes grow wide with fear.

"Drop the keys and back up slowly," I say. "Or I'll stick this straight in your throat."

She nods. The keys clank against the ground, and I advance toward her, my weapon extended toward her neck. I push her backward, into the room, and shove her down on the bed. She falls back and cries out.

Then I'm out the door, taking the keys with me. I pull the door shut as she flies toward it, her mouth open in a scream. We struggle for a moment, her trying to yank it open while I get the key into the lock and hear the metal click.

My hands are shaking as I sort through the keys, trying to find the right one to open the next door. I don't really know what to expect when I step through. A hospital hallway, nurses and doctors? Will someone be there to drag me back to that tiny room?

No.

There's no way I'm going back. I'll hurt anyone who tries to stop me from getting out of here.

I don't see a hospital or staff or anyone else when I open the door. What I see instead is a very impressive wine cellar. Dusty bottles sit in hundreds of little holes. It smells of ferment and dirt. A staircase runs up one side of the cellar. There is a door at the top.

I run for the stairs, stubbing my toe hard on the concrete and feeling the wet blood run over my foot. I almost slip on it, but I catch onto the railing in time.

The top of the stairs opens to a kitchen, a single light illuminating the counters and floors. I don't pause to look around. I need to find…a door! I grab the handle, and this time it's not locked. I cry out in triumph as it flies open. The night air hits me in the face. I breathe it in gratefully.

Then I run.

31

Silas

"You can't trespass, Silas!" Landon yells.

I'm trying to scale the gate, but my foot keeps slipping. "Help me over," I yell down to him.

He walks up to me and offers his hands, palms up, despite the fact that he's still verbally trying to stop me from climbing over. I step into his hands and he hoists me higher, allowing me to grab the bars toward the top of the gate.

"I'll be back in ten minutes. I just want to check out the property." I know he doesn't believe a word I've said today, so I leave out the fact that I think this Cora girl knows something. If she's inside that house, I'm going to force her to talk to me.

I finally make it to the top and down the other side. When my feet hit the dirt, I stand up. "Don't leave until I get back."

I turn and take a look at the house. It's about two hundred yards away, hidden behind rows of Weeping Willow trees. They look like long arms, swaying toward the front door, coercing me to move forward.

I slowly make my way down the path that leads to the porch. It's a beautiful house. I can see why Charlie missed it so much. I look up at the windows. Two of them are lit up on the top floor, but the bottom floor is completely dark.

I'm almost to the porch that extends across the entire front of the house. My heart is racing in my chest so fast that I can actually hear it. Other than the occasional insect noise and the pounding of my pulse, it's completely quiet out here.

Until it's not.

The bark is so loud and so close, it rumbles in my stomach and vibrates through my chest. I can't see where it's coming from.

I freeze in my tracks, careful not to make any sudden movements.

A deep growl rolls through the air like thunder. I slowly look over my shoulder without turning my body.

The dog is standing behind me, lips pulled back in a snarl, teeth so white and sharp they look like they're glowing.

He rears back on his hind legs, and before I can run or look around for something to fight him off, he's in the air, lunging toward me.

Straight for my throat.

I can feel his teeth pierce the skin on the back of my hand, and I know if I hadn't covered my throat, those teeth would be in my jugular right now. The massive strength of this animal knocks me to the ground. I can feel the flesh give way on my hand as he thrashes his head from side to side and I try to fight him off.

But then something slams into it or on top of it—a whimper and then a thud.

And then silence.

It's too dark to see what just happened. I take a deep breath and try to stand.

I look down at the dog, and a sharp piece of metal is protruding from his neck. Blood is pooling around his head, tinting the grass the color of midnight.

And then a strong scent of flowers...*lilies*...surrounds me in a rush of wind.

"It's you."

I recognize her voice immediately, even though it comes out in a whisper. She's standing to the right of me, her face illuminated by the moonlight. Tears are streaking their way down her cheeks, and her hand is cupped over her mouth. She's wide-eyed, staring at me in shock.

She's here. She's alive.

I want to take her in my arms and hug her and tell her it's okay, that we're going to figure this out. But she more than likely has no idea who I am.

"Charlie?"

She slowly lowers her hand away from her mouth. "My name is Charlie?" she asks.

I nod. The terrified expression on her face slowly transforms into relief. She steps forward and throws her arms around my neck, pressing her face against my chest. Sobs begin to rack her body now.

"We need to leave," she says through her tears. "We have to get out of here before they find me."

Find her?

I wrap my arms around her long enough to hug her, and then I take her hand and we run toward the gate. When Landon sees Charlie, he rushes to the gate and begins to shake the locks. He tries to find a way to get us out so she doesn't have to climb over, but he can't.

"Use my car," I tell him. "Bend the gate. We have to hurry."

He looks back at my car and then again at me. "You want me to break open the gate? Silas, that car is your baby."

"I don't give a shit about the car!" I yell. "We need out!"

He acts fast, running straight to the car. As he climbs inside, he yells, "Get out of the way!" He puts the car in reverse and backs up, then slams on the gas.

The sound of iron on metal isn't nearly as loud as the sound my heart makes seeing the car being torn to shreds. At least I wasn't that attached to it. I've only known it less than two days.

He has to back up and drive forward two more times to bend the iron enough for Charlie and me to slip through. Once we're on the other side of the gate, I open the back door to Landon's car and help her inside.

"Just leave my car here," I tell him. "We can worry about it later."

When we're all in the car and finally heading away from the house, Landon picks up his cell phone. "I'll call Dad and tell him you found her so he can notify the police."

I grab the cell phone from his hands. "No. No police."

He slams his hand against the steering wheel in frustration. "Silas, you have to tell them she's okay! This is ridiculous. You're both being completely ridiculous with this."

I turn in my seat and stare at him pointedly. "Landon, you have to believe me. Charlie and I are going to forget everything we know in a little over twelve hours from now. I have to get her to a hotel so I can explain everything to her, and then I need time to make notes. If we notify the police, they might split us up for questioning. I need to be with her when this happens again. I don't care if you don't believe me, but you're my brother and I need you to do this for me."

He doesn't respond to my request. We're at the end of the road now, and I can see the roll of his throat as he swallows, trying to decide whether to turn left or right.

"Please," I ask him. "I just need until tomorrow."

He releases a pent-up breath and then turns right—the opposite direction from our homes. I breathe a sigh of relief. "I owe you one."

"More like a million," he mutters.

I look in the backseat at Charlie, and she's staring at me, obviously terrified by what she's hearing.

"What do you mean this will happen again tomorrow?" she asks, her voice trembling.

I crawl into the backseat with her and pull her to me. She melts against my chest, and I can feel her heart racing against mine. "I'll explain everything at the hotel."

She nods, and then, "Did he call you Silas? Is that your name?"

Her voice is raspy, like she's screamed herself hoarse. I don't even want to think about what she's been through since yesterday.

"Yeah," I tell her, rubbing my hand up and down her arm. "Silas Nash."

"Silas," she says softly. "I've been wondering what your name was since yesterday."

I immediately stiffen and look down at her. "What

do you mean you've been wondering? How do you remember me?"

"I dreamt about you."

She dreamt about me.

I pull my short list of notes from my pocket and ask Landon for a pen. He pulls one out of his console and hands it to me. I make a note about the dreams and how Charlie knew me without having memory of me. I also note that my own dream about her felt more like a memory. Could our dreams be clues to our past?

Charlie watches me as I write down everything that has transpired in the last hour. She never questions me, though. I fold the paper up and slide it back into my pocket.

"So what's the deal with us?" she asks. "Are we like… in love and shit?"

I laugh out loud for the first time since yesterday morning. "Yeah," I say, still laughing. "Apparently I've been in love and shit with you for eighteen years now."

I told Landon to come to our hotel room at eleven thirty tomorrow morning. If this happens again, we'll need time to adjust and read the notes to get acclimated to our situation. He was hesitant, but he finally agreed. He said he would tell Dad he's been out looking for us all day with no luck.

I feel bad for making people worry until tomorrow, but I'm not about to put myself in a situation where I let her out of my sight again. Hell, I wouldn't even let her shut the door when she said she wanted to take a shower. A *warm* shower, she clarified.

When we got to the hotel, I told her everything I knew. Which, once I laid it all out, didn't seem like much.

She told me what had happened to her since yesterday morning. I'm relieved it was nothing too serious, but disturbed that they were holding her in the basement. Why would The Shrimp and her mother be keeping Charlie against her will? The woman was obviously trying to mislead me yesterday when she said, *"The answers to your questions lie with someone who is very close to you."*

Yeah, I'd say. The person with answers was *very* close to me. A mere two feet away.

I feel like this information is one of the best leads we've gotten in the past week, but I have no idea why they were holding her captive. That's the first thing I want us to figure out tomorrow. Which is why I'm ensuring our notes are detailed and precise, so we can get an even better head start.

I've already made a note for Charlie to go to the police station and ask for all her belongings to be returned to her. They can't keep them now that she's no longer missing, and we desperately need those letters and journals. The key to everything could be written in there somewhere, and until it's all back in our possession, we're completely stuck.

The bathroom door opens wider, and I hear her walking toward the bed. I'm sitting at the desk, still writing notes. I glance up at her as she sits on the mattress, her feet dangling off the edge of the bed as she watches me.

I expected after her ordeal that she'd be more shaken up, but she's tough. She listened intently when I explained everything I knew, and she never once doubted me. She even threw out a few theories herself.

"Knowing me, I'll probably try to run tomorrow if I wake up in a hotel room with a guy I've never met," she says. "I should probably write myself a note and stick it over the door handle, telling myself to wait until at least noon before I hightail it out of here."

See? Tough *and* smart.

I hand her a piece of paper and a pen, and she writes herself a note and then walks it to the hotel room door.

"We should try to get some sleep," I tell her. "If this does happen again, we need to be well rested."

She nods in agreement and climbs onto the bed. I didn't even bother asking for two beds. I don't know why. Not that I have any ideas about how the night's going to play out. I think I'm just extremely protective of her. The thought of not knowing she's right next to me makes me too uncomfortable, even if it would have been a different bed just two feet away.

I set the alarm for ten thirty in the morning. That'll give us time to wake up and prepare, while hopefully giving us a good six hours of sleep. I turn out the lights and crawl into bed beside her.

She's on her side and I'm on mine, and I'm doing everything I can to not scoot over and spoon her, or at least put my arm around her. I don't want to freak her out, but it also somehow feels natural for me to do those things.

I fluff my pillow and turn it over so the colder side is against my cheek. I face the wall and keep my back to her to make sure she doesn't feel uncomfortable having to share a bed with me.

"Silas?" she whispers.

I like her voice. It's comforting yet electric. "Yeah?"

I can feel her roll over to face me, but my back is still to her. "I don't know why, but I feel like we'll both sleep better if you have your arms around me. Not touching you seems more awkward than touching you."

Even though it's dark in the room, I try to fight my smile. I immediately roll over, and she scoots back against my chest. I wrap my arm around her and pull her closer, her body curving perfectly into mine, her feet locking around my feet.

This.

This must have been why I felt an unwavering need to find her. Because until this very second, I didn't know Charlie wasn't the only one missing. When she disappeared, part of me must have disappeared right along with her. Because this is the first time I feel like me—like Silas Nash—since the second I woke up yesterday.

She finds my hand in the dark and slides her fingers through mine. "Are you scared, Silas?"

I sigh, hating that she's falling asleep thinking about it. "I'm worried," I tell her. "I don't want it to happen again. But I'm not scared, because this time I know where you are."

If it were possible to hear a smile, hers would be a love song. "Goodnight, Silas," she says quietly.

Her shoulders rise and fall when she lets out a deep sigh. Her breathing begins to taper off after only a few minutes, and I know she's asleep.

Before I close my eyes, she readjusts her position slightly and I catch a glimpse of her tattoo. The silhouette of trees is peeking out of the top of the back of her shirt.

I wish there was a letter that would have described the night we got these tattoos. I would give anything to have that memory back—to see what it was like between us when we loved each other enough to believe it was forever.

Maybe I'll dream about that night if I fall asleep

thinking about it. I close my eyes, knowing this is exactly how it's supposed to be. Charlie and Silas.

Together.

I don't know why we ever started drifting apart, but I'm certain of one thing: I'll never allow it to happen again.

I press a soft kiss into her hair. Something I've probably done a million times, but the drunken, one-winged moths fluttering around in my stomach make it feel like the very first time.

"Goodnight, Charlie baby."

32

Charlie

I wake up to sunlight.

It's streaming through the window and warming my face. I roll over to look for Silas, but his pillow is empty.

For a moment, I'm afraid that he's left me, or that someone has taken him. But then I hear the clink of a cup and the sound of him moving. I squeeze my eyes shut gratefully. I can smell food. I roll over.

"Breakfast," he says. I crawl out of bed feeling self-conscious about the way I must look. I comb my fingers through my hair and wipe the sleep from my eyes. Silas is sitting at the desk, sipping on coffee and writing something down on paper.

I pull up a chair and seat myself across from him and grab a croissant, tucking my hair behind my ears. I don't want to eat, but I do anyway. He wants us to be well rested and fed before the clock strikes 11am. But my stomach is full of nerves, thinking about how it felt waking up with no memory two days ago. I don't want that to happen again. I didn't like it then, and I won't like it this time.

Every few seconds, he glances up at me and our eyes lock before he goes back to work. He looks nervous too.

After the croissant, I eat bacon, then the eggs, then a bagel. I finish off Silas's coffee, drink my orange juice, and push my chair back from the table. He smiles and taps the side of his mouth. I reach up and dust the crumbs off my face, feeling warmth rise to my cheeks. He's not laughing at me though. I know that.

He hands me a toothbrush still in its package and follows me to the bathroom. We brush our teeth together, eyeing each other in the mirror. His hair is standing on end, and mine is tangled. It's sort of comical. I can't believe I'm in the same room as the boy from my dreams. It feels surreal.

I look at the clock as we leave the bathroom. We have ten minutes to go. Silas has his notes ready, as do I. We lay them out on the bed so it's all circling us. Everything we know is here. This time is going to be different. We're together. We have Landon. We're going to figure this thing out.

We sit, facing each other on the bed, our knees touching. From where I sit, I can see the red letters of the alarm clock hit 10:59.

One minute. My heart is racing. I'm so afraid.

I begin the countdown in my head. *59...58...57...56...*

I count down to thirty, and Silas suddenly leans forward. His hands cup my face. I can smell him; feel his breath on my lips.

I lose the time. I have no idea what second I'm supposed to be on. "Never never," he whispers. His warmth, his lips, his hands.

He presses his mouth to mine and kisses me deeply and I...

PART 3

33

Charlie

The first thing I notice is the pounding in my chest. It's so fast it's painful. Why would a heart need to pound this hard? I breathe deeply through my nose and open my eyes on the exhale.

Then I throw myself back.

Luckily, I'm on a bed and I tumble onto a mattress. I roll away from the man staring intently at me, and land on my feet. I squint at him while backing up. He's watching me, but he hasn't moved. This eases the pounding in my chest a little. *A little.*

He's young. Not quite a man, maybe late teens or early twenties. I have the urge to run. A door… I need to find a door, but if I take my eyes off him, he may…

"Who the hell are you?" I ask. It doesn't matter who he is. I just need to distract him while I find a way out of here.

He's quiet for a moment as he sizes me up. "I was about to ask you the same thing," he says.

His voice makes me stop shuffling sideways for a few seconds. It's deep…calm. Deeply calm. Maybe I'm overreacting. I make to answer him—which would be the reasonable thing to do when someone asks you who you are—but I can't.

"I asked you first," I say. Why does my own voice sound so unfamiliar?

I raise a hand to my throat and wrap it around my neck.

"I…" he hesitates. "I don't know?"

"You don't know?" I say in disbelief. "How could you not know?"

I spot the door and edge closer, keeping my eyes on him. He's on his knees on the bed, but he looks tall. His shoulders are wide and pull against the t-shirt he's wearing. If he comes at me, I doubt I'd be able to fight him off. My wrists look small. *Look* small? Why don't I know that my wrists *are* small?

This is it. I have to do it.

I dart for the door. It's only a few feet away; if I can get it open I can run for help. I scream as I run. It's bloodcurdling, a real ear sore. My hand wraps around the knob and I look back to see where he is.

He's in the same spot, his eyebrows raised. "Why are you screaming?"

I stop. "Why…why aren't you coming after me?" I'm right in front of the door. Technically I can open the door and run out of here before he's even off the bed. He knows that, and *I* know that, so why isn't he trying to stop me?

He passes a hand over his face and shakes his head, sighing deeply. "What's your name?" he asks.

I open my mouth to tell him it's none of his business,

and then realize that I don't know. I don't know what my freaking name is.

In that case… "Delilah."

"Delilah…?" he asks.

It's pretty dark, but I swear he's smiling. "Yeah…is that not good enough for you?"

He shakes his head. "Delilah's a great name," he says. "Listen… *Delilah.* I don't know exactly what we're doing here, but right behind your head there's a piece of paper stuck to the door. Can you pull that off and read it?"

I'm afraid that if I turn around he'll attack me. I reach a hand back without looking and feel around. I pull the piece of paper off the door and bring it in front of my face.

Charlie! Don't open this door yet! That guy in the room with you…you can trust him. Walk back to the bed and read all the notes. They'll explain everything.

"I think it's for you," I tell him. "Is your name Charlie?" I look back up at the guy on the bed. He's reading something too. He looks up and holds a small white rectangle toward me.

"Look at it," he says.

I take a step forward, and then another, and then another. It's a driver's license. I study the picture and then his face. Same person.

"If your name is Silas, who is Charlie?"

"You are," he says.

"I am?"

"Yes."

He bends to pick up a piece of notebook paper from

the bed. "It says so right here." He holds the paper out to me and I hand him back his driver's license.

"Charlie isn't a girl's name," I say. I start to read what's written on the pages and everything else falls away. I drop heavily to the edge of the bed and sit down.

"What the hell?"

The Silas guy is reading too. His eyes trace over the paper he holds in front of his face. I sneak looks at him while he's reading, and when I do, my heart beats a little bit faster.

I read more. I grow more and more confused. The notes are supposedly from me and this guy, but nothing makes any sense. As I'm reading, I grab a nearby pen and copy the paper I found on the door, to see if I really *did* write it myself.

The handwriting is a perfect match.

"Whoa, whoa, whoa!" I say. "This is nuts!" I put the page down and shake my head. How can any of this be true? It's like reading a novel. Lost memories, fathers who betrayed their families, voodoo. *My God.* Suddenly I feel like I want to barf.

Why can't I remember who I am? What I did yesterday? If what these notes say are true…

I'm about to voice this when Silas hands me another sheet of paper.

You only have 48 hours. Do not focus on why you can't remember things or how weird it all feels. Focus on figuring this out before you forget again.

Charlie

It's my handwriting again. "I'm convincing," I say. He nods.

"So…where are we?" I turn around in a full circle, noticing the freshly eaten food on the table. Silas points to one of those little paper tents on the nightstand. A hotel. In New Orleans. *Great.*

I'm walking toward the window to take a peek outside when there's a knock at the hotel door. We both freeze and look in that direction.

"Who is it?" Silas yells at the door.

"It's *me!*" a voice replies.

Silas motions for me to go stand on the other side of the room, away from the door. I don't.

I've only known myself for a few minutes, but I can tell I'm stubborn.

Silas unlatches the deadbolt and pulls the door open just a little. A scruffy brown head bobs around the door.

"Hey," the boy says. "I'm back. 11:30 sharp, just like you said."

He has his hands stuffed in his pockets and his face is red like he's been running. I look from him to Silas, and back to him. They look alike.

"You know each other?" I ask.

The younger, lookalike version of Silas nods his head. "We're brothers." He says this loudly while pointing first to Silas and then himself. "I am your brother," he says again, looking at Silas.

"So you said," Silas says with a slight grin on his face. He glances at me, then back at Landon. "Mind if I take a look at your ID?"

The boy rolls his eyes but pulls a wallet out of his back pocket.

"I like that cool rolling-your-eyes thing you have going on," Silas says as he opens the boy's wallet.

"What's your name?" I ask him.

He tilts his head, narrowing his eyes at me. "I'm *Landon*," he tells me, as if I should know this. "The better-looking Nash brother."

I smile weakly as Silas looks over Landon's ID. He's a good kid. You can tell by his eyes.

"So," I say, looking at Silas. "You don't know who you are, either? And we're trying to figure this all out together? And every forty-eight hours we forget again?"

"Yeah," he says. "Sounds about right." This feels like a dream. Not reality.

And then it hits me. *I'm dreaming.* I burst into laughter, just as Landon hands me a sack. I think my laughter caught him by surprise.

"What's this?" I ask, opening the sack.

"You asked me to bring you a change of clothes."

I look down at the gown I'm wearing, and then at the clothes. "Why am I wearing this?"

He shrugs. "That's what you were wearing last night when Silas found you."

Silas pushes open the bathroom door for me. The clothes have tags on them, so I pull them off and begin to change. A cute black top with long sleeves and jeans that fit like they were made for me. *Who gets new clothes in their dreams?*

"I love this dream!" I yell through the bathroom door.

When I'm finished changing, I swing open the door and clap my hands together. "All right, boys. Let's go. Where to?"

34

Silas

I make a quick check of the hotel room as Charlie and Landon file out. I grab the empty trash sack out of the small can under the desk and shove all of our notes into it. When I'm certain I have everything, I follow Charlie and Landon outside.

Charlie is still smiling when we reach the car. She honestly thinks this is a dream, and I don't have the heart to tell her it isn't. It's not a dream. It's actually a nightmare and we've been living it for more than a week now.

Landon climbs inside the car, but Charlie waits for me by the back door. "You want to ride in the front with your *brother*?" she asks, forming air quotes with her fingers.

I shake my head and reach around her to open the door. "No, you can ride in the front." She begins to turn when I grab her arm. I lean down to her ear and whisper. "You aren't dreaming, Charlie. This is real. Something is happening to us and you need to take it seriously so we can figure it out, okay?"

When I pull back, her eyes are wide. The smile is gone from her face and she doesn't nod. She just gets in the car and closes the door.

I claim my spot in the backseat and pull my phone out of my pocket.

There's a reminder set on it, so I open it.

Go to the police station first. Get the backpack and read every note and journal entry you can... as fast as you can.

I close out the reminder, knowing I'll get about five more reminders in the next two hours. I know this... because I remember setting every single one of them last night.

I remember writing all the notes in this small hotel trash bag that I have clutched tightly in my hand.

I remember grabbing hold of Charlie's face right before the clock struck 11:00am.

I remember whispering *never never* to her, right before I kissed her.

And I remember ten seconds after our lips touched... she pulled back and had no idea who I was. She had no memory of the last forty-eight hours.

Yet... I remembered every single minute of the last two days.

I just couldn't tell her the truth. I didn't want to scare her, and making her believe I was in the same situation as her seemed to be the more comforting option.

I don't know why I didn't forget this time, or why she did. I should be relieved that whatever the hell has been going on with us seems to be over for me, but I'm not relieved at all. I'm disappointed. I would rather have lost my memory again with her than to have her be alone in this. At least when we were in it together, we knew it was something we could work out together.

What seemed to be a pattern has now been broken, and I feel like this just makes it even more difficult to figure out. Why was I spared this time? Why was she not? Why do I feel like I can't be honest with her? Have I always shouldered this much guilt?

I still don't know who I am, or who I used to be. I only have the last forty-eight hours to go by, which isn't much. But it's still better than the half hour of memories Charlie has.

I should just be honest with her, but I can't. I don't want this to scare her, and I feel like the only comfort she has right now is knowing she's not alone in this.

Landon keeps glancing back at me, and then looking at her. I know he thinks we've lost our minds. We sort of *did* lose our minds, but not in the way he's thinking.

I like him. I wasn't sure if he'd show up this morning like I asked him to, since he's still doubtful. I like that he doubts us, but his loyalty to me trumps his reasoning. I'm sure very few people have that quality.

We're mostly quiet on the way to the police station, until Charlie turns to Landon and glares at him.

"How do you know we aren't lying to you?" she asks him. "Why would you even humor us unless you have something to do with what's happened to us?" She's more suspicious of him than she is of me.

Landon grips the steering wheel and glances at me in the rearview mirror. "I *don't* know that you both aren't lying. For all I know, you're getting a kick out of this. Ninety percent of me thinks you two are full of shit and have nothing better to do. Five percent of me thinks maybe you're telling the truth."

"That's only ninety-five percent," I pipe in from the backseat.

"That's because the other five percent of me thinks *I'm* the one who has gone crazy," he says.

Charlie laughs at that.

We pull into the police station and Landon finds a parking spot. Before he turns off the car, Charlie says, "Just to be clear, what do I need to say? That I'm here for my backpack?"

"I'll go in with you," I tell her. "The note said everyone thought you were missing and that I was suspected in your disappearance. If we go in together, they'll have no reason to pursue anything further."

She gets out of the car, and as we're walking into the police station, she says, "Why don't we just tell them what's going on? That we can't remember anything?"

I pause with my hand on the door. "Because, Charlie. We specifically warned ourselves in the notes *not* to do that. I'd rather trust the versions of ourselves we don't remember than trust people who don't know us at all."

She nods. "Good point," she says. She pauses and cocks her head to the side. "I wonder if you're smart."

Her comment makes me chuckle.

There's no one in the lobby area when we walk in. I approach a glass window. There's no one behind the desk, but there's a speaker, so I press the button next to it, hearing it crackle to life.

"Hello?" I ask. "Anyone here?"

"Coming!" I hear a woman yell. A few seconds later, she appears behind the desk. Her eyes grow alarmed when she sees Charlie and me.

"Charlie?" she asks.

Charlie nods, wringing her hands together nervously. "Yeah," she says. "I'm here for my stuff. A backpack?"

The woman stares at Charlie for a few seconds and her eyes drop to Charlie's hands. The way Charlie is standing makes her look nervous…like she's hiding something. The woman tells us she'll go see what she can do, and she disappears around the desk again.

"Try to relax," I whisper to Charlie. "Don't make it look like I forced you to do this. They're already suspicious of me."

Charlie folds her hands over her chest, nods, and then brings her thumb to her mouth. She begins to bite the pad of it. "I don't know how to look relaxed," she says. "I'm *not* relaxed. I'm confused as hell."

The woman doesn't return, but a door to our left opens and a uniformed officer appears in the doorway. He looks over at Charlie and then me. He motions for us to follow him.

He walks into an office and proceeds to sit behind his desk. He nods at the two chairs opposite him, so we both take a seat. He doesn't look at all pleased when he leans forward and clears his throat.

"Do you realize how many people we have looking for you right now, young lady?"

Charlie stiffens. I can feel the confusion roll off of her. I know she's still trying to grasp what's happened in the last hour, so I answer for her.

"We're really sorry," I say to him. His eyes remain on Charlie for a few seconds, and then slide to me. "We got in a fight. She decided to disappear for a few days to process everything. She didn't know anyone would be looking for her, or that she would be reported missing."

The officer looks bored with me. "I appreciate your ability to answer for your girlfriend, but I'd really like to hear what Ms. Wynwood has to say." He stands, towering over us, and motions toward the door. "Wait outside, Mr. Nash. I'd like to speak to her alone."

Shit.

I don't want to leave her alone with him. I hesitate, but Charlie places a reassuring hand on my arm. "It's fine. Wait outside," she says. I look at her closely, but she seems confident. I stand up a little too forcefully and the chair makes an awful screeching sound as it scoots backward. I don't look at the officer again. I walk out, close his door behind me, and begin pacing the empty lobby.

Charlie emerges a few minutes later with a backpack slung over her shoulder and a smug grin on her face. I smile back at her, knowing I never should have believed that her nerves would get the best of her. This is the fourth time she's started from scratch, and she seems to have made it through the first few times okay. This time shouldn't be any different.

She doesn't sit in the front seat this time. When we approach the car, she says, "Let's both sit in the back so we can go through all this stuff."

Landon is already annoyed that he thinks we've carried out what he thinks is a prank for so long, and now we're forcing him to chauffer us around.

"Where to now?" Landon asks.

"Just drive us around until we figure out where we want to go next," I say.

Charlie unzips the backpack and begins rifling through it. "I think we should go to the prison," she says. "My father might have some sort of explanation."

"Again?" Landon asks. "Silas and I tried that yesterday. They wouldn't let us speak to him."

"But I'm his daughter," she says. She glances over at me as if she's silently asking for my approval.

"I agree with Charlie," I say. "Let's go see her father."

Landon sighs heavily. "I can't wait until this is over," he says, making a sharp right out of the driveway of the police station. "Ridiculous," he mutters. He reaches for the radio and turns up the volume, drowning us out.

We begin pulling items out of the backpack. There are two separate stacks I remember making a couple of days ago when I first began going through these items. One of them is useful to us, one is not. I hand Charlie the journals and I begin sorting through letters, hoping she doesn't notice I'm skipping some of the ones I know I've already read.

"All these journals are full," she says, flipping through them. "If I wrote this much and this often, wouldn't I have one that's current? I can't find one from this year."

She makes a good point. When I was in her attic taking all of this stuff, I didn't notice anything that looked like she was actively using it. I shrug. "Maybe we missed it when we grabbed all of these."

She leans forward and talks over the music. "I want to go to my house," she says to Landon. She falls back against the seat, clutching the backpack to her chest. She doesn't continue going through the letters or journals. She just quietly stares out the window while we approach her neighborhood.

When we arrive at her house, she hesitates before opening the car door. "This is where I live?" she asks.

I'm sure she wasn't expecting this, yet I can't reassure

her or warn her about what she'll find inside because she still believes I lost my memories, too.

"Do you want me to go inside with you?"

She shakes her head. "That's probably not a good idea. Our notes said you should stay away from my mother."

"True," I say. "Well, the notes said we found all this stuff in your attic. Maybe check your bedroom this time. If you had a journal you actively wrote in, it's probably near where you sleep."

She nods and then exits the car and begins walking toward her house. I watch until she disappears inside.

I can see Landon watching me suspiciously in the rearview mirror. I avoid eye contact with him. I know he already doesn't believe us, but if he finds out I have any memory of the last forty-eight hours, he'll *definitely* think I'm lying. And then he'll stop helping us.

I find a letter I haven't read yet and begin to open it when the back door opens. Charlie tosses a box inside the car and I'm relieved to see she found more stuff, including another journal. She slides into the car when the front door opens. I glance in the front seat to see Janette joining the party.

Charlie leans over until our shoulders are touching. "I think she's my sister," she whispers. "She doesn't seem to like me very much."

Janette's car door slams shut and she immediately turns around in her seat and glares at me. "Thanks for letting me know my sister is alive, asshole." She faces the front again and I catch Charlie suppressing a laugh.

"Are you serious?" Landon says, staring across the front seat at Janette.

He doesn't seem at all pleased that Janette is tagging along.

She rolls her head and groans. "Oh, come on," she says to Landon. "It's been a year since we broke up. It's not going to kill you to sit in the same car with me. Besides, I'm not staying home all day with Loco Laura."

"Holy shit," Charlie mutters. She leans forward. "You two used to date?"

Landon nods. "Yeah. But it was a loooong time ago. And it lasted like a week." He throws the car in reverse and begins backing out.

"*Two* weeks," Janette specifies.

Charlie looks at me and raises an eyebrow. "And the plot thickens…" she says.

I personally think Janette's presence will be more intrusive than helpful. At least Landon knows what's going on with us. Janette doesn't seem like she would take something like this very well.

She pulls a tube of lip-gloss out of her purse and begins applying it in the passenger mirror. "So where are we going?"

"To see Brett," Charlie replies nonchalantly as she rifles through the box in the backseat.

Janette spins around in her seat. "Brett? As in *Dad*? We're going to see *Dad*?"

Charlie nods as she pulls out her journal. "Yes," she says. She looks up at Janette. "If you have a problem with that, we can take you back home."

Janette clamps her mouth shut and slowly turns back around. "I don't have a problem with it," she says. "But I'm not getting out of the car. I don't want to see him."

Charlie raises an eyebrow at me and then settles back in her seat, opening the journal. A folded letter falls out and she begins to open that one first. She inhales a breath and then looks at me and says, "Well. Here we go, *Silas baby*. Let's get to know each other." She opens the letter and begins to read.

I open a letter I've yet to read and settle into my seat as well. "Here we go, *Charlie baby*."

35

Charlie

Charlie baby, My mom saw my tattoo. I thought I'd be able to hide it for a couple of years, but dammit if I wasn't taking off the bandage this morning when she walked into my room without knocking.

She hasn't walked into my room without knocking in three years! I think she assumed I wasn't home. You should have seen her face when she realized what I had done. The tattoo alone was bad enough. I can't imagine what would have happened had she realized it was a representation of you.

Thank you for that, by the way. Hidden meanings of our names was a much better suggestion than actually tattooing each other's names. I told her the strand of pearls was a symbol of the pearly gates of heaven, or some shit like that. After that explanation, she couldn't argue much, seeing as she's in church every time the doors are open.

She wanted to know who did my tattoo since I'm only sixteen, but I refused to tell her. I'm surprised she didn't guess because I'm pretty sure it was just last month that I mentioned Andrew's older brother was a tattoo artist.

Anyway. She was upset, but I swore to her I wouldn't get another one. She told me to make sure I never take off my shirt in front of Dad.

I'm still a little shocked we both went through with it. I was half kidding when I said we should do it, but when you seemed excited, I realized how serious I was. I know people say to never get a tattoo in honor of someone you're in a relationship with, and I know we're only sixteen, but I just don't see anything ever happening in this life that could make me not want you all over my skin.

I'll never love anyone like I love you. And if the worst is to ever happen and we do grow apart, I'll never regret this tattoo. You've been a huge part of my life for the sixteen years I've been alive, and whether we end up together in the end or not, I want to remember this part of my life. And maybe these tattoos were more of a commemorative thing than an assumption that we'll spend the rest of our lives together. Either way, I'd hope that fifteen years from now, we will look at these tattoos and be grateful for this chapter in our lives, and there won't be an ounce of regret. Whether we're together or not.

I will say, I think you're much tougher than me. I was expecting to have to be the one to calm you down and reassure you that the pain was only temporary, but it turned out to be the other way around. Maybe mine hurt more than yours. ;)

Okay, it's late. I'm about to call you and tell you goodnight, but true to form, I had to get all my thoughts out to you in a letter first. I know I've said it before, but I love that we still write letters to each other. Texts get deleted and conversations fade, but I swear I'll have every single letter you've ever written me until the day I die. #SnailMailForever

I love you. Enough to camouflage you into my skin.

Never stop. Never forget.

Silas

I glance across the seat at Silas, but he's engrossed in his own reading. I would like to see this tattoo in person, but I don't feel comfortable enough yet to ask him to take off his shirt.

I flip through more letters until I find one I've written to him. I'm curious to see if I'm half as in love as he seems to be.

Silas, I can't stop thinking about the other night when we kissed. Or your letter explaining how you felt about it.

I'd never kissed anyone before. I didn't close my eyes. I was too scared. In movies they close their eyes, but I couldn't make myself do it. I wanted to know if your eyes were closed, and what your lips looked like when they pressed against mine. And I wanted to know what time it was so I could always remember the exact moment we had our first kiss (it was 11 o'clock, by the way). And you kept your eyes closed the entire time.

After I left, I went home and I just stared at the wall for an hour. I could still feel your mouth on mine even if you weren't there anymore. It was crazy and I don't know if that's supposed to happen. And I'm sorry I ignored all your phone calls after that. I didn't mean to worry you, I just needed time. You know that about me. I have to process everything, and I have to do it alone. And you kissing me was something that definitely needed processing. I've wanted this to happen for a long time, but I know our parents are going to think we're crazy. I've heard my mother say people can't really be in love when you're our age, but I don't think that's true. Adults like to pretend that our feelings aren't as big and important as theirs—that we're too young to really know what we want. But I think what we want is similar to what they want. We want to find someone who believes in us. Who will take our side and make us feel less lonely.

I'm so scared that something will happen and it will change the fact that you're my best friend. We both know there are a lot of people who call themselves your friends and then don't act like it, but you've never been that way. I'm totally like rambling. I really like you, Silas. Like so much. Maybe more than green apple cotton candy, and the pink Nerds, and even Sprite! Yeah, you heard me.

Charlie

It's sweet. I was sweet—a girl falling for a guy for the first time. I wish I could remember what the first kiss felt like. I wonder if we did more than just kiss. I flip through more letters, scanning over each of them. I come to one with a word in it that catches my eye.

Dear Silas, I've been trying to write this letter for like thirty minutes and I don't know how to say any of it. I guess I just have to find a way, huh? You always say things so well and I'm always the tongue-tied one.

I can't stop thinking about what we did the other night. That thing you do with your tongue... it makes me want to pass out just thinking about it. Am I being too honest? Showing my cards? That's what my dad always says to me. "Don't show people all of your cards, Charlie."

I don't have any cards that I want to hide from you. I feel like I can trust you with all of my secrets. Silas, I can't wait for you to kiss me like that again. Last night after you left I had all of these irrational, angry feelings toward every girl on the planet. I know that's stupid, but I don't want you to ever do that thing with your tongue to anyone else. I don't feel like I'm a jealous person, but I'm jealous of anyone you've wanted before me. I don't want you to think I'm crazy, Silas, but if you ever look at another girl like you look at me, I'm going to gouge out your eyes with a spoon. I'd also possibly murder her and frame it on you. So, unless you want to be a blind prison mate, I'd suggest you keep your eyes on me. See you at lunch!

Love you!

Charlie

I blush at that one and sneak a glance at Silas. So we've... I've had...

I stick the note under my leg so he can't read that one. How embarrassing. Doing that with someone and not remembering it. Especially since he's apparently so good at that thing with his tongue. *What thing?* I sneak another look at him, and this time he's looking at me too. I immediately feel hot all over.

"What? Why do you have that look on your face?"

"*What* look?" I ask, looking away. It's then I realize that I don't know what my face looks like. Am I even nice to look at? I dig through the backpack until I find my wallet. I take out my ID and stare at it. I'm...*okay.* I notice my eyes first, because they look just like Janette's. But I feel like Janette might actually be a little prettier than me. "Do you think we look more like Mom or Dad?" I ask Janette.

She kicks her feet up on the dash and says, "Like Mom, thank God. I would die if I was born as pale as Dad."

I sink into my seat a little with that answer. I was hoping we looked more like our dad, so when I see him in a little while, he'll feel a tiny bit familiar. I pick up the journal, wanting to distract myself from the fact that I remember nothing about the people who gave life to me.

I flip to the very last day I wrote in my diary. It's probably the thing I should have read first, but I wanted some context. There are two entries for this day, so I start with the first one.

FRIDAY, OCTOBER 3RD

Day your dog gets run over.

Day father goes to prison.

Day you have to move out of your childhood home and into a dump.

Day your mother stops looking at you.

Day your boyfriend punches someone's dad.

All the shittiest days of my life. I don't even want to talk about it. By next week everyone else will be, though. Everything just keeps getting worse. I am trying so hard to fix things, make them right. Keep my family out of the gutter, even though that's exactly where we're heading. I feel like I'm swimming against this big wave and there's no way to win. People at school are looking at me differently. Silas says it's all in my head, but it's easier for him to believe that. He's the one with the father. His life is still intact. Maybe it's not fair of me to say this, but I get so mad when he tells me everything is going to be all right—because it's not. Clearly it's not. He thinks his father is innocent. I DO NOT! How can I be with someone whose family despises me? My dad isn't around for them to hate so they transferred it all on me. My family made their precious family look bad. My dad is rotting in prison while they walk around and carry on with their lives, like he doesn't even matter. What they did to my family matters and everything is not going to be all right. My dad hates Silas. How can I be with someone who is tied to the person who locked him up? It makes me feel so sick. Despite all of this, it's so hard for me to walk away from him. When I get angry he says all the right things. But I know deep in my heart that this isn't good for either of us. Silas is so stubborn though. Even if I tried to break up with him he wouldn't let me. It's like a challenge to him.

I act like I don't care? He acts like he doesn't care. I start cheating on him with his mortal enemy?

He starts cheating on me with his mortal enemy's sister.

He hears I'm at the diner with friends? He shows up with his friends.

We're volatile together. We weren't always like this. It all started when everything came to a head with our fathers. Before that, if anyone would have told me I'd do everything I could to get rid of him one day, I would have laughed in their face. Who would have thought that our lives that fit so perfectly together would—almost overnight—become unrecognizable?

Silas's and Charlie's lives don't fit together anymore. It's too hard now. It's taking more effort than either of us is capable of.

I don't want him to hate me. I just don't want him to love me anymore.

So... I've been acting different. It's not that hard to act different, because I actually am different after all of this. But I've been letting him see it in-

stead of hiding it. I'm mean. I didn't know I was capable of being this mean. And I'm distant. And I'm letting him see me flirt with other guys. A few hours ago, he punched Brian's dad when he overheard him tell another customer that I was Brian's girlfriend. I'm not sure we've ever gotten in that big of a fight before. I wanted him to yell at me. I wanted him to see me for what I really am.

I wanted him to see that he can do so much better.

Instead, right before they threw him out of the diner, he took a step toward me. He bent until his mouth was at my ear and he whispered, "Why, Charlie? Why do you want me to hate you?"

My sob caught in my throat as he was pulled away from me. He held my gaze as he was escorted outside. The look in his eye—it was one I've never seen before. It was full of...indifference. As if he finally stopped having hope.

And based on the text I just received from him before I began this journal entry... I think he's finally done fighting for us. His text said, "I'm on my way to your house. You owe me a proper break-up."

He's finally fed up with it all. And we are over. Really *over*. And I should be glad, because this was my plan all along, but instead I can't stop crying.

36

Silas

Charlie has been extremely quiet as she reads. She's not taking notes or telling me anything that might be of use to us. At one point, I saw her swipe her hand under her eye, but if it was a tear, she hid it well. It made me curious what she was reading, so I peeked over and tried to read from the journal.

It was about the night we broke up. What happened between us just a matter of a week or so ago. I want nothing more than to scoot over and read the rest of it with her, but instead, she tells Landon she has to pee.

He pulls over at a gas station about an hour from the prison. Janette remains in the car and Charlie sticks by my side as we enter the store. Or maybe it's me who sticks by *her* side. I'm not sure. The desire to protect her hasn't left me at all. If anything, I've become more involved. The fact that I remember everything from the last two—almost three—days has made it harder for me to forget that I'm not supposed to know her. Or love her.

But all I can do is think about the kiss from this morning—when we thought we weren't going to remember
each other when it was over. The way she allowed me to
kiss her and hold her until she wasn't Charlie anymore.

It took all I had not to laugh when she pretended she
knew her name. *Delilah?* Even without her memory,
she's still the same, stubborn Charlie. It's amazing how
a few pieces of her personality still shine through today
just as they did last night. I wonder if I'm at all similar
to who I was before all this started.

I wait for her until she emerges from the restroom. We
walk to the refrigerated cases of drinks and I begin to
reach for a water. She grabs at a Pepsi and I almost catch
myself telling her that I know she prefers Coke based
on something I read in one of the letters yesterday, but
I'm not supposed to remember yesterday. We take our
drinks to the register and set them down.

"I wonder if I even *like* Pepsi," she whispers.

I laugh. "That's why I got water. Playing it safe."

She grabs a bag of potato chips from a display and
places them on the counter for the cashier to scan. Then
she grabs a bag of Cheetos. Then a bag of Funyuns. Then
Doritos. She just keeps piling chips onto the counter. I'm
eyeing her when she glances over at me with a shrug.
"Just playing it safe," she says.

By the time we return to the car, we're carrying ten
different bags of chips and eight different types of sodas.
Janette shoots Charlie a look when she sees all the food.
"Silas is really hungry," she says to Janette.

Landon is seated behind the wheel, his knee bouncing
up and down. He drums his fingers on the steering wheel
and says, "Silas, you remember how to drive, right?"

I follow his gaze and see two police cars pulled over on the side of the road in front of us. We'll have to pass them to get out, but I'm not sure why this is making Landon nervous. Charlie is no longer missing, so we have no reason to be paranoid of the police.

"Why can't *you* drive?" I ask him.

He turns around to face me. "I just turned sixteen," he says. "I only have a permit. I haven't applied for my license yet."

"Great," Janette mutters.

In the grand scheme of things, driving without a license isn't really a priority on my list of things to worry about.

"I think we have bigger issues than getting a ticket," Charlie says, voicing my thoughts aloud. "Silas doesn't need to drive. He's helping me sort through all this shit."

"Going through old love letters is hardly important," Janette says. "If Landon gets a ticket with a permit, they'll deny his license."

"Don't get pulled over, then," I say to him. "We still have another two hours to go and a three-hour drive back. I can't waste five hours just because you're worried about your license."

"Why are you two acting so weird?" Janette says. "And why are you reading old love letters?"

Charlie is staring down at the journal when she gives Janette a halfhearted response. "We're experiencing an unusual case of amnesia and can't remember who we are. I don't even know who *you* are. Turn around and mind your own business."

Janette rolls her eyes and huffs, then turns around. "Weirdos," she mutters.

Charlie grins at me and then points down at the journal. "Here," she says. "I'm about to read the very last entry."

I move the box that separates us and I scoot closer to her so I can read the last entry with her. "Is it weird? Sharing your journal with me?"

She gives her head a slight shake. "Not really. I kind of feel like we aren't them."

FRIDAY, OCTOBER 3RD

It's only been fifteen minutes since I last wrote in this journal. As soon as I closed it, Silas texted me and said he was outside. Since my mother doesn't allow him in our house anymore, I walked outside to hear what he had to say.

He caught my breath and I instantly hated myself for it. The way he was leaning against his Land Rover—his feet crossed at the ankles, his hands shoved in his jacket pockets. A shiver ran over me, but I blamed it on the fact that I was in a pajama top with spaghetti straps.

He wouldn't even look up when I walked to his car. I leaned against it next to him and folded my arms over my chest. We stood there for several moments, suspended in silence.

"Can I just ask you one question?" he said.

He kicked off his car and stood in front of me. I stiffened when his arms came up beside my head and caged me in. He dipped his head a couple of inches until we were eye to eye. The position we were in was nothing new. We'd stood like that a million times before, but this time he wasn't looking at me like he wanted to kiss me. This time he was looking at me like he was trying to figure out who in the hell I was. He was scrolling over my face like he was looking at a complete stranger.

"Charlie," he said, his voice raspy. He pulled his bottom lip in and bit down on it while he composed what he was about to say next. He sighed and then closed his eyes. "Are you sure this is what you want?"

"Yes."

His eyes popped open at the steadfastness in my response. My heart ached for what he was trying to hide in his expression. The shock. The realization that he wasn't going to talk me out of it.

He tapped his fist on the car twice and then shoved himself away from me. I immediately stepped around him, wanting to go inside my house while I still had the strength to let him leave. I kept reminding myself why I was doing this. We aren't a good match. He thinks my father is guilty. Our families hate each other. We're different now.

When I reached my front door, Silas said one last thing before getting into his car.

"I won't miss you, Charlie."

His comment shocked me, so I turned and looked at him.

"I'll miss the old you. I'll miss the Charlie I fell in love with. But whoever this is you're turning into..." He waved his hand flippantly up and down my body. "Is not someone I'm going to miss."

He climbed inside his car and slammed his door. He backed out of the driveway and peeled away, his tires screeching against the streets of my slum neighborhood.

And now he's gone.

A small piece of me is angry that he didn't try harder. Most of me is relieved that it's finally over.

All this time, he's done everything he can to remember how things used to be between us. He's convinced himself that they can be that way again one day.

While he spends all of his time trying to remember... I spend all of my time trying to forget.

I don't want to remember how it feels to kiss him. I don't want to remember how it feels to love him.

I want to forget Silas Nash, and everything in this world that reminds me of him.

37

Charlie

The prison is not what I expected. And what was I expecting exactly? Something dark and rotting, set across a backdrop of gray skies and barren land? I don't remember what I look like, but I do remember what a prison should look like. I laugh as I climb out of the car and smooth out my clothes. The red brick is bright against the blue sky. There are flowers growing along the grass, dancing a little when the breeze hits them. The only thing ugly about this setting is the barbed wire that runs across the top of the fence.

"This doesn't look so bad," I say.

Silas, who gets out behind me, raises an eyebrow. "You're not the one locked in there."

I feel warmth rise to my cheeks. I may not know who I am, but I do know that was an extremely stupid thing to say. "Yeah," I say. "I guess Charlie is an asshole."

He laughs and grabs my hand before I can protest. I glance back at the car where Janette and Landon are watching us through the side windows. They look like sad little puppies. "You should stay with them," I say. "Teen pregnancy is a thing."

He snickers. "Are you kidding me? Did you not see how they fought the whole way here?"

"Sexual tension," I sing, as I swing open the door to the main reception area.

It smells like sweat. I crinkle my nose as I walk up to the window. A woman stands in front of me, a child tugging on each of her hands. She swears at them before barking her name at the receptionist and passing them her ID.

Shit. How old did you even have to be to visit someone in this place? I fumble for my driver's license and wait my turn. Silas squeezes my hand and I turn to smile weakly at him.

"Next," a voice calls. I step up to the window and tell a stern-faced woman who it is I'm here to see.

"Are you on the list?" she asks. I nod. The letters indicated that I had been to visit my father several times since he was incarcerated.

"What about him?" She nods toward Silas, who produces his driver's license.

She pushes back his ID and shakes her head. "He ain't on the list."

"Oh," I say. It takes her a few minutes to get everything into the computer, and then she hands me a visitor's badge.

"Leave your bag with your friend," she says. "He can wait out here."

I feel like screaming. I don't want to go in there alone and talk to some man who's supposed to be my father. Silas has his shit together. I want him to come with me.

"I don't know that I can do this," I say. "I don't even know what to ask him." He grabs both of my shoulders and bends his head to look me in the eyes.

"Charlie, based on his manipulative letters, this guy seems like kind of an asshole. Don't buy into his charm. Get answers and get out, okay?"

I nod. "Okay," I say. I look around the dingy waiting area—the yellow walls and painfully-trying-too-hard potted plants. "You'll be waiting out here?"

"Yeah," he says softly. He's looking in my eyes, a slight grin on his lips. It's making me feel like he wants to kiss me, and it freaks me out. Stranger danger. Except I already know what it feels like to kiss him. I just can't remember.

"If it takes a while, you should go wait at the car with Landon and Janette," I say. "You know…teen pregnancy and shit."

He smiles reassuringly.

"Okay," I say, taking a step back. "See ya on the other side."

I'm trying to look big and bad as I walk through the metal detectors and a guard pats me down. My legs feel shaky. I look back at Silas, who is standing with his hands in his pockets, watching me. He nods his head to urge me forward, and I feel a little surge of bravery.

"I can do this," I say under my breath. "Just a little visit with Daddy-o." I am taken to a room and told to wait. Twenty-odd tables are scattered throughout. The woman who was in front of me in line is sitting at a table with her head in her hands while her kids play in a corner, stacking blocks. I sit as far away from them as possible and stare at the door. Any minute my so-called father is going to walk through those doors, and I don't even know what he looks like. What if I get it wrong? I'm thinking about leaving, just running out and telling the others that he didn't want to see me, when suddenly he walks in. I know it's him because his eyes immediately find me.

He smiles and walks over. *Walks* is not the word to describe what he does. He saunters. I don't stand up.

"Hey, Peanut," he says. He awkwardly hugs me as I sit stiff as a board. "Hi… Dad."

He slides into the seat across from me, still smiling. I can see how easy it would be to adore him. Even in his prison jumpsuit, he's set apart. It looks all wrong—him being here with his bright white teeth and neatly combed blond hair. Janette was right. We must look just like our mother, because we don't look anything like him. I have his mouth, I think. But not his pale skin tone. I don't have his eyes. When I saw my picture, that's the first thing I noticed. I have sad-looking eyes. He has laughing eyes, though he probably doesn't have anything to laugh about. I'm lured in.

"You haven't been here in two weeks," he says. "I was beginning to think you girls just left me here to rot."

I shrug off the daddy vibes I was getting a minute ago. *Narcissistic prick.* I can already tell how he works and I just met him. He says things with laughing eyes and a grin, but his words lash out like a whip.

"You left us destitute. The car is a problem, so it's hard for me to drive this far. And my mother is an alcoholic. I think I'm mad at you for that, but I don't remember."

He stares at me for a minute, his smile frozen on his face. "I'm sorry you feel that way." He folds his arms across the table and leans forward. He's studying me. It makes me uncomfortable, like maybe he knows more about me than I know myself. Which is probably the case in my current situation.

"I got a phone call this morning," he says, leaning back in his seat.

"Oh yeah? From who?"

He shakes his head. "It doesn't matter who it was from. What matters is what they told me. About you."

I don't offer him any information. I can't tell if he's baiting me. "Is there anything you want to tell me, Charlize?"

I tilt my head. What kind of game is he playing? "No."

He nods a little and then purses his lips together. His fingers come up in the form of a steeple under his chin while he stares across the table at me. "I was told you were caught trespassing onto someone's property. And that there is reason to believe you're under the influence of drugs."

I take my time before I respond to him. Trespassing? *Who would tell him I was trespassing?* The tarot reader? It was her house I was in. To my knowledge, we didn't tell anyone what had happened. We just went straight to the hotel last night, according to our notes.

So many things run through my mind. I try to sort through them all. "Why were you on our old property, Charlie?"

My pulse begins to quicken. I stand up. "Is there anything to drink here?" I ask, spinning around in a circle. "I'm thirsty." I spot the soda machine, but I don't have any money on me. Just then, my father shoves his hand into his pocket and pulls out a handful of quarters. He slides them across the table.

"They let you have money here?"

He nods, eyeing me suspiciously the entire time. I grab the change and walk over to the soda machine. I insert the quarters and glance back at him. He's not looking at me. He's staring down at his hands folded together across the table.

I wait for my drink to plummet to the bottom, and even then, I stall another minute while I open it and take a sip. This man makes me nervous and I don't know why. I don't know how Charlie looked up to him like she did. I guess if I had memories of him as my father, maybe I would feel differently about him. But I don't have memories. I can only go by what I'm seeing, and right now I see a criminal. A beady-eyed, pale excuse for a man.

I almost drop my soda. Every muscle in my body weakens with the realization. I think back to a description either me or Silas wrote in our notes. A physical description of The Shrimp. Of *Cora*.

"They call her The Shrimp because she has beady eyes and skin that turns ten shades of pink when she talks."

Shit. Shit, shit, shit.

Brett is Cora's father?

He's staring at me now, probably wondering why it's taking so long for me to make my way back to him. I head in his direction. When I reach the table, I eye him hard. Once I'm seated, I lean forward and don't allow a single bit of my trepidation to seep through my confidence.

"Let's play a game," I tell him.

He raises an amused brow. "Okay."

"Let's pretend I've lost my memory. I'm a blank slate. I'm putting things together I may not have seen otherwise, in my prior adoration of you. Are you following…?"

"Not really," he says. He looks sour. I wonder if he gets like this when people don't fall all over themselves to please him.

"Did you happen to father another daughter? I don't know, maybe one with a crazy mother who would hold me against my will?"

His face turns white. He immediately starts to deny, turns his body away from me, and calls me crazy. But I saw the panic on his face, and I know I'm onto something.

"Did you hear the last part of my sentence or are you just focused on keeping up appearances?" He turns his head to look at me, and this time his eyes are no longer soft. "She kidnapped me," I say. "Kept me locked in a room in her—*our*—old house."

His Adam's apple bobs as he swallows. I think he's deciding what to tell me.

"She found you trespassing on her property," he says finally. "She said you were acting irate. You had no idea where you were. She didn't want to call the police because she's convinced you're doing drugs, so she kept you to help you detox. She had my permission, Charlie. She called me as soon as she found you in her house."

"I'm not on *drugs*," I tell him. "And who in their right mind would hold someone against their will?"

"Would you rather she called the police on you? You were talking crazy! And you broke into her house in the middle of the night!"

I don't know what to believe right now. The only memory of that experience I have is in the notes I wrote to myself.

"And that girl is my half sister? Cora?"

He stares at the tabletop, unable to meet my eyes. When he doesn't respond, I decide to play his game. "It's in your best interest to be honest with me. Silas and I came across a file that Clark Nash has been desperately searching for since before your trial."

He doesn't even flinch. His poker face is too perfect. He doesn't ask me what file I have. He just says, "Yes. She's your half sister. I had an affair with her mother years ago."

It's like this is all happening to a character on a television show. I wonder how the real Charlie would take this. Burst into tears? Get up and run out? Punch this dude in the face? From what I've read of her, probably the latter.

"Wow. Oh, wow. Does my mother know?"

"Yes. She found out after we lost the house."

What a sorry excuse for a man. First, he cheats on my mother. Impregnates another woman. Then he hides it from his wife and kids until he gets caught?

"God," I say. "No wonder she's an alcoholic." I lean back in my seat and stare up at the ceiling. "You never claimed her? Does the girl know?"

"She knows," he says.

I feel hot anger. For Charlie, for this poor girl who has to go to school with Charlie and watch her live the life she didn't get to have, and for this whole screwed-up situation.

I take a moment to gather myself while he sits in silence. I wish I could say he was wallowing in guilt, but I'm not so sure this man is capable of feeling guilt.

"Why do they live in the house I grew up in? Did you give it to them?"

This question turns him a light shade of pink. He pops

his jaw as his eyes dart left to right. His voice is quieter when he speaks, so that only I can hear him. "That woman was a client of mine, Charlie. And a mistake. I broke it off with her years ago, a month before she found out she was pregnant. We came to an agreement of sorts. That I would be present financially, but nothing else. It was better for everyone that way."

"So what you're saying is, you bought her silence?"

"Charlie…" he says. "I made a mistake. Believe me, I've paid for it tenfold. She used the money I'd been sending her all those years to purchase our old house in auction. She did that just to spite me."

So she's vindictive. And maybe a little bit crazy. And my father is to blame for that?

Jesus. This just gets worse and worse.

"Did you do what they say you did?" I ask him. "Since we're telling the truth, I think I have a right to know."

His eyes dart around the room again to see who's listening.

"Why are you asking all of these questions?" he whispers. "This isn't like you."

"I'm seventeen years old. I think I have the right to change." This guy. I want to roll my eyes at him, but first I need him to give me more answers.

"Did Clark Nash put you up to this?" he asks, leaning forward with accusation in both his words and his expression. "Are you involved with Silas again?"

He's trying to turn it around on me. He can't get to me anymore.

"Yes, Daddy," I say, smiling sweetly. "I'm involved with Silas again. And we're in love and very happy. Thank you for asking."

Veins bulge at his temples. His hands tighten into angry fists. "Charlie, you know what I think about that."

His reaction sets me off. I stand up and my chair scoots back with a screech. "Let me tell you what *I* think, Dad." I take a step away from the table and point at him. "You've ruined a lot of lives. You thought money could take the place of your responsibilities. Your choices drove my mother to drinking. You left your own daughters with nothing, not even a role model in their lives. Not to mention all the people you swindled money from in your company. And you blame everyone else. Because you're a really shitty human. And an even shittier father!" I say. "I don't know Charlie and Janette very well, but I think they deserve better."

I turn and walk away, tossing a couple of final words over my shoulder. "Goodbye, Brett! Have a nice life!"

38

Silas

I'm sitting cross-legged on the hood of the car, leaning against the windshield and writing down notes when she returns. She was in there for more than an hour, so I did what she said and came to wait out here to keep an eye on our siblings. I sit up straight when I see her. I don't ask her if she found out anything; I just wait for her to say something. She doesn't look like she wants to be spoken to at this point.

She's heading straight for the car. She makes brief eye contact with me as she passes me. I turn my head and watch her as she walks swiftly to the rear of the car and then back to the front again. Then to the rear. Back to the front.

Her hands are clenched in fists at her side. Janette opens the front door and steps out of the car.

"What'd the world's greatest prison-dad have to say?"

Charlie stops in her tracks. "Did you know about Cora?"

Janette pulls her neck back and shakes her head. "Cora? Who?"

"The Shrimp!" Charlie says loudly. "Did you know he's her father?"

Janette's mouth drops open and I immediately jump off the hood of the car.

"Wait. *What?*" I say, walking toward Charlie.

She pulls her hands up and rubs them over her face, then makes her fingers into a steeple as she breathes in slowly. "Silas, I think you were right. This isn't a dream."

I can see the fear in every part of her. The fear that hasn't settled in since she lost her memories again several hours ago. It's all just now hitting her.

I take a slow step forward and reach my hand out. "Charlie. It's okay. We'll figure this out."

She takes a quick step back and begins shaking her head. "What if we don't? What if it keeps happening?" She begins pacing again, this time with her hands locked behind her head. "What if it happens over and over until our lives waste away!" Her chest begins to heave in and out with the deep breaths she's taking.

"What's wrong with you?" Janette asks. She directs her next question at me. "What am I missing?"

Landon is standing next to me now, so I turn to him. "I'm taking Charlie for a walk. Will you explain to Janette what's happening to us?"

Landon presses his lips together and nods. "Yeah. But she'll think we're all lying."

I grab Charlie's arm and urge her to walk with me. Tears begin streaming down her cheeks and she swipes at them angrily. "He was living a double life," she says. "How could he do that to her?"

"To who?" I ask. "Janette?"

She stops and says, "*No*, not Janette. Not Charlie. Not my mother. To *Cora*. How could he know he fathered a child and refuse to have anything to do with her? He's an awful person, Silas! How did Charlie not *see* that?"

She's worried about The Shrimp? The girl who assisted in holding her *captive* for an entire day?

"Try to take a breath," I tell her, grabbing her shoulders and forcing her to face me. "You probably never saw that side of him. He was good to you. You loved him based on the person he pretended to be. And you can't feel sorry for that girl, Charlie. She helped her mother hold you against your will."

She begins shaking her head back and forth feverishly. "They never hurt me, Silas. I made it a point to stress that in the letter. She was rude, sure, but I'm the one who broke into their house! I must have followed her there the night I didn't get in the cab. She thought we were on drugs, because I had no memory of anything, and I don't blame her! And then I forgot who I was again and I probably started to panic." She exhales sharply and pauses for a moment. When she looks up at me, she looks calmer. She folds her lips together and moistens them. "I don't think she had anything to do with what's happened to us. She's just a crazy, bitter woman who hates my father and probably wanted some sick revenge for how I treated her daughter. But they got brought into the fold by us. This whole time we've been looking at other people...trying to blame other people. But what if..." She exhales a breath, and then, "What if we did this to each *other*?"

I let go of her shoulders and take a step back. She sits down on the curb and holds her head in her hands. There's no way we would have done this to ourselves on purpose. "I don't think that's possible, Charlie," I say, taking a seat next to her. "How could we do this? How do two people just simultaneously stop remembering at the same time? It has to be something bigger than what we're capable of."

"If it has to be bigger than *us*, then it also has to be bigger than my father. And Cora. And Cora's mother. And my mom. And your parents. If *we* aren't capable of causing this, then no one else should be capable of it, either."

I nod. "I know."

She brings her thumb up to her mouth for a second. Then, "So if this isn't happening to us because of other people…what could it be?"

I can feel the muscles in my neck tighten. I bring my hands up behind my head and look up at the sky. "Something bigger?"

"What's bigger? The universe? *God?* Is this the beginning of the apocalypse?" She stands up and paces back and forth in front of me. "Do you think we even believed in God? Before this happened to us?"

"I have no idea. But I've prayed more in the last few days than I probably have in my entire life." I stand up and grab her hand, pulling her in the direction of the car. "I want to know everything your father said. Let's head back and you can write down everything he told you while I drive."

She slides her fingers through mine and walks back to the car with me. When we return, Janette is leaning against the passenger door. She's glaring at both of us. "So you seriously can't remember anything? Either of you?" Her attention is focused solely on Charlie now.

I motion for her and Landon to sit in the backseat this

time. I open the driver door as Charlie responds to her. "No. We can't. And I swear I'm not making this up for kicks, Janette. I don't know what kind of sister I've been to you, but I *swear* I wouldn't make this up."

Janette eyes Charlie for a moment and then says, "You've been a really *shitty* sister the last couple of years. But I guess if everything Landon just told me is true and you really can't remember anything, then that explains why not a single one of you dick faces has told me happy birthday today." She opens the door to the backseat, climbs inside, and then slams it.

"Ouch," Charlie says.

"Yeah," I agree. "You forgot your little sister's *birthday*? That's pretty selfish of you, Charlie."

She slaps me playfully in the chest. I grab her hand, and I swear there's a moment that passes between us. A single second where she looks at me like she can feel what she once felt for me.

But then she blinks, pulls her hand from mine, and climbs in the car.

39

Charlie

It's not really my fault that the universe is punishing me. *Us.*

Silas and me.

I keep forgetting that Silas is screwed too, which probably means I'm a narcissist. *Great.* I think about the sister in the car with me who is having a really shitty birthday. And the half sister who lives in my old house with her questionable mother. According to my journals, I've been torturing that girl for a decade. I am a bad person, and an even worse sister.

Do I even *want* to get my memories back?

I stare out the window and watch as we pass all of the other stupid cars. I don't have any memories, but I can at least make sure Janette has some of this day.

"Hey, Silas," I say. "Can you put something into that fancy GPS for me?"

"Yeah," he says. "Like what?"

I don't know the girl in the backseat at all. She could

be super into role-play video games for all I know. "An arcade," I say.

I see Landon and Janette perk up in the backseat. *Yes!* I congratulate myself. All pubescent humans like video games. It's a thing.

"Kind of a weird time to want to go play games," Silas says. "Don't you think we should—"

"I think we should play games," I interrupt. "Because it's Janette's birthday." I make my eyes really wide so he understands this isn't up for discussion. He makes an "O" face and gives me a really lame thumbs up. Charlie hates thumbs up, I can tell by her body's immediate reaction to it.

Silas finds an arcade not far from where we are. When we get there, he pulls out his wallet and digs around until he finds a credit card.

Janette makes eyes at me, like she's embarrassed, but I shrug. I barely even know this guy. What does it matter that he's spending his money on us? Besides, I don't have any money. My father lost it all and Silas's father still has some, so it's fine. *Not only am I a narcissist; I'm also good at justification.*

We carry our tokens in paper cups, and as soon as we're inside the arcade, Janette and Landon walk off to do their own thing. *Together.* I make eyes at Silas and mouth *See.*

"Come on," Silas says. "Let's get some pizza. Let the kids play." He winks at me, and I try not to smile.

We find a table to wait for our pizza, and I slide into a booth, wrapping my arms around my knees. "Silas," I say. "What if this keeps happening to us? This endless loop of forgetting. What will we do?"

"I don't know," he says. "Find each other over and over. It's not that bad, right?"

I glance over at him to see if he's joking.

It isn't that bad. But the situation is. "Who wants to spend their life not knowing who they are?"

"I could spend every day getting to know you all over again, Charlie, and I don't think I'd get sick of it."

Heat climbs up my body and I quickly look away. That's my go-to with Silas: *don't look at him, don't look at him, don't look at him.*

"You're dumb," I say. But he's not dumb. He's a romantic and his words are powerful. Charlie isn't, I can tell. But she wants to be—I can tell that too. She desperately wants Silas to show her it's not all a lie. There's a pull inside of her every time she looks at him. It feels like a tugging, and I want to brush it away every time it happens.

I sigh and rip open a sugar packet, emptying the powder onto the table. Being a teenager is exhausting. Silas silently watches me draw patterns in the sugar until he finally grabs my hand.

"We'll figure it out," he assures me. "We're on the right track."

I dust my hands on my pants. "Okay." Even though I know we aren't on any track. We're just as lost as we were when we woke up in the hotel today.

I'm also a liar. *A narcissist, a justifier, a liar.*

Janette and Landon find us just as the pizza arrives. They slide into our booth, rosy cheeked and laughing. In the entire day I've known Janette, I've never even seen her come close to laughter. I hate Charlie's father more right now. For screwing up a teenage girl. *Two* teenage girls if I count myself. Well...*three*, now that I know about Cora.

I watch Janette bite into her pizza. It doesn't have to be this way. If I could just come out of this...*thing*... I could take care of her. Be better. For both of us.

"Charlie," she says, setting down her slice. "Will you come play with me?"

I smile. "Yeah, of course."

She beams at me and my heart suddenly feels so big and full. When I look over at Silas, he's staring at me, glassy eyed. The corner of his mouth lifts in a small smile.

40

Silas

It's dark when we pull into Charlie and Janette's drive-way. There's an awkward moment where I should prob-ably walk Charlie to the door, but based on the way Landon and Janette have been flirting in the backseat, I don't know how all four of us are supposed to do this at the same time.

Janette opens her door, and then Landon opens his, so Charlie and I wait in the car.

"They're exchanging numbers," she says, watching them. "How cute."

We sit in silence watching them flirt until Janette disappears inside the house.

"Our turn," Charlie says, opening her door.

I walk slowly with her up the sidewalk, hoping her mother doesn't see me here. I don't have the energy to deal with that woman tonight. I feel bad that Charlie's about to have to do just that.

She's wringing her hands together nervously. I know

she's stalling because she doesn't want me to leave her alone tonight. Every single memory she has consists of me and her. "What time is it?" she asks.

I pull my phone out of my pocket to check. "It's after ten."

She nods and then glances behind her at the house. "I hope my mother is asleep," she says. And then, "Silas…"

I interrupt whatever she's about to say. "Charlie, I don't think we should split up tonight."

Her eyes meet mine again. She looks relieved. I'm the only person she knows, after all. The last thing we probably need right now is to be distracted by people we don't know. "Good. I was just about to suggest that."

I nudge my head to the door behind her. "We need to make it look like you're home, though. Go inside. Make like you're going to bed. I'll go drop Landon off at my house and then come back to get you in an hour."

She nods. "I'll meet you at the end of the road," she says. "Where do you think we should stay tonight?"

I think about that. It's probably best if we stay at my house, so we can see if there's anything we missed in my room that might help us. "I'll sneak you upstairs to my bedroom. We have a lot to go over tonight."

Charlie's eyes drop to the ground. "Upstairs?" she says curiously. She inhales a slow breath, and I can hear the air sliding through her clenched teeth. "Silas?" She lifts her eyes to mine, and they're narrowed. She has an accusatory look about her and I have no idea what I've done to provoke this look. "You wouldn't lie to me, would you?"

I tilt my head, not sure if I heard her right. "What do you mean?"

"I've been noticing things. *Little* things," she says.

I can feel the descent of my heart. *What did I say?* "Charlie… I'm not sure what you're getting at."

She takes a step back. Her hand covers her mouth for a moment, and then she points at me. "How do you know your bedroom is upstairs when you haven't even been to your house yet?"

Shit. I did say *upstairs*.

Shaking her head, she adds, "And you made a comment earlier at the prison. About how you've prayed a lot in the last few days, but we're both only supposed to remember *today*. And this morning…when I told you my name was Delilah? I could see you trying not to smile. Because you knew I was lying." Her voice begins to falter between suspicious and scared. I hold up a reassuring palm, but she backs another step closer to the house.

This is a problem. I'm not sure I know how to respond to her. I don't like knowing that she would rather run inside a house that terrified her five minutes ago than be standing near me. *Why did I lie to her this morning?*

"Charlie. Please don't be scared of me." I can tell it's already too late.

She darts for her front door, so I lunge forward and wrap my arms around her, pulling her against my chest. She starts to scream, so I cover her mouth with my hand. "Calm down," I say against her ear. "I won't hurt you." The last thing I need is for her not to trust me. She grabs my arm with both hands, trying to free herself from my grasp. "You're right. Charlie, you're right. I lied to you. But if you'll calm down for two seconds, I'll explain why."

She lifts a leg while I'm still holding on to her from behind. She presses her foot against the house and kicks as hard as she can, sending both of us tumbling backward. I lose my grip on her and she begins to crawl away from me, but I'm able to grab her again and push her onto her back. She's looking up at me wide-eyed, but she isn't screaming this time. My hands are pressing her arms against the ground.

"*Stop* it," I tell her.

"Why did you lie?" she cries. "Why are you pretending this happened to you too?" She struggles some more, so I tighten my hold.

"I'm not pretending, Charlie! I've been forgetting, just like you have. But it didn't happen to me today. I don't know why. But I can only remember the last two days, that's it. I swear." I look her in the eyes and she holds my stare. She's still mildly struggling, but I can tell she also wants to hear my explanation. "I didn't want you to be afraid of me this morning, so I pretended it happened again. But I swear, up until this morning, it's been happening to both of us."

She stops struggling and just lets her head fall to the side. She closes her eyes, completely exhausted. Emotionally *and* physically. "Why is this happening?" she whispers in defeat.

"I don't know, Charlie," I say, releasing one of her arms. "I don't know." I brush her hair out of her face. "I'm about to let go of you. I'm going to stand up and get in my car. After I drop Landon off, I'll come back for you, okay?"

She nods her head but doesn't open her eyes. I release her other arm and slowly stand up. When I'm no longer pinning her to the ground, she quickly sits up and scoots away from me before standing up.

"I was lying to protect you. *Not* to hurt you. You believe me, right?"

She rubs the spots on her arms where I was holding her down. She produces a meek "Yeah." And then, after clearing her throat, "Be back in an hour. And don't lie to me ever again."

I wait for her to walk back inside her house before I head back to the car.

"What the hell was that all about?" Landon asks.

"Nothing," I reply, staring out the window as we pass her house. "Just telling her goodnight." I reach into the backseat to grab all of our things. "I'm going back to Jamais Jamais for my Land Rover."

Landon laughs. "We sort of wrecked it last night. Tearing down a gate?"

I remember. I was there. "It might still drive okay, though. It's worth a shot, and I can't keep using...whose car is this, anyway?"

"Mom's," he says. "I texted her this morning and told her yours was in the shop and that we needed hers today."

I knew I liked this kid. "So... Janette, huh?" I ask him.

He turns toward the window. "Shut up."

The Land Rover's front end was a debacle of twisted metal and debris. But apparently the damage was only cosmetic, because it cranked right up.

It took all I had not to go inside the gate again and scream at that psycho woman for leading us in the wrong direction, but I didn't. Charlie's dad has caused enough of a shit storm in her world.

I calmly drive my car to Charlie's house and wait for her at the end of the road like I said I would. I text her to let her know I'm in a different vehicle.

I begin to turn theories over in my mind while I wait for her. It's hard for me to suspend belief in order to give our circumstances an explanation, but the only things I can come up with are otherworldly.

A curse.

An alien abduction. Time travel.

Twin brain tumors?

None of it makes sense.

I'm making notes when the passenger door opens. A rush of wind follows Charlie inside the car, and I find myself wishing it would push her all the way to my side. Her hair is damp and she's in different clothes.

"Hey."

She says, "Hi," and pulls the seatbelt into place. "What were you writing?"

I hand her the notebook and pen and then back out of the driveway.

She begins reading over my summary.

When she's finished, she says, "None of it makes sense, Silas. We got into a fight and broke up the night before this started. The next day we can't remember anything other than random stuff, like books and photography. It keeps happening for a week, until you *don't* lose your memory and I *do*." She pulls her feet up on the seat and taps the pen against the notebook. "What are we missing? There has to be something. I have no memory before this morning, so what happened yesterday that made you *stop* forgetting? Did anything happen last night?"

I don't answer her right away. I think about her questions. How all along, we've been assuming other people had something to do with this. We thought The Shrimp was involved, we thought her mother was involved. For a while, I wanted to accuse Charlie's father. But maybe it's none of that. Maybe it has nothing to do with anyone else and everything to do with us.

We reach my house no closer to the truth than we were this morning.

Than we were two days ago. Than we were last week.

"Let's go through the back door in case my parents are awake." The last thing we need right now is for them to see me sneaking Charlie into my bedroom to stay the night. The back door won't take us past my father's study.

It's unlocked, so I make my way in first. When all is clear, I grab her hand and rush her through the house, up the stairwell, and to my bedroom. By the time I shut the door behind us and lock it, we're both breathing heavily. She laughs and falls onto my bed. "That was fun," she says. "I bet we've done that before."

She sits up and brushes the hair out of her eyes, smiling. She begins to look around my room, through eyes that are seeing it again for the first time. I immediately get that longing in my chest, akin to how I felt last night at the hotel when she fell asleep in my arms. The feeling that I would do absolutely anything to be able to remember what it was like to love her. *God, I want that back.* Why did we ever break up? Why did we let everything that happened between our families come between us? From the outside looking in, I'd almost believe we were soul mates before we let it all fall apart. *Why did we think we could intervene with fate?*

I pause.

When she looks at me, she knows something is going on in my head. She scoots to the edge of the bed and tilts her head. "Do you remember something?"

I sit in the desk chair and roll toward her. I take both of her hands in mine and I squeeze them. "No," I say. "But… I might have a theory."

She sits up straighter. "What *kind* of theory?"

I'm sure this is about to sound crazier coming from my mouth than it does swimming around in my head. "Okay, so…this might sound stupid. But last night… when we were at the hotel?"

She nods, encouraging me to continue.

"One of the last thoughts I had before we fell asleep was how—while you were missing—I didn't feel whole. But when I found you, it was the first time I felt like Silas Nash. Up until that point, I didn't feel like *any*one. And I remember swearing to myself right before I fell asleep that I would never allow us to drift apart again. So I was thinking…" I release her hands and stand up. I pace the room a couple of times until she stands up, too. I shouldn't be embarrassed to say this next part out loud, but I am. It's ridiculous. But so is every other thing in the whole world right now.

I rub the nerves out of the back of my neck while I lock eyes with her. "Charlie? What if…when we broke up…we screwed with destiny?"

I wait for her to laugh, but instead, a rush of chills covers her arms. She makes to rub them away as she slowly takes a seat back down on the bed. "That's ridiculous," she mutters. But there's no conviction in her words, which means maybe a part of her thinks this theory is worth exploring.

I sit down in my chair again and position myself in front of her. "What if we're supposed to be together? And messing with that caused some sort of… I don't know…rift."

She rolls her eyes. "So what you're implying is, the universe wiped away all of our memories because we *broke up*? That seems a little narcissistic."

I shake my head. "I know how it sounds. But yes. Hypothetically speaking…what if soul mates exist? And once they come together, they can't fall apart?"

She folds her hands together in her lap. "How does that explain why you remembered this time and I didn't?"

I pace the room some more. "Let me think for a minute," I say to her.

She waits patiently while I rub the floor raw. I hold up a finger. "Hear me out, okay?"

"I'm listening," she says.

"We've loved each other since we were kids. We obviously had this connection that has lasted our entire lives. Up until external factors started getting in our way. The thing with our fathers, our families hating each other. You holding a grudge against me for believing your father was guilty. There's a pattern here, Charlie." I grab the notebook that I wrote in earlier and look at all the things we naturally remember and all the things we don't. "And our memories…we can remember things that weren't forced on us. Things we had a passion for all on our own. You remember books. I remember how to work a camera. We remember lyrics to our favorite songs. We remember certain things in history, or random stories. But things that were forced on us by others, we forgot. Like football."

"What about people?" she asks. "Why did we forget all the people we've met?"

"If we remembered people, we'd still have *other*

memories. We'd remember how we met them, the impact they've had on our lives." I scratch at the back of my head. "I don't know, Charlie. A lot of it doesn't make sense still. But last night, I felt a connection with you again. Like I had loved you for years. And this morning… I didn't lose my memories like you did. There has to be significance in that."

Charlie stands up and begins pacing the room. "*Soul* mates?" she mutters. "This is almost as ridiculous as a curse."

"Or two people developing in-sync amnesia?"

She narrows her eyes at me. I can see her mind working as she chews on the pad of her thumb. "Well then, explain how you fell back in love with me in just two days. And if we're soul mates, why wouldn't I have fallen back in love with *you*?" She stops pacing and waits for my answer.

"You spent a lot of your time locked up inside your old house. I spent all that time looking for you. I was reading our love letters, going through your phone, reading your journals. By the time I found you yesterday, I felt like I already knew you. For me, reading everything from our past somehow connected me to you again…like some of my old feelings had come back. But for you… I was barely more than a stranger."

We're both sitting again. Thinking. Contemplating the possibility that this might be the closest we've come to any sort of pattern.

"So what you're suggesting is…we were soul mates. But then external influences ruined us as people and we fell out of love?"

"Yeah. Maybe. I think so."

"And it'll keep happening until we set things right again?"

I shrug, because I'm not sure. It's just a theory. But it makes more sense than anything else we've come up with.

Five minutes pass while neither of us says a single word. She finally falls back onto the bed with a heavy sigh and says, "You know what this means?"

"No."

She pulls up onto her elbows and looks at me. "If this is true…you only have thirty-six hours to make me fall in love with you."

I don't know if we're on to something, or if we're about to spend the remainder of our time chasing a dead end, but I smile, because I'm willing to sacrifice the next thirty-six hours for this theory. I walk over to the bed and fall onto it beside her. We're both staring up at the ceiling when I say, "Well, Charlie baby. We better get started."

She throws an arm over her eyes and groans. "I don't know you very well, but I can already tell you're gonna have fun with this."

I smile, because she's right.

"It's late," I tell her. "We should try to get some sleep, because your heart is going to get a serious workout tomorrow."

I set my alarm for 6am so that we can be up and out of the house before anyone else wakes up. Charlie sleeps closest to the wall and is out cold in a matter of minutes. I don't feel like I'll be able to fall asleep anytime soon, so I pluck one of her journals from the backpack and decide to read some before I fall asleep.

Silas is crazy.

Like...legit crazy. But my god, I have so much fun with him. He started a game he forces me to play sometimes called Silas Says. It's exactly the same as Simon Says, but...you know. With his name instead of Simon's. Whatever. He's way cooler than Simon.

We were on Bourbon Street today and it was so hot and we were both sweating and miserable. We had no idea where our friends had gone off to and we weren't supposed to meet them for another hour. When it comes to me and Silas, I'm always the whiney one, but it was so hot this time, even he was whining a little.

Anyway, we walked past this guy who was propped up on a stool and he had painted himself silver, like a robot. There was a sign leaning against his stool that said, "Ask me a question. Get a real answer. Only 25 cents."

Silas handed me a quarter, so I dropped it in the bucket. "What's the meaning of life?" I asked the silver man.

He made a stiff turn of his head and looked me square in the eye. In a very impressive robot voice, he said, "That depends on the life of which you search for meaning."

I rolled my eyes at Silas. Just another hack job scamming the tourists. I clarified my question so that at least the quarter wouldn't go to complete waste. "Fine," I said. "What's the meaning of my life?"

He took a rickety step down from his stool and

bent at a ninety degree angle. With his silver robot fingers, he plucked my quarter out of the bucket and placed it in my palm. He glanced at Silas and then to me and smiled. "You, my dear, have already found your meaning. All there is left to do now...is dance."

Then the silver dude started dancing. Like... legit dancing. Not even in a robot style. He just had this big, goofy grin on his face and held his hands up like a ballerina and danced like no one was watching him.

At that point, Silas grabbed my hands and said in mock-robot voice, "Dance. With. Me." He tried to pull me into the street to dance with him, but hell no. Embarrassing. I pulled away from him, but he wrapped his arms around me and did that thing where he puts his mouth right on my ear. He knows I freaking love that, so it was really unfair. He whispered, "Silas says dance."

I don't know what it was about him in that moment. I don't know if it was because he honestly didn't care that anyone was watching us, or if it was because he was still talking to me in that silly robot voice.

Whatever it was, I'm pretty sure I fell in love with him today. All over again. For like the tenth time.

So I did what Silas said. I danced. And you know what? It was fun. So much fun. We danced all around Jackson Square and we were still dancing when our friends found us. We were covered in sweat and out of breath, and if I were watching us from the sidewalk, I would probably be the girl *crinkling up my nose, muttering "Gross" under my breath.*

But I'm not that girl. I never want to be that girl. For the rest of my life, I want to be the girl dancing with Silas in the street.

Because he's crazy. That's why I love him.

I close the journal. *Did that really happen?* I want to read more, but I'm afraid if I keep going, I'll come across things I don't want to remember.

I set the journal on my nightstand and roll over so that I can wrap my arm around her. When we wake up tomorrow, we'll only have one day left. I want her to be able to let go of everything that's going on between us so that she can genuinely focus on me and our connection and nothing else.

Knowing Charlie…that's going to be hard. It'll take some crazy skills to be able to accomplish that.

But luckily… I'm crazy. *That's why she used to love me.*

41

Charlie

"Okay, so how does this work exactly?" I ask as we walk toward his car. "Do we float down the bayou in a rowboat while little critters sing 'Kiss the Girl'?"

"Don't be a smartass." Silas grins. Then he stops me before I reach the car, grabbing my hand and pulling me back. I look up at him in surprise. "Charlize," he says, looking first at my lips, and then in my eyes. "If you give me half a chance I can make you fall in love with me."

I clear my throat and try not to look away even though I want to. "Well…you're off to a good start. So there's that."

He laughs. I feel so awkward, I don't know what to do with myself, so I pretend to sneeze. He doesn't even say *bless you*. He just smiles at me, like he knows it was a fake sneeze.

"Stop it," I say. "You're staring at me."

"That's the point, Charlie. *Look into my eyes.*"

I burst into laughter. "You've got game, Silas Nash," I say, walking toward my side of the car.

When we're both buckled in, Silas turns to me and says, "According to a letter you wrote, the first time we had sex was—"

"No. I don't want to go there. Where did you find that letter? I thought I hid it."

"Not well enough." Silas grins.

I think I like flirty Silas. Even if we forget everything again tomorrow, at least I'll get one good day out of this. "Let's go somewhere fun," I say. "I can't remember the last time I had fun."

We both start laughing at the same time. I like him. I really do. He's so easy to be around. He laughs too much, maybe. Like, we're totally screwed right now, and he's still always smiling. Worry a little, dude. He makes me laugh when I should be worrying.

"Okay," he says, glancing at me. "I really would rather go to that place in the letter where I did that thing with my tongue, but…"

It's automatic—it must belong to Charlie—but as soon as the words are out of his mouth, my hand reaches across the space between us and I slap his arm. He grabs my hand before I can pull away and holds it to his chest. This too feels like something that's been done before, something that belongs to them—Charlie and Silas, not me and this guy.

It makes me feel tired to be held against him like this, even if it's just my hand. I can't afford to be tired, so I tug away from him and look out the window.

"You're really fighting this," he says. "That kind of defies the point."

He's right. I reach over and grab his hand. "This is me falling in love with you," I tell him. "Deep, soul love."

"I wonder if you're less ridiculous when you have your memory."

I turn on the radio with my free hand. "Doubt it," I say.

I like making him smile. It doesn't take much to make the corners of his mouth twitch, but to actually get his lips to curve all the way up, I have to be extra sassy. His lips are fully curved now as he pulls into traffic and I am able to watch him without him watching me. We're acting like we know each other even though our conscious minds don't know each other. Why is that?

I reach for the backpack, to search for the answer in their letters or journals.

"Charlize," Silas says. "The answer isn't in there. Just be with me. Don't worry about that."

I drop the backpack. I don't know where he's driving. I don't know if he knows where he's driving, but we end up in a parking lot just as it starts to rain. There are no other cars around and it's coming down too hard for me to see what's in the buildings around us.

"Where are we?"

"I don't know," Silas says. "But we should get out of the car."

"It's raining."

"Yes. Silas says get out of the car."

"Silas says…? Like *Simon* says?"

He just stares at me expectantly, so I shrug. Honestly, what do I have to lose? I open the car door and step into the rain. It's warm rain. I tilt my face up and let it hit me.

I hear his door slam and then he runs around the front of the car and stands in front of me.

"Silas says run around the car five times."

"You're weird, you know that?" He stares at me. I shrug again and start running. It feels good. Like with every step some of the tension is leaving my body.

I don't look at him when I run past him; I stay focused on not tripping. Maybe Charlie ran track or something. Five car laps later I stop in front of him. We are both soaked through. Drops of water are dangling from his eyelashes and running down his tanned neck. Why do I have the urge to touch my tongue to those lines of water?

Oh, yeah. We were in love. Or maybe it's because he's freaking hot. "Silas says go into that store and ask for a hotdog. When they tell you they don't have hotdogs, stomp your foot really hard and scream like you did in the hotel this morning."

"What the—"

He crosses his arms over his chest. "Silas says."

Why the hell am I even doing this? I give Silas the dirtiest look I can and stomp off in the direction of the store he pointed me to. It's an insurance agency. I swing open the door and three grouchy-looking adults raise their heads to see who has walked in. One of them even has the audacity to scrunch up their nose at me, like I don't already know I'm dripping water everywhere.

"I'd like a hotdog with everything," I say.

I'm met with blank stares. "Are you drunk?" the receptionist asks me. "Do you need help? What's your name?"

I stomp my foot and let out a bloodcurdling scream, at which all three of them drop whatever they're holding and look at each other.

I take their moment of surprise to run out. Silas is

waiting for me outside the door. He's laughing so hard; he's bent over at the waist.

I punch him on the arm and then we both run for the Rover.

I can hear my own laughter blending with his. That was fun. We jump into the car and peel away just as Grouchy One, Two, and Three walk outside to watch us.

Silas drives for a few miles before he pulls into another parking lot. This time I can see the glowing sign advertising "The Best Coffee and Beignets in Louisiana!"

"We're soaking wet," I say, not seeming to be able to wipe the smile from my face. "Do you know how messy beignets will be?"

"Silas says eat ten beignets," he says stoically.

"Ugh. Why do you have to act like a robot when you play this game? It's creeping me out."

He doesn't respond. We get a table near the window and order coffee and two dozen beignets. The waitress doesn't seem bothered by our wet clothes or the fact Silas is speaking in a robot voice.

"The waitress thinks we're cute," I tell Silas. "We are."

I roll my eyes. This is fun. *Would Charlie think this was fun?*

When our beignets come, I am so hungry I don't care about my wet hair or clothes. I dive in, moaning when the warm pastry hits my tongue. Silas watches me in amusement.

"You really like those, huh?"

"They're actually really gross," I say. "I'm just really into this game."

We eat as many as we can until we're covered in white

powder. Before we leave, Silas rubs some of it across my face and hair. Not to be outdone, I return the favor. God, this guy is fun. Maybe I kind of see what Charlie sees in him.

42

Silas

She's into this. She hasn't smiled nearly enough in the last few days I've had with her, but now she can't *stop* smiling.

"Where are we going now?" she says, clapping her hands together. She still has powdered sugar on the corner of her mouth. I reach across the seat and wipe it off with my thumb.

"We're going to the French Quarter," I tell her. "Lots of romantic places there."

She rolls her eyes, scrolling through her phone. "I wonder what we actually used to do for fun. Besides take selfies."

"At least they were all good selfies."

She shoots me a look of pity. "That's a contradiction. There are no such things as *good selfies*."

"I've been through your camera roll. I beg to differ."

She ducks her head and looks out her window, but I can see the pinks of her cheeks grow redder.

* * *

After we park, I have absolutely no plan. We filled up on so many beignets for breakfast, I'm not sure she's quite ready to have lunch yet.

We spend the first part of the afternoon walking up and down every street, stopping in almost every store. It's as if we're both so fascinated by the scenery, we forget we have a goal today. I'm supposed to make her swoon. She's supposed to swoon and fall in love with me. *Get back on track, Silas.*

We're on Dauphine Street when we walk past what claims to be a bookstore. Charlie turns around and grabs my hands. "Come on," she says, pulling me into the store. "I'm pretty sure the way to my heart is in here."

There are books stacked floor to ceiling, every which way. Sideways, top to bottom, books used as shelves for more books. A man sits behind a cash register to the right, which is covered in even more books. He nods a greeting as we enter. Charlie heads to the back of the store, which isn't very far away. It's a small store, but there are more books than a man could read in his entire life. She runs her fingers along the books as she passes them, looking up, down, around. She actually twirls when she gets to the end of the aisle. She's definitely in her element, whether she remembers or not.

She's facing a corner, pulling a red book off the shelf. I walk up behind her and give her another Silas Says task.

"Silas says…open the book to a random page and read the first few sentences you see…"

She chuckles. "That's easy."

"I wasn't finished," I say. "Silas says read the sentences at the top of your lungs."

She spins around to face me, eyes wide. But then a mischievous grin drags across her mouth. She stands up tall while holding the book out in front of her. "Fine," she says. "You asked for it." She clears her throat, and then, as loud as she can, she reads, "'IT MADE ME WANT TO MARRY HER! MADE ME WANT TO BUY HER A MAGIC AIRPLANE AND FLY HER AWAY TO A PLACE WHERE NOTHING BAD COULD EVER HAPPEN! MADE ME WANT TO POUR RUBBER CEMENT ALL OVER MY CHEST AND THEN LAY DOWN ON TOP OF HER SO THAT WE'D BE STUCK TOGETHER, AND SO IT WOULD HURT LIKE HELL IF WE EVER TRIED TO TEAR OUR- SELVES APART!'"

Charlie is laughing when she finishes. But when the words she read begin to register, her laughter fades. She runs her fingers over the sentences like they mean some- thing to her. "That was really sweet," she says. She flips through the pages of the book until she comes to a stop with her finger on a different paragraph. Then, in just barely a whisper, she begins reading again. "'Fate is the magnetic pull of our souls toward the people, places, and things we belong with.'"

She stares at the book for a moment and then closes it. She places it back on the shelf, but she moves two books out of the way so that this book can be displayed more prominently. "Do you believe that?"

"Which part?"

She leans against a wall of books and stares over my shoulder. "That our souls are pulled toward the people we belong with."

I reach out to her and pull at a lock of her hair. I run my fingers down it and twirl it around my finger. "I don't know if I normally believe in soul mates," I tell her. "But for the next twenty-four hours, I'd bet my life for it to be true."

She rolls her shoulder until her back is pressed against the wall of books, and she's facing me. I would *absolutely* bet my life on fate right now. I somehow have more feelings for this girl than will fit inside of me. And I want more than anything for her to feel the same thing. To *want* the same thing. Which…in this very moment… is for my mouth to be on hers.

"Charlie…" I release her lock of hair and bring my hand to her cheek. I touch her gently…tracing her cheekbone with my fingertips. Her breaths are shallow and quick. "Kiss me."

She leans into my hand a little and her eyes flutter. For a moment, I think she might actually do it. But then a smile steals her heated expression and she says, "Silas didn't say." She darts under my arm and disappears down the next aisle. I don't follow her. I grab the book she read from and tuck it under my arm as I head for the register.

She knows what I'm doing. The whole time I'm at the register, she's watching me from down the aisle. After I purchase the book, I walk outside and let the door shut behind me. I wait a few seconds to see if she follows me immediately out, but she doesn't. Same stubborn Charlie.

I pull the backpack off my shoulder and shove the book inside of it.

Then I pull out my camera and turn it on.

She stays inside the bookstore for another half hour. I don't mind it. I know she knows I'm still out here. I take picture after picture, engrossed in the people who pass by and the way the sun is setting over the buildings, casting shadows on even the smallest of things. I take pictures of all of it. When Charlie finally makes it back outside, my battery is almost dead.

She walks up to me and says, "Where's my book?"

I hoist the backpack over my shoulder. "I didn't buy that book for you. I bought it for me."

She huffs and follows after me as I make my way down the street. "That's not a good move, Silas. You're supposed to be thoughtful. Not selfish. I want to fall in love with you, not become irritated with you."

I laugh. "Why do I feel like love and irritation go hand in hand with you?"

"Well, you *have* known me longer than I've known myself." She grabs my hand to pull me to a stop. "Look! Crawfish!" She yanks me in the direction of the restaurant. "Do we like crawfish? I'm so hungry!"

Turns out, we do *not* like crawfish. Luckily, they had chicken strips on the menu. We both like chicken, apparently.

"We should write that down somewhere," she says, walking backward down the middle of the street. "That we hate crawfish. I don't want to have to go through that awful experience again."

"Wait! You're about to..." Charlie falls on her butt before the rest of the sentence can make it out of my mouth. "Walk into a pothole," I finish.

I reach down to help her up, but there's not much I can do about her pants. We had finally dried off after the rain from earlier today, and now she's soaking wet again. This time from muddy water. "You okay?" I ask, trying not to laugh. *Trying* being the key word here. Because I'm laughing harder than I've laughed all day.

"Yeah, yeah," she says as she attempts to wipe mud from her pants and her hands. I'm still laughing when she narrows her eyes and points down at the mud puddle. "Charlie says sit in the pothole, Silas."

I shake my head. "No. No way. The game is called *Silas* Says, not *Charlie* Says."

She arches an eyebrow. "Oh, really?" She takes a step closer to me and says, "Charlie says sit in the pothole. If Silas does what Charlie says, Charlie will do whatever *Silas* says."

Is that an invitation of sorts? *I'm liking flirtatious Charlie.* I glance down at the pothole. It's not *that* deep. I turn around and lower myself until I'm sitting cross-legged in the puddle of muddy water. I keep my eyes on Charlie's face, not wanting to witness the attention we're probably attracting from bystanders. She swallows back her laughter, but I can see the pleasure she's getting out of this.

I stay sitting in the pothole until it even starts to embarrass Charlie. After several seconds, I lean back onto my elbows and cross my legs. Someone snaps a picture of me in the pothole, so she motions for me to stand. "Get up," she says, glancing around. "Hurry."

I shake my head. "I can't. Charlie didn't say."

She grabs my hand, laughing. "Charlie says *get up*, you idiot." She helps me to my feet and grabs my shirt, pressing her face against my chest. "Oh, my God, they're all staring at us."

I wrap my arms around her and begin to sway back and forth, which is probably not what she was expecting me to do. She looks up at me, my shirt still clenched in her fists. "Can we go now? Let's go."

I shake my head. "Silas says dance."

Her eyebrows crinkle together. "You can't be serious!"

There are several people stopped on the street now, some of them taking pictures of us. I sort of don't blame them. I'd probably take pictures of an idiot who willingly sat in a mud puddle, too.

I unclench her fists from my shirt and make her hold my hands as I force her to dance to non-existent music. She's stiff at first, but then she seems to let the laughter take over the embarrassment. We sway and dance down Bourbon Street, bumping into people as we go. The whole time, she's giggling like she doesn't have a care in the world.

After a few minutes, we come to a break in the crowd. I stop twirling her long enough to pull her to my chest and sway softly, back and forth.

She's looking up at me, shaking her head. "You're crazy, Silas Nash," she says.

I nod. "Good. That's what you love about me."

Her smile fades for a moment and the look she has in her eyes causes me to stop swaying. She places her palm over my heart and stares at the back of her hand. I already know she's not feeling a heartbeat inside my chest. It's more like a drumline in mid procession.

Her eyes meet mine again. She parts her lips and whispers, "Charlie says…kiss Charlie."

I would have kissed her even if Charlie didn't say. My hand wraps in her hair a single second before my lips meet hers. When her mouth parts for mine, it feels as though she punches a hole straight through my chest and makes a fist around my heart. It hurts, it doesn't, it's beautiful, it's terrifying. I want it to last for eternity, but I'll run out of breath if this kiss goes on for just one more minute. My arm wraps around her waist, and when I pull her closer, she moans quietly into my mouth. *Jesus.*

The only thing I have room for in this head of mine right now is the firm belief that fate *absolutely* exists. Fate…soul mates…time travel…you name it. It *all* exists. Because that's what her kiss feels like. *Existence.*

We're momentarily jolted when someone bumps into us. Our mouths separate, but it takes effort to free ourselves from whatever hold just took over. The music from all the open doors along the street comes back into focus. The lights, the people, the laughter. All the external things that ten seconds of her kiss just blocked out are rushing back. The sun is setting, and nighttime seems to transform this entire street from one world to another. I can't think of anything I want more than to get her out of here. Neither of us seems to be able to move, though, and my arm feels like it weighs twenty pounds when I reach for her hand. She slides her fingers through mine and we begin walking in silence back toward the parking lot where my car is.

Neither of us speaks a word the entire walk back. Once we're both inside my car, I wait a moment before cranking it. Things are too heavy. I don't want to start driving until we get out whatever it is we need to say. Kisses like that can't linger without acknowledgment.

"Now what?" she asks, staring out the window.

I watch her for a moment, but she doesn't move. It's as if she's frozen.

Suspended in time between the last kiss and our next one.

I buckle up and put the car in drive. *Now what?* I have no idea. I want to kiss her like that a million more times, but every single kiss would end just like that one did. With the fear that I won't remember it tomorrow.

"We should go back home and get a decent night's sleep," I say. "We also need to make more notes in case…" I cut myself off.

She pulls on her seatbelt. "In case soul mates don't exist…" she finishes.

43

Charlie

During our drive to Silas's house, I think about everything we've learned today. I think about my father and how he isn't a good human. Part of me is scared that being a good person is inherent. I've read enough about how I used to be to know that I didn't treat people very well. Silas included. I can only hope that the person I turned out to be was the result of outside influences, and not because that's who I'll always be. A vindictive, cheating shell of a person.

I open the backpack and begin reading more notes while Silas drives. I come across something about files that Silas stole from his father, and how we suspect they might implicate my father. Why would Silas steal those from his father? If my father is guilty, which I believe he is, why would Silas want to hide that?

"Why do you think you stole those files from your father?" I ask him.

He shrugs. "I don't know. The only thing I can come

up with is that maybe I hid them because I felt bad for you. Maybe I didn't want your father to go to prison for longer than he already was, because it would have broken your heart."

That sounds like something Silas would do. "Are they still in your room?" I ask him.

Silas nods. "I think so. I'm pretty sure I read somewhere that I keep them near my bed."

"When we get to your house tonight, I think you should give them to your father."

Silas glances at me across the seats. "Are you sure about that?"

I nod. "He's ruined a lot of lives, Silas. He deserves to pay for that."

"Charlie didn't know you had these?"

I'm standing outside Silas's father's study. When we walked in the door and he saw me with Silas, I thought he was going to hit him. Silas told him to give him five minutes to explain. He ran upstairs and got the files and brought them back down to his father.

I can't hear their entire conversation. Silas is explaining to him that he hid them to protect me. He's apologizing. His father is quiet. And then...

"Charlie? Can you come in here, please?"

His father scares me. Not in the way my father scared me. Clark Nash is intimidating, but he doesn't seem evil. Not like Brett Wynwood.

I walk into his office and he motions for me to take a seat next to Silas. I do. He paces the length of his desk a few times and then stops. When he faces us, he's looking directly at me.

"I owe you an apology."

I'm sure he can see the shock in my expression. "You do?"

He nods. "I've been harsh on you. What your father did to me—to our company—that had nothing to do with you. Yet I blamed you when the files went missing, because I knew how fiercely you stood by him." He glances back at Silas and says, "I'd be lying if I said I wasn't disappointed in you, Silas. Interfering with a federal investigation…"

"I was sixteen, Dad. I didn't know what I was doing. But I do now, and Charlie and I both want to make things right."

Clark Nash nods and then walks around his desk to take a seat. "So does this mean we'll be seeing you around more often, Charlie?"

I glance at Silas and then back at his father. "Yes, sir."

He smiles a little bit, and his smile looks just like Silas's smile. Clark should smile more often.

"Very well, then," he says.

Silas and I both take that as our cue to leave. As we're walking up the stairs, Silas pretend-falls, sinking down on the top stair as he clutches his chest. "Christ, that man is terrifying," he says.

I laugh and pull him back to his feet.

At least if things don't work out in our favor tomorrow, we'll have done one good deed.

"Charlie, you were a good sport today," Silas says, tossing me a t-shirt. I'm sitting cross-legged on his floor. I catch it and shake it out to see what's on the front. It's a camp t-shirt. He doesn't offer pants.

"Is that your way of flirting with me?" I ask. "Bringing sport into your compliments?"

Silas makes a face. "Look around this room. Do you see anything sports related?"

It's true. He seems to be more into photography than anything else. "You're on the football team," I say.

"Yeah, well, I don't want to be."

"Charlie says quit the football team," I tell him.

"Maybe I will," he says. With that, he swings open his bedroom door. I can hear him rushing down the stairs two at a time. I wait a moment to see what he's up to, and then shortly thereafter, he's running back up the stairs. His door swings back open and he smiles. "I just told my father I quit the football team," he says proudly.

"What did he say?"

He shrugs. "I don't know. I must be scared of him, because I ran back upstairs as soon as I told him." He winks at me. "And what are *you* quitting, Charlize?"

"My dad." My answer comes easy. "Charlie needs to walk away from things that stunt her emotional growth."

Silas stops what he's doing to look at me. It's a weird look. One I'm not familiar with.

"What?" I suddenly feel defensive.

He shakes his head. "Nothing. It was a good thought, that's all."

I hug my knees and stare at the carpet. Why was it that when he complimented me my entire body went into overdrive? Surely his opinions couldn't matter that much to Charlie. To *me.* Surely I would remember if they did. Whose opinions were really supposed to matter in life, anyway? Your parents'? *Mine were screwed up.* Your boyfriend's? *If you weren't dating a saint like Silas Nash, that could go very wrong.* I think about what I would tell Janette if she were asking this question.

"Trust your gut," I say out loud.

"What are you talking about?" Silas asks. He's digging around in a box he found in his closet, but he leans back on his haunches to look at me.

"Trust your gut. Not your heart, because it's a people pleaser, and not your brain, because it relies too heavily on logic."

He nods slowly, never taking his eyes off of me. "Charlize, it's really sexy when you get deep and say stuff like that. So unless you want to play another round of Silas Says, you might want to lay off the deep thinking."

I put down the t-shirt and stare at him. I think about today. I think about our kiss and how I would be a liar if I said I wasn't hoping he would kiss me like that again tonight. This time in private, without a dozen eyes on us. I reach down and tug at a piece of the carpet. I can feel my face grow warm.

"What if I *do* want to play another round of Silas Says?" I ask.

"Charlie..." he starts, almost as if my name is a warning.

"What would Silas say?"

He stands up and so do I. I watch him run a hand across the back of his neck, my heart pounding like it's trying to break free and run out of the room before Silas can get to it.

"Are you sure you want to play?" he asks, raking over me with his eyes.

I nod. *Because why not?* According to our letters, it won't be the first time we've done this. And chances are, we probably won't even remember it tomorrow. "I'm positive," I say, attempting to come off way more confident than I feel right now. "It's my favorite thing to do."

He suddenly looks firm, more planted in his own skin. It's thrilling to watch.

"Silas says…take off your shirt."

I raise my eyebrows, but do as I'm told, lifting the hem of my shirt over my head. I hear his intake of breath, but I can't seem to meet his eyes. The strap of my bra slips down my shoulder.

"Silas says…lower the other bra strap."

My hand shakes a little as I do. He takes a slow step toward me, staring down to where my arm is still crossed over my chest. His eyes flicker up to mine. His mouth turns up at the corner. He thinks I'm about to quit playing this game. I can tell.

"Silas says…open the clasp."

It's a front clasp. I keep my eyes locked with his as I unlatch it. His Adam's apple bobs as I shrug off my bra and hold it on the tip of my finger. The cold air and his eyes make me want to turn away. His gaze follows my bra as it falls to the floor. When he makes eye contact with me again, he's smiling. But he's not. I don't know he does that—looks so happy and so serious at the same time.

"Silas says come here."

I'm not able to turn away when he looks at me like that. I walk toward him, and when I'm near enough, he reaches for me. He puts his hand behind my head and threads his fingers through my hair.

"Silas says—"

"Shut up, Silas," I interrupt. "Just kiss me."

His head dips and he catches my lips in a deep kiss that tilts my head up to meet him. He presses his mouth against mine in a soft kiss, once, twice, three times before parting my lips with his tongue. Kissing Silas feels rhythmic, like we've had more than just this afternoon to figure it out. His hand tightly gripping my hair at the scalp makes me weak in the knees. I am out of breath and my eyes are glazed.

Do I trust him?

I trust him.

"Charlie says take your shirt off," I say against his mouth.

"This game is called *Silas* Says."

I run my hands up the warm flesh of his stomach. "Not anymore."

44

Silas

"Charlie baby," I whisper, sliding an arm over her. I press my lips against the curve of her shoulder. She rustles, then pulls the covers over her head. "Charlie, it's time to wake up."

She rolls over to face me but stays under the blanket. I lift it over my head until we're both covered. She opens her eyes and frowns. "You smell good," she says. "No fair."

"I took a shower."

"And brushed your teeth?"

I nod, and her brow furrows.

"That's not fair. I want to brush my teeth."

I lift the covers from her head and she puts a hand over her eyes and groans. "Then hurry up and brush your teeth so you can come back and kiss me."

She crawls out of the bed and makes her way to the bathroom. I hear the sink begin to run, but that's quickly drowned out by the noises that come from downstairs.

Pots and pans clanking together, cabinet doors slamming. It sounds like someone is cleaning. I look at the clock and it's almost 9am.

Two more hours.

My bathroom door opens and Charlie runs across the room and hops onto the bed, quickly pulling the covers over herself. "It's cold out there," she says, her lips quivering. I pull her to me and press my mouth to hers. "Better," she mumbles.

And this is what we do while I try my best to lose track of time. We make out.

"Silas," she whispers as I'm working my way up her neck. "What time is it?"

I reach over to the nightstand and look at my phone. "Nine fifteen." She sighs, and I know exactly what she's thinking. I'm thinking it too.

"I don't want to forget this part," she says, looking at me through eyes that look like two broken hearts.

"Me neither," I whisper.

She kisses me again, softly. I can feel her heart racing through her chest, and I know it isn't because we're kissing under my covers. It's because she's scared. And I wish I could make it to where she isn't scared anymore, but I can't. I just pull her to me and hold her. I would hold her here forever, but I know there are things we need to be doing right now.

"We can hope for the best, but I think we should prepare for the worst," I tell her.

She nods against my chest. "I know. Five more minutes, okay? Let's just stay under the blanket for five more minutes and pretend we're in love like we used to be."

I sigh. "Pretending isn't necessary for me at this point, Charlie." She grins and presses her lips to my chest.

I give her fifteen minutes. Five isn't enough.

When our time is up, I crawl out of bed and pull her up. "We need to eat breakfast. That way if 11am hits and we freak out again, it'll be a few hours before we have to worry about food."

We get dressed and head downstairs. Ezra looks like she's cleaning up breakfast when we walk into the kitchen. She sees Charlie rubbing sleep out of her eyes and she raises an eyebrow in my direction. She thinks I'm pushing my luck having Charlie in this house.

"Don't worry, Ezra. Dad says I'm allowed to love her now." Ezra returns my smile.

"You two hungry?" she asks.

I nod. "Yeah, but we can make our own food."

Ezra waves a hand in the air. "Nonsense," she says. "I'll make your favorite."

"Thanks, Ezra," Charlie says with a smile. A mild look of surprise passes over Ezra's face before she walks to the pantry.

"My God," Charlie says under her breath. "Do you think I really used to be that awful? That it was shocking to ever hear me say thank you?"

About that time, my mother walks into the kitchen. She stops short when she sees Charlie. "Did you spend the night here?" My mother doesn't seem very pleased.

"No." I lie for Charlie. "I just picked her up this morning."

My mother's eyes narrow. I don't have to have memory of her to know she's suspicious. "Why aren't you two at school right now?"

We're both quiet for a moment, but then Charlie blurts out, "It's a flex day."

My mother nods without question. She walks to the pantry and begins speaking to Ezra.

"What's a flex day?" I whisper.

Charlie shrugs. "I have no idea, but it sounded good." She laughs and then whispers, "What's your mother's name?"

I open my mouth to respond, but I draw a complete blank. "I have no idea. I'm not sure I ever wrote it in any notes."

My mother peeks her head out of the pantry. "Charlie, will you be joining us for dinner tonight?"

Charlie looks at me, and then at my mother. "Yes, ma'am. If I can remember."

I laugh and Charlie smiles, and for a split second, I forget what we're about to go through again.

I catch Charlie staring at the clock on the oven. I can see the worry, not only in her eyes, but in every single part of her. I grab her hand and squeeze it. "Don't think about that," I whisper. "Not for another hour."

"I have no idea how anyone could possibly forget how magnificent this is," Charlie says, taking the last bite of whatever it was that Ezra cooked for us. Some might call it breakfast, but food like this deserves its own category.

"What is this again?" Charlie asks Ezra.

"Nutella French toast," she responds.

Charlie writes *Nutella French toast* down on a piece of paper and scribbles two hearts next to it. Then she adds a follow-up sentence that says, *You hate crawfish, Charlie!!!*

Before we leave the kitchen and head back to my room, Charlie walks over to Ezra and gives her a big hug. "Thank you for breakfast, Ezra."

Ezra pauses a moment before hugging her back. "You're welcome, Charlize."

"Will you make that for me next time I'm here for breakfast? No matter if I can't remember eating it today?"

Ezra shrugs and says, "I guess."

As we're walking upstairs, Charlie randomly says, "You know what? I think money is what made us mean."

"What are you talking about?" We reach my bedroom and I close the door behind us.

"It just seems like maybe we were ungrateful. A little bit spoiled. I'm not sure our parents taught us how to be decent humans. So in a way... I'm grateful this happened to us."

I sit on the bed and pull her back against my chest. She rests her head on my shoulder and tilts her face up to mine. "I think you were always a little nicer than me. But I don't think either of us can be proud of who we were."

I give her a quick peck on the lips and lean my head back against the wall. "I think we were a product of our environment. Inherently, we're good people. We might lose our memories again, but we're still the same on the inside. Somewhere deep down, we want to do good. *Be* good. Deep down we love each other. A lot. And whatever this is that's happening to us, it's not touching that."

She slides her fingers through mine and squeezes. We sit in silence for a little while. Every now and then I'll glance at my phone. We have about ten minutes left until 11am, and I don't think either of us knows how to spend that time. We've already written more notes than we'll be able to comprehend in the next forty-eight hours.

All we can do is wait.

45

Charlie

My heart is beating so hard, it's losing rhythm. My mouth is dry. I grab the bottle of water sitting on Silas's nightstand and down a big drink. "This is terrifying," I tell him. "I wish we could speed up the next five minutes and get this over with."

He sits up straighter on the bed and grabs my hand. "Sit in front of me."

I sit in front of him. We're both cross-legged on the bed, in the same position we were in at the hotel room two days ago. Thinking of that morning makes me ill. I don't want to acknowledge the possibility that in a few minutes, I might not know who he is.

I have to have faith this time. This can't go on forever. *Can it?*

I close my eyes and try to control my breathing. I feel Silas's hand reach up and brush the hair from my eyes.

"What's the one thing you're the most scared of forgetting?" he asks.

I open my eyes. "You."

He brushes his thumb over my mouth and leans in to kiss me. "Me too. I love you, Charlie."

And without hesitation I say, "I love you, too, Silas."

When his lips meet mine, I'm no longer scared. Because I know that whatever happens in the next few seconds...it'll happen with Silas, and that brings me comfort.

He threads our fingers together and says, "Ten seconds."

We both inhale deep breaths. I can feel his hands shaking, but they aren't shaking nearly as badly as mine.

"Five...four...three...two..."

46

Silas

The only sound I hear is the thrashing of my heart. The rest of the world is chillingly silent.

My lips are still resting softly against hers. Our knees are touching, our eyes are closed, our breath is mingling between us as I wait to make my next move. I know for a fact that I didn't lose my memory this time. That makes twice in a row…but I have no idea about Charlie.

I slowly open my eyes so that I can see what's in hers. Her eyes remain closed. I watch her for a few seconds, waiting to see what her first reaction will be.

Will she remember me?

Will she have no idea where she is?

She begins to pull back, slowly, and her eyelids flutter open. There's a mixture of fear and shock in her expression. She pulls back a few more inches, studying my face. She turns her head and looks around the room.

When she glances back at me, my heart plummets

down my chest like the drop of an anchor. *She has no idea where she is.*

"Charlie?"

Her tear-rimmed eyes swing to mine and she quickly covers her mouth with her hand. I can't tell if she's about to scream. I should have put a note on the door like we did last time.

She looks down at the bed and lowers her hand to her chest. "You were wearing black," she whispers.

Her gaze falls to the pillow next to me. She points at it. "We were right there. You were wearing a black t-shirt, and I was laughing at you because I said it was too tight. I said it made you look like Simon Cowell. You pinned me to the mattress, and then…" Her eyes meet mine. "And then you kissed me."

I nod, because somehow… I remember every single moment of that. "It was our first kiss. We were fourteen," I say. "But I had been wanting to kiss you like that since we were twelve."

She slaps her hand over her mouth again. Sobs begin to rack her entire body. She lunges forward, wrapping her arms around my neck. I pull her down to the bed with me and everything comes rushing back in waves.

"The night you got caught sneaking in?" she says.

"Your mom went after me with a belt. Chased me right out of your bedroom window."

Charlie starts laughing between her tears. I'm holding her against me, my face pressed against her neck. I close my eyes and sort through all the memories. The good ones. The bad ones. All the nights she cried in my arms over the way things turned out between her mother and father.

"The phone calls," she says quietly. "Every single night."

I know exactly what she's talking about. I would call her every night and we would stay on the phone for an entire hour. When our memories left us, we couldn't figure out why we had talked for so long every night if our relationship was falling apart.

"Jimmy Fallon," I tell her. "We both loved Jimmy Fallon. And I would call you every night when his show would come on, and we would watch it together."

"But we never talked," she says. "We just watched the show together without speaking and then we'd go straight to sleep."

"Because I loved hearing you laugh."

Not only are the memories flooding me right now, but the feelings. All the feelings I've ever had for this girl are unfolding, and for a second I'm not sure if I can take it all in.

We hold each other tight as we rake through a lifetime of memories. Several minutes pass as we both laugh at the good memories and then more minutes pass as we succumb to the not so good ones. The hurt our parents' actions inflicted on us. The hurt we've caused each other. The hurt we've caused other people. We're feeling every bit of it, all at once.

Charlie clenches my shirt in her fists and buries her face in my neck. "It hurts, Silas," she whispers. "I don't want to be that girl again. How can we make sure we're not the same people we were before this happened to us?"

I run my hand over the back of her head. "But we *are* those people," I say to her. "We can't take back who we've been in the past, Charlie. But we can control who we are in the present."

I lift her head from my shoulder and hold her face in

my hands. "Charlie, you have to promise me something."
I wipe her tears away with my thumb. "Promise me you
will never fall out of love with me again. Because I don't
want to forget you all over again. I never want to forget
a single second with you."

She shakes her head. "I swear. I'll never stop loving
you, Silas. And I'll never forget."

I dip my head until my mouth meets hers. *"Never
Never."*

EPILOGUE

Charlie

Silas is bringing dinner home. I wait for him at the kitchen window while I pretend to wash vegetables for a salad. I like to pretend I'm washing things at the sink just so I can see when he pulls into the driveway.

His car pulls in ten minutes later; my fingers are pruned from the water. I grab for a dishtowel, feeling those damn butterflies in my stomach. They never went away. From what I've heard, that's a rare thing after this many years of marriage.

The kids get out of the car first. Jessa, our daughter, and then her boyfriend, Harry. Normally my eyes would go to Silas next, but something makes me linger on Jessa and Harry.

Jessa is just like me: stubborn, mouthy, and aloof. I'd cry, but she mostly makes me laugh with her one-liners. I like Harry; they've been together since freshman year and plan on going to the same college when they graduate next year. They're usually the epitome of teen love, all glassy eyed and touchy like Silas and I used to be. *Still are.* But today, Jessa stands off to the side of the driveway, her arms folded across her chest.

Harry gets out of the car too and goes to stand next to her. *They must be fighting,* I think. Jessa sometimes likes to flirt with the neighbor kid, and Harry gets upset.

Silas walks in a minute later. He grabs me from behind, wrapping his arms around me and kissing my neck.

"Hey, Charlie baby," he says, breathing me in. I lean into him.

"What's up with those two?" I ask, still watching them out the window.

"I don't know. They were really weird on the ride home. Barely spoke."

"Uh, oh," I say. "Must be the hot neighbor boy again." I hear the front door slam, and I call Jessa into the kitchen. "Jessa, come here!" She wanders in, slowly, without Harry in tow.

"What's up?" I ask her. "You look shell shocked."

"Do I?" she asks.

I look at Silas and he shrugs.

"Where's Harry?"

Jessa jabs a thumb over her shoulder. "He's in there."

"Okay, well, you two get ready for dinner. We'll eat as soon as the salad is done."

She nods, and I swear she's going to start crying.

"Hey, Jessa," I say as she turns around to leave.

"Yeah?"

"I was thinking we could go to Miami for your birthday next month. Does that sound okay to you?"

"Yeah," she says. "Cool."

When she's gone I turn to Silas, whose eyebrows are drawn together.

"I didn't know we were going to Miami," he says. "I can't get time off for work that quick."

"Silas," I say sharply. "Her birthday isn't for six more months."

The line between his eyes relaxes and his mouth opens. "Oh, yeah," he says. And then realization hits. "Oh. *Oh.*" He brings a hand up to the back of his neck. "*Shit*, Charlie. Not again."

* * * * *

ACKNOWLEDGMENTS

THANK YOU TO OUR READERS.
YOU MEAN THE WORLD TO US.
~TARRYN AND COLLEEN

COLLEEN HOOVER
colleenhoover.com
Facebook.com/authorcolleenhoover
Twitter.com/colleenhoover
Instagram.com/colleenhoover

TARRYN FISHER
tarrynfisher.com
Facebook.com/authortarrynfisher
Twitter.com/darkmarktarryn
Instagram.com/tarrynfisher

THE
ASTROLOGICAL PROFILE
OF
CHARLIE
WYNWOOD

&

SILAS
NASH

SILAS

Birthday: December 7th
Sun Sign: Sagittarius

Sagittarians are the explorers of the zodiac. Wild and adventurous—and sometimes curious to a fault—they are on a perpetual quest to discover not only the world around them, but the world within them, too. They have an insatiable appetite for knowledge and truth and can be relentless in their pursuit to get what they want. They know that while external knowledge is easy to come by and useful to an extent, self-knowledge holds more value and more power in the long run. It's no surprise that Silas uses photography to capture the world around him, and to hold on to memories in a more tangible way. One of the Fire Signs, Sagittarians burn bright and are up for anything, wanting to live life to the fullest, and will never turn down a chance to have fun. They are lovers of spontaneity and excitement to the point of reckless-ness and hate the idea of settling down to a predictable life. As a result, they don't fall in love easily but badly want someone willing to go on their journey with them. This could not be more evident than in Silas's relationship with Charlie. While he's loved her since he could walk, when they lose their memories, it forces them to go on a different kind of journey together. Sagittarians are the supreme realists of the zodiac, and will always choose their values over their feelings, yet will often form opinions based on their fierce emotions.

At their best, Sagittarians are courageous and honest, and are the most loyal friends. They're the life of the party, and endless fun to be around. They are one of the most generous signs in the zodiac, and their boundless optimism is infectious. At their worst, Sagittarians can be erratic and unfocused, never finishing what they start. Intense and energetic, Sagittarians speak their mind, and their brutal honesty can get them into trouble. They rebel against authority and won't be told what to do, and their natural confidence can be taken as arrogance. Silas is a true Sagittarius in every way, and he never fails to fight for Charlie.

CHARLIE

Birthday: March 21st
Sun Sign: Aries

Aries is the first sign in the zodiac, and ruled by the House of Self, which makes them brave and dazzling, but there's an aggressive quality to the first house that can make them demanding and diva-like. With the responsibility of leading the zodiac, Aries feel compelled to pick up the torch and lead the way. Aries are driven by a desire to prove themselves and their strength, and naturally take charge and are competitive and ambitious. This fire sign has the ability to move mountains; they throw themselves at the world with the impulsiveness, energy, and persistence of the Ram that represents them. Charlie acts impulsively throughout the book, and yet her confidence always allows her to move through situations to get the answers she needs.

Unafraid of conflict, Aries do what they want, and do things their way. They aren't afraid to make the first move when it comes to love and friendships. One of the most passionate signs of the zodiac, they are fearless, and won't let the idea of failure stop them from chasing after their wildest dreams. While Aries enjoy competition, they don't like to play games. They are highly self-aware, have strong opinions, and don't like to waste time. Even without her memories, Charlie picks a path and follows it, trusting her gut. Charlie isn't a damsel in distress—when she senses that something is wrong, she doesn't wait around to be rescued.

At their best, Aries are courageous and confident, hard-working with a high sense of duty. They appreciate honesty above all else. Aries are enthusiastic about everything in life, and put their whole heart and soul into all their undertakings. Not content to sit back and wait, they go out and make their own luck. At their worst, Aries are impatient, jealous, and hotheaded. Known for their fiery tempers, they do not apologize for their anger. When they say "I don't care," they mean it. Aries often cause their own turmoil; they want to feel things intensely, which is why they can sometimes react out of heightened emotion. In true Aries fashion, Charlie embodies her feelings. When her father goes to prison, she pushes Silas away, doing everything she can to hurt him. But she shows her love for Silas just as intensely.

ARIES AND SAGITTARIUS
IN LOVE

What would a relationship between Aries and Sagittarius look like? Well, definitely something passionate and fiery! As friends or as lovers, Aries and Sagittarius are a perfect match. These two signs are similar in many ways—they're both adventurous, optimistic, and dynamic. There will never be a dull moment in the relationship; Aries and Sagittarius are able to match each other's strengths and desire for excitement and freedom. On the rare occasion they fight, things may become explosive as these two volatile signs risk saying hurtful things without thinking, but their anger will flame out as quickly as it sparks. The depth of their feelings will always reunite them, just as Fate continually resets Silas's and Charlie's memories at 11:00 a.m. every day, the time of their very first kiss.

When it comes to romance, neither Aries nor Sagittarius care about grand gestures. Chocolates and flowers? Not for these two! Instead, they are each other's ride-or-die. More subtle or permanent expressions of their loyalty, like tattoos, will hold more appeal for these signs. The quiet but meaningful time Charlie and Silas spend on the phone every night watching television, just to hear each other breathe, holds more value than any token they could buy. They will support each other, no matter what happens, and face any issue as a team. Together, they will feel unstoppable. Because this fire duo recognizes a little bit of themselves in each other, their mutual understanding and respect run deep. Sagittarius might be reluctant to settle down in a relationship just as Aries won't fall in love that easily. But even if they struggle to get on the same page about the depth of their feelings, it's a bond that can't be broken.

How far is too far to go when you're fighting to win back the love of your life?

———

Turn the page for an excerpt of The Opportunist, *book one in Tarryn Fisher's Love Me with Lies trilogy, now available for the first time in print!*

1

The Present

I am Olivia Kaspen, and if I love something, I rip it from my life. Not intentionally…not unintentionally either. I can see one of them now, a survivor of my tainted, acrid love. He's a hundred yards from where I stand, flipping through old records.

Caleb. His name rolls around my head like a barbed ball, slicing open feelings that have long since become scar tissue. My heart tries to punch its way out of my chest and all I can do is stand and watch him. It has been three years since the last time I saw him. His parting words to me were a warning to stay away. I suck sticky air into my lungs and try to rein in my sloppy emotions.

I want to go to him. I want to watch the hate surface in his eyes. Stupid. I start to leave and I am almost across the street and to my car when my feet fail me. The sharp tingle of agitation crawls up my fingertips. Clenching my fists, I march back to the window. This is my side of town. How dare he show his face here?

His head is bent over a cardboard box of CDs and as he turns to look at something over his shoulder, I catch a glimpse of his offbeat nose. My heart clenches. I still love this boy. The realization scares me. I thought I was over it. I thought I could handle something like this— an impromptu run-in. I've had therapy. I've had three years to...

~~Get over him.~~
Fester in my guilt.

I muck around in my emotions for a few more seconds before turning my back to the music store and to Caleb. I can't do it. I can't go back to that dark place. My foot is lifted to step down from the curb when the clouds that have been lurking around Miami for a week suddenly groan like old plumbing. Before I get two steps, the rain is assaulting the pavement, drenching my white shirt. I back up quickly and huddle underneath the music store's awning. I stare at my old Beetle through the sheets of rain. Just a short run and I'll be on my way home. A stranger's voice interrupts my moment of escape. I pull back, not sure if he's speaking to me.

"The sky is red—means trouble."

I spin on my heels and find someone standing directly behind me. He is closer than what is deemed socially acceptable. I make a surprised sound in my throat and back up a step. He is at least a foot taller than I am, all muscle, though not in an attractive way. He holds his hands at an odd angle with his fingers tensed and spread apart. My eyes are drawn to a mole that sits like a target in the center of his forehead.

"What?" I shake my head, confused. I am trying to peer over his shoulder to catch a glimpse of Caleb. *Is he still there? Should I go in?*

"It's an old sailor's superstition." He shrugs.

I lower my eyes to his face. He looks vaguely familiar, and as I consider telling him to screw off, I try to remember where I have seen him before.

"I have an umbrella." He holds up a floral thing with a plastic handle in the shape of a daisy. "I can walk you to your car."

I look at the sky, which does appear to be a dusky red, and I shiver. I want him to leave me alone and I am about to tell him so, when I think—*What if this is a sign? The sky is red. Get the hell outta here!*

I study the chipped polish on my thumbnail and consider his offer. I am not one for omens, but he does have a way to keep me dry.

"No, thanks," I say. I jerk my head toward the store behind me and realize I had already made up my mind.

"Okay. Hurricane's coming, but suit yourself." He shrugs again and steps out into the rain, not opening his umbrella.

I watch him go. His broad back curves against the downpour like a ledge for the rest of his body. He is truly huge. In seconds, the rain has swallowed him and I can no longer see his silhouette. I know him from somewhere, but surely I would remember such a large guy if I had met him before. I turn back to the shop. The sign above the door reads *Music Mushroom* in bright curlicue letters. I look beyond the glass and search the aisles for him. He is right where I left him, his head still bent over what looks like the reggae section. Even from where I am standing, I can make out a slight furrow in his brow.

He can't make up his mind. I realize what I am doing and cringe. I don't know him anymore. I can't make assumptions about what he is thinking.

I want him to look up and see me, but he doesn't.

Since I don't want to lurk underneath the awning like a creeper any longer, I gather my guts, compose myself, and walk through the door. The air-conditioning is icy against my damp skin, and I shiver. I spot a tall shelf of bongs to my left, duck behind it, and pull out my compact to check my makeup.

While I spy on him through the slats in the shelves, I use a finger to scrub at the smudged mascara beneath my eyes. I have to make running into him look accidental.

In front of me, there is a bong in the shape of Bob Marley's head. I look into Bob's glass eyes and practice a surprised face. I am disgusted by how low I can stoop. Pinching my cheeks for color, I step out from my hiding place.

Here goes everything.

My heels bite into the linoleum, snapping loudly as I make my approach. I might as well have hired a trumpeter to announce my arrival. Surprisingly, he doesn't look up. The air conditioner clicks on when I am a few yards away. Someone has tied lime green streamers to the vents. As they begin to dance, I smell something. It is Caleb's smell: peppermints and oranges.

I am close enough to see the scar that curves itself gently around his right eye—the one I used to trace with my finger. His presence in a room is like a jarring physical impact. To prove this, I see women—old and young—shooting him looks, bending toward him. The whole world bends for Caleb Drake and he is charmingly unaware of it. It is truly disgusting to watch.

I sidle up next to him and reach for a CD. Caleb, oblivious to my presence, moves down the alphabetized line of artists. I trace his steps, and just as I move a few feet behind him, his body turns in my direction. I freeze

and there is a brief second when I have the urge to run.
I grind my heels down and watch as his eyes trace my
face like he's never seen it before and land on the plastic square in my hand. And then, after three long years,
I hear his voice.

"Are they any good?"

I feel the shock rush from my heart to my limbs and
settle like lead in my stomach.

He still speaks with the same diluted British accent
I remember, but the hardness I was expecting to hear
isn't there. Something is wrong.

"Ummm…"

He looks back at my face and his eyes touch each
of my features as if he's seeing them for the first time.

"I'm sorry? I didn't catch that."

Shit, shit, shit.

"Err, they're okay," I say, shoving the CD back on the
rack. Seconds of silence flick by. I decide he is waiting
for me to speak.

"They're not really your style."

He looks confused.

"They're not my style?"

I nod.

"What exactly do you think my style is?" His eyes
are laughing at me, and there is a hint of a smile around
his mouth.

I run my eyes over his face, looking for a clue to the
game he is playing. He has always been so good at facial
expressions, always the right one at the right time. He
looks placid and only remotely interested in my answer.
I feel safe so I say, "Umm, you're a classic rock kind of
guy…but I could be wrong." People change.

"Classic rock?" he repeats, watching my lips.

I shiver involuntarily as a memory of him looking at my lips that way comes rushing back to me. Wasn't that look how it all started?

"I'm sorry," he says dropping his eyes to the floor. "This is awkward, but I…uhhh…don't know what my style is. I have no memory of it."

I gape at him. Was this some type of sick joke—some way of getting back at me?

"You don't remember? How could you not remember?"

Caleb runs his hand across the back of his neck, the muscles in his arms flexing. "I lost my memory in an accident. Sounds corny, I know. But, the truth is—I have no idea what I like. Or liked, I guess I should say. I'm sorry. I don't know why I'm telling you this."

He turns to leave, probably because my face is so full of shock it makes him uncomfortable. It feels as if someone has taken a potato masher to my brain. Nothing makes sense. Nothing fits together. Caleb doesn't know who I am. *Caleb doesn't know who I am!* With every step he takes toward the door, I become more desperate. Somewhere in my head I hear a voice scream, *"Stop him!"*

"Wait," I say. My voice is barely audible. "Wait… *wait*!" This time I scream and several people turn to stare. Shutting them out, I focus on Caleb's back. He is almost to the door when he turns to face me. *Think fast. Think fast!* Holding up a finger, indicating for him to wait where he is, I set off in a trot for the classic rock section. It only takes a minute to find what used to be his favorite CD. I return with it clutched tightly in my hands, stopping a few feet away from where he is standing.

"You'll like this," I say, tossing him the copy. My

aim is off, but he catches it with grace and smiles almost sadly.

I watch him walk to the register, sign his credit card receipt, and disappear right back out of my life.

Hello—Goodbye.

Why didn't I tell him who I am? Now it is too late and the moment for honesty has passed. I stay rooted in his wake, my heart beating sluggishly in my chest, as I try to process what has happened. He forgot me.

2

The Present

At some point during the fifth grade, I watched a murder mystery on television. The detective, who I had a ridiculous crush on, was named Follagyn Beville. A modern-day Jack the Ripper was targeting prostitutes. Follagyn was hunting him down. He was interrogating an especially ratty-looking hooker, with stringy blond hair that was stained black at the roots. She was curled up on a mustard yellow couch, her lips sucking greedily on a cigarette. *Wow, what a terrific actress!* I remember thinking. *She should, like, win an Emmy for being so pathetic.* She held a rocks glass in her hand and was taking quick, birdlike sips of whiskey. I watched her movements, hungry for the drama, memorizing everything she did. Later that night I filled a glass with ice and Pepsi. I took my drink back to the windowsill and lifted an imaginary cigarette to my lips.

"No one listens to me," I whispered so that my breath frosted the glass. "This world—it's cold." I took a sip of Pepsi, making sure that I rattled the ice.

A decade and a half later and I still have my sense of the dramatic. The day after my run-in with Caleb, Hurricane Phoebe ripped through town and spared me from having to call in sick to work. I am in bed, my body curled possessively around a bottle of vodka.

Around midday, I roll out of bed and shuffle to the bathroom. There is still electricity, despite the Category 3 hurricane that is rattling my windows. I take advantage by running myself a bath. As I sit in the steaming water, I replay the whole thing in my mind for the millionth time. It all ends with, *he forgot me.*

My pug, Pickles, settles herself on my bath mat and watches me carefully. She is so ugly that it makes me smile.

"Caleb, Caleb, Caleb." I say it to see if it still sounds the same.

He used to have a weird habit of reversing people's names when he heard them for the first time. I was Aivilo and he was Belac. I thought it was ridiculous, but eventually I found myself doing the same thing. It became a secret code that we used when gossiping.

And now he doesn't remember me. How could you forget someone you loved, even if I did rip his heart to shreds? I pour some vodka into my bathwater. How am I ever going to get him out of my head now? I could make being depressed my full-time job. That's what country singers did. I could be a country singer. I belt out a couple verses of "Achy Breaky Heart" and take another swig.

I pull the chain to the plug with my toe and listen to the water gurgle into the drain. I get dressed and plod to the fridge. Cheap liquor sloshes around in my empty belly. My emergency hurricane food supply consists of two bottles of ranch dressing, an onion, and a block of sharp cheddar cheese. I cut up the cheese and onions and toss them into a bowl, pouring fat-free ranch over the top. I put on the coffee pot and hit *play* on the stereo. In it was the same CD I had given to Caleb in the Music Mushroom. I drink a lot more vodka.

I wake up on the kitchen floor with my face pressed into a puddle of drool. In my fist is a picture of Caleb that has been ripped and taped back together. I feel pretty damn good, even though there is a mild throbbing in my temples. I make a decision. Today I am going to start from scratch. I am going to forget what's-his-name and buy healthy crap to eat and move on with my damn life. I clean up my drunken mess, pausing briefly to toss the torn and taped picture into the trash. Goodbye yesterday. I grab my purse and head to the nearest health food store.

The first thing the healthy crap store does is puff patchouli-scented air into my face. I scrunch up my nose and hold my breath until I pass the service desk where a girl my age is snapping gum and meditating behind the counter.

Grabbing a cart, I head for the rear of the store, pushing past the bottles of Madame Deerwood's Aura Cleanser (it doesn't work), the Eye of Newt, and the bags of Gotu Kola.

As far as I am concerned, this is a normal grocery store and not a supply haven for every new age weirdo in a twenty-mile radius. Caleb and I were never here together, making the Meccan market a memory-free zone for me.

I throw some seaweed cookies and baked chips into the cart and head for the ice cream aisle. I pass a woman wearing a shirt that says "I am Wiccan, see me broom." She isn't wearing shoes.

Turning down the ice cream aisle, I shiver.

"Cold?"

I swing around so fast my shoulder upsets a display

of waffle cones. I watch in horror as they crash to the ground, scattering and skidding like my thoughts.

Caleb!

I watch him pick up the boxes one by one, stacking them in his free hand. He smiles at me, and I get the feeling he is amused by my reaction.

"Sorry, I didn't mean to scare you."

So polite. And there was that damn accent again.

"What are you doing here?" The words tumble from my mouth before I can stop them.

He laughs. "I'm not stalking you, I swear. Actually, I wanted to thank you for the music suggestion in the store the other day. I liked it—a lot actually." His hands are in his pockets and he is bouncing up and down on his heels.

"Wine," he says, spinning his thumb ring with his forefinger. He used to do that when he was nervous.

I stare at him blankly.

"You asked me what I was doing here," he says patiently, as though he were speaking to a child. "My girlfriend likes this wine, and one can only get it here… organic." The last word makes him laugh.

Girlfriend? I narrow my eyes. How is it that he remembers *her* and not me?

"So…" I say casually, opening one of the coolers and grabbing the first thing I see. "You remember your girlfriend?" I was trying to sound nonchalant, but I couldn't have sounded more strangled if he had his hands around my throat.

"No, after the accident—I didn't remember her."

I feel a little bit better.

I immediately think back to the first time I set my blues on her, three years ago when I was performing the ritual of post-breakup spying. I decided that I needed to see my replacement for closure. It was crazy really, but we are all entitled to a little bit of stalking.

I wore my grandmother's red derby hat because it had a ridiculously wide rim that would hide my face, and it was as melodramatic as my personality. I took Pickles for support.

Leah Smith. That was the little beast's name. She was as rich as I was poor, as happy as I was miserable, as redheaded as I was dark-haired. Caleb met her at some swanky party about a year after we broke up. Apparently, they hit it off right away, or maybe he hit *it* right away, I can't be sure.

Leah worked in an office building ten minutes from my apartment. By the time I slid my car into a parking spot, I had an hour to spare before her shift was over. I spent it convincing myself that my behavior was normal.

Leah walked out of the building at exactly 6:05 p.m. with a Prada purse swinging cheerfully on her forearm. She walked like a woman who knew she had the world staring at her breasts. I watched her clip-clop along the sidewalk in her green stilettos, while I sat strangling the steering wheel. I hated her long red hair that hung in fat curls down her back. I hated the way she waved good-bye to her coworkers with a tinkling of her fingertips. I hated the fact that I liked her shoes.

Searching his eyes for answers, and trying to get my head out of the past, I ask, "So, what—you guys are still together even though you don't know who she is?"

I expect him to be defensive, but instead he slyly smiles. "She's really torn up over the whole thing and is a great girl to stick with me through all of this." He doesn't look at me when he says "this."

Like any girl in her right mind would let *him* get

away—except me, of course—but I have never claimed to be in my right mind.

"Would you like to grab a cup of coffee?" he asks. "I can fill you in on my whole sob story."

I feel a tingle start at my feet and work its way up my body. If he remembered anything about me, this would not be happening. It was crazy—exactly the type of situation that I could completely take advantage of.

"I can't." I feel so proud of myself that I stand up a little taller. He takes my response the same way he'd taken all of my rejections over the years we dated—smiling like I couldn't possibly be serious.

"Yes, you can. Think of it as a favor to me."

I cock my head.

"I need some new friends—good influences," he presses.

My mouth opens, and lets out an extended *Pffffffff-ing* sound.

Caleb raises an eyebrow.

"I'm not a good influence," I say, blinking rapidly.

I shift from one foot to the other, distracting myself with a bottle of maraschino cherries. I could grab the bottle, toss it at his head, and run, *or* I could go get coffee with him. It was only coffee after all. Not sex, not a relationship, just some friendly jabber between two people who supposedly didn't know each other.

"Okay, coffee." I hear the excitement in my voice and cringe. I. Am. Disgusting.

"Good." He smiles.

"There's a coffee shop two blocks from here on the northwest corner. I can meet you there in thirty minutes," I say, calculating the time it would take for me to get home and de-slobbify. *Say you can't make it. Say you have other things to do...*

"Thirty minutes," he repeats, watching my lips. I purse them for effect and Caleb ducks his head to hide a smile. I turn and walk calmly down the aisle. I can feel his eyes on my back, making me tingle.

I abandon my shopping cart as soon as I am out of sight and gallop toward the front of the store. My flip-flops slap against my heels as I run.

I reach home in record time. My neighbor Rosebud is knocking on my door with an onion in her hand. If Rosebud catches me, I will be involved in a two-hour one-sided conversation about her Bertie and his struggle with gout. I hide in the bushes. When she gives up five minutes later, my thighs are burning from crouching and I need to pee.

The first thing I do when I walk through my door is rescue the picture of Caleb from the trash. Dusting it free of eggshells, I shove it in my silverware drawer.

In fifteen minutes, I am walking out the door feeling so nervous I have to make a conscious effort not to trip over my own feet. The three-block drive is torturous. I swear at myself and twice swerve into the turning lane to go home. I make it to the parking lot with a mild case of whiplash.

The coffee shop is full of dark blue walls and mosaic patterns. It is intense and depressing and warm all at the same time. With a Starbucks only three blocks away, this place is reserved for a more serious crowd—artsy-fartsy types that brood over their MacBooks.

"Hey, Livia." The little punk boy who works the counter waves at me.

I smile at him. As I pass the bulletin board, something catches my eye. A printout of a man's face is tacked among the flyers. I walk closer, feeling prickles of recognition. Along the bottom of his face the word WANTED stands out in bold letters. It's the man from the Music Mushroom—the one with the umbrella!

Dobson Scott Orchard, born September 7, 1960.

Wanted for kidnapping, rape, and assault.

Distinguishing feature: birthmark on forehead.

The mole! That is the birthmark the poster is referring to. What would have happened had I gone with him? I shake the image out of my head and memorize the number at the bottom of the page. If I hadn't seen Caleb that day, I might have let him walk me to my car.

Dobson escapes out of my head when I see Caleb.

He is waiting for me at a small table in the back corner, staring absently at the tabletop. He lifts a white porcelain cup to his lips, and I get a flashback of him doing the same thing in my apartment years ago. My heart accelerates.

He spots me when I am a few feet away.

"Hi. I got you a latte," he says, standing up. His eyes sweep from my feet to my face in one quick motion. I clean up well. I swipe a dark strand of hair out of my eyes and smile. I am jittery; my hands are trembling. When he extends a hand toward me, I hesitate before reaching out to shake it.

"Caleb Drake," he says. "I would say that I usually tell women my name before I ask them out for coffee, but I don't remember."

We smile awkwardly at his terrible joke as I allow my small hand to be swallowed in his. The feel of his skin is so familiar. I close my eyes for a brief second and allow the absurdity of the situation to wash over me.

"Olivia Kaspen. Thank you for the coffee."

We sit down awkwardly and I begin pouring sugar into my cup. I watch his face. He used to tease me about my coffee being so sweet it made your teeth hurt. He drinks tea hot, the way the British drink it. I used to think it was charming and distinguished. I still do, actually.

"So what did you tell your girlfriend?" I ask, taking a sip.

I am swinging my shoe off the end of my big toe, which is something that used to annoy him when we were together. I see his eyes reach my foot, and for a second, I think he's going to grab it to stop the motion.

"I told her I needed some time off to think. It's a horrible thing to say to a woman, isn't it?" he asks.

I nod.

"Anyway, she burst into tears the minute the words were out of my mouth, and I didn't know what to do."

"I'm sorry," I lie.

Strawberry Freckle Face is cuddling with rejection tonight. It is a wonderful thing.

"So," I say, "amnesia."

Caleb nods, looking down at the table. He absently traces a pattern of circles with his finger.

"Yes, it's called selective amnesia. Doctors, eight of them, have told me it's temporary."

I suck thoughtfully on the word *temporary*. It could mean my time with him is as temporary as hair dye or an adrenaline rush. I decide I'll take either one. I am having coffee with a man who formerly hated me; *temporary* doesn't have to be a dirty word.

"How did it happen?" I ask.

Caleb clears his throat and looks around the room like he's gauging who can hear us.

"What? Too personal?" I can't keep the laughter out of my voice.

It feels strange that he is hesitating to tell me. When we were together, he told me everything—even the things that most men would be embarrassed to share with their girlfriends. I can still read his expressions after all these years, and I can tell that he is uncomfortable sharing the details of his amnesia.

"I don't know. It seems like we should start with something simple before I tell you my secrets. Like my favorite color."

I smile. "Do you remember what your favorite color is?"

Caleb shakes his head. We both laugh.

I sigh and fidget with my coffee cup. When we first started dating I'd asked him what his favorite color was. Instead of just telling me, he'd forced me into the car, saying he needed to show me.

"This is ridiculous, I have a test to study for," I complained.

He drove for twenty minutes, blaring the terrible rap music he liked to listen to, and finally pulled up beside the Miami International Airport.

"That," he said, pointing to the lights lining the runway, "is my favorite color."

"That's blue," I said. "So what?"

"That's not just any blue. It's Airport blue," he said. "And don't you ever forget it."

I turned back to the runway to study the lights. The color was eerie; it looked like fire when it burned at its hottest and turned blue. Where was I going to find a shirt in that color?

I look at him now, the memory clear in my mind and gone from his. What would it be like to forget your favorite color? Or the girl that smashed up your heart?

Airport blue haunts me. It's become a brand to me, a

trademark of our broken relationship and my failure to move on. Airport fucking blue.

"Your favorite color is blue," I say, "and mine is red. Now we're best friends, so tell me what happened."

"Blue it is," he says smiling. "It was a car accident. A colleague and I were on a business trip in Scranton. It was snowing heavily and we were on our way to a meeting. The car skidded off the road and wrapped around a tree. I sustained serious head injuries…" He rattles it off as if he is bored with the story. I imagine that he has recited it hundreds of times already.

I don't need to ask what he does for work. He is an investment banker. He works for his stepfather's company, and he is rich.

"And your coworker?"

"He didn't make it." His shoulders slump.

I bite my lip. I'm not good with death and the words that you're supposed to offer as condolence. When my mother died, people said stupid things that made me angry. Soft, fluffy words that carried no weight: "I'm sorry—" when it clearly wasn't their fault, and "if there is anything I can do—" when we both knew there was nothing. I change the subject, rather than offer empty words.

"Do you remember the accident?"

"I remember waking up after it happened. Nothing before that."

"Not even your name?"

He shakes his head.

"The good news is the doctors say I'll remember. It's just a matter of time patience."

The good news for me is that he doesn't remember. We wouldn't be talking if he did.

"I found an engagement ring in my sock drawer." His confession is so sudden—I choke on my coffee.

"Sorry." He pats me on the back and I clear my throat, eyes watering. "I really needed to tell someone that. I was getting ready to ask her to marry me, and now I don't even know who she is."

Wow...wow! I feel like someone just plugged me in and threw me in the bathtub. I knew that he had moved on with his life—I spied on him enough to know that—but marriage? It made me itch just to think about it.

"What do your parents think about your condition?" I ask, steering the conversation in a more palatable direction. The thought of Leah in a white dress makes me want to laugh. She is better suited for slutty lingerie and a stripper pole.

"My mother looks at me like I've betrayed her in some way, and my father keeps patting me on the back, saying, 'You'll get it back soon, buddy. Everything's going to be fine, Caleb.'" He imitates his parents to a T and I smile.

"I know it sounds selfish, but I just want to be left alone to figure things out—you know?"

I don't, but I nod anyway.

"I keep wondering why I can't remember. If my life was as great as everyone keeps telling me it was, why doesn't any of it feel familiar?"

I don't know what to say. The Caleb I knew was always in control. I always thought Jewel had him pegged—he was fashionably sensitive, but too cool to care. This Caleb is confused and broken and spilling his guts to someone he thinks is a perfect stranger. I want to kiss his face and smooth out the furrows in his brow. Instead, I sit frozen in my chair, fighting the urge to tell him everything that tore us apart in the first place.

"So what about you, Olivia Kaspen? What's your story?"

"I...uhh... I don't have one." I am so thrown off guard by his question, my hands start shaking.

"Come on... I've told you everything," he pleads.

"Everything that you remember," I point out. "How long have you had amnesia?"

"Three months."

"Well, for three months of *my* life I've done nothing but work and read. There's your answer."

"Somehow, I think there's quite a bit more to you than that." He scans my face and I get the impression he is generating a history from what he sees there.

I wish he wasn't doing that—trying to see past my walls. I was never skilled at pretending with him.

"Look, when you get your memory back and can divulge all your secrets from the past, we'll have a sleepover and I'll tell you everything; but, as far as I'm concerned, until that day arrives, we both have amnesia."

He laughs a full-bodied laugh and I hide my contented smile behind the rim of my coffee cup.

"Well, that doesn't sound so bad for me then," he teases.

"Oh? Why is that?"

"Well, because you've just given me permission to see you again, and now I have a sleepover to look forward to."

I blush and decide that I can never tell him. He will remember eventually and this whole charade will come crashing down around me like a bad game of Jenga. Until then, I have him back and I am going to hold on to that for as long as I can.